"YOU SMELL LIKE GRASS," HE MURMURED. "AND MOONLIGHT."

Where had that come from? He didn't know, but it was true. There was a wild night perfume that was driving him to speak, to act.

"Paul?" Torie whispered his name. But she didn't move away. Didn't retreat this time. He shoved the past away and focused on the now.

"You're safe here, Torie. I don't want you to think otherwise, but I need to—"

"To what?"

"This," he said, leaning into her, pressing his lips to hers. He wanted to snatch her up, devour her, pull her into her arms and fill himself with her.

BOOK YOUR PLACE ON OUR WEBSITE AND MAKE THE READING CONNECTION!

We've created a customized website just for our very special readers, where you can get the inside scoop on everything that's going on with Zebra, Pinnacle and Kensington books.

When you come online, you'll have the exciting opportunity to:

- View covers of upcoming books
- Read sample chapters
- Learn about our future publishing schedule (listed by publication month *and author*)
- Find out when your favorite authors will be visiting a city near you
- Search for and order backlist books from our online catalog
- Check out author bios and background information
- Send e-mail to your favorite authors
- Meet the Kensington staff online
- Join us in weekly chats with authors, readers and other guests
- Get writing guidelines
- AND MUCH MORE!

**Visit our website at
http://www.kensingtonbooks.com**

DARK and DEADLY

Jeanne Adams

ZEBRA BOOKS
Kensington Publishing Corp.
http://www.kensingtonbooks.com

ZEBRA BOOKS are published by

Kensington Publishing Corp.
119 West 40th Street
New York, NY 10018

All Kensington titles, imprints, and distributed lines are available at special quantity discounts for bulk purchases for sales promotion, premiums, fundraising, educational or institutional use.

Special book excerpts or customized printings can also be created to fit specific needs. For details, write or phone the office of the Kensington Special Sales Manager: Kensington Publishing Corp., 119 West 40th Street, New York, NY 10018. Attn. Special Sales Department. Phone: 1-800-221-2647.

ISBN-13: 978-1-4201-0430-1
ISBN-10: 1-4201-0430-6

First Printing: June 2009
10 9 8 7 6 5 4 3 2 1

Printed in the United States of America

Acknowledgments

As always, I want to thank my beloved family for their unflagging support. You're the best.

In addition, I'd like to thank Kenneth I. Korenblatt, Battalion Chief, Montgomery County Maryland Fire and Rescue, Fire and Explosives Investigations for the information he provided about arson investigation and Molotov cocktails. I'd also like to thank Barbara Watkins of State Farm Insurance for her assistance in figuring out timelines on the insurance issues. Last but not least, I want to thank Laura Graham Booth, fellow author and Washington Romance Writers member, for her insider's knowledge of Philadelphia.

Trust me, any errors, missteps, oddities, or omissions in this work are mine!

No dedication would be complete without acknowledging the amazing and wonderful support of my fellow readers and writers: The Avocats, the wonderful Banditas at The Romance Bandits' blog, http://www.romancebandits.blogspot.com; and the fab ladies Romance Novel TV and Romance Buy The Book. You rock, ladies! Nor could I ever go without thanking my fabulous editor, Kate Duffy; and my wonderful agent, Laurie McLean.

DARK *and*
DEADLY

Prologue

"What do you mean we can't get married?" Torie's words were a panicked screech. "Todd, there are five hundred guests in the church. The music's started. They've seated our mothers, for God's sake." She gestured, and rose petals flew from her bouquet, drifting to the floor like snow.

Panic filled her. Half of Philadelphia was waiting for her to walk down the aisle. Her sorority sisters were there. His fraternity brothers, mostly sober, were there. Even the lawyers from his new firm, and her boss from the engineering firm, were there to see her marry Todd.

"I know, I know. But, I can't do it Torie. I can't. Not now."

"What changed, Todd, between Monday, when I left the conference in Raleigh and today?" Torie's heart stuttered. "Oh, my God. You slept with someone. You had a fling."

"No, no, no," Todd protested, his face stricken, grabbing her waving hands, bouquet and all. "I didn't, I swear. What happened is—"

"Tell me," she insisted. "I have a right to know."

"I won the jackpot," he blurted. "Three hundred and sixty-eight million dollars. I never expected, I mean, you know, I always buy a ticket on special days."

He did. She knew that. They'd always talked about what they'd do if they won.

Her mind whirled. Oh, good Lord, he'd won.

"You won?" she managed faintly. "All that money?"

They would never have to scrimp. Her mother's complaints about Todd's spendthrift habits and frat-boy ways would be nothing against that kind of income. They could—

Torie went very still as his words sank in. He was choosing the money over her, over the life they'd planned.

Devastation came first. Then hot anger boiled in her veins. He didn't want to share a new, financially prosperous life with her.

She wasn't good enough.

Oblivious to her reaction, he just shook his head. "I know, it's crazy. But you understand, right? This changes everything in my life."

"You son of a bitch," Torie snarled as she balled up her fist.

The door from the bride's room to the church opened, but Torie barely heard it, and didn't look around. The bouquet disintegrated, and the best man gasped as Torie decked her groom.

Chapter One

Five years later

Grunting with the effort, he hefted the bundle from the trunk and into the wheelchair. He hadn't expected the body to be this heavy. It wasn't like the guy was fat or anything.

He was sweating like a pig by the time he got to the church door. Nudging it open, then kicking it shut behind him, he let the wheelchair topple as he dragged Todd's solid weight backward toward the altar. The round hole in the corpse's forehead stared at him accusingly, like an eye from another world.

He ignored it.

As much as he'd enjoyed the actual killing, he hated having to go to the worst parts of town to buy unregistered, illegal guns. Dealing with those people was distasteful.

"You may have had everything, you prick," he grunted to the dead man, finally tossing him on the steps leading to the pulpit. "And because of you, I got nothing. But thanks to *me*—" he laughed now, still wheezing from the effort as he arranged Todd's limp hands—"you never got to enjoy it. Not one bit. Not really."

He placed one of Todd's hands at his crotch, the other at his forehead like a fainting woman. He giggled, thinking that when the body went into rigor mortis the coroner wouldn't be able to move the hands from their position. What a great picture for the police file. Todd would look as silly in death as he'd made others feel in life.

"There now. A fitting tribute. You got to fuck the woman I wanted, and you were always whining like a stupid bitch over the details." He pitched his voice high like a girl's. "*Is it legal?* Blah, blah, blah. Now everyone will mourn you. Hell," he giggled again, "I'll mourn you. No one will ever guess. Hee hee."

Uncapping a bottle, he sprinkled blood on Todd's shirtfront, then rubbed some blood on the knuckles as well. It hadn't been easy to get it, but blood drive volunteers, especially well-known ones, weren't watched that closely.

Ripping open an envelope he pulled from inside his jumpsuit, he plucked a series of long blond hairs from it, draping one across the lapel of the designer suit Todd wore. He then dropped the others around the body, making sure at least one stuck in the blood on Todd's knuckles.

With a skipping step, he practically danced over to the thermostat. Setting the controls to the lowest possible air-conditioning setting, he then programmed it to come back up to regular temperature within twenty-four hours. The body would probably be found on Saturday of course, when parishioners came to the church to prep for the Sunday service. Then again, it could be Sunday morning. Nice thought. Either way, if all the TV shows and books were right, the cold temperatures would delay determination of time of death.

Perfect for what he wanted.

Within minutes, he'd stashed the wheelchair and relocked the church. It took only two more minutes to park the car he'd used to transport the body at the gas station on the corner. He slipped through the concealing shadows to his own car four blocks away. The first layer of gloves he'd stripped off went into a plastic bag. He'd dispose of them across town.

So many idiots left evidence too close to the crime scene. Stupid. Then again, most criminals were morons. The crime shows were sensationalized, of course, but most were built on brainless things people had actually done, like dropping gloves or weapons a block or less away. No wonder they got caught.

The second rental car was parked in the public lot downtown. He'd parked his own car on the street and put enough quarters in the meter to get him past the time the meters were in effect. Snapping on another pair of latex gloves, he popped the trunk on the junky car to be sure the pipe bombs and Molotov cocktails were still in their protective cushioning. Grinning at them, he carefully shut the trunk. He didn't want the fireworks to start early.

As he drove off the lot and turned north, he couldn't stop laughing. He cranked the radio, and sang along to the songs as they came on. He felt so free. No one would ever know.

It wasn't the perfect crime because there was no way now he could get the money. In some ways, that made it better; there was no obvious motive for him to do anything to anyone.

It was revenge at its purist. He didn't profit, but neither of *them* would have it, or each other.

At this point, that was enough.

He'd practiced and practiced tossing the bombs and bottles. He knew it would work faultlessly because he'd had plenty of time to perfect his technique. Five long years to plan, to decide, to study. To practice.

He dabbed his forehead and neck with his handkerchief. He was still sweating from moving the body, drat it. He'd worked out with a trainer to prepare, but he really needed to get more exercise, as annoying and disgusting as it was.

He hated it, but he needed to go to the gym more often. Otherwise, how could he possibly manage his new life, once his revenge had run its course?

Two left turns got him onto the quiet Society Hill side street where *she* lived. To his delight, his scan for dog walkers and busybodies showed nothing. No one was out.

That would change quickly, he decided with another giggle. It was the work of seconds to jump out, throw the bombs, light the bottles and throw them, then dive back into the car.

The devices arched through the air, breaking the windows just as he'd envisioned it. Perfect. Everything was perfect. He tossed the last pipe bomb hard enough to break the windows in her car where it sat out front.

Fire blossomed with a roar in the house as he sped away.

"What a total rush!" he exalted.

Behind him, the boom of the explosives he'd tossed in both house and car shattered the calm night. "Woooo-hoooo!" he screamed, laughing like a loon.

The only thing that would be better was if he could stay and watch.

That's how real criminals were exposed though, he reminded himself. His work was about justice. Not crime. So he knew better than to make low-class, uneducated mistakes.

Slowing to a sedate pace, he drove to another lot on Chestnut, switched the plates to a different rental car, and dropped that rickety junker back at a third, unrelated agency four blocks away. Peeling out of the workman's coverall he was wearing, he packed the clothes, gloves, and wig into a plastic bag, and put that in a plain black gym bag. He threw the second pair of gloves into a McDonalds' trash can as he walked up to Fifth and hailed a cab. There were always cabs in Society Hill, even at night. The bars and nightspots were popular, and since both the Phillies and the Flyers were playing at home, the town was busy.

His elegant suit was only slightly rumpled, and it got him immediate attention.

"Where to, sir?" the cabbie inquired.

"Market and Ludlow, over by the Shops at Liberty Place. My car's on the street there. I had to bring an, uh, mmm, tipsy friend home."

"Oh, yeah," the cabbie nodded with sage understanding and a glance at the gym bag. As hoped, the cabbie assumed he had been unlucky in love. "Bummer. You want I should drop you at the car, or somewhere else?"

"I think this was enough of a letdown that I'll head on home." Pretending to be tired was far more difficult than he'd imagined. Delicious joy pulsed within him.

Todd was dead. Hopefully Torie was, too.

They deserved it. Every bit of it.

Now, there was only one last thing to do. He nearly giggled aloud at the thought. He was so high, it would be easy. *Easy peasy rice and cheesy,* he singsonged the playground chant in his mind.

What a wonderful day.

Torie dropped her keys on the hall table and headed back to the kitchen. Stopping only long enough to plunk her purse and grocery bags on the counter, she continued through her townhouse to the stairs.

"I'm coming, I'm coming," she called to the dog whining behind the baby gate across her bedroom door. Her young Labrador retriever was wiggling in doggie ecstasy as she approached, as if to say, "You're home! You're home!"

Torie kicked off her shoes in the hall and grabbed the dog's collar before she disengaged the gate. Hanging on for dear life, she managed to keep Pickle's feet mostly on the ground, preserving her skirt and blouse.

"C'mon, Pickle, let's get you outside, girl."

With the dog bounding around the small backyard, Torie hurried upstairs to change. For the first time in weeks, she hadn't brought work home. She was going to cook herself a nice dinner, and spend the evening with the dog and a good book.

She was tired of work, tired of being everyone's go-to girl. She figured she'd beat her mother to the punch, call early and get off the phone right away. As much as she loved her mother, the prospect of an evening free of questions about her dating habits and marital prospects was worth the pain of being the first to call. Now that her mother was in assisted living, her chief entertainment was calling Torie and bedeviling her only daughter about her social life.

Torie decided jeans and a sweatshirt would withstand Pickle's enthusiasm. Her bare feet were silent on the lovely wood floors as she padded to let the dog in. She was absorbing the licks and absolute happiness of the dog's greeting when she heard it.

The crash was loud. The sound of breaking glass was unmistakable. So was the pungent smell of gasoline. And fire. What on earth? Had someone hit her car? The house? Struggling to her feet, she held Pickle's collar. The dog barked frantically as they started toward the living room.

Then the world exploded.

Flung backward, she and the dog slammed against the wall. It was a moment before the sounds and smells penetrated her shock. The roar of flames, the nauseating smell of burning curtains and upholstery.

Phone. The phone. She had to get it, call nine-one-one.

A whimper made her pause. Pickle was struggling to rise as well, and Torie scooped her up with a grunt, grabbed her purse, and ran for the back door.

The second explosion threw them through the door and into a heap on the back deck. She saw stars as her head connected with the edge of the concrete planter.

Sirens wailed in the darkness as Torie groaned and tried to get up. Someone had seen the flames. Thank God. Still, she fumbled for her purse. The phone— she had to get to the phone. Wrestling it from her bag, she dialed nine-one-one.

"Philadelphia Dispatch. What is the nature of your emergency?"

"Fire," Torie croaked, giving her address. "Ambulance. I'm on the back deck. I need my vet." Pickle was whimpering in pain, her leg at an awkward angle. She managed to stutter out the vet's name before the pain in her head registered. "Oh, shit," she mumbled as the dispatcher firmly requested her status. Staring at the red liquid covering her hand. "I'm really bleeding. A lot." Her vision wavered and her forehead throbbed.

She hated blood.

The roar of sirens and heavy engines filled her ears. Or was that the blood rushing out? How could you tell?

The dispatcher's voice was getting farther and farther away. Everything narrowed to the blood on her hand. She pressed her head again, and her palm came away wetter and redder.

"Fascinating," she whispered a moment before she pitched forward onto the deck next to the whimpering dog.

Everything was swimming and swaying. Voices echoed in her head and all around her. She couldn't identify any of it.

"Wha . . ." she tried to speak, to sit up.

Firm hands held her down. "Be still, ma'am. We're taking you to the emergency room now. They'll check you out, get some stitches in that cut."

"Cut?"

"Yes, ma'am. You have a pretty serious cut on your forehead."

"My dog," Torie struggled to sit up again. "Pickle. My dog. She was hurt."

"Please, ma'am. Don't try to sit. I don't know about

the dog, but I'm sure the firefighters got her, and are looking after her."

The wait was interminable—the wait for the doctor, for the numbing agent to work on her head, the wait for word on Pickle. Waiting for everything.

No one would talk to her about what had happened. Her stomach was in knots, her head was pounding so hard she could hardly see. They wanted to give her a pill to kill the pain, then keep her overnight, but she needed to know about Pickle, and her house. And she needed to know *why?* Why would anyone set fire to her house?

"Miss?" she called out to a passing nurse. "I'm sorry to bother you, but has anyone from the fire department come or called yet?"

The nurse had pity in her eyes. It was the third time Torie had asked. Every nurse on the floor probably knew about the pitiful woman who was worried about her dog and her house.

"I'm sorry," the nurse replied, stepping to the side of the bed to fluff the flat pillow. "If you could relax for a bit, I'm sure someone from the police will be along to let you know. We're going to move you upstairs as soon as we can." She unclipped the chart and frowned. "Why don't you go ahead and take the pain medication? We'll wake you up when the officers arrive."

Frustrated, Torie shook her head. She regretted the gesture immediately. She moaned as her vision blurred, and her stomach rebelled at the swimming sensation. "Oh, God, I think I'm going to be sick."

The nurse shoved an emesis basin into her hands, but also pressed the webbing at the juncture of her thumb and forefinger. The relief wasn't immediate, but the nausea backed off.

Closing her eyes with relief, she relaxed into the flat pillow. The nurse adjusted the bed to support her.

"What did you do? That pressure thing?" Torie managed to ask.

"Acupressure. I learned it when I was pregnant and had constant morning sickness. Sometimes it helps. Luckily, it did for you. It's no fun to be sick when you've got a concussion and an impressive set of stitches in your forehead."

Torie was beginning to feel the pins-and-needles sensation in her skin as the local anesthetic wore off. The pain medication would be good, but she hated to take it, hated to feel so out of control. She needed to know something, anything, about her house, about what had happened.

Before she completed the thought, she heard several male voices beyond the curtain, and she heard her name.

"There. Finally," the nurse commented. "You can get your answers, and then get some rest."

Two men slipped through the curtains. One was short but lean, like a greyhound. The other was tall, a bit on the bulky side. The tall one looked, ironically, like a bulldog, all jowls and attitude.

"Ms. Victoria Hagen?"

"Yes. Can you tell me about my dog? She was out on the deck with me, I asked the dispatcher . . ."

The short one interrupted. "I'm Battalion Chief Marsden, I'm a fire investigator. The dog was taken to the ASPCA shelter hospital. They'll take good care of her, I'm sure."

"The shelter? But they might put her to sleep, or

think she's abandoned," Torie exclaimed, once again struggling to sit up. Her swimming head warned her to stop. Right now.

She sat still. She had to get her stomach calmed down so she could manage a call to her vet. Now.

Well, maybe when they moved her to a room. She squinted against the light, her head still pounding. There would be a phone in the room. Yes. That's what she would do. She'd call Karen, the vet, from the room.

"Uh, no, ma'am," the tall investigator spoke slowly and shook his head as well, as if she couldn't understand the words he was saying. "They won't hurt her. They know you're her owner and what the circumstances are. She'll be looked after."

"Do you know if she's okay?"

"No, ma'am, but I'm sure she is. We need to ask you some questions."

Of course they did. Her own questions flooded her mind and poured out in a rush. "What about my house? Is it okay? They were able to put the fire out, right? Oh, God," she managed, when the two men exchanged glances. "My laptop. My photos. Granny's bible. Oh, God. Did it . . . did it . . . burn to the ground?" The words came out in a choked whisper.

"No ma'am. But there is a lot of damage. Our team of arson investigators are there now. The fire's out, and once the team's done they'll do an overhaul and check, but they'll see to the building tonight. We won't know till morning the extent of the damage. You'll need to call your insurance company right away, of course."

"Uh, didn't look like a total loss, ma'am," the shorter man, Chief Marsden interjected.

"Not a total loss," Torie managed weakly. Squeezing

her eyes shut to block the glare, she imagined the devastation. *Not a total loss* left a lot of room for destruction.

"Please Ms. Hagen, the doctor has restricted our time with you, and we do need the information while it's fresh in your mind."

Oh, it was fresh all right. The smell of fire and blood lingered in her hair. She could even smell it on her skin.

Fear. She smelled that, too. Her own fear. How many times would her life be turned upside down?

"Ms. Hagen?"

"Yes. What do you need to know, Detective . . . ?"

"Oh, sorry. I'm Investigator Sorrels. Walk us through what happened. Tell us everything you remember."

Step by step, she took them through the events. They wanted to know about her day, the time leading up to when she got home.

"I left work late. Grabbed a . . . drink with a friend." No need to tell the police what else she and Pam had grabbed. She needed to call Pam. Shit, when was she going to do that? "Um, I, um, stopped and got some groceries. Came home."

"A neighbor said you had a visitor when you got home."

Surprise must have been written all over her face because the taller man smirked. "Your neighbor's the curtain-peeking sort, I believe."

"Missus Bellfort. Yes, she is," Torie managed, gritting her teeth at a new wave of pain in her head. *Snarky old biddie. It just figured she'd be watching everyone on the block. As usual.*

"I hope she saw something useful." Irritation made the headache worse. "The visitor was Dev, my cousin from New Orleans. He stopped by, wanted to come in, but I told him it wasn't convenient."

"You don't get along with this cousin?" Marsden's voice sharpened, every bit of his attention focused on Torie. It was weird to watch the switch from laconic to on-point.

"No, it's not that." Torie wondered how on earth to explain. "Dev's my fourth cousin, a couple times removed. He's in town on a conference. I knew he was going to be in town, we talked about getting coffee or something, but no firm plans. We share a great-grandmother. She sent a message that he felt needed to be delivered in person."

"What are you leaving out?" This from Sorrels.

Crap. Mama had always said she was too easy to read. Torie sighed. "He wanted to take me out for dinner or drinks to catch up. I'd just come in from . . ." she hesitated, telling herself again that she had to call Pam, make sure their stories were straight. "Drinks with my friend, as I said. I just wanted to spend the rest of the evening in."

"And you didn't invite your cousin in as well?"

"It wasn't, um, convenient. And he wanted to go out. He's kind of a party guy."

Men who came into her house got hurt.

Or worse.

She'd been trying to protect Dev as best she could. Besides, she had been tired.

"Ms. Hagen?"

"Sorry. My head's hurting a lot. Anyway, Dev delivered my great-grandmother's message, and headed back to his conference. I went into the house to put the groceries away, change, and take Pickle out."

"Pickle?"

"My dog."

"And your cousin's full name? And the name of the convention, too, if you remember?"

"Devereaux Chance. The convention's for green building technologies." Marsden made a note, of course.

"And what happened then?"

Torie told them about the sound of breaking glass, the smell of gasoline, how she'd headed toward it, then been blasted back by the explosion. The two exchanged glances.

"You're very lucky, Ms. Hagen. If you'd gotten into the room, you would have been severely injured." She got the strong sense that Sorrels really meant she'd have been killed.

"Did anything else happen today? Anything unusual?"

"Nothing that I can think of. I got up, went to work, basic stuff."

"Is there anyone who would want to hurt you? An ex-husband? Ex-boyfriend? Anyone with whom you work?" Sorrels probed.

"Old boss? Ex-fiancé?" Marsden chimed in.

When her eyes flew open at the last words, Marsden's face took on that sharp look again.

"Tell me about the ex-fiancé," he said, his gaze intense.

"Oh, not Todd. He would never hurt me. He can hardly kill bugs." She rubbed at her forehead, which hurt more and more with each passing second. Her rubbing at it didn't help. "He's got this reverence-for-life thing going. Went to Tibet to find himself. He got back into town again, and called me yesterday. We were going to have lunch tomorrow after he met with his lawyer." She had to remember to cancel that.

Todd's face popped into her mind's eye, the way she'd last seen him. Right next to him, looming large in her memory was Paul Jameson, Todd's gorgeous, irritating frat brother, and lawyer. She never thought about Paul without reliving the horrible moment when he'd walked into the bride's room as she punched Todd.

The images were accompanied by the terrible swimmy feeling in her senses, along with the pounding behind her eyes. "Wow, my head really hurts."

The nurse had been silent up to this point, a chaperone in scrubs, but at Torie's complaint, she cleared her throat. "I think you need to wrap it up, gentlemen. Ms. Hagen needs to rest."

"What's the ex-fiancé's full name?"

"Todd Alan Peterson."

"When did you, dum . . . uh, call off the wedding?"

Torie scrunched her eyes against the pain, which grew worse by the minute. "Five years ago," she managed to grind out. "Exactly five years to the day, this Saturday."

There was a lot of beeping and the sound of pings from the machines behind her head. The bed suddenly went flat and her head spun with dizzying force. It was the last straw for her stomach.

With a heave, she vomited. Then choked.

The last thing she heard was the nurse hollering in the loudest voice Torie had ever heard. It rang in her head for hours.

"I need a doctor in here. Stat!"

Chapter Two

There were flowers everywhere. It was only the next morning, but people had already heard about her house, her injuries. Torie counted no less than eight bouquets. They'd begun arriving early in the morning, once she'd been installed in a regular room. There were roses from her brother, who had also called. She'd reassured him that coming home from Russia wasn't necessary.

There wasn't much he could do really, and it wouldn't help his business to fly home and do nothing. The office had sent a plant, and each of the divisions had sent flowers as well. Two of her major clients from TruStructure, her engineering firm, had sent flowers, and one had sent a really interesting looking cookie-tower-thingie from Harry & David.

Other than the fact that she had a concussion, had almost choked to death, hurt all over, and had a partially destroyed house, she felt pretty good.

"Alive and hurting is better than the alternative," she said into the quiet of the room. She needed to hear something besides beeping.

Pickle was in the gentle and competent hands of her very own vet, thank goodness, so she didn't have to worry about that anymore. Pam knew to cover for her for their little excursion after drinks and before the grocery.

A niggle of worry wormed its way into her thoughts. What about Dev? Her great-grandmother, GoodMama, had sent a warning. It had been about fire. Surely he'd heard from her, or heard about it on the news. And Todd. Where was he? Even after the horrible way things had ended, they'd somehow managed to stay friends. She'd left a message about lunch on his cell phone, saying she was in the hospital. She'd left the number, too. It wasn't like him to not call. She looked at the bouquets again. None of them were from Todd, and he was a champion flower buyer.

"How's my patient this morning?" a cheery voice called from the doorway. Her doctor, a spritely woman in her sixties, bounced into the room.

"I'm good, Dr. Suz, when can I go home?"

"When I say you're ready." Suz Pierce smiled and deflected Torie's protests with the ease of long practice. "A concussion's nothing to fool with young lady. Not to mention that you've got a lot of work ahead of you to get your house in order, so to speak. You don't need to start on that until you're fit for duty."

"I'm bored," Torie sulked. Even she could hear the petulance in the words. "Sorry, but I am."

"Better bored than unconscious. Too hard to read?"

Nodding, Torie grimaced. Her head still hurt if she made too many sudden movements. "My iPod's at the house, probably a pile of plastic goo, same as my laptop." She managed to talk even as the doctor checked her eyes and gently examined the lump and cut on her head. The nurse who had checked her vital signs not ten minutes before came trotting through the door in time to hear Dr. Suz say, "Any friends coming to visit today? Maybe they could get you some magazines or something."

"Or our volunteers keep a supply, if you'd like some," the perky woman chimed in.

"I forgot about that," Dr. Suz said. "Why don't you see if Nancy can find something from this century, preferably the last few months."

"She already has some visitors," Nurse Perky chirped as she held a tray to receive the dressing the doctor was changing. To Torie, she said, "They'll be able to come back when Dr. Pierce is finished, and you're ready."

"Thanks." The idea of visitors cheered her immensely. Maybe Pam had come. Or Dev. Or Todd. She'd left a message at Todd's hotel as well.

Hopefully Todd was smart enough not to bring the odious Paul Jameson with him.

To her dismay, the first two people in her door were the fire investigators.

"Good morning, Ms. Hagen, how are you feeling?" Sorrels began as soon as he made eye contact.

"Okay, all things considered. Have you been by my house? How does it look?"

The investigators glanced at one another.

"That bad?"

"No, but it doesn't look good. It's better than it might be, with the fire department being so close. Structurally, we'll have to wait for the city inspector to let us know. Evidently, you've got some kind of fire retardant in your insulation? That seems to have given some protection to the structure."

"Oh, I had the house reinsulated several years ago."

Torie was delighted and surprised that the stuff had been of some use. It hadn't been as insulating as she'd been promised, but if it saved her house, she'd never regret the expense again.

"That might be it. Anyway, your insurance adjuster has been by, and your neighbors have asked after you. Evidently, the whole neighborhood knows you."

"I used to run the neighborhood association," Torie explained.

"Ah. That makes sense."

She wondered what they thought she was up to, by the looks of relief. Drug smuggling? Gang activity? Prostitution? The last thought nearly made her giggle. All the possibilities skittered through her mind as the men continued to comment on the neighborhood and the house.

"There is one thing we need to tell you, Ms. Hagen. It may be a bit concerning to you."

"Concerning?"

"Yes, your cousin—" Sorrels began.

"Have you talked to him?" Torie interrupted. "I can't get a hold of him."

"There's a reason for that." The grave look on Marsden's face had Torie leaping to a terrible conclusion.

"Oh, Lord, something happened to Dev? What? What happened?"

"He was stabbed several times. The attack occurred in a park near the hotel where he was evidently staying."

"Stabbed?" she screeched. "Is he alive? Is he okay? Where is he?"

Both inspectors made calming motions as they stumbled over their words, reassuring her.

"I'm sorry to break it this way," began Marsden.

"He'll be fine. He's two floors down on the third floor," Sorrels soothed.

"Who would do that sort of thing? Oh, God, poor Dev."

"What's important," Marsden recovered his composure to continue. "He's not the one who bombed your house."

"Of course he isn't," Torie replied, highly indignant. "I don't know why you'd even suspect him."

"Motive and opportunity," snapped Sorrels. "I checked your name in our database, Ms. Hagen. You seem to have an unfortunate number of accidents happening around you."

Torie felt all the blood drain from her face. No one had ever put it quite so boldly before. In fact, she didn't think anyone but Pam had realized how many of her boyfriends, dates, and lovers had had serious or life-threatening accidents or injuries over the last few years. All within weeks or months of dating her, or breaking up with her.

She was cursed. She knew it.

That's why she'd turned Dev away, why she'd stopped dating. Why she eluded her friend Pam's attempts at matchmaking, and basically went to work and came home to her dog.

"It's true," she stuttered the word. "I don't know why, but a lot of the people . . . men . . . I've dated, have had accidents or . . . or . . ."

"Another man died."

"Yes."

"You don't know why this is happening?"

"No. I tried to talk to someone about it, at the police department, but all they did was ask about me. Did I have a stalker or someone who had threatened me, that's all they asked about. I didn't. I don't. I haven't ever been threatened."

"Is it possible that your cousin is another victim of this pattern?"

Unable to speak, Torie could only nod.

"We still haven't located Mister Peterson. His lawyer has reported him missing. Do you know anything about where he might have gone?"

Pulled away from her thoughts about Dev, she frowned, which pulled at the stitches. It hurt.

"No, I don't. He'd never stand Paul up for a meeting. They were roommates and fraternity brothers. They're both lawyers, and they worked together at Pratt and Legend before Todd won all the money."

"Did he have any other kind of relationship with this friend of his?" The words were straightforward, and the detective's bland countenance gave her no hints to his meaning.

"What do you mean?"

"Was the lawyer involved with your former fiancé, in a relationship of any kind?"

"A relationship? Paul was Todd's lawyer. Paul was Todd's best man at our wedding. He was Todd's best friend. They'd talked about going into business someday, but other than that, I don't know." The look of sly innuendo on Sorrell's face led her to another conclusion.

"Oh, no, not that. You mean like lovers? No way." The idea gave her the creeps. Having slept with Todd, she knew he liked women. As to Paul, he'd been the campus lothario—known as Love-'em-and-leave-'em-Jameson. She told the detectives about both men's proclivities with as straight a face as she could manage.

"So what do you think of Jameson?"

Cheap shot. Marsden could obviously read body language and tone.

"I don't like him, but you've obviously guessed that. He never approved of me, or of my relationship with Todd."

She tried to be brief, but Marsden kept prodding her.

"How do you know he didn't approve?"

She stalled, but he pressed. Finally she gave in.

"In a drunken rant back in our college days, he told Todd that he was a fool to date me. Then later in grad school, he told Todd he was crazy to marry me, and that we'd be miserable together.

"Even up to the day of our wedding, he tried to talk Todd out of it. When Todd came to tell me he was backing out of the wedding, I thought Paul was to blame and I socked Todd and told him to tell Paul Jameson to," Torie hesitated, but decided since she'd said this much, she might as well get the rest of the sorry, embarrassing story on the table. "Well, I told him to tell Paul to get, uh, screwed. Except I used the other word, the f-word. I'm afraid the whole church heard it because Paul walked in as I hit Todd."

"Wow. I'll bet that caused an uproar." Sorrels's eyes were dancing with humor, but his face remained bland. She thought she caught the barest twitch of a smile. She was still mortified to have cussed in church, and to have had virtually everyone in the world she cared about hear her do it.

"Understatement of the century, I'm afraid. So Paul still doesn't like me, nor I him."

"And Todd called off the wedding because?"

"He won the Lotto jackpot."

"And didn't . . . ah . . ." Marsden stopped mid-sentence and busied himself making notes. Evidently he was drawing his own conclusions as to why Todd had called it off.

"I believe we'll want to talk to Mister Jameson a bit more about your situation, and about Mister Peterson's whereabouts."

"It isn't unusual," Sorrels spoke now, "for one party in a situation to have . . . unrequited feelings . . . for another man. It's possible that Mister Jameson may know more than he's telling."

The very idea was ludicrous, and she very nearly told them so. But even all these years later, she still held a grudge against Paul. She was sure that his antipathy had been a factor in the decisions Todd had made when he'd won the money. The first and only person Todd told about his winnings before he told Torie had been Paul.

Given that, she could see why the detectives would see Paul in a skewed light, but the idea that Paul was gay nearly made her laugh out loud. His bearing and demeanor was all male—all red-blooded male. He was very determinedly heterosexual. She knew that intimately. Of course that knowledge was connected with a lot of bad memories.

Then and now, the intensity of his sensuality, the way he sometimes looked at her made her terribly uncomfortable. Between that and his repeated, public declarations that she was all wrong for Todd, Torie disliked him intensely. When she and Todd moved in together before the wedding, she'd asked Todd not to invite him to parties or dinners at their house. Nor did she ever want to be left alone with him.

She didn't hate him. He made her feel and remember things that she wasn't prepared to deal with.

Just one more reason Paul hated *her*.

As if he'd read her thoughts, Sorrels spoke. "So do you know why Mister Jameson doesn't like you or why he would try to break up your relationship?"

"I don't know."

"I'm sure you have some idea." Sorrels shot her a knowing look. "Most women have an inkling about that sort of thing."

"I don't know for sure. He thought Todd would stray. Wouldn't be able to be faithful. Or so he said. I never thought that at all. Todd kept his word, so I thought Paul was being, I don't know, overprotective."

"Of you?"

Torie frowned. That angle hadn't occurred to her. "No, like I said, he doesn't like me. I guess he was protecting Todd from the possibility of an expensive divorce later. He *is* a lawyer."

"Did you and Mister Peterson have a prenuptial agreement?"

"A what? No, that wasn't Todd's style. Or mine. Besides, it doesn't matter now, does it? It was five years ago."

"Maybe it matters to Mister Jameson."

Paul Jameson's face leaped into her mind. Lean and tan, as it had been in their college days. Everybody's pal. Everyone except her. He'd been so attractive, so ready to go out or make out with anyone. Just not her. Until after that one night.

Steering away from that thought, she shifted to wondering about her cousin. Ironically, Dev was a similar type. Very masculine, very much the easygoing friendly playboy sort. But he didn't set her teeth on edge.

Dev.

Oh, Lord.

"Do you need anything more from me? I need to find out about my cousin, go see him if I can."

"I don't think so. We'll keep you up to date on our findings, Ms. Hagen. Please let us know if you think of anything else. However, before you go anywhere, there's another officer who wants to speak to you about your cousin's incident."

Incident? Nope. It was an attack. How could she expect these men to understand the curse? But she hadn't dated Dev. Why had he been a victim? Good-Mama was going to be so upset. Not only had Torie not heeded the warning about the fire—although honestly she hadn't had any time to do so—but Dev had gotten hurt as well. GoodMama would be frantic, and further upset and outraged that Torie had embroiled her favorite great-grandson in her own personal curse, sending him to the hospital.

Oh, man she was in *so* much trouble. She'd be lucky if GoodMama didn't put her own curse on her troublesome great-granddaughter.

She was so caught up in her thoughts as the investigators left that she barely registered when her best friend Pam slipped into the room.

"Girl, you look like a thundercloud."

"Jeez!" Torie yipped in surprise. "You scared the crap out of me."

Pam set the bakery box of doughnuts on the table, dropped her fat purse in the chair, and stretched over the bed to give Torie a firm, best-friend hug. "Don't know why, it's like Grand Central in here, all the comings and goings. Who were the two stuffed shirts? They looked like insurance salesmen or cops."

"Ding, ding, ding. Give the lady a prize," Torie joked as she returned the pressure. Having Pam there to support her brought her to tears. Pam was so strong, such a great friend. With everything that had happened to her over the past five years, and even before when they were in college, Pam had been and still was her anchor to sanity.

Torie wiped her eyes as Pam plopped into the chair. "So, tell me everything," she demanded, digging a can of Diet Pepsi from her purse. After unwrapping a straw, she took a long drink, and grabbed a doughnut. "Well?"

"They're the fire inspectors assigned to my case. My house was torched, no accident."

"You need a lucky clover or rabbit's foot, girlfriend. No, scratch that, everyone around you, the males at least, need a clover. Better yet, I need to rub your shoulder for luck. You manage to end up okay when everyone around you is getting knocked for a loop."

"Yeah, well, I got the loop knocked out of me this time," Torie pointed to her bandaged head. "And Dev. Oh, Pam, Dev's been hurt." Torie reached for her hand. "You have to find out how he is. They said he was here in this hospital, on the third floor."

"Oh, man, really? Dev?" Pam sat forward, drink forgotten. "The sexy-cousin-from-New-Orleans-Dev? Don't tell me he's one of the *men fatales.*" *Men fatales* was the moniker Pam had hung on the men who had dated Torie, and suffered for the privilege.

"I don't know. I think so, but we never actually *dated.*"

"You didn't date Jorge either. He fixed your plumbing and your roof, was at your house for a few meals, and viola, he's left with a broken leg from a hit-and-run."

"Exactly."

"Okay, item one on the agenda is to see about Devastating Cousin Devereaux." Pam made a check mark in the air. "Item two, we need to talk about how to deal with the cleanup of you-know-what."

"They can't find out about that."

"Who?"

"The investigators. I told them you and I went out for a drink after work, then I came straight home after getting some groceries."

"We did have a drink." Pam shot her a wicked grin. "And a chaser."

Torie groaned, but smiled. "Yeah, we chased, and got chased, but nobody knows it was us, right? We have to keep it that way."

"No worries. I have the mangy dog stashed at Carlos's house." Pam had a legion of friends, mostly male, who would do anything for her, up to and probably including murder. She attracted men like bees to honey, and even when she didn't date them, or even acknowledge them, they still hung around, doing her favors at the slightest whiff of a whim.

"Is he okay?"

"Yeah, Carlos knows what to do, and how to handle him."

"Thank goodness for Carlos. Will he keep it quiet?"

"For me? Of course. I promised to bake him my special German chocolate cake."

When Torie dated a man he ended up in mortal peril; with Pam, they got cake. And probably coffee, too.

"So I'll go see about Devereaux. By the way, what's his last name?"

"Chance. Like take-a-chance."

"I'd love to," Pam quipped, picking up her bag.

"Har, har. Would you mind getting me something to read too? Like a magazine or something?"

"Your wish is my command." Pam dug around in

her capacious purse and pulled out a *People* magazine, along with an *InStyle* and the *Moore Manor* spring issue.

"The *Moore Manor*'s the most interesting, of course. Wait till you hear who they picked for Fall. Enjoy. I'll be back in a jiff."

Pam skipped out the door, a woman on a mission. Torie was about to buzz the nurse when another man walked in. Unfamiliar, but obviously a cop. He was gray-haired, but fairly young. As evidence, he immediately flashed a badge.

"Sorry to bother you, Ms. Hagen, but I'm Officer Tibbet. I'm here about your—" he consulted a notepad. "cousin, is it? Mister Devereaux Chance?"

"Yes, do you know how he is? My friend's gone to check on him."

"He's been out of surgery for a while now, and the nurses say he's doing great, considering."

"Surgery," Torie managed weakly, envisioning all manner of terrible things.

"Yeah. You knew he was stabbed, yes?"

"Yes. The other officers, the fire investigators, they told me."

"He got some licks in, too, evidently. Your cousin's no slouch in the self-defense area, I'm guessing."

"No, I'm sure he's very proficient. I know he did a stint with some kind of bodyguard business, or something."

"Hmmm, yeah, I'm figuring it's the 'or something' part, but either way, he fought back. Problem was he got a whack on the head as part of the package, so he didn't get a look at his attacker."

The officer took her through the same time line the detectives had, but he dug deeper into her dating habits and her situation with Todd, searching for a link among the men she'd dated. A link other than her.

"The investigators gave me their data, what they pulled out of the database. This is the run of all the guys who uh," he cleared his throat. "Anyway, I wonder if you'd look over this list, and see if I've left anyone off."

She looked. Read the notes he'd penciled in next to each name: burglary, vandalism, arson. Arson. Two hit-and-run accidents, identity theft issues—although that one had been weird. The culprit had actually closed everything and told the credit bureaus the guy was dead.

The only one missing from the list was Christian.

Closing her eyes against the continued pain in her heart, she told him about her dates with Christian, and what had happened.

"Hit-and-run?"

"That's what they told me."

Tibbet took Christian's name and last address, and jotted down the date of his death.

Where was Todd? Paul Jameson paced the lush confines of his office, worrying over the whereabouts of his best friend. He was sure that Todd was in trouble, just as he was sure that Torie Hagen had something to do with it. He'd told the police, when he reported Todd missing that *she* was the one with the most to gain by Todd being in trouble.

After all, she stood to inherit everything.

Not that she knew that. Unless Todd had been stupid enough to tell her.

He hoped Todd hadn't been that rash.

The woman was a menace. Everything she touched—especially Todd—was damaged. He'd been glad when Todd had left her. There had been a time when he wanted her for himself. Even now he could see her, picture her athletic build and her twinkling brown eyes. Thinking about her, though, brought him around to the memory of her terrified face, from the incident in college to the look on her face as she socked Todd at the church.

Neither memory was pleasant, and pretty much negated any feelings of warmth he'd ever had for her in the first place. And, of course, after the disaster at the church, she'd run away, leaving Todd and Paul to clean up the mess.

"Mister Jameson? There are two investigators here about a fire." His starchy assistant sounded affronted at the very idea of the officers.

"A fire? Todd?" Paul hurried toward her and the door. "Send them in."

"Of course," she said, unbending enough to add, "I hope everything's all right with Mister Peterson."

"I do, too, Martha. I do, too."

"Gentlemen." Martha ushered the two men into the office, where Paul shook their hands and showed them to the chairs opposite his desk. "How can I help you? Have you heard from Todd? Found him?"

"We're not missing persons, Mister Jameson. We're fire investigators. I'm Investigator Sorrels, he's Chief Marsden. We're here about a fire at Victoria Hagen's home. Could you tell us where you were between six and eight p.m. last night?"

"Torie? A fire? Oh, my God. Is she okay?"

"You seem concerned, Mister Jameson," Chief Marsden drawled. "I've been given to understand that there's bad blood between the two of you."

"Bad blood?" Paul could hear the harshness of his own words. "Not so much that I'd torch her house. As to your question, I was here, working on a deposition with a client, a stenographer, and my assistant until nearly nine."

"If I could get the stenographer's name?"

It pissed him off, but Paul gave them the woman's name. The sooner they ruled him out, the better. "Is Torie okay?"

"She's in the hospital." This was from the chief again, Marsden. "She got a conk on the head, a nasty cut. We're investigating who might have wanted to hurt her. Do you know anyone else who bore her a grudge, Mister Jameson?"

"You say that as if you think I bore her one. I didn't."

"And yet you didn't want her marrying your best friend. Why?"

"There were a lot of reasons. What does that have to do with anything now? That was five years ago."

"Humor us." Sorrels smiled. "Never know when things are connected."

"I didn't think they were well matched."

"Were you interested in Mister Peterson, and didn't want Torie to marry him?" Sorrels shot back.

"Interested . . ." Paul threw his head back and laughed. Wait till he told Todd. "Uh, no. Did Torie tell you that?" He hadn't thought she'd be that petty.

"No, actually she didn't. Quite the opposite. Did you prefer her for yourself?"

Paul tamped down his anger at the question. These

were experienced investigators. No need to give them anymore ammunition to look his way.

"No, but I did see that she was a far more serious, settle-down kind of girl. My friend was and is a happy-go-lucky sort. He didn't need to get married that young. Then things changed, and he didn't." Paul sighed. "Regardless, that was years ago. Todd has moved on with his life, and so, I presume, has Torie."

"Ms. Hagen indicated that she and Mister Peterson were to have lunch today, after he had a meeting with you. Were you aware of that?"

Paul frowned. Damn Todd and his endless need to *make it up* to Torie. Hadn't he done enough in apology for leaving her?

He shut down that line of thinking, since it was particularly fruitless. He'd never been able to convince Todd that Torie wasn't damaged for life by being left at the altar.

It served nothing to lie to the men before him, so Paul answered with the truth.

"No, I didn't know that. I would have tried to talk him out of it if I had. That's probably why he didn't tell me."

"Do you have any idea why he'd want to meet with her, and hide it from you?"

"He knew I wouldn't approve."

"And was your approval so important to him?" This from the taller one, Sorrels.

"We were friends, Inspector. I was also his counsel. Todd hasn't had an easy life, even with the money he won. I assume you know about the money?"

"Yes," Marsden replied. "Ms. Hagen indicated that he'd won a considerable sum, and that the win was the reason he called off the wedding. Do you agree with her assessment?"

"I do. I think he also had cold feet. He was worried about her mother's interfering ways, and about his own ability to be faithful. His eyes wandered a lot when they were dating. He never cheated on her, but I believe he thought about it."

Paul closed his eyes. He remembered how he'd once pulled Todd back from the brink when his flirting had nearly gone too far with a waitress in a bar. Paul hadn't wanted to see either Todd or Torie hurt. That had been the first time Paul had tried to talk him out of the marriage.

Unfortunately, Torie had walked in on that discussion.

"Anyway, he didn't cheat. Then he won the jackpot. He came to me with the news, and wondered how on earth he was going to tell Torie. I asked if she would be happy about it, and he said he didn't know."

"He didn't know if his fiancée would be happy about several million dollars?"

Chapter Three

Sorrels seemed surprised. Paul smiled.

"You see why I was worried?" Paul shrugged. "I kept asking him why he felt she wouldn't be happy about it. He said he wondered if she'd want to leave her widowed mother behind, travel the world." Paul remembered Todd's boyish excitement about the prospect of honest-to-goodness world travel. "I knew that anyone, especially a woman, would be happy about money coming in, but if he was worried, I was worried."

"Especially a woman? You thought she was a gold digger?"

"Oh, no, not in the sense you mean. Before the big win, her family had far more money than Todd's. Her father owned some sort of manufacturing business, did pretty well. He passed away a few years before they were to be married, and the business was sold, but at the time, they were doing well."

"So why else did you dislike Ms. Hagen? She indicated that there was an antipathy long before the aborted wedding."

Once again Paul squelched the instant spurt of

anger. How did you admit that kind of pain to a couple of strangers, both of whom had already decided you might be gay?

"We'd had a confrontation over some college . . ." he hesitated. Torie had been adamant about the situation then, and given the trouble it was still causing, he'd better choose his words with care. "Pranks. We argued about it. Very loudly. And she heard me tell Todd I thought he shouldn't get married. In typical fashion, she thought I was dissing her. I wasn't." He stated it flatly. Truthfully. It had never been about Torie, despite what she believed. "After that, she asked Todd not to invite me to their house. It wasn't very pleasant to be excluded, but hey, we were adults. I got over it. It was hard to see my friend put in the middle of a tug of war, though."

"I see," Sorrels made a series of scrawling notes. Paul wondered what inference the man had drawn from the simple words. Obviously Torie was up to her old tricks, pouring out the poison. How had he ever wanted her so badly, seen her as the pinnacle of everything desirable?

"It's old news, gentlemen. I didn't have anything to do with Torie's house being burned, and I'm sure Todd didn't either."

"You reported him missing."

"We were supposed to go to the Flyers game on Wednesday. He didn't call to cancel, and he didn't show up. When I couldn't get him on the phone, I went by the Ritz, where he was staying. The manager checked the room, the bed hadn't been slept in, so I reported him missing this morning."

"Cell phone?"

"No answer."

"Would he hate Ms. Hagen enough to burn her house down, flee the country? Was he someone who acted rashly?"

"Rashly? Todd? No. He was considerate, usually thought things to death. And he didn't hate Torie. Ever."

"Hmmm." Marsden's comment wasn't articulate. Sorrels took one last note, and closed his book.

"Thank you for your time. If you hear from Mister Peterson, please let us know."

"Will do."

Paul ushered the men out, only to find another officer, this time a cop, waiting to see him. Detective Tibbet was less annoying, but covered the same ground. At least he was more focused on Todd's being missing, rather than Torie's fire. Paul's imagination of that event was a little too vivid, and he didn't want to think about it.

They were about ten minutes into their conversation when Tibbet got a call.

"Scuze me," he said, flipping open his phone to take it. His end of the conversation was unenlightening. Neither was his expression at the end of the call.

"Tell me again where you were for the last two nights?"

Frustrated, Paul went over his activities yet again.

"Good to know. I'll need names and numbers." Tibbet sighed. "Hate to tell you, but you're going to get another bunch of cops in here. Your friend's been found."

Paul was on his feet in an instant. "Where? Is he okay?" He knew as soon as he said the words that Todd wasn't okay. Tibbet's face, stony as it was, told him the story. "No. Please tell me he's okay."

"I'm sorry, Mister Jameson, but your friend's been found dead."

"Oh, hell." The bad luck which had dogged Todd since he'd left Torie at the altar had finally caught up with him. "How? Where?"

"Oh, my God. He's what?"

"Dead," Pam managed through her tears, collapsing into the chair by Torie's hospital bed. "You know, I thought I hated him for leaving you like he did, being such a prick, but . . . but . . ."

"No." Torie couldn't fathom that Todd was gone. Dead. Not Todd, with his infectious laugh and booming voice. He couldn't be gone, forever. "How?"

Pam gulped and averted her eyes. "Pam, what aren't you telling me?"

"He was . . . he was . . . murdered," she whispered. "At the church."

"Nooooo," Torie wailed as her heart shattered into a million tiny fragments. It was her fault. Everything she touched turned to ash. To death. First Christian, now Todd. And if Dev hadn't been as strong and as fierce as he was, he, too, would be dead because of her.

Did *she* have to die to end this curse?

Two weeks later, she still couldn't fathom Todd's death.

The prayer ended and the pastor motioned for her to come forward. When she sat paralyzed, the funeral director touched her elbow, a concerned look shadowing his features.

"Ms. Hagen? Are you all right?" he whispered.

Torie shook her head *no*, but managed to stand anyway. She wasn't okay.

It had been two weeks. Two long weeks had not been enough for her to begin to come to grips with the losses, the double blow of her house burning and Todd dying.

She wasn't sure she would ever be okay again. Grief carved a hollow in the core of her body. She felt empty.

Straightening her skirt as she rose, she tried to adjust the suit jacket as she stood behind the podium. The clothes were new, the shoes uncomfortable; everything she owned was in the house, covered in soot and saturated with smoke. The woman at her insurance agency warned her she might have to replace her entire wardrobe.

As it was, until the fire investigators released the scene, she couldn't go back in. She had nothing.

Torie forced her mind away from that terrible, wandering path.

The church looked so solemn. Not that she usually saw it from the pulpit, but the difference was obvious. Everyone was in black or a somber color. The sea of tear-streaked faces, pale and grim, made a horrible contrast with the gorgeous riot of flowers surrounding the casket situated in front of the altar.

Many of the people here today had been in these very seats five years ago, waiting for the bride to appear, for *her* to appear.

"I don't know why Todd wanted me to be the one to speak today," she began. She really didn't know. She cleared her throat. "The last time I was in this church, many of you were, too . . . when Todd and I . . . when Todd left me at the altar."

Torie hadn't meant to say it so bluntly. The pages of her carefully prepared speech quivered in her cold fingers.

"Todd . . ." she began, but had to stop, fight the tears. "Todd hated to let anyone down."

Yes. That was it. Focus on that. "We'd only been dating six weeks when my father died. He hardly knew me or my family, but he was there for me. For us." She saw her brother nod, felt the small smile of encouragement warm her.

"When my father's long estranged relatives from New Orleans came for the funeral, he helped us cope. He organized many of you, his fraternity brothers and friends, to shuttle people to and from the airport, he brought groceries, he even fixed meals." She saw nods and smiles from some of the brothers she recognized.

"When one of the brothers from his pledge class was diagnosed with cancer, he took every spare moment he had from classes to call every other brother to raise money for medical expenses." Torie heard a muffled sob, saw a man drop his head, saw his wife put a comforting arm around his shoulders.

"When he came into his fortune, he didn't change." The words brought fresh memories: she'd come home from what was to have been her honeymoon, which had turned into her escape from the debacle at the church. The townhouse had been cleared of Todd's things, and it was as clean as a whistle. Her car had been full of gas, the fridge full of groceries. The wedding presents had all been returned, with a note from Todd. He'd paid his secretary two thousand dollars to do it, and spare Torie the pain.

Two days later, the deed to the house and the title to her car, paid in full, had arrived by courier. Neither she nor her family had ever received a bill or a complaint from any of the vendors associated with the wedding.

A cough from the funeral director brought her back to the moment. She'd lost her place, fogged by the memories.

"He asked me to give him another chance. I said no. All I could see, all I could remember," she managed the words through the rising sobs. "All I could remember was the feeling of horror, standing in the bride's room, with all of you out here, knowing he didn't want me." The words, ripe with pain, escaped, even though she had willed them not to.

In the front pew, Pam sat crying. She saw Steven and Dev turn from either side to comfort her friend.

"He would call me," Torie managed to continue, to drag her gaze and thoughts away from Pam's grief, "at weird times of the day or night. From weird places in the world." Looking at the back of the church, she saw a few more nods, smiles. She focused on those last rows. She didn't recognize many people sitting there, and that helped. She could not, would not look at Pam, or Paul Jameson sitting with the pallbearers on the other side of the church, in the front. "He'd send me presents, out of the blue. I know he did that to many of you as well."

She saw one of Todd's frat brothers elbow another, bend his head to share a story. It made her smile. "Once he called me from the golf course at St. Andrews. I was annoyed because I was on a date, and here was Todd, calling me." That memory was so clear, she was able to push back the tears. Her date had been outraged. "But I had to laugh because he wanted to tell me he'd seen an eagle and had thought of me, and that he'd won ten thousand dollars on a hole-in-one and was going to give it to a wildlife conservation group."

Wiping her eyes, she was able to echo the smiles she saw before her. "It was so like him. When I hung up, I didn't even care that the date was a bust."

There were actual chuckles as she finished, and it helped her regain her composure.

"He hated to come home at times. It seemed like bad luck plagued him if he were in the states. He said he had to keep moving so it didn't catch him."

Torie looked at her brother as she said the next part. "When my grandmother for whom I was named passed away, Todd flew thirty-seven hours to be here for her service. He just did that sort of thing. The right thing. I know most of you have the same kind of stories to tell about him. He did the right thing, and with very few exceptions, he managed to make it fun."

Tears welled again, fell like rain onto the shiny wood of the pulpit. "I was never his wife, but I was his friend. I never managed to forgive him for being strong, doing the right thing, and not going through with our wedding. Now, remembering so many things, so many good things, I wish I'd done that before now. Told him . . . told him . . ."

It took seemingly forever to pull her composure back from where it flew at those words, those thoughts. She knew her voice was shaking, but she managed to wrap up her speech.

"I will miss him, and I know all of you will, too."

Stepping down from the pulpit, she fumbled her way around the flowers, approached the casket covered in roses. Pressing her hand to her lips, she carried a last kiss for Todd with them as she touched the cool oak.

She didn't remember going back to her seat. She didn't hear the music, or remember leaving the church to follow the casket out. That was all a blur.

The next thing that registered was Paul Jameson taking her arm at the graveside, leading her back to the family car. He'd stood next to her as they'd buried Todd next to his mother and father.

She'd been there. She simply didn't remember much of it. What she remembered were flashes of the sky's amazing azure crispness, the trees beyond the tent blowing in the March breeze, the deep comforting warmth of Paul's hand on her arm, or at the small of her back.

Her brother drove her to the hotel where she was staying until the insurance company helped her find a rental. After she put Steven on a plane back to Russia, she called in sick. The following day, she pulled every string and every favor she could muster to get her projects covered. Assured by the vet that Pickle was on the mend, she turned the car toward the airport, and got on a plane herself.

When she pulled another rental car up at the hotel in Nags Head, North Carolina, it was like coming home. A refuge in the storm. The same one she'd found after the wedding.

That's where Paul Jameson found her.

She was on the beach. No towel, no chair, not even a jacket to block the whipping wind. The sea spray was a bitter gall to his lips as he strode toward her. Irritated, he stopped long enough to take off his shoes.

He'd looked everywhere in the small town. It was still off-season, so there weren't that many places to look. His last resort had been the beach.

He could feel the sand weighing down the cuffs of his dress pants. Great.

"Torie," he called.

Either she didn't hear him, or she was ignoring him. He repeated the call, louder this time, and saw her frown, but she didn't turn.

"TORIE!"

Her head whipped around and her mouth dropped open in an O of surprise. At least he'd finally gotten her attention.

"Paul, what are you doing here?" She struggled to her feet, untangling and brushing at the full skirts she wore. They were a bright whirl of gypsy colors. He'd never seen her wear that style before. She was usually more conservative.

"Looking for you, of course. What else?"

It pissed her off, he could tell. Well, good. He was plenty pissed off himself to have to hunt her down. Again. Not to mention that the cops were all over him about Todd's affairs. She was smack in the middle of everyone's questions, and wasn't there to be the target of them.

Each part of the jumbled puzzle connected to Torie. To have to find her so *she* could answer the damn questions, and get *her* to be the center of the maelstrom, infuriated him

"Why?"

"Don't play stupid, Torie, it doesn't suit you."

"Stupid? You arrogant prat," she fired up. "I ask a simple question, a logical one, and you call me stupid? What the hell do you want from me?"

"Logical? Todd's dead, your house is a wreck, and you run off to North Carolina? Yeah, and don't expect someone to come looking for you? That's logical?"

She threw up her hands. "Yes, it's logical. With Todd gone, you don't ever have to see me again since you despise it so much. And my house isn't any concern of yours, now is it? What does it matter that I'm in North Carolina, North Dakota, or the north quadrant of hell?"

"You need to be home for the reading of the will," he said, ticking the points off on his fingers. "Second, your friends are worried. Third, you're a murder suspect."

She went pale, and staggered as if she'd been shoved from behind. "I'm a . . . a what?"

"Murder suspect." For some reason, the vindictive relish he'd felt when hearing that news dimmed in the face of her reaction. She looked as if she'd been punched.

"But I would never . . . You know I wouldn't . . . couldn't . . ."

"It doesn't matter what I know or what I think. It's about what the police think. I managed to find out some things. They have your hair and blood at the crime scene, or so I've been told." He crossed his arms over his chest. "I'm not saying I believe you or them, but I do know you need to come back. Whatever trouble there is, you've got other matters to attend to."

"What other matters?"

"Not my business to tell you, but Todd left you something in his will." He frowned to think of all she was going to inherit. He really didn't think she was capable of putting a bullet in Todd, but he didn't like her, or trust her either.

"What?" She strode toward him, standing in front of him, her own arms crossed. "What could he possibly leave me? He long ago paid any debt to me, which I never thought he owed in the first place, by the way. You know I never expected anything from him."

"You took it, though," he snapped.

"I offered to pay him back, every time I saw him," she fired back. "I've saved a lot of money, thinking that one day he'd take me up on it."

"Not Todd." That thought broke his anger. It was stupid to blame Torie. Todd did what he wanted to do. Paul knew it, but Torie was a handy target for his grief.

"No." She shook her head, turned to look at the sea. He followed her gaze and they both watched a V of pelicans skim the wave tops and disappear around the spit of land toward town. "But thanks to him, I have a great retirement fund."

Paul nearly told her she wouldn't need it.

"Come on, let's get out of this wind." He took her elbow and steered her toward the parking lot. His car was the only one there, so she must have walked. She waited unspeaking, as he shook the sand out of his cuffs. She kept a cautious distance between them as they walked to the car.

"Get in." He held open the door, but she shook her head.

"I'll walk. It's about a block. I'm all sandy." She pointed to a bed-and-breakfast facing the street with blue shutters and a Canadian flag flapping in the breeze below the North Carolina flag. "I'm staying at the inn."

"It's a rental," he indicated the car. "It'll manage some sand."

"No."

His blood pressure spiked as she turned and left. He had to forcibly stop himself from grinding his teeth.

He let her get a bit of a start as he brushed more sand off his clothes, then got the car turned toward the hotel. He needed time to compose himself. She still got under his skin every time. The years hadn't dimmed his response to her. He still wanted her.

The difference was now he knew better than to come anywhere near her.

Especially now when he was, for all intents and purposes, her lawyer.

Oh, and there was that murder suspect thing. The sarcastic thought got him past his anger, and with a sigh, he parked the car. He had to stop thinking of her as anything but a client in trouble at this point. He had to divorce himself from the Torie with whom he had a past, think of her as someone else.

Pacing the porch he cleared his mind, tried to see her in a different way, to separate her from Todd, from college, grad school, and from his life. Clean slate. It took him a few moments, but he managed to adjust his attitude, at least a little bit, by the time he walked in.

Remember, she's a client. Remember, she's a client. Clients pay the bills. Clients are good, ergo, Torie is good.

The image which leapt to mind about Torie being good had nothing to do with virtue and everything to do with vice.

"Stop it," he muttered to himself as he opened the door. "Remember, she's a client."

She'd waited for him in the lobby, and they mounted the generous main steps to a lovely sitting area. A fire burned in the fireplace, taking the chill off the room.

"Torie?"

"In a minute. You want coffee?"

"Yeah, that'd be good." He leaned on the mantel as she poured from a thermal carafe, added two sugars, and handed it to him. "You remember how I take it?"

Torie looked at him, surprised. "Yeah, that's one of the crazy things about me. I forget a lot of things, and like anyone, there's things I'd prefer to forget that I can't, but I always remember phone numbers and how people take their coffee or tea." She sipped from her mug. "Go figure."

He tamped down a snarky comment and went for bland. "Handy if you want to go into politics or catering, I guess."

She laughed. "There's a thought, if I ever want to give up engineering. Problem is I'm a horrible cook."

"Good businesswoman, though, from what I hear."

Her face was a study in surprise. "Thank you, I guess. Who'd you hear that from?"

"From Todd, of course, and from some clients who use our services and also use your firm, and from the Chamber folks."

"The Chamber of Commerce guys? Alex and Tom?"

"Yeah, you get saddled with a lot of the public relations, I take it."

She grimaced, and he had to smile. He'd forgotten how mobile her face was, how quickly she could go from looking like a calm society debutante to making a goofy face. She'd entertained Todd to no end with the impressions she could do.

Thinking about it made his heart clench. His best friend was dead, and he was standing alone in a room with the woman suspected of murdering him.

"How quickly can you pack?" he asked, trying to keep his thoughts out of his voice.

Torie looked at him, her eyes sad. She set the cup down. "I won't be long. Make yourself at home."

Spinning on her heel, she left the room. Because the house was so quiet, he heard the rattle of the door opening and closing. Muffled and distant, he heard the unmistakable sound of her blowing her nose.

Crap. He hadn't meant to make her cry.

Or maybe he had. God. She'd already driven him to drink on more than one occasion. Maybe he needed therapy.

The only trace of tears he could see when she came out, though, was in her refreshed makeup and slightly reddened nose.

"Okay. Let's go." She hefted a briefcase onto her shoulder.

"Just like that?"

She looked exasperated. "You want me to hurry, then you ask me how I can be ready so quickly? Which is it, Paul? What, do you want me to give you another reason to dislike me by being slow?"

"No, not at all." He sighed. "I don't dislike you, Torie. You know that."

"Oh, sure," she scoffed. "I know that by the way you avoid me, make such *friendly* remarks when you do see me, and generally speak ill of me to all and sundry."

"I do not," he protested, stung, as he picked up her rolling bag.

"Um hmm." Her muttered rejoinder was as mocking as any biting words. She excused herself at the bottom of the stairs to locate the innkeepers and check out. She efficiently settled her bill and joined him in the lobby. He loaded her bag into her rental car for her, and they drove separately to the Wilmington airport.

"I don't know when the next flight out is. I'll be on it and back in Philly as soon as I can."

"I booked you on the same flight as mine."

A mutinous look crossed her face, but she didn't speak. It was interesting to watch the feelings skate across her mobile features. Irritation, anger, hurt, and finally resignation.

"Fine."

"We've got a bit of time before the flight. Let's get some dinner."

"I'm not particularly hungry."

It took everything he had not to snap at her. Lord, the woman brought out the worst in him at every turn. "Torie," he said through gritted teeth, "humor me. This is a small airport. I'd rather talk with you in the confines of a booth at an airport restaurant than in the general seating area. Okay?"

She closed her eyes. He guessed that she, too, was holding onto temper. Instead, tears sparkled when she opened her eyes again.

"Whatever," she managed, hauling her suitcase onto the shuttle bus from the rental car return.

They sat in silence for the entire ride. She spoke to the clerk at the ticket counter, showed her license, but said nothing to him or anyone else until they were through security and he had guided her into a small pub in the moderately decorated concourse. Wilmington didn't have a lot of gates, and they'd be changing planes in Charlotte, a short hop before the flight back to Philly.

He decided to try a neutral topic. "You love it here in the Carolinas don't you?"

She nodded without looking at him. "It's beautiful. The people are friendly. The beach is wide and clean. What's not to love?"

"Hmmm, I agree. I've never been down here in winter." He'd never been down in summer, either. Torie had done a series of graduate classes at North Carolina State University in the summer before she and Todd were to have been married. She'd been in Raleigh when he won the lottery, Paul remembered, so Todd had come to Paul's house first to share his news, double-check the winning sequence on the computer, and get advice.

"It's peaceful," she said softly. "Serene."

"I see that." The concourse was quiet. The waitress from the bar strolled over to see if they wanted anything. Torie ordered coffee. Paul ordered a beer and a sandwich. He'd missed lunch. "You sure you don't want something to eat?"

She shook her head. "Not hungry."

It was his turn to frown. Now that he'd achieved his objective of getting her to the airport, he really looked at her. She was pale, and there were circles under her big, expressive eyes. If he wasn't mistaken, she'd lost weight.

She'd never been a small woman, something he'd enjoyed about her. Usually he thought of her as more statuesque than fragile, but the contrast of the hollows under her high cheekbones, a slight slumping curve to her broad shoulders, and the pallor in her striking coloring made her look like a strong wind could blow her down.

He was used to noticing behavior, managing his clients through the subtle body language clues they offered. Her posture and demeanor said sorrow, despair, overwhelm. It irritated the shit out of him to realize that he was dreading what he was about to do. In fact, he was about to pile another load on her, overwhelm her even further.

So, uncharacteristically, instead of going straight to the punch and talking about the will, or that he'd pretty much dragged her from her sanctuary, he tried a different tack.

"So, are you still rooting for those losers down in DC?"

Chapter Four

The look she shot him was pure venom. And pure Torie. It lightened his heart.

"Losers? The changes they've made this year will see them to the playoffs. The stats from spring training . . ." she trailed off, narrowing her eyes. Spearing a finger his way, she growled. "What? What is it that you want to distract me from?"

He laughed. He couldn't help it. She had a sharp mind.

"Well, I guess it was pretty lame if you caught on that easily." He delayed any further answer by taking another bite.

"Lame? Yeah, well, I guess. Spill it, Paul."

"I just thought you looked . . . weary. I hate to add to it, be the bearer of worse news."

"Not just bad, eh?"

"No, it's bad. Not much worse than being named as a murder suspect, is there?"

The stricken look was back. "No, especially in this situation."

"Exactly. And you have to deal with me, something

you've always despised. I'm sure that's no picnic. I thought I'd try and distract you with something else."

"Well, since you root for those lousy Phillies, you don't have a lot of room to rejoice, now do you?"

It was a poor attempt for her. Her comebacks were usually so sharp, so sassy, they cut you off at the knees and left you puzzled as to how she'd done it. It irked him as much as it intrigued him.

"True. They sucked last year and aren't looking too good this year either, with Adams being traded to the Cubs."

They traded halfhearted barbs about baseball for a while as he finished his sandwich and beer. When their flight was called, he dropped a twenty on the table, waved at the waitress and offered Torie his arm.

"We might as well board and head back with as much energy as we can muster."

She looked at his waiting arm, and then into his face. Something flickered in her eyes, and she shook her head.

"Thanks, I'll walk on my own. I'm not that feeble. Not yet, anyway."

A sharp bite of pain, like a twisted muscle, pierced his chest. For the barest instant, he wondered if he were having a heart attack. It subsided and he moved aside to let her go ahead to the gate. In silence they boarded, sitting next to one another for the short up and down flight to Charlotte without a word exchanged.

They checked in at Charlotte, where he picked up voice mail and turned on his PDA for the brief layover. Thirty-seven emails had piled up, and fourteen voice mails clogged his in-box. Better than half of them were about Torie, or the situation surrounding her. She sat across from him, holding a glossy fashion magazine.

He knew she wasn't reading it because she hadn't turned a page in five minutes. As he watched, she closed her eyes, squeezing them to block some inner anguish to which he wasn't privy.

Was it possible that she had killed Todd? Even wondering it made him feel ill. He'd loved Todd like a brother, which had made him feel ten times worse when he'd met Torie, been attracted to her. Could he have misjudged her that much? Had her disappointment, her bone-deep embarrassment, her fear and her anger built so fiercely and deeply over the intervening years that she could plot Todd's death, carry it out?

He had no idea. The inability to judge her, to get a handle on who she now was pissed him off. Worse yet, it made his gut roil. God, he was going to have to resort to the prescription meds for his stomach again at this rate.

The overhead announcement of their boarding call relieved him of his angst. They hadn't been able to get adjoining seats on the flight from Charlotte to Philly, so he merely touched her shoulder as they boarded, moving beyond her to sit in the exit row.

Looking at her from this vantage point, Paul saw nothing about her body language. The thought that she might be sitting there in misery only made his stomach hurt more.

Just as well he couldn't see her. He had work to do, and knowing she was there was distracting enough; it would have been worse if she'd been sitting next to him. He mentally thanked his secretary for not getting them adjoining seats as he rummaged in his briefcase for the antacids.

* * *

On the ground in Philadelphia, Torie was still wrestling with the notion that she, of all people, could be accused of killing Todd. Tears threatened, and she forced them back. No. She'd cried enough.

Torie pulled her sunglasses out of her purse as they walked through the terminal toward baggage claim. Neither she nor Paul had spoken, which was just as well.

Beyond the security gates, she could see throngs of people waiting for their loved ones. It was sad that no one was waiting there for her.

"Stop." Paul put a hand on her arm to enforce the command. "Hang here for a second." Without explanation, he strode forward toward the exit. She was about to follow despite his warning when he turned back. His face looked like a storm cloud, and she could hear him cursing under his breath. "C'mon, let's find the American Airlines lounge."

"What? Why?"

"The press is waiting out there for you."

"What?" Torie couldn't believe it. "You're kidding, right?"

"Torie." Paul stopped as he said her name, forcing her to turn and face him. "You are a murder suspect. It's a colorful story. The press has been digging. I didn't think anyone would figure out that I was going to get you, but someone did and someone talked. And when I find out who . . ." He let the words dangle. The look in his eyes told Torie someone was in for an ass-whipping.

"But, but . . . who? How?"

Paul managed a wry grin. "This is the first time I've ever heard you speechless."

"Don't get used to it," she snapped back. "But I don't understand."

"Not that complex, honey. Todd won big five years ago. That was in the files. Todd donated to a lot of Philly charities, so his name's well-known. He's dead. You did his eulogy. You're news, too, around here."

"Not that much," she protested.

"More than you know."

"But still," she managed, denying his comment, "I'm just a small fish."

"They figured out, or the cops leaked the fact that your dates haven't fared so well." His face was closed down now, almost shuttered. "They learned about your boyfriend, the one who was killed."

"Christian," she whispered.

"Yeah, and they've put it together with Todd. Some other guy said he'd nearly been run down after dating you a couple of times. They're calling you the Black Widow."

"The *what*?"

"You heard me." He pushed open the door to the quiet lounge. "Follow me." He showed the desk clerk his access card, and led her to a kiosk with a computer desk and a phone. "Sit. I have to make some calls."

Torie sank down, letting her heavy carry-on bag drop to the floor. Never in a million years could she have imagined this as part of her life. Murder suspect. Black Widow. How could it get worse?

"Cancel, cancel," she muttered, knowing it *could* get worse, and that was the last thing she needed or wanted.

Yanking out her own cell phone, she called Pam.

"Honey, are you okay?" Pam didn't bother with hello before launching in. "Where are you? Are you all right?"

"I'm with Paul. He came and got me at the beach. I . . . I don't know if I'm all right or not. Pam, they're saying things, horrible things."

"I know, honey, but they aren't true. We both know that. Sticks and stones, love."

"Pretty ugly stick to hit me with," Torie said, fighting tears.

"That's God's truth, but I'm here for you. You'll get through this." There was a long pause. "You want some good news?"

"There's good news in the world right now?" Torie tried to joke.

"You bet. Tax cut to boost the economy. Three houses sold on my block for full-asking price. That's not bad."

"Yeah? That's the good news?"

"Um, no. Good news is your cousin is okay and on the mend. He's, uh, really nice."

Torie heard the underlying excitement in Pam's voice. Oh, no. She could not let her friend fall for Dev. He was the quintessential ever-philandering flirt. Her sexy cousin was also a marked man, if the cops were to be believed. He was part of her curse.

"Pammie, girl, don't go and fall for Dev. He's not the marrying kind."

"I know, but damn if he's not one of the hottest men I've ever met. Seriously. I mean *damn*, girl. How could anyone resist that smile? And you wouldn't even go to dinner with him."

Torie said flatly. "I go to dinner with him, he's a target Pammie. He's my cousin—that already makes him a target. Which would make you one, too. Please, please, don't go there. And be careful."

"You know I will, either way. But I can't *not* help your cousin, girlfriend. Since you're a big fat target for the press right now, you're not going to be able to. There are newshounds all over the place. They've been showing photos of your house, and they're trying to dig up all the guys you've dated. I think one of those cops let loose with his theory that you were some kind of—"

"Black Widow. Yeah, Paul told me that charming tidbit."

"Oh, the other piece of good news is that package we picked up—the night everything went down?"

Torie had forgotten about their little criminal detour. "Yeah?" she said cautiously.

"Doin' fine. I baked that cake and all is well."

Cake. Life was simple when all it took was baking a cake. Why couldn't she be more like Pam? Torie cut off that line of thinking. If she'd thought it once, she'd thought it a hundred times.

"That's good. Any idea where we can send the package from here?"

"May have already found a place to stash it. I'll keep you posted."

Paul had come back, and was waiting impatiently to talk to her.

"Uh, I have to go, Pam. Paul's back. I'll let you know what's up as soon as I know, okay?"

"'kay, see ya, and love ya, girl."

"You, too."

Torie flipped shut the phone, and turned to face Paul. For the first time, she actually looked at him, really looked. His face was drawn and pale. The lines around his eyes and mouth were more pronounced. As she watched, he downed two tablets, chasing them with water from a bottle he held.

"Are you okay?" she asked, honestly concerned. "You look . . ."

"That bad, huh?" Paul said, frowning. He rubbed his eyes, which just made them redder, and made him look even more haggard.

"Yeah. That bad."

"Tell me what you really think. Seriously," he quipped. "Don't mince words."

Torie smiled. "Sorry. It's just I've never seen you so out of sorts, I guess. You always seem to be in that 'I'm in charge' mode."

He grimaced. "Thanks, I guess. Although that really doesn't sound like a compliment."

"True. I'm just not used to you being, um, human."

That made him laugh. "Oh, I'm human all right. Damnably so."

Torie had no idea what he meant. She was about to ask when his cell phone rang. He held up a finger, motioning her to be quiet.

"Okay, great. We're in . . . yeah, okay. Officer Rhodes. Yes. Thanks."

"What was that all about?"

"Airport security is happy to escort us out of a private entrance in order to get all the reporters out of the airport. They don't like it, they don't like doing it, but the press has access to the public areas of the airport just like anyone else, and the TV vans and so forth can circle all day long. They'd rather have us out of here and get it over with."

"Ooookay. Our luggage?"

"Will be picked up from the carousel and brought

to us at the door. Another officer will round up a driver for us."

"You didn't drive?"

"No, took a shuttle."

They both heard footsteps, and Paul stood up to greet a uniformed man. "Officer."

"Mister Jameson?"

"Yes, sir."

"If you and your guest would come with me, please."

"Sure," Paul said as he picked up his briefcase and hefted Torie's carry-on bag. He made a soft oofing noise and glanced at her as if to say, "What have you got in this, rocks?"

"Running shoes. Books."

"How many?"

"I expected to be there for a while longer."

"Uh huh."

She thought he muttered something about her being a crazy woman, but the words were lost in the throng of the airport's noisy passageways. The officer led them down the concourse, then ducked into a bland passageway. Three doors led in different directions, but all were marked with "No Admittance" signs.

Rhodes took the central door, sliding a keypass over an electronic plate. He ushered them into what looked like a gray tunnel, which led down two sets of steps before leveling out. Torie was so turned around and confused by it all, she had no idea where in the airport they could possibly be.

"Here you are. Your luggage."

Their bags sat by an equally unremarkable exit door. Beyond it, a dark sedan idled in the sunshine.

"The driver doesn't know who you are or where you're going. I'd suggest you not go straight home or to your office," Rhodes said as he once again uncoded the door. "These drivers usually try to sell information to the press before the car door's closed behind you."

"Good advice," Paul muttered, offering the man his hand. "Thanks."

"No problem."

He shook Torie's hand as well, and they were on their way. She glanced back, but Rhodes was already gone from the door. The driver, his eyes alive with curiosity, held open the door for her, then helped Paul load the luggage in the trunk.

"Where to?"

"The city. Market Street and Fourth. The Bourse Shops."

Torie started to speak, but Paul shushed her and motioned to his PDA.

"I'll have my secretary pick us up."

"Good idea."

Nothing else was said for the entire ride. The driver attempted some conversation, but when neither of them picked up the gambit, he finally fell silent. That didn't stop him from constantly checking them out in the rearview mirror. Evidently, Rhodes had been correct. No way they could trust this guy to keep their destination a secret.

"She'll be waiting on the Independence Mall side," Paul said quietly. "We'll get you home, and then you can come to the office tomorrow, okay?"

"Do I need to call the police or anything?" Torie whispered.

"No, I'll take care of that. I'm your lawyer now, like it or not."

"But you . . ."

"Don't argue with me right now, Torie. Please."

She probably would have continued but for that one word. She'd seldom heard it from him. In fact, she tried to remember the last time she had heard it. Those thoughts occupied her the rest of the ride. They paid the driver and got out at the corner. Paul's secretary waved from a nearby coffee shop. Paul waved back, but waited to walk over until the sedan from the airport had pulled into traffic and moved off down the long one-way street.

"Let's get going, quickly," Paul said as he took her arm and marched her across the street to the shop. "Hey, Martha, thanks for coming on such short notice.

"Torie, I'd like you to meet my assistant, Martha Prinz. Martha, this is Torie Hagen."

"I was happy to help." Martha smiled at Paul and gave a brisk nod toward Torie. Evidently, Paul's attitude was echoed by his assistant. "Hello, Ms. Hagen. I'm glad you got here safely. Let's get both of you under wraps."

Walking around the block, pulling her luggage with her carry-on piled on top, Torie wondered what the hell had happened to the tidy, boring life she'd tried to build. Nothing about the past five years had been tidy, but this was even worse.

"I've arranged to get Ms. Hagen home," Martha said as they walked. "You did leave your car at your hotel didn't you, ma'am?"

"Please, call me Torie. And yes, I did."

"Well, we'll be sure one of our trustworthy car services get you home quickly. No press will find out anything from the people we hire."

"That's good to know." What else was there to say? She couldn't imagine the press knowing where she was staying, or working, or anything. She couldn't imagine the trouble she was in.

Torie frowned at Paul's back. They were descending into the depths of a parking garage, with Paul and Martha at the front of the car. How could she be a murder suspect?

"Paul," she began, just as the doors opened.

"Hold that thought," he cautioned, checking outside the doors before letting her get off.

"You're acting as if there were a raft of reporters waiting at every turn."

"There could be. Todd was well loved in our fair city, and you were not only his jilted bride, but rumors are already floating about what happens to his estate."

"His estate?" Torie was flabbergasted. What did that have to do with her?

"Hush, now. We don't want anyone to overhear us discussing anything of the sort." Martha was the voice of caution. She led the way to a silver Mercedes with faintly tinted windows. Paul piled their luggage in the trunk, and helped her into the backseat.

"You won't be seen back here. Martha often picks me up, so hopefully no one will think you're in here."

She nodded. Right now, she had so much to think about that she didn't want to talk, or be seen.

Torie closed her eyes and dropped her head onto the smooth leather of the headrest. How was she going to explain this to her boss? Or her Mama? Her brother would know immediately that it was all crazy. Pam obviously thought so already. Dev probably didn't care as long as he could get as far away as possible from her. Lord only knew what GoodMama would think.

"Torie," Paul said as they pulled into the garage at

his office. "I want you to stay here with Martha for a few minutes until I'm sure there's no one waiting upstairs. Will you do that for me?"

"Sure." Torie managed the word without lifting her head. Her mind was fogging over with all the thoughts and ideas, the details and ramifications of Todd's death. Who would she call when she wanted crazy advice? For solid business advice, she had always called her brother. Even though he was younger than she, he'd been a suit-and-tie businessman from the time he was twelve. But when she wanted off-the-wall, go-for-it kind of advice, she'd called Todd.

Paul stood there for a moment, looking at her. It was unnerving because she could swear he was reading her mind. He didn't say anything, just turned and walked away. Martha, in the driver's seat, never looked back. She kept her eyes on Paul as he walked through the door to the elevators, and she kept her gaze there the whole time he was gone.

Mercifully, Paul returned within five minutes. "We're good. Why don't you come on up, Torie? We'll talk."

"Talk?"

"I'll fill you in on what the police have, or at least what they've shared."

"Okay."

"Mister Jameson," Martha began.

"It's okay, Martha. You can head out. I'll send for the car for Torie."

Martha didn't say anything, but Torie was sure she disapproved, just by her body language.

Paul confirmed it once they got to his office. "Don't mind Martha. She's overprotective."

"Why? Surely you've already shared with her how much you dislike me."

"I don't dislike you, Torie. And no, I don't share my opinions with my assistant."

"Ha. Yeah, like she doesn't know your opinion. She probably knows it before you do," Torie said as she walked into the spacious office. Framed photos of beach scenes, in haunting black and white, graced the walls. They were of empty stretches of sand, or twisted driftwood. No people. No color. They made her sad, and she said so.

"Really? I find them restful," Paul replied. He seemed surprised. "Nothing but sand and waves and peace."

"You crave peace?" There was a surprise. Paul had always struck her as the quintessential party animal.

He smiled. "Sometimes. The older I get, you know the line."

"Yeah, I guess."

"So, have a seat. Let's get this over with."

Nice. He couldn't wait to get rid of her. Suddenly the thought of her empty, cheerless Extended Suites room made her want to cry. She longed for the comfort of her home, her things. Her dog. All of which were currently covered with soot, and under investigation, or in veterinary care.

"What do I need to do to convince them I didn't do this?"

"Explain how either your blood or hair got to the church, and all over Todd."

"What?" Shocked, Torie just stared at him. "My blood? My hair?"

"That's what I've heard."

"But I haven't even *seen* Todd in six months. I wasn't supposed to see him until Friday night. How

could anything of mine be anywhere near Todd? I
don't even have a cut." Torie looked at her hands,
thinking that surely she'd see something, hear something that made some sense, because nothing Paul
was saying made any.

"I don't know. Officially, I don't know that much.
They want you to submit to a voluntary DNA sam-
pling. That tells me there's either blood or hair, and
I'd think that if they want DNA, it's probably blood."

"But, I haven't been anywhere near Todd. I haven't
bled on anything of his. What?"

Paul was pointing at her arm. A long shallow
scratch showed through the gap at her wrist. "How'd
you get that?"

"I think I got it when I fell on my deck after the explosion. I have a bunch of cuts on my shoulders and
back, too, from the flying glass."

There was a quaver in her voice and she fought to
suppress it. She'd gotten that particular cut on her
little mission with Pam. Their creepy little escapade
was taking on a more sinister tone with each passing
day. She wished now that she'd told the officers about
it, despite the fact that it wasn't legal. In the face of
murder charges, it was definitely the lesser of the evils.

Then again, since she did have cuts and scrapes
virtually everywhere from the explosion, it was logical.

"Give blood recently?"

"Yeah, you know I did. You and all your staff went
that day, too, to the Chamber blood drive. I saw
Melvin Jr. and Pratt Sr. there. Melvin was volunteer-
ing, wasn't he?"

Paul flipped open his calendar, noted the date.
"Yeah, Pratt Sr. set that up as a fund-raiser. Nearly
two weeks ago. Blood doesn't last that long, so

maybe my contact's wrong. It could be hair, or skin, or something. Who knows. But," he said as he turned back to her, "that's one thing they're asking for. The other is a detailed, written time line of your activities that day. Also, they want to know more about this whole Black Widow thing." Paul leaned forward, but his dark eyes gave away none of his feelings. "What's that about, Torie? Where'd they get this idea about you being some kind of man-eater?"

"Oh, Lord. Paul, it's been going on since Todd and I split up. I'm cursed. I know it," she said, shaking her head at the disbelief written on his features. "It sounds absolutely nuts. But ever since the wedding, or the not-wedding, it's been this way. Anyone I go out with, no matter how casually, ends up getting hurt in some way."

As thoroughly as she could, she told him what had happened to her dates, especially Christian. She told him about the officer who'd asked her all about it as well. "The only thing I can think of is that that guy, Tibbet, told the press. I don't know, Paul. All I know is that I gave up on dating. I refused to even go out to dinner with my cousin just before my house got torched. Before he got back to the conference center, he was attacked."

"Damn. That's crazy, Torie."

"I know. It sounds insane. I mean, who am I? Why the hell would someone obsess over me?" The look Paul gave her was so strange, it made her shiver. "What? What do you know?"

"Nothing. It's just that Todd has had terrible luck ever since he won the money. Every time he came home to Philly, he'd have problems. His car windows were smashed one night. Someone slashed the tires another time. It ranged from nuisance stuff, like the rental car getting key-scratched, to the smash-up incident. And he'd always have trouble wherever he stayed, even the Ritz. He'd come back to his room, and there'd be no towels. Or all the linens would be gone off the bed and the mattress would be on the balcony. It was weird."

"He never mentioned any of that to me."

"I wonder why. I guess he didn't want to worry you."

"That would be like him," Torie agreed. It was all she could do not to cry. Paul seemed oblivious to her wavery answer.

"I know you're tired, but here's what I need you to do," he said, pulling a lined yellow pad out of a desk drawer. "Take this, and list every event, every time something happened to you or to someone else. I kept a list of the things that happened to Todd. We need to compare them, see if there's a pattern."

"A pattern?" Torie was so tired, so confused, that it didn't make sense.

"Yes, yes, a pattern," Paul insisted. "If there was someone after both of you, it makes this good evidence that you weren't after Todd, but that someone is after both of you."

"Both of us? But why?"

"We'll get to that, but for now, just go to the hotel and get started on that list, okay? I'll send a car for you in the morning, too. Will nine o'clock work?"

Baffled, Torie agreed. She wasn't expected back at work for another two days, so she could do as he asked. She wasn't sure she could remember everything without her notes, which were on her computer, which was melted at her house.

"You're exhausted, aren't you?" Paul asked, as he came around the desk, sitting on the edge nearest her chair.

"Yeah. I didn't sleep much at the B and B."

"Hmmm. Well, let's get you home, such as it is."

"Thanks."

Paul didn't ask any more questions or give her any more instructions before helping her into the dark sedan that pulled to the curb in front of his office. "I'll see you in the morning. We'll go over the list, okay?"

"Okay."

Paul started to say something, then stopped. Instead, he bestowed an awkward pat on her shoulder, and shut the car door.

Paul had given the car service the address, so Torie didn't have to do anything, which was good. She was wrung out.

At the apartment, she offered to pay the driver, but he declined, saying Paul had taken care of it. He helped her with her luggage, pulling the larger suitcase from the trunk and popping the handle up so she could set her carry-on bag on top and wheel them both behind her. She bid him good night as she turned toward the building.

The shattering of the sedan's car windshield had her spinning around, but she immediately obeyed the driver's shout: "Get down!"

Chapter Five

"Stay down," the driver yelled again, motioning her over to the car. He was simultaneously yelling into his cell phone, giving the address of the Extended Suites, and babbling about gunfire.

In shock, Torie stared at the pile of pebbled glass at her feet. Her skirt was sprinkled with the octagonal shards, darkly tinted and jagged.

"Shit!" the driver said as two more thwacking pops sounded.

Torie had no idea what the sound was. "What's happening? Why did the windows break?"

The driver looked at her like she was insane. "That's gunshots, lady."

"What? Gunshots?"

"Gunshots. I'm a South Philly boy, born and raised. If I tell you somebody's shooting at us, then somebody's shooting."

"Good God!" Torie gasped, frantically looking around.

"Stay down," the man hissed. "Cops're coming but we don't know where this guy is. He may be gone, but we can't take a chance."

No sooner had the words left his lips, than another snick and pop sounded, and she smelled a hard, sharp scent.

"Move!" The driver was up and running for the dubious safety of the building. "C'mon, lady!" he yelled over his shoulder. "That hit under the hood, it could blow!"

Blow? *Shit. As in blow up?*

Still dragging her bags, she sprinted after the driver. She stumbled and fell as she passed him, scrambling up to huddle under the metal stairs. Her knees stung, as did her hands, but she dug out her own cell phone. Her fingers were shaking so badly she misdialed four times, but the sound of sirens helped her steady.

"Paul?" she whispered. "Paul, are you there?"

She thanked heaven when he picked up. "What's up, Torie?" he sounded impatient. "Why are you whispering?"

"Someone shot at us outside the hotel. The driver's called the police but his car . . . his car is all—"

The explosion was enormous. From more than forty feet away, protected by the stairs, she could feel the heat. The noise was a terrible roar.

"Torie? Torie?" Paul's voice seemed to be tiny, mouselike and far away. "Torie! Talk to me!"

"Car blew up," she squeaked. "Can you—"

"I'm on my way. Sit tight and don't talk to the police about anything. Nothing. You hear me?"

"Hear you." Oh, God. Someone wanted her dead. Someone wanted to not only ruin her life and destroy her things, but kill her. She'd done the impossible as well.

She'd called Paul Jameson for help.

"The devil, you know," she whispered to herself

as she watched the flames engulf the car. "The devil, you know."

"Well, we are certainly not happy to see you again, young lady." The nurse who had been on duty when she came in before greeted her, pulling the curtain closed. "What's up this time?"

"Someone, someone shot at the car I was in," Torie said, her voice hitching. Reaction was setting in. The ambulance arrived before Paul, and the officers and EMTs insisted she be checked out. She'd dragged her luggage to her room, thrown it inside, then gone back downstairs to comply. When they discovered she'd been in the hospital with a concussion, the EMTs loaded her into the ambulance, and sent her to the ER. Torie was too shell-shocked to disagree.

"Shot at you? Good heavens. And weren't you in a house fire? Girl, you are not in a happy way, are you?"

"Nooooo. I feel like I'm in a movie."

"A bad one, yeah." The nurse stepped in to shine a light in her eyes, flicking it to either side. "Do you have any cuts, or bruises? Does your head hurt?"

"No, but my hands do." Torie held out her palms, which were scraped and scratched. Her manicure was toast. "I fell when I was running away from the car."

The nurse was cleaning her hands when she heard Paul's voice outside the curtain.

"Torie?"

"I'm here, Paul."

"Boyfriend?"

"Attorney."

"Ah." The nurse grimaced as she twitched the curtain aside to let Paul in.

"You okay, Torie? How bad is it?" He directed the last question to the nurse. The nurse's eyebrows winged up, but she kept her voice level as she answered.

"She's got some scrapes on her palms, but there's no evidence that the concussion has been triggered again, or that she's in any pain or distress."

"Of course she's in distress," he argued. "Someone just shot at her."

The nurse took a deep breath, shooting Torie a look. "Yes sir, but what I meant was, medically, she's not in any distress."

"Oh, okay." The reply was lame, even to Torie's ears. Before she could think anymore about that, however, he stepped to her side. "Who have you talked to, Torie?"

"No one. I put my stuff away and got in the ambulance. How's the driver?" This time it was Torie who directed a question to the nurse. "I think he got hit with some flying glass. Is he okay?"

One more person hurt by her curse.

"He's fine. Hasn't stopped talking on that cell phone, though. Trying to get the insurance company to come in the morning to see the car, get it replaced," the nurse said as she bent to examine Torie's palms. She applied a cool gel as she spoke. "This is an antibiotic ointment. It's also got an analgesic, should take some of the sting out."

"He's an industrious guy," Paul said of the driver, without taking his gaze from Torie. "And a tough one. It's also his livelihood. I'm sure he wants to get back out there as soon as possible."

"I'm going to get the doctor to stop in so we can release you, Ms. Hagen. And please," the nurse said, smiling to take the sting from the words, "don't come see us again, okay?"

"I'll do my best." Torie managed to return the smile, but lost the will for it as soon as the woman disappeared.

"You didn't talk to the police? To the EMTs?"

"No, Paul, I didn't. You said not to. Besides, I didn't have time."

"That's good." He ran a hand through his hair, then dropped it into his pocket to jingle the change that rested there. "We need to get you moved out of that place. Whoever's after you obviously knows where you're staying. It isn't safe for you. Do you have a place you can go tonight?"

Torie shook her head. "No. I'm not endangering anyone else I know just for a room for the night. I'll switch hotels if I have to, but I'm not staying with anyone who could get hurt," she said, thinking of Pam. Pam would be pissed not to be called, but between her interest in Dev and being friends with Torie, Pam was in enough danger.

Paul looked exasperated. "Just for the night."

"No. I'll find another hotel, or just go back to the one I'm at. Surely whoever it is wouldn't do it again, in the same night? I mean," she said as she closed her eyes, thinking about what had happened, "he could have just as easily killed me tonight. He shot the car first, but I was standing outside it, on the sidewalk."

"Don't even think that," Paul said, gripping her arms. "Much less say it."

"What?" Torie was baffled. "Say what?"

"That you could have been killed."

"But . . . I could have." Torie stopped. The blazing anger in Paul's eyes brooked no argument. "Okay.

So, maybe you could talk to the police. I'll call the insurance agent."

"Insurance?"

"I gotta know if I'm covered on the move."

"Torie, if it's a matter of money, I'll pay."

"No, it's not that. It's making sure about the house. It's all connected," she said, frustrated that she was too tired to make sense. The way she said it made it sound like she was some penny-pinching miser, but the truth was, she was learning that the insurance was tricky on what it covered when it came to the house.

"The insurance can wait. Don't bother checking out, just go to another hotel for now. I'll book the room."

Too weary to argue, Torie just nodded. Having gotten that acquiescence, Paul left her alone.

The beeping and droning of machines, the wails of a baby, and the curses of what sounded like a teenager all closed in on her. She wanted to curl up and go away, leave the ugly reality of what was going on behind. With all that had happened, as bad as it had been, even in college, she'd pushed through it, gone on with her life. This was almost more than she could bear.

For the first time in her life she understood why someone would take Valium or get high on something. Escape. Oblivion seemed pretty appealing because right now, reality just plain sucked.

Before she could give that any more attention, she heard Paul's voice arguing with other people.

"She didn't see anything."

"We'd like to hear that from her, Mister Jameson."

"Of course." Paul's voice was cold, hard. She knew that distant, professional tone. It was usually directed her way, so she could easily imagine the icy stare that accompanied it.

"Ms. Hagen? May we come in?"

Torie nearly laughed at the request. As if there was a door. Right.

"Sure."

The officers introduced themselves, and Paul moved to her side, making his allegiance obvious. "I've already given them the names of the officers working on the other cases, Ms. Hagen," Paul said, fully in the role of professional counsel. "I've informed them that you didn't see anything."

Torie didn't like anyone speaking for her, but in this case, she was grateful. "He's correct, gentlemen. The only thing I saw was flying glass from the wind-shield. The only way I knew I was in danger was because of the driver. His quick action saved my life. He told me to get down. There were more shots. When one hit the hood and he said to run, I ran. We both saw the explosion. He said a bullet must have hit the battery. I didn't see any other people, or cars, or anything. I was just too tired to be paying attention."

"Tired?"

"Ms. Hagen had just returned from a long trip and had been in our offices for a meeting for at least an hour. I arranged for the car to take her back to the hotel. As I mentioned, this is the second attack. Her home is still an unreleased crime scene. You'll want to talk to Sorrels and Marsden from Arson Investigation."

Torie winced at the mention that her home was off-limits, especially to her. It just added insult to injury that the officers were nodding, already familiar with the situation.

"We'll confer with the arson team in the morning.

In the meantime, Ms. Hagen, we need to ask that you not leave town again. Will you go back to the hotel?"

It was Paul who answered. "Only long enough to gather some belongings."

"We'll need to know where you are, Ms. Hagen."

"You can contact my office." Paul pushed a higher degree of authority into his tone, handing them his card. "Obviously, your department has been leaking information as it is, given the Black Widow inferences I've already seen in the press. I don't want to give her attacker any further chances to utilize loose gossip to get another shot at her."

Torie let the battle of words rage over her head. They were arguing technical points, like boxers, or umpires. She just wanted to go home.

Which was impossible, of course. Home didn't exist.

That thought brought her right back to thinking Valium was a good idea.

"Excuse me, but I need to get to my patient," a brisk voice said, as a short dark-skinned man pulled on the curtain. "All of you need to leave." In the face of his cross-armed stance and obvious medical authority, the police officers cleared out. Their parting shot was melodramatic, like something out of *Law & Order.*

"Stay available, Ms. Hagen."

"Yeah, right," Paul muttered, mustering a smile for her behalf.

"You need to leave, too, sir, unless you are family or her husband," the doctor stated.

Paul winced. "No, just her attorney." To Torie, he added, "I'll be right outside. I'll get you where you need to go."

She managed a nod, then looked at the doctor.

"Good, now that they've all gone, perhaps you can

tell me if your head hurts? Your eyes, are they sensitive to the light?" He flicked the tiny flashlight into her eyes, as the nurse had done. "No? Good. Our lovely Nurse Pickering has dressed your hands, yes? Let me look." She held out her hands and he peeled back the dressing just a fraction. "Good, good. Now, here is a prescription for a good antibiotic ointment. Some of those scrapes are sure to be painful, but they'll heal quickly. Probably won't even need the bandages by day after tomorrow. However, we don't want infection." He ripped a paper off and handed it to her. "There. Fill that tomorrow. But for now, get some rest. You look terrible."

"Thanks a lot," she muttered sarcastically, sliding off the table.

Grinning, he put out a hand, steadied her descent. "You're welcome. I always try to tell my patients the truth. You need sleep, and probably a good meal. Make him stop and get you something, yes? And wait." He pulled the curtain, but went behind the nurse's station, got the nurse to retrieve some tablets. "Take this. It will help you sleep. You won't need more than one, yes? But get some sleep tonight."

He pressed a two-tablet blister pack into her hands. Tylenol Three with codeine. Oh, yeah, she'd sleep. The stuff knocked her out.

"Thanks, Dr. Paresh."

"Most welcome. Now go." He handed her a sheaf of papers with his signature scrawled along the appropriate lines. "Get out of here before you catch something."

The doctor's humor was appreciated, but Torie couldn't even muster the energy to laugh. She managed to get out to the waiting area where Paul was talking to the police. He hurried to her. "You okay?"

"I guess."

"Let's get you out of here."

"Mister Jameson," one of the officers protested. "We need to—"

"You can talk to her tomorrow, my office. Ten A.M."

Paul hustled her out to a sleek Mercedes sedan and, holding open the door, held her purse as she got in. She'd never experienced Paul in this kind of solicitous mode. Gone was the joking or angry man. Here he was all concern.

"I made a reservation for you. It's under my name for now. I don't want anyone to be able to call around and find you."

"Okay."

She managed to answer his other scant questions, but was worn out by the time they pulled up under the portico of the Hilton.

"Wait here."

Like she could move.

Paul took care of the mundanities of checking her in. When he came back, he helped her out of the car and got her settled in her room.

"Give me your key to the other room at the Suites. I'll go get your bags from your trip. If you want to, go on to bed. I'll just set them inside the door."

"You'll need a key."

"I got one for this room, too."

"Oh."

"Go on. Get yourself to bed, Torie."

At this point, she couldn't find words to protest. She just nodded and headed for the bathroom. For once, she didn't mind following someone else's orders. With everything topsy turvy in her world, she just wanted to sleep.

Paul eased the door closed on the hotel room. He wished he could lock it from the outside, giving Torie another level of protection. Whipping out his PDA as he walked, he began texting, then calling the people he needed. With that done, he headed to the Extended Suites to get Torie's things.

A crowd of bystanders lurked beyond the yellow tape at the hotel, most of them holding beer bottles or soft drink cans. They were trading theories about the car, and what had happened.

"Yeah, I heard it blow," one young man drawled. "Didn't know it was a car though. Sounded like something bigger."

"Uh huh," his companion replied. "I didn't hear it, had my 'phones on." He pointed to the dangling earbuds attached to his slim music player. "Saw the flash. It was awesome."

Paul wanted to smack them both for being so nonchalant about what had happened. Another part of him reasoned that they had no way of knowing that it had been gunfire, or that his . . . client had nearly been killed. He had to keep thinking of her as his client, not as anything else. She'd looked so vulnerable, so young.

The memory of her, younger and equally vulnerable, rose to haunt him. He'd rescued her then. History seemed to be repeating itself.

"Jameson?"

Paul turned to see the same officer from the hospital standing by the curb.

"Yep. Any new info?"

"No, but we're pinpointing where the shots came from. We'll get the crime techs to pull the bullets out."

Looking at the burned car, Paul was dubious. Then again, you never knew what forensics could do. "Be interesting to see if they match the gun that killed my friend."

"Nah. I looked it up. Your church friend was killed with a small caliber weapon. This had to have more oomph."

"Looks like both my friends are targets."

"You'd better be careful, too, Jameson." Another voice joined the conversation. It was Tibbet, the detective who'd broken the news of Todd's death. "Looks like someone doesn't care much for your friends."

"You're right, Tibbet. And that worries me."

"Where's the woman, Hagen? Wasn't she here? They keep her at the hospital?" Tibbet was asking his officer, but Paul answered.

"Treated and released. I moved her to another hotel."

Tibbet took out his notebook. "Glad she's back in town. We'll need to contact her in the morning. Where can I reach her?"

"My office after ten."

Tibbet frowned. "I need her whereabouts, Jameson."

Paul shook his head. "I don't think so, Tibbet. Doesn't seem like your people can keep anything quiet. Who let the info out about what's happened to her, eh? No one should know that. I think you're the only one. Haven't you and your people totally compromised any effort at protecting her?" Paul stepped in towards the man angry now on Torie's behalf. "I brought her back for you, but for what? So she can be hounded by the press? Do you know what it took to get her out of the airport?"

"Act of Congress?" Tibbet quipped. "Look, Jameson, I don't make the rules, nor do I dictate the Freedom of Information Act."

"Bullshit. Information in an ongoing investigation isn't subject to the FIA. You can't tell me someone didn't leak that, because I know better. Only Torie and *your* staff knew about the guys she dated, and what happened to them. And how could *The Inquirer* have gotten *all* their names without access to someone in your office?"

"You're gonna want to step back, Jameson," Tibbet said blandly, although his body language was tense, that of a fighter.

"Yeah, and you're going to want to notify your department rep because we'll be filing a complaint tomorrow."

"Noted. Now step back before you compromise the scene."

Paul looked down. His feet were touching the edge of the scorched grass just outside the tape.

"Tomorrow, Tibbet."

"Your office, Mister Jameson."

Paul nodded. He pushed through the bystanders who looked at him with avid curiosity. It made him feel vaguely sick to look at the car, think about Torie, and imagine the explosion. To combat the feeling, he hurried to Torie's room, slipping the key card into the slot, and waiting for the green.

Pushing open the door, he stopped dead.

"Tibbet!" Paul called as he hurried back toward the curb. The burned-out hulk of the sedan was being loaded onto a flatbed tow truck and wrapped in a tarp. The tarp made it look like a huge package or present sitting on the back of the truck. Two techs were directing the process, muttering about preserving evidence and chain of custody.

"Tibbet," Paul huffed a bit as he reached the taciturn cop. "You're going to want to come with me."

"And why would I want to do that?"

"Torie's room."

Tibbet's eyes sharpened their focus, and he motioned for Paul to lead the way. They pushed through the fast-dispersing onlookers to climb the stairs to Torie's suite.

"I opened the door, so I guess I should tell you my prints are on it. That's her blood. She said she threw her things into the room before the cops showed up when the car blew."

"Yeah, duly noted."

Paul pushed the door open and stood aside to let Tibbet get the full effect.

"Damn," the cop breathed the word. "Someone hates this girl, bad."

"Ya think?" It was all Paul could manage through the haze of anger and fear for Torie which threatened to blind him.

Paint sprayed over the walls spelling, "You Lose!" The mattress was tossed off the bed, and Torie's belongings were scattered over the floor, smashed and broken. The suitcases were torn asunder, zippers dangling, the aluminum rods from the handles twisted and bent. A colorful shirt was shredded, and the scraps of it flung about the room like confetti. In the small kitchen, meager supplies were smeared on the counters, and part of a loaf of bread had been tossed randomly around the room. One piece had impaled itself on a lamp finial, giving the toppled light fixture a Dali-esque quality.

"So tell me again why you were back here?" Tibbet finally broke the silence.

"I put her in another hotel. Came back for her gear."

"Ah. Well, I guess you'll be buying her some stuff instead." He pulled a cell phone from his belt, and using it like a walkie-talkie, called the damage in. "Looks like we got us a secondary crime scene, gents."

There was a crackle of static and some generalized cursing before an affirmative and request for location came back through. Tibbet relayed and closed the phone.

"Give me a number where I can reach you, Jameson. Then go buy the lady something for the morning. I think the Target over off Snyder, on Mifflin, is still open."

Evidently, through some mysterious process of evidence and elimination, he and the detective had gone from adversaries to allies.

"Thanks," Paul said, rattling off his cell number. "I'll see you at ten o'clock, my office."

Taking the detective's advice, Paul agonized over what to get at the Target. He had no idea. Deodorant, yes, but socks or hose? And what size? Resigned to making bad choices all the way around, Paul picked jeans in several moderate sizes, grabbed both socks and hose, chose four blouses in various colors and sizes, and compromised on shoes by getting a pair of slip on sandals in a medium. It was the best he could do for now.

"What the hell do I know about women's sizes?" he muttered, plunking everything on the counter in a heap. When the teenaged checkout girl kept looking at him as she rung things up, he got more and more frustrated.

"Uh, sir? Uh, did you want the shoes too?" The girl pointed to the cart.

"What? Yes." He tossed those up on the belt and whipped out his credit card. By the time he got to his car and from there to the hotel, he was completely irritated.

Slipping into the hotel room, he called out. "Torie?"

In the main part of the room, lights blazing and television on, Torie lay sprawled on top of one of the beds. Momentarily frightened, Paul hurried over to check for a pulse. As soon as the thought crossed his mind, however, he noted the rise and fall of her chest. The motion rustled the wrinkled cotton blouse, exposing creamy skin where the shirt had ridden up.

"Don't go there, Jameson," he warned himself. "That is *so* off-limits."

To combat the images in his head, he turned down the covers on the other bed, flattening the pillows and turning down the blasting heat. Torie must have been cold when she came in, but the room had reached roasting levels now.

He turned on the bathroom light, but pulled the door closed. That would give her some ambient light if she woke in the night.

"Hey," he called softly, rubbing a hand down Torie's arm in an attempt to rouse her. "Torie, let's get you in bed. Come on, Torie, wake up, just a little."

Other than moaning as she turned over, coming precariously close to the edge of the bed, she didn't flicker an eyelid. The colorful skirt rode up her legs, showcasing long toned calf muscles. Her feet were bare, her toenails a coppery red.

"Damn." Paul looked away, focused on the late night comedian cracking jokes on TV. "Damn, damn, damn. Get a grip, dude," he warned himself.

With the utmost care, he slid one arm under her legs and the other behind her shoulders. Bracing his legs, he lifted her, pivoting to deposit her gently in the other bed. While not heavy, Torie was definitely no feather either. Solidly built, elegantly muscular, she was an armful of sexy, lean woman.

"I am not thinking about that now," he told himself out loud.

"Dev?" she muttered, clutching at the pillows, shifting against the sheets. "Oh, Dev . . . Good . . ."

His blood pressure rose at the soft moan of another man's name. Served him right, though, for thinking about her in any way other than as a client, or as Todd's former fiancée.

The mere thought of Todd brought him back to reality with a thud. Blocking everything else from his mind, he pulled the covers over Torie, turned off the lights and television, and left as quickly as he could manage.

He would have Martha call her first thing in the morning to wake her and tell her what had happened at the Extended Suites. He would keep his distance. He would not think about her as a woman. Or even feel sorry for her. After all, she could have killed his best friend.

"No." He stated it in the darkness of the car as the truth of it rang in his mind. He'd dealt with his share of criminals, and there was no way Torie could have killed Todd. No way she could have shot him and hauled his body into the church. Rumor had it that Todd's body had been staged in some way, and he couldn't bring himself to believe Torie would do that, either, not to Todd and not in the church they'd both loved.

He went to bed with the same resounding negative foremost in his mind. She wouldn't, and couldn't, have done it.

"Melvin, you're certainly cheery this morning." Martha greeted one of the other attorneys as she moved behind her desk to tuck her purse into the drawer. She was an early arrival at the office, but Paul had essentially never left. He watched the interaction from his desk.

"Why, yes, I am. I had dinner with the nicest woman last night. I'm quite taken with her," the man replied with a patronizing tone. "I've put some files here for Paul. If you'd let him know that my father would like to see him when he gets in? Wonderful."

Paul came out of the office. "What time would he like to see me, Melvin?"

"Oh, hi, Paul." Melvin smiled at him, but didn't offer a handshake. They'd had an unspoken truce since Melvin Sr. had hired Paul out of the same university as his son. They'd despised one another in law school, but managed a cordial distance now that they were older. Unfortunately, the truce was strained more and more frequently as Paul, not the purported heir to the firm, got the plum clients. To say that Melvin now despised him was much more accurate. Paul had ceased to care about Melvin.

"Around ten, I think."

"Martha, if you'll go in my office, I need to give you some notes. Melvin, thanks for letting me know."

"Of course." Melvin's smile was condescending, as

if he were the one doing the summoning. Or was the one in charge.

Shaking his head, Paul closed the door on Melvin's departing back. Didn't the little prick realize that his father had turned him into a glorified errand boy?

Dismissing the unctuous twit, Paul began rattling off information to Martha.

"After you left, I sent Ms. Hagen to the hotel by private car, the usual service," he said before she asked. "Discrete as always. However, when they got there, someone was waiting. They shot up the car."

Aghast, Martha squeaked, "Someone, *shot* at them?" Hand to her throat, Martha was aflutter and upset. "Gracious, are they all right? Do I need to send flowers? What—"

"First thing is to call Ms. Hagen at the Hilton. The room's in my name. Tell her to order room service and get a cab over here."

"A cab, sir? Is that wise?"

"Yes, actually. I think it would be harder to track a cab, don't you?"

"I . . . well, I guess. We do use the same service over and over. It might be easier to trace."

"Exactly my thought. Also, if you would, tell Torie I couldn't get into her suite at the Extended Suites, so I got her some clothes. They're in the Target bags I left for her."

Martha's eyes widened. "You went to Target?"

"Nothing else was open. Believe me, I didn't want to tell her that her room had become a crime scene, too, okay?"

"Oh, no," Martha's face fell. "That poor girl. More trouble?"

"I thought you didn't like her." He waited a beat,

but Martha didn't respond. "And yeah, someone trashed the room, right under the noses of the cops too. While they were investigating the shots fired and the burned car, someone spray-painted the walls in Torie's room, tossed the furniture around, ripped all her things to shreds."

With her hand to her throat again, all Martha could manage was another, "Gracious."

"That's one word. I've a few stronger ones. You'll need to move the meeting with Melvin Sr." He grimaced at Martha's immediate negative response. "Can't be helped, Martha. Torie will be here at ten, and so will the cops. I've got to review things before they get here."

Scribbling quickly, Martha noted the time, the changes, and added some other squiggles on her pad. "And if Melvin Sr. really needs you?"

"Explain the situation."

Martha rolled her eyes, and Paul felt serious sympathy. Neither Melvin Sr. nor his troll of a secretary, were known for their patience or equanimity when a summons was issued from The Big Office one floor up, then denied by an underling. Paul was actually the only one who got away with it, but only because he billed more hours for more money than virtually anyone in the firm other than Melvin Sr. himself. Together, they'd doubled the direct-line financial profits of the firm within the last five years.

On Paul's part, it was all thanks to Todd.

The phone rang and Martha picked it up. "Mister Jameson's office." She listened for a moment, her eyes widening. "Just a moment, please."

"Oh, my gosh," she gushed. "It's Carl Appleton."

Chapter Six

"The actor?" Paul asked, astonished.

"Yes." Martha still looked shell-shocked. Paul held out a hand for the phone.

"Mister Appleton? This is Paul Jameson. How may I help you?"

"I just got word that Todd Peterson was killed. I was out of the country and didn't get the news. I am just devastated." In Appleton's rich baritone, the words somehow managed to sound sincere rather than theatrical. "Is there a memorial fund, or is anything being done of that sort?"

"We're just beginning work on something, yes," Paul began, filling in what little he'd worked out in the few moments he'd had to think about it since Todd's death. He promised Appleton a call, getting his private line, when there was more information available.

Martha sat, practically twitching with excitement. "Oh, my. Did Mister Appleton know Mister Peterson?"

"They served on some charity committee together,

evidently. Played golf, too. Appleton wants to be part of whatever fund we set up for Todd."

"How wonderful."

"It will be," Paul agreed, but sorrow took that moment to hit him again at the loss of his friend. Todd had had so much to give. He had been so full of life.

"I know, Mister Jameson," Martha said, rising to pat his shoulder before she left. "We'll all miss him." She hesitated, as if to say something else, but didn't. "I'll get right on this with Mister Pratt Sr., and call Ms. Hagen. If I may suggest it, sir . . ."

"What?"

"You might want to let her detour to the mall or at least to a clothing store before she comes to the office."

Thinking of the tops and jeans he'd randomly selected, Paul nodded. "Good idea. I'll contact the cops and tell them ten forty-five."

"Eleven at the earliest, sir." Martha said firmly. "She'll need a bit of time."

Thinking of his sisters, Paul nodded. "Right. Eleven. Thanks."

As she closed the door, Paul pulled the detective's card from his wallet and dialed.

"Tibbet," the man answered with impatient irritation.

"Detective, this is Paul Jameson. I need to move our meeting to at least eleven."

"Why?"

"Ms. Hagen has nothing to wear."

Tibbet barked out a laugh. "Are you serious?"

"In this case, yes. Remember? House fire, no stuff. Suitcase in the Extended Suites destroyed? No stuff. Women have to have some stuff. Hell, in that situation even I'd have to have some stuff."

Tibbet was briefly silent, then laughed again. "Yeah,

even a guy would need to regroup. You think it's safe to let her do that, though? This guy's escalating already, so . . ." Tibbet let the sentence hang.

"I've got it covered. Private duty. Unobtrusive."

"Good. I'd say I'd help, but the budget sucks, you know? Anyway, I'll be there around eleven-fifteen. If she's not there yet, we'll go over some things."

"Is she still a suspect?"

"Don't know yet. Lab's not back in."

Hanging up, Paul shuffled through the papers on his desk. Ten folders, neatly aligned, contained all the info he and Todd had planned to discuss. He scooped them together and pulled out the fat legal-size folder with all of Todd's estate planning.

"Martha?" He waited for her to answer his hail before asking, "Is Myra available for a few minutes?"

"I'll see, Mister Jameson."

He wanted Myra, the firm's foremost estate planning specialist, to go over all of the estate issues with him one more time. He didn't want to be without answers if the police asked specific questions.

By the time he was done with Myra, it was eleven. There was no sign of Torie or Tibbet.

Which meant he had time for more coffee. He felt like he'd already drunk a gallon of it, but with so little sleep, the punch of caffeine was a necessary evil.

He was filling his mug when Martha found him.

"Detective Tibbet is here, Mister Jameson."

"Of course, I'll be right there. Would you check on Ms. Hagen's progress?"

"I will, yes. I'll just follow you with Detective Tibbet's coffee, then see if she's on her way."

"Thanks." They rounded the corner and he greeted

Tibbet. "And I believe Missus Prinz has coffee for you? Yes. Great, let's go into my office."

He sat down behind the desk, keeping the professional distance. What he wanted to do was grab Tibbet's annoying little notebook and read it. Or stuff it down the man's throat.

"So, Detective, what can you tell me about all of this?"

"Not much, Mister Jameson. Wheels turn slow, if you know what I mean. Nothing's back on the car yet. They're still running prints from the hotel room, but I don't know if they'll find anything. Hotel rooms are full of prints, especially if the maid service sucks."

"Did you get the notice of our complaint?"

"Yep. I guess you filed it first thing."

"As promised," Paul said. Reconsidering his tactics and his thoughts about allies, he decided to try for a more friendly approach. "I know the other part isn't on you, but I hope that whoever snagged the notes and let that shit leak gets at least a hand smack for blowing information to the press."

Tibbet's smile was sour. "Me, too."

"So, how can I help you? How can we figure out who the hell wants my client dead."

"Shots fired doesn't equal a hit."

"No, but if the same person's responsible for all the stuff going on with the guys in Ms. Hagen's life, he's escalated."

"Or she."

"You think it's a woman?" Paul was surprised. It made his theories spin a whole new direction. "But, I thought you said the body, Todd . . ."

"I didn't say anything, Mister Jameson. I'm just not ruling out anyone at this point. With each day, this whole thing gets more complex, if you know what I mean."

"Do I," Paul muttered as he looked at the notes he'd scribbled while talking with Myra.

"Now why don't you tell me where you were when the lady was fired on?"

Paul felt Tibbet's look all the way to his toes. The camaraderie was still there, but he was making sure to cross his Ts and keep his case tight. "Here, making calls, trying to get a bodyguard hired. I've got a guy with her this morning, but he can't stay more than today. Other commitments. I've also got to find her some place safe to live other than a hotel."

"Why? I thought there was an antipathy between you two. And did she choose you to be her attorney?"

"No, but Todd Peterson did," Paul said quietly.

Torie pulled herself from sleep to answer the phone. The tablet had done its work; she'd slept dreamlessly and deeply.

"'lo?" she managed.

"Ms. Hagen? This is Martha Prinz from Mister Jameson's office?"

Torie cleared her throat, hoped she'd sound less raspy. "Yes, ma'am?"

"Mister Jameson is ordering a taxi for you, to be there at nine. He wasn't able to get back into your room last night at the Extended Suites. The police have locked it off."

"Why?"

There was a pause, then Martha continued. "He didn't tell me all the details, Ms. Hagen. He did make some purchases for you at Target." Torie could hear the older woman's disdain. "However, I'm sure that you would prefer to purchase some additional things for yourself before having to be at our offices to meet with Mister Jameson and the police."

Scanning the room, Torie saw the Target bags piled on the low dresser next to the TV. She frowned, thinking that the TV had been on when she went to bed. Then again, Paul had been back, so he'd probably turned it off.

"Um, yes, okay. I would." Torie scrambled to keep up. No way was she meeting the police in the jeans she could see peeking out of the bag. She needed the armor of good clothes to help her get through it. "What time am I expected—"

Martha cut her off. "I was able to postpone the time of the meeting until eleven. It doesn't give you much more time, but you should be able to find a few things before you have to be here. Also, there will be someone watching out for you, a bodyguard. He'll be there to protect you, following you, but you need to get what you need and be done with it."

"Thank you ma'am." Torie managed to inject some warmth into her voice. Martha might not like her, but she'd protected Torie's interests by getting her enough time to go buy clothes. Of course, she was warning her not to dawdle at the same time, which was annoying, but Torie chose to ignore that part. "I appreciate the help."

"You're welcome. We'll see you then."

Scrambling out of the bed, Torie again experienced a momentary disorientation. Spinning in place she looked at the other bed. Hadn't she . . . ? Seeing the bedspread in disarray she decided that yes, she had been in the other bed, and Paul had evidently moved her or woken her enough for her to move herself. She didn't remember, but then again, she'd been so tired.

"Time, Victoria Marie," she reminded herself, as her mother would have. "It's marching on." She headed for the shower.

Minutes later, hair in a towel, she surveyed the pitiful mess of stuff Paul had purchased for her. He'd managed a toothbrush, toothpaste, and deodorant, but the rest was fairly useless. It was another cool day and he'd gotten short sleeves. The jeans were a ten, a fourteen, and a sixteen, and she wore a twelve. The socks worked, and she pulled those on, laughing at the five packages of hose, one in every size but queen. She piled all the rejects back in the large plastic bag, hoping he'd kept the receipt.

"He's probably already put it on my bill," she muttered to herself as she dug through the second bag. Sandals. Again, a cool day so they were a no-go, but surprisingly cute. Another pair of jeans, a size twelve this time, and another blouse with blessedly long sleeves.

"This would be more like it. Score one for the bad guys," she said, snapping the tags off the jeans. There was no underwear of course, but she at least had her bra. Now more than ever she appreciated the taciturn Martha for her thoughtfulness in allowing for time this morning.

"First stop, Macy's."

Barefaced but for a little mascara, and clad in the mishmash of clothes Paul had purchased, Torie climbed into the cab right at nine o'clock. The Center City Macy's opened at nine-thirty, thank goodness. She gave the cabbie the directions and sat back watching the miles pass. She wondered if she could spot the bodyguard. Taking out her phone, she turned it on.

Messages immediately popped up, twenty-seven of them. She scrolled through the list, looking for any that she knew. She recognized Pam's number, Paul's, one could possibly be Dev or GoodMama. She winced at the thought. She owed GoodMama a call and a thank you for the warning, though she hadn't had time to heed it. She also had to apologize for involving Dev in the mess of her life.

Oh, God, I have to call my mother.

She cringed at the thought as she continued to scan the list. The office had called four times. She frowned at that. She wasn't due back until tomorrow. Torie hoped there hadn't been a problem with a client.

"Here we are, Miss," the driver said, snugging up the car to the curb as he rattled off the fare. She dug out the money and handed it to him. "You have a good day now, ma'am. Please call me if you would like me to transport you again." He handed her his card, and before she'd barely shut the car door, he was off again.

Walking into Macy's was like walking into Nirvana. The thought of having clothes that fit, not to mention underwear and makeup, put a spring in her step. She had to do this anyway, thanks to the fire, so it was time to begin rebuilding her wardrobe.

When she finished shopping and piled into the cab to go to Paul's office, she felt human again. Cosmetics were a wonderful boost to the ego, or at least cosmetic saleswomen were. Good-looking pants and proper attire for a meeting made her feel like she could face Detective Tibbet, and whoever else needed to ask her questions. The warm boucle jacket in jewel-bright colors also made her feel feminine and capable, more normal than she had since the fire and Todd's death.

She'd never even seen the bodyguard.

Although she felt odd carrying four shopping bags into Todd's office, she hoped Martha would continue to be her ally and tuck them away for her until she could go back to the hotel.

"Good morning. May I help you?" the youthful receptionist chirped.

"I'm here for a meeting with Mister Jameson."

The young woman's eyes widened a bit, but she said nothing more than, "I'll let Missus Prinz know you've arrived."

"Thank you."

Before she could sit down, Martha strode purposefully around the corner. "If you'll come with me, Ms. Hagen?"

"May I put these somewhere for safekeeping?"

"Certainly. There's a closet in my office. We'll put them there."

"Thanks, and thank you for helping me with the timing so I could be presentable."

"You'll need all the help you can muster, Ms. Hagen," Martha said coolly as they entered her office. She said no more, just opened the closet door and motioned her to set down the bags. "I'll show you in, then get you coffee, if you drink it."

"I do. Sweet and black, please."

"Certainly. Would you care for anything else?"

"Is Detective Tibbet here already?"

"Yes."

"No, I'll just take coffee, ma'am."

With a curt nod, Martha turned away toward Paul's

office. "Here we are. Brace yourself, and put on your game face."

Torie couldn't believe the quiet murmur of advice had come from the sourpuss of an assistant. Nevertheless, she did put herself in negotiation mode, just as she would with a client. Construction clients were usually men, and a woman engineer had to be bold and take the initiative if she wanted to succeed.

Torie was very successful. So she put on her game face.

"Good morning, gentlemen," she said as she came into the room, taking charge by speaking first.

"Torie, good morning," Paul said, standing as she entered and coming to shake her hand. He squeezed it a bit, giving her an encouraging look while his back was to the detective. "Looks good on you," he whispered.

She simply smiled.

"Detective. I'd say good to see you again, but under the circumstances, it's not that good."

"I get that a lot," Tibbet said, but he grinned as he said it.

"Let's move to the table, shall we?" Paul directed them to a round table. With deliberate ease, he set their two chairs together a bit and set Tibbet apart on the other side of the table.

"Ms. Hagen, the detective and I have been going over a few things," Paul said. "However, he would like you to answer some of his questions directly."

"Of course." Torie crossed her legs and waited.

Tibbet ran her back through the usual questions about her whereabouts during Todd's murder, then progressed to the events of the previous night.

"I was quite serious last night, Detective. Having just gotten back from North Carolina, I was exhausted.

The only way I knew something was wrong was because of the driver. He's a hero, if you ask me. He saved my life."

"Indeed. We think we have an area pinpointed where the shooter would have been positioned."

"Do you have any leads?" Torie decided it was time to go on the attack herself. "And do you know who leaked the information to the press about the incidents with people whom I've dated?"

"That's being handled. Your lawyer here," Tibbet said, indicating Paul, "filed a complaint this morning. He's already offered to do it again several more times if you don't receive an official apology from the department."

Torie couldn't help it, she smiled at Paul. "Thank you."

"My job."

It was always the job with Paul. She turned back to Tibbet.

"We've already asked you about who might be interested in hurting you. So far we're following up on things there, but what about Mister Peterson? Do you know anyone who would have wanted to hurt him?"

Torie shook her head to emphasize her answer. "No. No one. In all seriousness, Detective, if there was anyone who did their level best to help people it was Todd. The money didn't change that one bit, did it, Paul?"

"No, it didn't." Paul was as adamant about that as she was.

"He gave a lot of money away, I know that. Of course, he was really good at investing it, too, so the money he won just continued to grow, or so he told me once. Then he'd win more stuff, like golf things. He won a car by doing a hole in one. He'd never shot a hole in one before, but he wanted to give a car as a prize to a charity for the church, and the next thing you know, he's shooting a hole in one at the Castico Open. You know, the one out the Main Line at the Lands End Course?"

Tibbet nodded, indicating he knew it.

"So without spending more than the fee to play, he was able to give that to the church for the raffle."

"Would there be anyone at the church who was jealous of the money, or who was pressuring him to give more?"

Glancing at Paul again to see if he had input, she said, "No, I don't think so. I don't get to church every week and I'm not in the sort of inner circle that plans things, but I don't think anyone was particularly upset. The opposite actually seemed to be true. He never minded if they hit him up to cover a shortfall. I think he told the deacon's committee that he'd match the annual donations."

Paul spoke up. "I can corroborate that. He was quick to give."

"Did you know of anyone who wanted more, Mister Jameson? Anyone who was trying to scam him, or get him to join them in some scheme or something?"

"As easygoing as he was, he was pretty sharp about that sort of thing. After all, he was a lawyer before he was a multimillionaire. He was generous, but not a soft touch."

"How so?" Tibbet paused, his pen hovering over his book.

"He got into it with this guy once. The guy had set up a meeting, seemed to be legitimate and all that. But when Todd and I began to question him, the guy didn't have good answers. We closed out the meeting, and Todd hired a private investigator. Shut the guy down. He was working for a legitimate charity, but was skimming huge amounts off the top."

"What's the guy's name?"

"He's still in jail."

"The name?"

Paul went to his desk and got out a file. Meanwhile Tibbet turned back to Torie.

"You know about this guy?"

"No, but I agree that Todd wasn't easily taken in."

Tibbet wrote the name Paul gave him, and promised to check it out. "So there's no one you know, no one you can think of that would want to hurt you, Ms. Hagen?"

"No, I really wish I could. I want to be able to tell you someone or give you a name because it would make it less frightening. I don't know anyone I've injured or upset enough that they would do this."

"I understand," Tibbet said as he closed his book. "If you think of anyone or anything, no matter how small, a sister of someone you dated that got hurt, a parent, a friend, anything, you let me know."

Torie nodded and stood to shake hands as Tibbet left. Paul showed him to the door and came back to the table. He pulled two yellow pads from a nearby stack.

"Okay. We're going to spend some time on a time line, all right? We're going to start from now and work backwards in time, as much as you can remember. I've got a file on the stuff that happened to Todd when he would come home. We're going to see if any of the dates match."

He handed Torie a pen and went to his desk for the file.

They worked for over two hours, plodding through her life, dissecting her dates and her work.

"Crap," she cursed as they reviewed a point that brought her work into play. "I had a call from the office. I need to check my messages."

Flipping over another page, she clicked over to voice mail and began to listen to what were now thirty-two messages.

Predictably, there were a lot of calls from the press.

"Any idea how the press might have gotten my cell phone number?"

"Does the Chamber have it?"

"Damn." She sighed. "Yeah, they do. My office does as well, so it could have come from there."

She jotted down the names and information of the various reporters.

"You're not obliged to call them back, Torie. They're just after a story or a scoop or some comment they can use against you."

Looking up from her notes, Torie managed to smile. "I know, but I guess I want to see who's calling and who has some decorum about contacting me. If there ever comes a time to talk to the press, I'll know who to pick."

Paul looked nonplussed for a moment, then laughed. "Very good. Really." He grinned at her. "That's perfect."

She smiled back. "I thought so."

She got to a message from her brother and stopped to text him, fill him in on the latest details. Within seconds, she had a ping with a reply.

"No, you goof," she murmured aloud, texting back. "I don't want you to fly home again."

"Your brother?"

Torie nodded. "Yes, he wants to be more of a big brother than a younger one, take care of me. I'm trying to explain that you can't fight shadows with no names."

"Good way to put it, as it's certainly what we've got." He pulled her pages over to his side of the table and began comparing them.

She listened to Pam on the message talking about Dev and how nice he was. Rolling her eyes, she deleted it, and picked up a message from Dev saying that Pam certainly was a hottie and he was glad Torie had introduced him to her.

The next one was from GoodMama. Bracing herself for the worst, Torie began to listen to the message.

"You call me, y'hear, little girl? I ain't got no mad on, so you call. I know you be thinkin' I'm mad about the boy, but I ain't. He had his own warning and didn't heed it, so's it's just as it's supposed to be anyhow. Now, fergit Devereaux Chance for a minute, and call your GoodMama."

Breathing a sigh of relief, she clicked the message into saved messages.

"You look like you got a reprieve from the gallows."

"Kinda. My grandmother, the one from New Orleans?"

"The tiny one, the one that had the—"

"The pet bobcat? Yes, that one." GoodMama had brought her pet bobcat from New Orleans in a cat carrier. In the interest of keeping the fragile peace brought about when GoodMama and Daddy had talked before he died, Torie and her mother said nothing about the cat. As she remembered, Dev and the other cousins who'd come had given the cat a wide berth.

"Does she still have the cat?"

"I don't think so. She hasn't mentioned Stiletto in a while," Torie said as she noted the number. "I guess I need to call her."

"Do you want to use the landline?" He pointed to the phone by his desk. "Save some battery or minutes?"

"Oh, sure."

Torie eased into the large leather chair, spinning it carefully to pick up the phone. When she'd dialed, she turned the chair so its back blocked her view of Paul. Talking to GoodMama was going to be nerve-wracking enough, much less with Paul listening in.

"'Bout time." GoodMama answered the phone without preamble. "I been waitin' on ya. Some reason you think to keep me waitin'?"

"I'm sorry, GoodMama, I just got the message."

"You saw it yesterday."

"I did, but I got shot at and nearly blown up yesterday, so I wasn't really up for talking."

"Hmmmmph. Well. Reckon that's true. You eatin'?"

"Eating? No, I haven't eaten yet, but it's not lunchtime."

"Breakfast, girl. Most important meal of the day. Didn't your mama teach you that?"

Torie smiled. "Yes, yes she did."

"Listening's a good skill to have, little girl." Good-Mama said it with a flat tone, like a warning. "You need to do a lot of it right now. I'm telling you that you need to look at everyone close to you. That Pam, she's not the one. Nor Dev. Nor that man sittin' there with you that thinks you mighty fine. Them you can trust. The others? Don't you trust no one else, you hear, little girl? Dev, he has to come home. Get him outta harm's way."

"I understand," Torie said. She hated the thought that Dev had been hurt, and she hoped he would go home, and out of the line of fire.

"Do you understand this ain't your fault?"

"What?" Torie was startled by the comment. "How do you mean?"

"Someone got a powerful mad on, hatin' mad. But it ain't you—it's that man you nearly hitched yourself to. Remember what GoodMama told you?"

"That gold was more powerful than affection."

"Still the case. But that hate's spillin' onto you. You look there, at that man. And watch for falling glass. I keep seeing falling glass. Not just this moment, but soon."

When she hung up with GoodMama, she hurried to the table to write everything down. Talking with the old woman was mesmerizing—you couldn't write things down while you were talking to her because she'd ask if you were listening or paying attention. But Torie knew she'd better get it down fast, because so far GoodMama had never been wrong.

"Did Granny WooWoo have some information?"

"Hush," Torie chided, scribbling away.

Before she could finish, a squealing whoop, whoop, whoop filled the air, along with a disembodied voice.

"This is not a drill. This is a fire alarm. Please exit the building immediately." Whoop, whoop, whoop.

Chapter Seven

"What the hell?" Paul growled. He snatched files from the table and from his desk, threw them in a drawer, and locked it. "Come on. We have to get out."

Paul was tugging on her arm, hauling her up and toward the door.

"But, but . . ." Torie was aghast. GoodMama said she had some time.

"It's probably nothing. We've had a couple of these recently, but you can't take a chance."

They hurried out of the office to join others hurrying through the suite of offices and out to the stairs. On the street, after a long descent, Torie, Paul, and other people from the building milled around, waiting for the firemen to give an all clear.

Martha scurried up, her sharp features set in disapproving lines.

"What is it?" Paul asked.

"Melvin Jr.," she whispered. "He said he was just checking to see that you were out, but I was helping Elsa get Mister Pratt Sr. down the stairs and saw him coming out of our offices."

"Really?" Paul frowned.

As they watched, Melvin Jr. pushed through the crowd to Paul's side. "Paul, I wanted to . . ." He noted Torie's presence, and his eyes widened. "Well, hello, Torie."

He held out a hand and Torie shook it, then let go as quickly as she could. Melvin, Todd, and Paul had all been in law school together, and in the same fraternity. Once Todd left the country, Melvin had asked Torie out several times.

She'd declined. He was just . . . unpleasant.

"Hello, Melvin. How are you?"

He smiled and motioned to indicate the crowd on the sidewalk. "I've been better. This is certainly not the way I'd expected to meet you again. I trust you've been well?"

"As well as can be expected, yes."

Melvin looked surprised for a moment, then seemed to remember she'd had troubles. "Oh, I'm sorry. I did hear about your house. And Todd, of course. My apologies. And my sympathy."

"Thank you."

"Melvin, I understand you were in my office?" Paul went right to the heart of the matter.

"Yes, I thought I saw someone in there. There was someone coming out of your office as I came out of the stairwell, and I yelled and he ran. I don't think anything was taken, but I can't be sure. I was coming to tell you before I found the police."

Melvin pivoted and scanned the crowd. "There, there's an officer. Let's go over. My father's over there as well. Good."

Torie and Paul exchanged glances behind Melvin's back.

"Do you believe him?" Torie whispered.

Paul simply shook his head in the negative.

They walked up in time to hear Melvin Sr. saying, "Yes, and my son saw someone coming out of one of our partner's offices."

Melvin Jr. froze in his tracks. Torie almost plowed into his back. Paul's hands steadied her, but she felt a tremble in them.

"Whose office would that be, Mister Pratt?" the officer asked.

"Ah, there he is. Thank you, Melvin, for fetching Paul for me." The older man had a wheeze to his voice, and coughed a bit. "Excuse me, I don't usually take the stairs, much less in haste." He coughed again, more vigorously this time. "Paul, you need to talk to the officer, and let him go into your office with you when we get the all clear. Melvin here says he surprised someone coming out of your suite."

"So, Mister, uh . . ."

"Jameson. Paul Jameson."

"You're a partner here at Pratt and Legend?"

"He is. Just got the promotion this morning, so he's not used to it yet," Pratt Sr. interjected. "Missed the meeting, Jameson. You could've gotten the news firsthand, otherwise . . ." The old man shot him a sly smile before he began coughing again.

"Sir, do you want to see the EMTs?" Torie moved to his side. She was concerned about how pale he was. Her father had gotten wheezy, coughed that way when his heart was acting up. "Perhaps just a whiff of oxygen will help you clear up that shortness of breath."

The cop didn't wait to hear the old man's answer, and Torie was glad of it. He tucked his notes away and hustled over to the waiting ambulance. The loitering EMTs snatched up some gear and came over.

"I'm fine, really," the senior lawyer complained.

"Sir," Torie said firmly, "you don't want your family to worry." She refused to look at Melvin Jr. "And," she lowered her voice, "if you let them give you oxygen now, you'll probably be able to walk back into the building. If you don't, they'll insist you go to the hospital."

The old man harrumphed and muttered, but he talked to the EMTs and allowed them to fit an oxygen mask over his face. His color cleared immediately and he began to breathe easily.

The older man gave Torie an appraising glance, and then, to her surprise, winked.

She smiled at him and looked away so she wouldn't laugh. It felt good to laugh. Heaven knew she hadn't had much reason for humor over the last few weeks.

"It's clear, gentlemen." A fire captain came over to give them the news. "We found where the alarm had been pulled."

"Damn pranksters," Pratt Sr. declared, pulling off the oxygen mask and carefully standing up. "Thank you, gentlemen," he said to the EMTs as he passed the mask back to them. One of the EMTs spoke quietly to him and he nodded, shooting a glance at Torie as he did. "I'll do that. Thank you," she heard him say.

"Now, let's get back in the building and use the elevator this time."

On their way into the building, Torie and Paul exchanged glances. "Are you going to call Tibbet?" she asked.

"Of course."

In Paul's area, the officer asked him to look around, without touching anything, to assess if anything was missing. "Officer, you may want to contact Detective Tibbet. My client," he said as he indicated Torie, "has had considerable difficulties in the last few weeks, and this might be another attempt to scare or intimidate her."

"Yes, sir. I'll contact the detective."

Torie was watching Paul. He was a good poker player, she was sure. Nothing showed on his face as he scanned the desk, the table where they'd been working, and the credenza behind his desk.

"Everything seems to be here," he said finally.

"But not at my desk," Martha said, coming in from the assistant's area. "My PDA is missing."

"Could you have taken it with you, or knocked it over in your haste to leave?" the officer asked.

Martha froze him with a look. "Absolutely not, young man. It was in a locked desk drawer, hooked to the charging station. It was deliberate."

The young officer blushed, but got busy calling Tibbet. Once done with that, he also summoned the crime scene techs, at Tibbet's request.

Martha's phone rang and she picked it up. Her eyebrows rose as she looked at both Torie and Paul, but she concluded the call quickly. "Mister Jameson, if we could speak in private for a moment?"

"Certainly. If you'll excuse us?"

Torie watched them, but could discern nothing from their body language. Although she'd slept well, she was beginning to fade. It was lunchtime, and she'd not eaten anything.

"Let's go," Paul said, taking her arm to ease her around the arriving officers. "Tibbet can come over to O'Briens if he wants to see us."

"Where are we going?"

"We're getting lunch. You're too pale, your hands are shaking, and I'm starving."

"Wait a sec," Torie said, remembering her shopping. "Missus Prinz," she said to Martha, "would you mind checking the items I left with you?"

Martha's lips tightened, but she turned to the nearly invisible closet door in the paneling. Opening it up, she gasped.

"No. No argument," Paul insisted as they left the building at the end of the day. They'd spent the afternoon with the police going over what had happened to Torie's things. The shredded garments from Martha's closet were now in Tibbet's hands. They'd been notified that they could pick up the few undamaged clothes from the Suites, since they were ready to release the room as a crime scene. According to Tibbet, there wasn't much left, so Torie would have to go shopping again.

"Until we can find you a new bodyguard, you aren't going anywhere alone, much less staying alone. I'd rather have you in my guest room than have both of us staying at some characterless hotel. We'll pick up your remaining things and head to my place."

"Paul, I don't want to stay with you. I can call Pam," Torie began. "And what about the bodyguard from this morning?"

Paul glared at her. "I thought Pam was your best friend."

"She is." Torie's whole body bespoke insult.

"Then don't get her hurt, dead, her house burned down, or anything else. The same reasons you had when you insisted on staying at the Hilton still apply."

"I don't think . . ." she stopped, and Paul nodded.

"Yes, you do. You think the same thing I do. Whoever this is, whatever it's about, it's directed at you." Paul ushered her into his car. Once he got in, he continued the thought. "Better to be with me, someone who knows what's up and can, hopefully help. Besides, the bodyguard from this morning could only work today. He has another gig, but he was able to cover you while you were out of my sight."

Torie frowned into the darkening day. She spoke very little until they had picked up her meager things at the hotel and were driving toward his house.

"I don't want anything to happen to you, either, Paul."

He laughed. "Oh, come on. Wouldn't it just be justice for something to happen to me? After all, I'm sure you've wished me dead or to the devil at least a hundred times since we met."

"No," she said. Her voice was quiet but firm. "I wouldn't wish this on anyone." She turned in the seat to look at him. Since the light was red, he turned to her, grinning.

"Oh, right. How better to get back at me?"

She shook her head. "That's not the way I work. Never has been."

"Right," he smirked, and drove on.

Her cell phone rang. Digging it out of her purse, she answered it.

"Hi, Pam."

"You've got to come, quick," Pam was panting the words. "It's the package. There's been a problem. You gotta come."

Torie looked at Paul. Crap. He'd never understand. Closing her eyes, she wondered why she cared. What did it matter what he thought of her? He'd made his decision a long, long time ago.

"Turn around, Paul. We've got to go to Germantown."

"What?" Paul snapped.

"It's a matter of life or death. I'm not kidding."

"You're kidding, right? Life or death in Germantown? It's a suburb."

"Pam and my cousin Dev are there. Yes. It's for real."

"I'm calling Tibbet," Paul said as he made a squealing U-turn and headed for the interstate.

"No," Torie screeched and snatched his phone away. "This isn't about that. It's something else. But we have to go."

"We're on our way, Pam," she said, cutting off Pam's stream of chatter. "Can't talk."

Slapping the phone closed, she grabbed the armrest as Paul whipped the car onto a side street, screeching to a halt at the curb.

"What the hell is going on?" Paul demanded.

"Pam and I had a little side incident, the day my house burned down. The, um, package, we delivered is really fragile, and . . ."

"Torie, if you don't speak English and tell me what the hell you and Pam did, I'm turning the car around and calling Tibbet."

"You can't. Really. Just trust me."

"*Trust* you?" His incredulity crushed her heart. "I can't believe you said that to me, of all people."

Her nerves, frayed to the point of breaking so many times over the past few weeks, finally gave way. The scream started low and rose until she let loose a howl worthy of a banshee.

Paul recoiled in reaction and she poked a finger into his bicep.

"I want you to shut the hell up. Trust. What the hell do you know about trust? I trusted *you,* you bastard. *You're* the one who told Todd, not me, and I'm supposed to *trust* you? Ohhhh, no. Then you go from helping me get away, asking me out, being *that* way with me, to shouting at me afterward? Telling people we were a one-date wonder? Then complain when, after six months, *six months,* that I'm dating your friend?"

She sat back into her seat with a whump, sat for all of two seconds, then fired up again. "I think you should be really watching who you ask to trust you, buddy. I've never been anything . . ." she shouted, turning back. She felt as if she could shoot fire from her fingertips, she was so mad, as she poked his arm again. "*Anything* but honest and truthful with you. You're the one who betrayed *my* trust. So suck it up, Jameson. If you want to protect me, fine. I'm going to help my friend since she asked, and has *never, ever* broken the bonds of friendship. So let's go. Drive." When he didn't put it in gear, she put her hand on the latch and picked up her purse. "Trust me on this, Paul, if nothing else. If I have to get out of this car and call a cab, I will."

Paul sat for several heartbeats more, just looking at her. His dark eyes betrayed turbulent emotions, but she couldn't tell what he was thinking or feeling. Her own outburst had her so wound up, so shaken, that she didn't really want to know.

"Damn it, Paul," she began, pulling the latch.

He slammed his hand down on the locking mechanism. "I'm driving."

The silence was fat and thick with unspoken pain,

with memories and bitter words from long ago rising to shake off the dust of time, to bite again. Torie sank into her seat. She'd gotten her way, but at what cost? Her resolve to never speak of those days again, her decision to not go there, was blown.

They pulled into the neighborhood; Torie gave terse directions to get them to Carlos's house. There were three cars in the driveway. Carlos's low-slung Jaguar was first, then Pam's SUV, then what looked like a rental car.

Paul pulled to the curb behind the rental. Torie got out before Paul could cut the engine.

"Where is he?" Torie called as Pam hurried out the door.

"Who?" Paul was quick to follow. "Where is who?"

"More like what, I think," a male voice drawled from inside. "Come in here, cher cousine and 'splain all this to your Dev, eh?"

She felt Paul jerk in reaction to Dev's voice, but she didn't have time to think about that. She whipped open the door and ran inside.

"Dev." She hugged him tightly, but carefully. "You're out of the hospital. Are you okay? Are you—"

He laughed and hugged her back as he interrupted her. "Hold on, little cuz. You go too fast. I'm fine. I mend quick, and I'd been better if I'd'a remembered GoodMama's warning to me. She tol' me not to go see you, to jus' call."

Torie caught her breath. "Oh, Dev."

"Yeah, call me a horse's ass. Might as well." He grinned a bright, wry grin. "She did, and a whole lot more."

"She told me to watch out for fire, but I didn't have time."

"I know." Dev's smile faded. "I'm sorry 'bout that."

"Not your fault."

"No, but . . ."

"Yeah. I get it."

"Besides, it's had some benefits." Dev turned his dazzling smile toward Pam. "I got to meet this lovely friend of yours."

Torie looked at Pam's face and her heart sank. Pam was hooked. Damn. On Dev of all people. This was *so* not good.

Paul cleared his throat.

"Oh, sorry. Paul, this is my cousin from New Orleans, Devereaux Chance, also known as Dev. And you remember Pam, don't you?"

"Your cousin?" Paul asked, looking relieved about something. "Pleased to meet you. I heard you were hurt."

"Dev was cut up pretty badly," Pam volunteered. "But he's healed with amazing speed." Torie saw the sly twist to her smile, just before Pam dropped her gaze. Crap, they were sleeping together. Pam never slept with anyone, she just dangled the lure and the men followed her anywhere.

The fact that she had actually slept with . . . no, she could not think about Dev in bed with her best friend. It was just . . . wrong. Not to do it, just for her to be thinking about it.

Cripes. There was that image again, popping into her head. Nope. Not going there.

Meanwhile, the two men were shaking hands.

"So, you're the attorney, eh?" Dev said, eyeing Paul. "The one that was the best man, right?"

"That was a long time ago, Dev. Water under the bridge."

"There are some long bridges, where I come from, cher cousine. Plenty of time to dip some water."

"No, there isn't," Torie said flatly. She was not going to referee some stupid male dominance battle, nor let her cousin defend her over long-ago slights. Much as he obviously wanted to, which was sweet. Hadn't she already dredged up enough of the past, shouting at Paul? "I let the water flow, Dev, and I've moved on."

"Hmmm."

She glared at him. "Water. Under the bridge. Done. Over. My battles, Dev. Remember?"

"Yeah, yeah, cher. I read you loud and clear," he said with a laugh. He shot Paul an amused look. "She defends you pretty good, counselor."

Paul nodded, but didn't respond. He nodded at Pam. "Pam, long time, no see."

"All the better," Pam managed without a smile.

"Pam, you said it was urgent." Torie redirected the budding blowup. She knew Pam and, new beau or not, she'd always wanted a chunk of Paul Jameson's hide. It had been Pam who had helped her pick up the pieces of her college life, Pam who had made sure she survived the heartaches. Pam was the one who had introduced her to Todd.

Instantly contrite, and distracted from Paul, Pam responded. "Oh, it is. He got away. I don't know how."

"Where's Carlos?" Now Torie was deeply worried.

"Out hunting him."

"How did he get out?"

"It was a mistake. He'd been doing so well." Pam was pacing now, her worry prompting her to move. "I wasn't ready to move him yet. I don't have a home lined up."

"The family in Harrisburg fell through?"

"Yeah, they paid more to someone else, but they got reliable merchandise, you know?"

"But this boy is reliable. We know that. You can't do all that, and oh . . ." Torie wanted to cry all over again. It was bad enough that her life was totally screwed. She hated that this little project was going to hell in a go-cart as well. "I had so hoped that home would work and work quickly. Carlos has done so much."

"Carlos hasn't minded the work. He used to be a tech, you know?" Pam replied. One part of Torie's brain noted that she was pitching her voice like Dev's, and using the same rhythm and speech pattern that her cousin used.

Bad sign.

"Stop."

Torie turned to Paul, reacting as much to his firm, irritated tone as she did to the word.

"What?"

"What are we doing here that's a matter of life and death? Who is Carlos, and what or who is he hunting?" Paul ticked the points off on his fingers. "Oh, and last but not least, what the hell do you have to do with it?"

Torie looked at Pam, who managed to look sheepish. Dev had crossed his arms over his chest and was looking amused, but was apparently just as interested in the answer as Paul was.

When she shot a questioning look Pam's way, her friend shrugged. "I hadn't had a chance to explain to Dev either. I just told him where to meet me. Carlos nearly took Dev out with a baseball bat before we got him to listen."

"I thought you said he was reliable?" Torie was

aghast. First her cousin was attacked because of her, now this.

"He is, but he's nervous now. There's been a lot of . . ." Pam glanced at Paul. "Snooping around. Neighbors and stuff."

"Torie, who the hell is Carlos, why is he looking for someone out in the dark, and why are you—" he turned a hot, angry look toward Pam—"involved in finding someone a home? For money?"

"It's not what you think."

"I sure as hell hope not, because what I'm thinking could get you twenty-five years in jail."

"No, it's—"

There was a banging from the back of the house, and within seconds, the door to the living room burst inward. An excited Carlos bounced into the middle of the fray. Torie barely recognized the suave restaurateur in the mud-covered, wild-haired man standing before her.

"Pam, you must, oh—" He stopped at the sight of Paul in his city lawyer suit, and Torie in her business attire.

"Carlos, this is my friend Torie, the one I told you about. And this is her . . . friend, Paul."

"You, I recognize you." Carlos looked at Paul. "You're a lawyer."

"Yes."

"I hate lawyers."

"So do I," Paul said, his tone flat, with no hint of humor.

Carlos stood for a moment, considering. Then smiled. Then laughed.

So did Dev.

Pam rolled her eyes, but Torie smiled. Male bonding was weirder than anything women came up with.

"Where is he?"

"Come, I'll show you."

She moved to follow, but Paul blocked her way.

"You are not going anywhere until you answer my questions."

"I'll back you up on that," Dev said, stepping up beside Paul. "I think we'd better hear this story from the beginning."

"There's no time," Torie said, attempting to push past them.

"No." Paul's voice was stone hard, and she could see Dev taking on the same stance.

Chapter Eight

"Oh, for heaven's sake," Torie began.

"It's a dog," Pam snapped. "Now get out of the way."

Together the two women pushed passed the gaping men to follow Carlos through the house, out the back door, and into the darkness.

"Well, damn," Paul said. He turned to Dev. "Did all that cloak and dagger talk sound like they were talking about a dog?"

"Hell, no."

"Jesus, she drives me insane. You coming?"

"No." Dev grimaced. "Not this mission, Kemo Sabe. I'll do more harm than good."

Paul grinned, suddenly struck by Dev's posing for Pam. "Not all that well yet, huh?"

Dev read exactly what Paul meant, and laughed. "Good enough for some things, eh? But not for chasing wily animals in the dark, you know? The stitches don't come out till next week."

"Got it. I better go if I want to keep up," Paul said as he was moved toward the door.

"Luck, brother."

"Thanks. With this caper, we're gonna need it."

Pushing open the back door, Paul was engulfed in darkness. Three bouncing lights were already at the back of the property, pausing at a large gate.

"Hang on," he called, moving quickly toward them. They waited, then went through the gate and into a long stretch of wild grass. The power line easement stretched out before them, rolling for miles as it meandered through neighborhoods and out into the countryside.

"He's holed up in a shed over on the other side of the easement," Carlos said. "Some kids found him and came and let me know."

"Kids?" Torie asked, amazed.

"Yeah, they know stuff. They keep me posted." Paul could see the flash of his grin in the dark. "I know everything going on in my 'hood, ladies. Everything. Kids see a lot more than anyone thinks, you know."

"I know," Pam muttered. The way she said it was striking. Paul, used to listening to jurors and clients for the meaning behind the words, had to wonder what might have happened to Pam, or what she'd heard as a child.

"Is he frightened again?" Torie asked, oblivious to the byplay.

"No, I don't think so, but the kids, they shut him in. I think he's just stuck," Carlos explained.

"Okay. Do the property owners know he's there? Should we tell them?"

"Naw. Those people are never home."

"As long as we don't get shot at again, I don't care," Pam muttered.

"Shot at?" Paul growled. "Torie."

"Later, Paul. I'll explain it all later. For now, we've got to get to Bear."

"Bear?"

"The dog."

"What is he, a Chihuahua?" His buddy in high school had named his Chihuahua Rambo, so he figured it might fit.

"No. He's a Rottweiler, and maybe an Australian Cattle Dog, crossbred with a Labrador retriever. Could be some Newfoundland, too, as big as he is."

"Holy shit."

"Big motherfu . . . sorry," Carlos aborted what he was about to say. "He's huge."

"Great."

They reached the other side of the cleared area, and Carlos took the lead again. A narrow dirt path opened up to a cement sidewalk, and they were able to move more quickly.

"Let me go in—he knows me."

"He's gonna be scared," Carlos temporized. "You sure you want to do that?"

"He knows me. I got him into this mess."

"Torie," Paul started.

"Shut up, Paul. Don't start with me. My life is so out of my control, I can't bear it. This, I can do. So shut up and let me."

The three waited five endlessly tense minutes for Torie to return. When she did, she was leading the biggest damn dog Paul had ever seen. The beast was pressed firmly to the side of her leg, eyes darting furtively around. When he caught wind of their presence, he didn't bark. He just stopped. Torie, caught off guard, stumbled to a halt as well.

"It's okay, Bear, they're with me."

Her voice, cheerful and pleasant, was like a live wire to the dog. Without warning, Bear bounded forward again, dragging Torie with him. He ignored Pam and Carlos, whom he knew, and focused on Paul.

Two enormous, dinner-plate sized feet planted themselves on his lapels. For several heartbeats, he and the dog stared at one another. There was the barest curl to the dog's lip that made Paul wonder if he was going to lose his face. Instead, a moment later, the biggest damn tongue he'd ever seen wrapped itself around his jaw.

"Get down, Bear," Torie managed, tugging on the lead.

Seemingly satisfied, Bear dropped down to all fours.

Pam let out a long breath. "Good Lord, I thought he was going to take your face off."

They started walking, and Paul answered her. "Me, too, Pam. Me, too."

When they finally arrived at Paul's house, it was after ten. Paul plopped the fast-food bags on the kitchen table and flipped on the lights.

"So. What's the story with the dog? Is that where you were with Pam? The night your place was . . ." Paul hesitated, not wanting to say torched, which was the first word springing to mind. "Damaged?"

Torie nodded. She was still standing in the doorway. She looked weary and a little bewildered. Asking about the dog brought a spark of interest to her eyes.

"He's a sweet dog, really. The owner lives next to a friend of Pam's. He chained the dog up short, only let him have water once a day or so. We're not sure how often he fed him."

"He's that big and not getting regular meals?" Paul whistled in astonishment. "Holy crap."

"Yeah." Torie smiled. "And he's sweet. We think the guy was trying to make him mean to use him in fights."

"He'd make a killing," Paul said, keeping his face poker straight.

Torie fired up, almost immediately. "You cannot tell me you would condone . . ." she trailed off, catching him in the lie. "I know you wouldn't, so what are you going to say, smart-ass?"

"The other dog would die of fright."

She laughed, as he hoped. Together they walked on through to the kitchen. He scanned the counters, glad to see he hadn't left anything sitting out.

"It's clean, I think. The housekeeper was here yesterday. I know there're clean sheets on the guest bed."

"That's fine. Just show me where. I feel like I could sleep for a week."

"Sounds good to me, too," Paul said, setting his briefcase on the floor. "But we both need to eat. You especially."

"Is that your way of saying I look like shit?" Torie retorted, as she plopped wearily into the chair at the table, and began rustling in the bags.

"No, it means you haven't eaten today, not breakfast, and not lunch. You've been shorting yourself on sleep and food, Torie. That's a bad combo. Believe me, I know."

"Yeah," was all she could manage.

"Here, let me help." He pulled plates from the cabinet, and found two cold Sprites in the fridge. He kept them for his niece and nephew, but he needed something wet, decaffeinated, and nonalcoholic. Setting them on the table, he managed to get the hamburgers set out, and the steaming French fries heaped onto a communal plate. "There. It's not haute cuisine, but it'll do for tonight. Dig in."

Together the plowed through the food. The appetite he'd always admired wasn't up to its usual standard, but Torie held her own. However, when she'd eaten the burger, the steam left her.

"I could put my head down right here on this table, and sleep."

"You'd get a crick in your neck," Paul observed, pushing his plate away. He'd stopped eating to watch her, and the last of the fries no longer appealed. The familiar gnawing in his gut was making the ketchup a bad choice as well.

"You sound like my mother." Torie's muffled voice came from the crook of her arm as she put her head down on the table. "I was right. I could sleep here."

Paul laughed and moved around behind her. "No way," he rubbed at her shoulders a bit. "You'll ruin my rep if anyone sees you at the table, asleep."

"I'll promise you anything if you keep rubbing my shoulders," Torie said on a groan.

Under his hands, her tight shoulders relaxed, and as he moved to her back, she sighed. Everything in his body went on high alert. Her soft moan had him gritting his teeth in a vain attempt to focus on something other than the thought of Torie's back, her body, what else might make her moan.

"C'mon, Tor," he said softly. "Let's get you to bed."

She opened one bleary eye. "You haven't called me that in . . . forever."

He hadn't. Damn it, now was not the time to slip up, with her in his house, close to him. She'd be sleeping in the other bedroom, for God's sake.

"Time for bed, Torie. You'll have to walk this time. I'm too frickin' tired myself to carry you that far."

She raised her head, and gave him a sleepy smile. It was the sexiest damn thing he'd ever seen, and his body responded. He could practically feel the blood pounding in his veins. It didn't get any better when she stood up, stretching all those lithe muscles, arching her back and bending forward to pick up her purse.

Damn. She had one of the finest asses he'd ever seen. He'd lusted after her for that one attribute since the first moment he'd seen her, sophomore year.

"You carried me, from one bed to the next, didn't you?" It was more statement than question, so he just nodded. Not trusting himself to speak.

"Thanks."

"You're welcome," his voice sounded weird, tinny, and high, but Torie didn't seem to notice. "Let's get you settled."

The thoughts running through his mind would have made a sailor blush, and it was all he could do to walk normally, switch on lights, and try to be a good host.

"Here. The guest bedroom. Uh, the bathroom's across the hall here." He turned on the light. "I think everything you need's in the cabinets. My sisters are okay with it, so it's been girl approved."

"Girl approved?" She laughed. "Sounds good. I just want to wash my face and crawl under the covers." Pausing, she looked uncomfortable for a moment, then dropped her eyes.

"What?" Had she seen how aroused he was? Damn it. He cursed his reaction to her, not for the first time either.

"I, uh, need something to wear to bed. The stuff I got today," she began, remembering the shredded bags, the torn clothing. "Uh, and none of the things left over from the Suites included pajamas. Or anything I could sleep in."

"I know. Never mind. I'll get you a T-shirt. Some boxers. Will that work?"

A look of relief and a smile were his answer.

"Okay, you get your face washed and I'll be right back."

It took him a few minutes to find something suitable, but he unearthed a clean, long sleeved Temple T-shirt and a pair of gym shorts with a drawstring waist. He refused to think about how erotic it was to have her wearing his clothes.

Refused. Not going there.

"Torie?" He tapped on the door. "You haven't fallen asleep on me, have you?"

She opened the door, her face freshly washed, the hair at her temples wet. A laugh sparkled in her eyes. He could watch that all day.

"I thought about it, but the bed seemed like a better idea."

"It is." He closed his eyes and winced. "What I mean is," he began.

"Shhh." She put a finger to his lips. "I know. You didn't mean anything by it."

Was there disappointment in her voice?

He wished he'd turned on the hall light. Now that she'd turned the bathroom light off, in the dim light coming from the bedrooms he couldn't tell if she was serious or . . .

She leaned into him and he wanted to groan. Out loud. She brushed his cheek with a kiss.

"Thank you," she murmured. "For being kind. I'm sorry I shouted at you earlier."

She took hold of the shirt and shorts, but he didn't let go.

"Paul?"

"I'm not that kind, Torie. I'm . . ." He didn't finish. He didn't know what he was.

"You're?"

He looked into her eyes and forgot about their argument, forgot that he'd wanted to justify his need to protect her. He couldn't see their expression, but he could see her lips and he wanted them. She was close enough for him to smell the soap she'd used to wash her face. He could smell the faint scent of dog, from Bear. And grass.

"You smell like grass," he murmured. "And moonlight."

Where had that come from? He didn't know, but it was true. There was a wild night perfume that was driving him to speak, to act.

"Paul?" Torie whispered his name. But she didn't move away. Didn't retreat this time. He shoved the past away and focused on the now.

"You're safe here, Torie. I don't want you to think otherwise, but I need to—"

"To what?"

"This," he said, leaning into her, pressing his lips to hers. He wanted to snatch her up, devour her, pull her into his arms and fill himself with her.

The temptation was overwhelming, but he locked it down. Instead, he savored. Gently. Carefully.

Somehow, the careful touch, the brush of their meeting lips, the slow progression to a deeper, more passionate kiss was incredibly arousing, more erotic than the headlong rush. He allowed himself to use one hand to slide under the heavy mane of her hair which she'd loosened, finally, from its strict arrangement.

With the other, he gripped the door jamb, willing himself to stay upright. Willing himself not to grab at her, like a greedy child. There would probably be impressions in the wood, he was squeezing so tightly.

"Ahhhhh," Torie sighed, leaning into his hand. The sensuous sound coiled around his body, tightening every muscle. He had to call on every bit of control he'd learned, as a man, as a lawyer, to slow down, to stop the mad rush he wanted to give in to.

He'd frightened her once, on their one lone date. They'd been so hot for each other, so consumed that they'd rushed into sex. They'd set each other on fire. He'd been so blown away, so shaken by the power of it, he'd backed away emotionally and physically. The wound of that came between them at every turn.

God knew if there were ever to be another chance, he had to take it slowly. Maybe, just maybe.

"Torie." He managed her name from a throat gone desert dry. "Torie." Just her name. If he said anything else, he'd lose it, start trying to explain the years away. Something.

So he just let himself say it, the way he wanted to say it.

"Torie."

He kissed her again, softly, then drew her in, letting her rest against him. When she pressed in, of her own accord, he felt her jolt just a little as she realized how aroused he was.

"Paul . . ."

"Shhhhh. It's okay." It was so much more than okay. She shifted, her soft breasts moving over his chest. He thought he was going to explode, like a green high school kid with his first crush. He eased back. If she did it again, he would embarrass himself, and her.

"It's been an emotionally charged day. We're both tired," he said, pressing the shirt and shorts into the hand that was on his chest. "Here, take these. To sleep in."

They stood in the dark, hovering mere inches apart for what seemed like an eternity. She didn't look at him; her eyes were closed. He took the opportunity to savor the look of her, the clean, sharp line of her cheekbones, the curve of her ear, the glint of gold from the new earrings. His hand, still cupping the nape of her neck flexed, and she rolled her head, rubbing into his fingers as a cat might do.

"We need sleep," she finally whispered. "We're too tired to think."

There were a lot of things running through Paul's mind, and his thinking was quite clear, but he knew what she meant.

Lowering his mouth to hers one last time, he kissed her, let himself drown in her lush, immediate response. Then, reluctantly, he pulled away.

The cool air rushed between them and in defense, she clutched the borrowed clothes to her body.

"Good night, Tor."

She said nothing, just stood, looking at him as if she'd never seen him before. He got to his own bedroom door and stopped.

She finally moved, turning into the guest room. Before the door closed, he heard her response.

"Good night, Sir Paul."

* * *

He hadn't slept. Big surprise. Paul woke up feeling like he was on the last day of a four-day drinking binge, without the benefit of the fun party beforehand. His empty stomach was already clenching at the thought of seeing Torie again. A recipe for instant indigestion.

He groaned, and slapped the alarm again. Lurching to his feet, he headed for the shower.

Feeling only marginally better, he dressed for work and listened for Torie. He heard the water running and presumed she was showering as well.

"No. Do NOT go there," he told his reflection. But the image of Torie, wet and soapy, in his guest shower wouldn't be denied. He felt the sweat begin to bead on his forehead.

Great. He was either sick or crazy.

He'd put money on crazy.

Doors opened and shut, and he waited long enough for her to not be in the hall when he made a break for the kitchen. He couldn't face running into her in the hallway where they'd kissed last night, fresh from a shower.

"Nonotgoingthere," he growled under his breath as he slapped the coffee machine. It spluttered as the last of the coffee ran into the carafe.

He poured a mug for himself, threw a bagel in the toaster, and wondered if he should ask her about breakfast. Did she eat breakfast?

He had no idea. She used to, when they were in school. The protein girl, Todd had called her, always ready for eggs and bacon. Wincing at the memory of his friend, Paul got out another mug.

"Just going to knock and ask about coffee," he lectured

his raging hormones. "Christ, Jameson, you are not seventeen. Cut it out."

He tapped a knuckle on the door. "Torie? You decent? How do you take your coffee?"

She didn't answer. He frowned, leaning in toward the door to try and catch any response.

"Torie?"

Now he was worried. Decent or not, he was going in.

He knocked one more time for form's sake, and twisted the knob. He'd only opened it an inch when she spoke.

"I'm okay, just . . ."

He knew that quaver. She was crying. Damn it. Steeling his nerves, reminding himself to be professional, he walked in.

She was sitting on the side of the bed, her cell phone cupped in between her hands. He could see the scroll of a text message. Her head was bowed, her loose hair camouflaging her expression.

"Really, I'm fine."

"You are not. You're crying." He sat down on the bed, making sure there was at least a foot, maybe more, between them.

Torie raised her face, and he could see the streaks of her tears. *Her mascara must be waterproof.* Why that would matter, he couldn't say, but her gorgeous eyes were reddened and as he watched, a tear escaped to run down her cheek.

"What is it, Torie? It's not Pam, is it? Or your cousin?"

She shook her head.

"The dog? Bear?"

She half-laughed, half-sobbed. "No, they're all okay."

"But you're not. Please, tell me. Maybe I can help."

He wanted to scoot closer, to touch her. He held back because if he touched her now, when she was upset and vulnerable, and something happened . . . He'd never forgive himself for screwing it up again.

"I don't think so, but thanks," she looked at the ceiling, and he decided she was doing it to keep from crying. Unfortunately, all it did was expose the long line of her throat, which directed his gaze straight to her gorgeous—

"Really. I want to." *Oh, I want to.* "Help, that is."

She looked at him, her smile forced. She held up the phone. "I was supposed to go back into the office today. I got an email from my boss. Seems like the HR team and the firm's principals decided I needed administrative leave. The phones have been ringing off the hook you see, from the press. They figure it'll die down if I take a week or so off." She pushed off the mattress, went to stand by the window.

For a moment, all he could focus on was the way she moved, all grace and flow. Then, in the light from the window, he could see the outline of her back, the curve of her waist through the lightweight shirt she'd put on. It was one that they'd picked up from the Suites, slightly wrinkled from being tossed off its hanger, thrown to the floor.

Paul shook off the haze of physical need, drilling in on what she'd said.

"I beg your pardon, but they did *what?*"

She laughed, half-turned, and Paul nearly groaned. The shirt was still opaque, but he could see the curve of her breast, and the snug fit of equally wrinkled pants was killing him.

"They put me on paid administrative leave for

two weeks. I guess they don't want a murder suspect cluttering up the office."

"Torie, no." He rose, went to her. He couldn't help it. The naked pain on her face, every line of her posture told him what a deep wound it was to be slapped down professionally for something over which she had no control. He wanted to tell her she had nothing to worry about, but he couldn't. Not until she was cleared.

"They don't believe I'm guilty, you understand." She failed miserably at the intended sarcasm. "They just think it's *for the best*." She outlined the last words with her fingers making quotations in the air.

"Well, we both hate that, don't we? Anyone thinking they know what's best?"

She stared at him for a heartbeat, then laughed. "Yeah, I guess we do."

He wanted to distract her, change the subject. Without thinking of the implications, he asked, "So how did you sleep?"

The answer spread over her face in a blush. Awww, crap.

"That bad, huh? Was it the bed?"

"No."

He looked into her eyes and saw something kindle, hot and wild. It might be his imagination, but she was looking at him. Really looking at *him*, for once.

Torie dropped her gaze, then crossed her arms over her chest. Unfortunately, not before he saw that she was aroused.

"Do I smell coffee?"

It was impossible to resist. That glimpse of fire, the sight of her pebbled nipples erect, and her breasts straining the buttons of her shirt. He knew it was wrong. It broke all the rules, everything he'd kept to for more than ten years.

He didn't care.

He took a step toward her, let his hand slide under her hair as it had the previous night. She froze, but didn't retreat.

A good sign.

"Torie?"

"Paul, this is a mistake. We both know it. We can't go there again."

"Is it a mistake? Torie? Was it?"

She turned her head, and her hair slid onto his arm, lay like gold on the starched blue of his shirt. He was going to need a new shirt before he headed to the office.

He smiled at the thought.

"Paul?"

"Come here," he urged, gently tugging her toward him. She eased in, not rushing, but not actually reluctant. "Let me hold you."

"We shouldn't."

"On the contrary," he murmured, lowering his head to look into her eyes, using the other hand to tuck her wayward hair behind one ear. "We should. We have every right to, no barriers this time, Torie. Whatever else there is, or isn't, there's always been this."

The kiss was slow, soft, exploratory.

Then she leaned into him, and the tight control he'd managed to keep the previous night shattered irrevocably. He captured her mouth, let himself taste her, fully and deeply. He could have kissed her for hours, maybe days.

The brush of her breasts on his arms, her hands gripping his waist, all of it was almost unbearably erotic. When she dug into the fabric, holding on, it pulled his trousers snug and he groaned at the pressure.

"Let me touch you," he whispered. He wasn't sure why, but the quiet was mesmerizing. He wanted to take things slowly, softly. He tugged the shirt from her pants, letting his hands slide up the soft skin of her back. When she arched like a cat, pulling away from his mouth, he actually moaned. Here was her elegant neck to feast on, to explore.

"Oh, my God," she mumbled. "That feels so, so . . ."

"What? Tell me what you're feeling."

"Hot, powerful. Sexy."

"Oh, you're all that, and more," he managed to say, bringing her back to his mouth, forgetting everything in the turbulence of her kiss, in the feel of her body.

"I need to touch you, too," she said, her hands restless now at his waist, tugging the belt free from its silver fittings, her fingers nipping the buttons open so fast he barely knew what she was doing. "Ohhhh." She let the word vibrate against his lips, while her hands danced over his skin.

The involuntary shiver had him pulling her nearer, molding her to him, pressing her amazing ass to lock them more intimately together. Now it was his turn to gasp.

Here, finally, was Torie. Glorious, amazing, supple, and powerful.

He fumbled the buttons, but got them undone. He wanted to rip the shirt off, but restrained himself. He didn't want to frighten her. Never again.

That nearly brought him up short, nearly had him pulling away from her to be sure.

She was having none of that. "No, no regrets," she

said, her fingers plunging into his hair, bringing his mouth back to hers. "Not this time."

She was taking charge, and he was in heaven. She pushed his shirt away, and he popped the cuff buttons getting it off. He kicked off his loafers, and she stepped out of the pumps she'd put on.

She turned him as they undressed each other, and before he knew what she was about, they were at the bed.

"I've wanted to—" Paul began.

"Years—" she muttered.

"Years?" *Really?*

They fell to the mattress. He'd think about that years thing later. For now, he had to . . .

"Oh, sweet heaven." He hardly managed the words as she shimmied down his body to take him into her mouth. "Don't, I can't take it." He didn't want to explode, even as he was dying to climax with her fabulous hands wrapped around him.

To prevent it, he lifted her up, capturing her mouth once again and rolling them both. Reality yanked at him for one brief moment.

"Protection, we've got to—"

"I'm protected. Come here," she insisted, panting now and as eager and ready as he was. "I need you. Oh Paul, please, just—"

"This?" She answered him with a long, drawn-out growl of pleasure. "Oh yes, let me see you, Torie, let me taste you." He kissed her mouth, her neck, everything within reach as they came together in one swift stroke.

He paused, quivering with the effort not to come, not to launch himself into her ready heat, not to let himself sink too deeply, too quickly.

She twisted her gorgeous body, pressing into him, and backing off. The friction of her curls, the wet power of her eager response was overwhelming.

"Slowly, Tor," he managed. "Let me be there for you, too. Show me what you like."

She opened her eyes and looked at him, shifting her hips to gather him more deeply in. "I like what you're doing. Do it some more. Now. Please."

He laughed and complied. Gently, with deliberate ease, he stroked her body, matched her arching hips with his own.

"Oh, Paul." His name was drawn out, like a battle cry, and he felt her body tense. She twisted, pulling at his shoulders as her hips shot up, pinning him as she reached the peak of her orgasm.

The sight of her, the freedom of her response, the years of wanting all coalesced into a hot, flashing point of release.

It felt like a scream. Like an echoing shout of triumph across the misunderstandings and sharp rejections. It was a balm to all things in that brilliant moment.

Everything was hot. The long ache in his heart, and in his body, burst free. He felt as if he were exploding into nothingness as he braced himself above her, and into her and around her.

It was all about her.

Chapter Nine

"It's all about her," Paul said to Melvin Pratt Sr. "The whole thing surrounds Torie. Everything that's happened to both Todd and Torie began when they called off their wedding." He laid the neatly typed sheets on the desk in front of his boss and mentor. Martha had taken the two time lines and noted all the intersecting mishaps. There was definitely a pattern.

"So," the older man began, leaning back in his chair and eyeing Paul. "You think there's something more here? An attempt to frame her?"

"I do."

"Interesting," Pratt murmured as he looked at the list again. "Does she know how much you care about her?" he said without looking up from the paper.

Paul froze. He and Torie had been so late coming into the office that he had expected questions. They hadn't talked about it. They'd dressed in the hazy, powerful aftermath, and driven in, each submerged in their own thoughts.

To his surprise, everyone assumed he'd taken her

shopping to replace the items damaged in the previous day's vandalism.

He wished he'd thought of that. She'd been incredibly quiet. She was, however, off shopping for replacements while he was talking to Pratt. He'd managed to get a second bodyguard to shadow her, but again, only for a short time frame. He had to find someone who could focus on it.

Just one more thing on the to-do list.

He realized Pratt was waiting for him to answer the question. His collar felt tight as he cleared his throat.

"I don't think so, sir." Hard as it was, he kept his tone level. Pratt obviously had him dead to rights, but there was no reason to give him more ammunition. He'd be stupid to argue that he felt nothing for her. His poker face wasn't good enough, especially since he could still imagine her in his arms.

"You might want to keep it that way until she's cleared of murdering her former fiancé." He winked at Paul as he handed the list back to him. "I'm presuming you don't think she did it."

"She didn't," he said with conviction. Now that he knew about Bear, he knew she wouldn't have had time to murder Todd and put him in the church. "Timing's off, personality type doesn't fit."

"Because you don't want it to? Or because you think the DNA swab they took this morning will clear her?"

Paul hesitated. He'd questioned that. A lot. Ever since he'd gotten the news. He'd been disconcerted to find a technician at the office, ready to swab Torie's cheek the minute they walked in the door.

Pratt waved at a chair. "Before you answer that, take a seat."

Paul sat. Waited while Pratt stared. It was a tactic he recognized, and he wasn't going to fall for it.

The older man finally smiled. "So, no cat and mouse. Tell me your thoughts on this, Paul. And tell me why you haven't told her how much Todd left her in his will."

Clearing his throat, Paul began. "I haven't told her because she is still a suspect. The inheritance just adds fuel to that fire."

"Press hasn't got wind of it, have they?"

"Not officially, but there's gossip. One of the tabloids already has a reporter here. He's been digging old pictures out of the society pages from back when . . . well, their engagement picture, and all that."

"Hmmm. Yes. That's unfortunate. That type can dig out a lot of information in too short a time span. I often wish they worked for us. Or for the police, rather than some rag of a grocery-store newspaper."

"Good point. We could use those kind of research skills."

"Indeed. So far she's avoided the press, yes? When are you planning to tell her?"

"Yes, they're focusing on the men, and on her office. As to when to tell her about the money, I don't know. One of the things I need to ask you, though, as a point of law—can I represent her? Do I need to get Myra or—" a terrible thought crossed his mind—"You don't want Melvin Jr. in on this, do you?"

Pratt looked irritated, then sad, before quickly covering it up with a smile. "No, Melvin's better suited to corporate work. I think Myra would be superb for handling the estate matters with you. You stay on as defense council while she needs it. I think it would be best to recuse yourself for the estate matters." Pratt laughed suddenly. "After all, we'll be billing for two sides of the cookie. You'll be closing out Todd's affairs, Myra will be handling Ms. Hagen's. A nice fee for us."

Hating the sound of it, as Pratt put it in terms of billable hours, Paul nonetheless nodded. "True. Though he's gone, I still represent Todd."

"Exactly." Pratt nodded and looked satisfied. "I didn't think I was going to need to remind you of that. You are going to have to tread very carefully between being in conflict of interest and in being downright over the line."

"For the firm's sake," Paul said, choosing his words with care, "do I need to disconnect entirely, turn her case over to someone else?"

Pratt cocked his head, and focused his entire attention on Paul. The old man was intimidating most of the time. The weight of years and skills gave him an aura of power and knowledge that no amount of joviality could mask. It was an uncomfortable feeling, like talking to The Powers That Be or something.

"Can you walk that thin line?"

Paul waited before answering. Thought about it. Could he? Now that he'd touched her again, tasted her again, held her again? Could he defend her?

Absolutely.

Could he keep his work for Todd's estate separate?

That he wasn't so sure about.

"I think so, sir. However, I will understand if you want to put someone else in the saddle."

"You'd hate that worse than being fired," Pratt said bluntly.

Paul couldn't help it; he grinned. "Well, yes."

Pratt returned the smile, and Paul could see him

relax into his chair. "You know, that's what got you promoted to partner so quickly. You have just enough killer instinct, tempered with what works for the long-term good. You balance them both," Pratt said, holding out heavy gnarled hands to pantomime a tipping load. "Too much one way and you become a shark, dedicated to the thrill of closing cases. Too much the other way, and you might as well be working for the state."

Paul laughed. "The state doesn't bill enough hours. You know that."

It was an old joke between them. Pratt had asked why he wanted private general law, instead of the more high-profile defense positions available with law enforcement or government agencies. He'd always claimed he liked keeping score with billable hours.

"Here's the compromise. I want you to report to me every few days. If I think the balance is tipping—" he let his hands slide down to the desk—"then we'll talk about a second set of eyes on everything, and another set of ears in the discussions. Until then, you're point."

"Thanks." Paul rose to take his leave, extending his hand to shake the older man's hand.

"One more thing," Pratt said, gripping his hand, and giving it an extra squeeze. "Well, three more, actually. You need this." He handed Paul an envelope. "That's something you can put away for a rainy day, or celebrate with. The press releases will go out today. The dinner is scheduled with the senior and junior partners for late next week. We usually do that at the Ritz, and invite everyone to stay the night. Have Martha talk to my assistant, get all the details finalized. The word's already on the street, by the way. Give marketing a list of anyone you want to personally send a note to, and they'll handle it."

"Got it." Thank God Martha could handle that. He saw the dismissal in Pratt's nod, and turned to leave. He was nearly at the door when he made the count. Pratt had said three things. "Sir? What's the third thing?"

Pratt didn't smile this time. He looked deadly serious.

"Be very, very careful, Paul."

Everything jumbled together in Torie's mind as she tried to focus on picking out clothes. What had she done? She'd started everything by kissing him last night. She hated him. Didn't she? Oh, Lord, had she really slept with Paul? Again?

Was she insane? Hadn't college taught her anything? Sleeping with him then had been a mistake, too.

Not that sleep had anything to do with what had happened. Her lips curved in memory. His body was so strong, so lean and sexy.

They'd been like sleepwalkers afterwards, helping one another to dress. It was that fierce desire that had frightened her so in college. That intensity of attention and focus. When she was younger, to have it turned her way so powerfully had been terrifying after all she'd been through at the frat party.

Now, it was incredible. Commanding. Orgasmic.

She felt her body heat just conjuring the images. His face. His hands.

"Miss? Did you need help finding anything?"

The clerk's interruption was like a bucket of cold water.

"No, thanks. Oh, just the dressing room?"

She caught sight of a man sitting nearby, reading the paper. He met her gaze, gave a slight nod.

The bodyguard.

It shifted her thinking away from Paul, thank goodness. Hopefully Paul's house would be secure, if she agreed to stay there. She felt like a hunted animal moving from hotel to hotel, from the fire to the beach, only to return to bullets and destruction. She was looking over her shoulder at every turn.

Everything was crazy. Upside-down. The world had surely gone mad when she of all people needed a bodyguard. Then there was her job. How could they? One part of her understood. It was hellish enough to meet deadlines, and answer RFPs, and beat the competition at the engineering and architecture game in the best of times. If the press were breathing down your corporate neck about an employee, it would be strategic to neutralize that employee.

"Except it's me," she muttered, shifting around the racks, looking for the right size.

Piling items into the saleswoman's arms, Torie made her weary way to the dressing room. She loved shopping as a rule, but having done this same thing several times over the last few weeks, it was getting old. It was also dreadful to try to start over. She kept thinking about a special shirt or skirt that would work with an item, then felt a hard pang when she realized that shirt or skirt was no longer available to her.

Torie had discarded five skirts and as many shirts when her cell phone rang. Sitting down on the bench, she tugged it from her purse and answered it.

"Ms. Hagen? This is Investigator Sorrels, from the Philadelphia Fire Department?"

Like she wouldn't remember who he was. "Yes, Inspector Sorrels, how may I help you?"

"We'd like you to come down to the scene, identify some items for us, if you can."

"Okay, I can be there in . . ." She looked at her watch, a cheap pink Timex picked up from a street vendor. "Thirty minutes? Is that soon enough?"

"That'll be fine."

As soon as they hung up, Torie began wondering what they wanted her to identify. Nothing she came up with seemed probable, but it reminded her to call her insurance agent. She'd been so busy getting shot at and recovering, and then, Paul.

Instant arousal had her leaning her head back onto the cool wood of the dressing room partition. She'd been so wanton, so over-the-top with Paul. They'd been so good together, fit so well. Nothing, not even her terrible memories, had come between them.

For the first time in nearly a decade, she felt free.

"Miss? Did you need a different size? Can I find anything else for you?"

The clerk was efficient and helpful, sensing a big sale. Torie stared at the remaining items she needed to try on. She didn't want to bother, but she had to. For once it was true that she had little to nothing she could wear.

With a grunt, Torie stood up. Her muscles were slightly sore, but the twinge made her smile. She'd instantly regretted the action, and been horrified to give in to the desire she'd repressed all this time. The result was . . . spectacular.

"Uh, I need a larger size in this," she said, passing a too-small sweater set over the partitioned door.

"And a smaller one in this." A skirt joined the sweater. "Otherwise, I'm okay for now."

With another new suit, two skirts, and several sweaters bagged and wrapped up, Torie hurried to Paul's Mercedes. He'd loaned it to her, arguing that her own vehicle might be a target. He figured that the rental car might be marked by now.

It was a short ride to her house. She wanted to weep at the sight of her once-lovely little row house with its boarded-up windows and smoke-blackened siding. A huge pile of trash was heaped in the front yard, including her great-aunt's settee, which had been in the front room. The blackened hulks of the matching chairs were on the side of the pile. Her bookcases and the twisted wreck of her plant stands lay on top.

All of it was soggy and disgusting. Soot stained everything. Her flowers and grass were a ruin as well, trampled by the firemen.

Not that she regretted their fabulous response, just the necessity for it.

Sorrels and Marsden waited for her outside the house. Belatedly, she realized she should call Paul. Curling her earpiece around her ear, she used the speed dial for his office.

"Mister Jameson's office."

"Good afternoon, Missus Prinz," Torie said, uncomfortable at talking to the eagle eyed assistant. "Is he in, please?"

Should Torie call him Paul or Mr. Jameson when talking to Martha? How the hell did she address her attorney? How the hell did she address her lover? Was he her lover?

What the hell had she gotten herself into now?

Before she could wind herself up anymore, Paul came on the line.

"Hey, you all right?"

"I'm fine. I'm over at my house." She heard the quiver in her own voice. Damn it, she had to get over it. It was just a house.

"You're where? Torie, why?"

"Sorrels and Marsden. They wanted to meet me here, ask some questions about things."

"I'll be there in fifteen minutes."

"But I have your car," she protested.

"I'll be there." He hung up without another word.

Miffed, but somehow reassured, she dropped her phone into her purse and got out of the car.

"Ms. Hagen, thanks for meeting us here."

"Sure." Torie looked at the gloppy pile in the yard. "That's just awful, isn't it?"

Sorrels nodded. "Yeah, they have to tear out so much drywall to be sure they've gotten to all the fire, then soak it down. It makes one damn-all mess."

Marsden cleared his throat.

"Oh, sorry," Sorrels offered.

"For what?"

"Language," Sorrels said.

Torie laughed. "I work with engineers, gentlemen. Language doesn't bother me."

They looked relieved, even as they were moving toward the house. "We have the key to the padlocks here, since it is still a crime scene," Sorrels said, unlocking the thing and swinging the makeshift plywood door away from the jamb. The shattered storm door creaked like doom when they pushed it open.

Torie couldn't suppress a horrified gasp as they crossed the threshold and she saw the devastation.

Virtually nothing was left of her living room. The lovely hardwood floors were blackened and hacked. The walls were stripped to the studs, all the wallboard torn away to insure the fire hadn't spread. The ceiling joists were exposed; some of them were blackened as well, showing where the fire had roared through the ceiling when the bomb went off.

"Oh, my God," Torie murmured, reaching for the newel post to steady herself. With total disregard for her new pants, she lowered herself to the steps. "This is . . . this is . . ."

"Horrible. Yes, it is. Fire always is, but one that's set? With intent to harm? That's worse." Sorrels said it with matter-of-fact calm, but Torie heard the intensity of his conviction.

She managed to nod, but couldn't speak. It looked like a war zone, like a movie set. It was so different, so surreal, it hardly seemed to be her house at all.

Marsden picked a careful way through the maze of broken floorboards. "We think the bomb landed here, then exploded," he stated, turning to spread his hands in a wide pattern to mimic the blast.

"Can you tell us where you were when it went off?"

Torie corralled her chaotic thoughts which all centered on how terrible everything looked and smelled. She decided the smell of soaked floors, soggy drywall, and possible mildew were nearly as bad as the smell of the fire.

"I think I was here," she said as she managed to make herself move toward the kitchen, tripping a bit over the warping floorboards. "I had just let the dog back in and I heard the noise." She shuddered at the memory, the odor of gas. "I smelled gas, I went toward the living room," she continued. Looking at the two men, she grimaced. "I guess that was really stupid."

"It's a natural response." Marsden temporized his response. "But dangerous."

"I guess. Anyway, that's when the first explosion went off."

"First?"

"There were two. Pickle and I were thrown back and we hit the door. When I heard another crash, I grabbed my purse to get the phone." She pointed to where it had been, on the counter. The twisted, melted, and mangled plastic of her grocery bags were a bizarre sculpture on the counter. "I got the door to the deck open. The second blast knocked through the door, out onto the deck."

Sorrels nodded. "That's what we wanted to know."

From the doorway, Paul cleared his throat. Torie jumped at the sound. "Oh, Paul. Inspector, Chief, you know Mister Jameson, don't you?"

"Yes, indeed," Sorrels commented, shooting looks between the two of them. "Obviously you two have come to some sort of truce?"

Torie nodded and prayed she wasn't blushing, though she felt her cheeks heat. "Common enemy, it seems."

"Yes, Ms. Hagen's correct. I believe whoever killed our friend is responsible for this as well, and the additional attempts on Ms. Hagen's life."

"So you're a detective now, too?" Marsden said, sarcasm tingeing his voice.

"No, but I'm a trained observer, Chief. And in talking with both of you, with Officer Tibbet, and with the officer who worked the scenes at the hotel, I can put a lot of pieces together."

Paul turned to Torie, extended a hand as if to brush her arm, but changed the gesture at the last minute. Instead of a caress, he rested his hand on the door jamb. If the others found it odd, they didn't show it. "So, Ms. Hagen, I know this is difficult." His gaze was hot, but his tone cool. It was a strange combination.

With a grimace, Torie shook her head. "We've known each other for nearly twelve years, Paul. The inspectors know that."

Paul smiled. "True, but I wanted to be sure you were comfortable." He looked around, stepping away from the stairs and gazing into the trashed living room. "What a disaster."

Marsden nodded. "The smallest fire can cause tremendous damage, and this was no small event."

"May I take anything out of the house?" Torie finally gathered the courage to ask. "Or can I at least go upstairs and see if anything is left of my clothes?"

Sorrels and Marsden exchanged looks, but Sorrels spoke. "Yeah, but be careful. We don't want you landing on our heads, okay?"

"I'll come with you," Paul said, following her up the stairway. The pictures on the wall were cracked and the glass blackened from the blast. She couldn't tell if any of them were still whole. That alone broke her heart. The large picture of her grandparents was one of the only ones still hanging in place, but along with everything else, it was dark with soot, the black dust obscuring the seated couple.

The damage was only slightly less obvious upstairs. The scent of smoke permeated everything. Water stained the walls, and the enormous gaping hole in the floor and ceiling of her guest room showed the path of the flames. Plywood covered the windows here as well, making the room dark and dank. Everything in it was surely a total loss.

"Where do you want to start?" Paul said, his voice neutral, urging her to keep moving.

"The office," Torie said, moving that way. She'd turned the third bedroom into an office overlooking the narrow garden in the back of the house. The windows here, unboarded, let in the spare sunlight. The trees and pretty bushes still stood, unmoved by the destruction in the house. At least the back was salvageable. "Oh."

Stopping dead in her tracks, Torie surveyed the wreckage that had been her neat, pretty office. Soot and water stains were less visible here, with the fire concentrated in the front, but they were nevertheless present.

The large window overlooking the backyard was a haze of cracked panes. A storm front was blowing up outside, and the cloudy day made the formerly cheerful room seem sinister and murky.

"I don't think anything in there will be useable," Paul murmured, his voice ripe with sympathy.

"I have to see if my files are here. I have a fireproof box," she managed, then stopped again, realizing that it alone would be undamaged.

Fetching it from the soot-covered drawer, she cradled it in her arms.

"I'll hold onto that for you if you want to check on the things in your room."

Not daring to look at him, knowing the least bit of pity would have her either flying into sobs, or the opposite, roaring into anger, Torie handed him the case. It was like a tackle box, only metal and bright red.

"You're a smart woman," he complimented, following behind her as she moved past him into the hallway. "Most people never get around to this sort of protection."

She suppressed a shudder. "I never thought I'd need it."

When she had to stop in the doorway to her room, he moved up behind her, his free hand pressing her shoulder in a reassuring squeeze. If nothing else had happened between them, if all were still wretched and horrible, that gesture alone would have gone miles toward mending things.

As it was, his presence, his comfort unlocked something frozen within her, something dark and powerful. Something primitive. She wanted to forget everything that had happened between them. Take back the words about trust and pain she'd spewed to him in the car. Make him . . .

"Torie?"

She couldn't speak for a moment. Emotion choked her, both about her house, and about him. Clearing her throat, she managed a brief, "Thank you."

"For?"

"Being here."

He said nothing, just squeezed her shoulder again.

That gave her the courage to move forward into the disaster area that had once been her tidy, restful master bedroom.

Damn. Close calls were not part of the plan. Stories of an intruder weren't part of the plan either.

Slipping into the back entrance of the hotel near his condo, he took the elevator to the business center.

Logging on with the usual code, he quickly hacked into the Pratt website and database. There was a lot to be done in a short amount of time. In order to finish, eliminate any traces, he'd have to do the last of it from a remote location. He didn't want any log-ons from any one place in the downtown area. Tonight he could drive out to the 'burbs. There was a cybercafe across the river in Camden that he'd used to good effect before. That would confuse things, to use a New Jersey address.

He had to be more careful now. No one should have been in the building to see him when he went to check Jameson's office. That had been a narrow escape.

He hated to have to run.

His cell phone rang. He ignored it the first time, but when it chimed twice more in quick succession, he picked it up.

"Hey, baby," she purred.

"Why are you calling me?" he hissed. He hated the whine. It made a red haze of anger rise within him. Just the sound of it made him grind his teeth. He'd started dating her after she was fired from the office, just to get information. She'd proved a useful tool, but she wasn't what he wanted. It would be fun to flaunt her, though.

"Don't call me. I'll call you."

Hurt silence replaced the whine.

"Don't pout. I'm working, and you know it makes me short-tempered," he said, attempting to soften his tone. He needed her. Besides, she liked to fuck.

"I do understand," she said. Thankfully, the whine was gone, replaced by ridiculous hauteur. "Lose the temper and the attitude before you stop by."

That was more like it. She didn't realize how she

betrayed her need for recognition, for attention, by
that very attitude. He knew how to work that.

"Got it."

"How long?"

"Two, maybe three hours."

"I'll be waiting. I'll wear—" Throaty laughter
purred through the phone's small speakers, and he
felt himself harden into instant desire.

That laugh always did it to him. Probably why he'd
always wanted Torie, until Todd had gotten ahold of
her. He would give anything to hear Torie laugh that
way with him, need him.

Shaking off the thought, he focused on the words.
Smiled. Felt a heightened arousal at the realization
that he was the one in charge.

No one knew it. That just made it more delicious.

"You'll come by—"

"I said," he emphasized, "I'll be there. Let me finish
this, so I can come . . . to you." He let the double en-
tendre hang between them, tantalizing.

As he did it though, his fingers were flying over the
keys, entering codes and inserting the specially
designed virus to slowly erode the law firm's source
files. Within days, Paul Jameson's files would disappear one by one.

They'd be able to reconstruct the list, if they had
time.

He didn't plan on giving them time.

Chapter Ten

With Paul's help, Torie carried three trash bags of clothes out to his waiting car. Piling them in the trunk, she worried about how much they stank. Would she ever get them clean? A fourth bag contained her laptop, which she hoped would either still work, or that the hard drive would be salvageable.

Sorrels and Marsden, who had checked over and listed everything she'd removed, were locking up the house.

They came over to the car, eyeing the sleek, expensive vehicle, one with disdain, the other with admiration.

"Ms. Hagen, I think we'll be able to release your house as a crime scene within the next few days. We've got a report to write, but other than that, it should be pretty routine. After that, you can start getting folks in here to help you clean up."

"Thank you, Inspector Sorrels." She glanced at the house, looked away. It was so forlorn. "Can I get the settee out of the trash pile? Start work on that?"

"Settee?" Marsden looked back at the soggy mess. "You think you'll be able to salvage that?" Everything about his statement bespoke doubt that she could manage it.

"I need to try, Inspector. That's been in my family a long time."

He shook his head, but said, "Good luck. You can get it started, but don't touch anything on the house until you hear from us. Got it?"

"Got it."

They said their good-byes, and Torie climbed into the car. Before Paul closed her door, she saw him salute toward a distant, unremarkable Toyota SUV. The lights flashed but the car didn't move.

Paul didn't mention it when he got behind the wheel. Instead, he talked about Sorrels and Marsden.

"That was tough on you. Do you have any idea what they wanted? I mean, what they really wanted?"

"No, not entirely. They seemed focused on asking me where I was and what I heard. Sorrels seemed satisfied when I said two breaks of the glass, two thuds, two explosions."

"Hmmm. Coordinating their findings."

"What does that mean for me?"

"Faster resolution, maybe."

"So what was all the cloak and dagger stuff with the SUV?"

Paul grinned. "Cloak and dagger? Isn't that painting it a bit grim?"

"Everything in my life is grim right now," Torie replied, feeling as if it were true.

At the stoplight, Paul sent her a searing look. "Everything?"

His implication was obvious, and it lightened her heart. It also turned her on. "Not everything," she admitted.

"That was today's bodyguard."

"Today's? What do you mean?"

"I could only get short-term again today. I think I've got someone who can do it, though, for the next week or so."

She shuddered. "I hope I don't need it that long."

Paul didn't say anything. She let it go, not wanting to think about the alternative. "I need to call Barbara, my insurance lady." She pulled a notepad from her purse. "Do you mind?"

"No, go ahead."

Paul listened to Torie's side of the conversation, making mental notes of what he needed to ask her. He also needed to suggest several workmen, firms who had helped him with small jobs, as well as one company he'd heard of who remediated smoke and water damage. He hadn't ever used them himself, thank goodness, but he knew their reputation.

"I see, yes. I'm at a friend's house. Yes. They're both crime scenes. Yes. I don't know. Just a minute, my friend should know." She held the phone to her chest, covering the receiver to mask her question. "Barbara wants to know if I'm still being charged by the hotel. For the room. They let me get the rest of my things, but I don't think I officially checked out. Can they do that?"

Paul nodded, but added. "We'll run by there and take care of it."

"Okay." She went back to the call saying she'd check out. "Yes, I'll be in touch with someone. Can you email that to me? Yes, my computer is, well, toast, but I have my PDA. I'm taking the computer to the repair—" She stopped to listen. "Oh, okay. I will. Yes."

They hung up, and Torie took time to jot everything down. With a weary sound, she turned to Paul.

"You know, I'm a detail person, but this level of note-taking is going to drive me bats."

"Where to?"

"Oh, sorry, two blocks over, the dry cleaner on Washington Street."

He helped her haul in the bags, and waited as she haggled with the clerk about when things would be ready and what to do if they decided something couldn't be returned to smoke-free usefulness.

"I'm going to need to do some more of this kind of thing," she said as they walked back to the car. "Do you want me to take you back to the office after we go to the hotel? Oh," she said, remembering suddenly, "the rental car is at the hotel. I should—"

Paul interrupted. "No, it's been impounded. It was damaged, too. Martha took care of notifying the rental car place. She said you took out the extra insurance, right?"

Torie sat for a moment, just staring. The rental car, too. "How bad was it, in the hotel room at the Extended Suites?" she asked, knowing she'd been hiding her head in the sand about that since it happened. She hadn't asked, hadn't wanted to know. Until this moment, she wasn't sure she could handle it.

Paul looked at the road, and without facing her said, "It was bad, Torie. The damage and the destruction are escalating. And Tibbet is worried because this person's getting bolder." He glanced at her, as if to gauge her reaction. "The fire alarm, the shooting, everything. Before he was just taking his anger out on you and Todd in random ways, malicious mischief if you want the technical term."

"I think running someone over with a car and killing them is more than malicious mischief," she said, gripping her hands together so tightly the knuckles cracked.

"Yeah, Tibbet thinks so, too. He's worried about you." Paul took a hand off the steering wheel and covered her clenched fingers. "I'm worried, too."

Taking a deep breath, Torie asked the question that was looming in her mind, and had been hovering all day. "Is that what this morning was? Between us? Worry? Stress?"

With a quick twist of the wheel and a squeal of tires behind him, Paul pulled to the curb and slapped on the four-way flashers. "Oh, no, Torie. That wasn't worry."

His eyes were boring into hers, and his strong palm closed more snugly over her folded hands.

"That was . . ." He hesitated, stopped.

Torie waited for him to continue, unsure of what she would hear, what she wanted to hear. When the silence dragged out, she had to fill it.

"What? Right? Wrong? Good? Bad?"

He laughed, but it wasn't like a belly laugh, or filled with humor. "Bad? Oh, no. Never bad, not with you. Bad *for* us, maybe. The worst thing we could do, since you're a suspect and I'm your lawyer." He looked at her, and she saw desire shimmer in his eyes. It was as reassuring as it was exciting. "But never, never bad. It couldn't be."

When she couldn't speak, couldn't respond, he smiled. It was a little smug, which irritated her, but when he unlatched the seat belt and swooped in to kiss her, all thought of irritation fled.

In fact, she stopped thinking all together.

The world narrowed to the sensation of his mouth

on hers, of his hand on her face, drawing her closer. Nothing seemed real except those two things.

When he broke it off, sat back and relatched his seat belt, she felt bereft.

"Never bad, Torie," he reiterated. "Not with you."

Pulling away from the curb amidst honking horns, he took her hand, lacing their fingers together. It was an intimate gesture. Lover like.

Into the deepening silence he asked, "And what did you think about it?"

How did she put it into words? She had asked for it, initiated it. The result, the chance to finally touch him, be with him, had been mind-blowing in so many ways. The fact that she'd been able to trust him enough to find her own release, not just kind of moan and fake it, was actually scary.

"Torie?" He pulled into the parking deck at his office, and parked. "Talk to me."

"It wasn't a mistake," she said, struggling to keep her voice level. "It was—"

"What?" he interrupted, sounding anxious.

Looking at him, facing him, she told the truth. "Beyond my wildest expectation. Incredible. What do you want me to say?"

He smiled. A true smile that twinkled in his eyes. "That works."

People were coming and going in the garage, and he glanced at them. His newly upgraded parking space was second row center, close to the elevator. Way too visible to do what he was obviously thinking about.

"It works for you? I'm so glad," her reply was half-pleased, half-sarcastic.

His smile stayed in place, but he sighed. "It's not

going to be a picnic, Torie. It's already so complicated with all you have going on, just with the fire. That alone is terrible. When you add in everything else, it's so complex, it's mind-boggling."

"Todd," she whispered. "The shootings."

"Everything from Todd to the vandalism. It's all directed at you now. It's the worst time for any kind of additional complication, especially for something between the two of us."

"You say that like everything is my fault."

"No," he said sharply. "It's not about fault. This isn't your fault. Someone has fixated on you, Torie, and that's dangerous." He frowned, looking away. "There are so many things we need to get out. Clear the air."

"Secrets," she began.

Before they could continue, both their phones rang.

"Yes. We need to talk. When we can be alone. You'll stay at my house again tonight. We'll talk then." He whipped out his phone and answered it. "It's what?" He flicked a glance her way. "I'm in the garage. I'll be right up."

Torie listened to her insurance agent detail the next steps she needed to take, taking in as much of it as she could manage. Part of her mind was still thinking about Paul, about what he'd said. She heard his surprise and looked over. He looked like a storm cloud, angry and fierce.

"Um, Barbara, may I call you back? Thanks." To Paul, she said, "What? What is it?"

"Somebody hacked into the firm's files. Everything in every file which mentions you or Todd has been deleted or corrupted. I have to get up there and see how much

I have in the paper files, be sure none of them were tampered with in the break-in the other day."

"Oh, my gosh. How?"

"We don't know. Now I've got more police to talk to. Cybercrimes, this time."

Torie sighed, leaning back into the seat for a moment. "I want to say 'what next?' but I don't dare."

"No, please. Nothing more." Paul laughed ruefully. He hesitated. "Take the car, do what you need to do. Call me, let me know where you are, okay?"

"Okay." She tried to disentangle her hands from his, but they were firmly planted on hers. "What?"

"Be careful. Really careful. Whoever this is, whoever wants to hurt you, isn't sane."

A shudder ran up her spine. "I know."

"I need to . . ."

"I know. Go. I'll manage. It's what I've learned to do."

Paul was about to say something, but his phone rang again and he shook his head. "We'll talk. Just be careful. Don't drive too fast, either. Let Marco keep up."

"Will do."

She came around the front of the car as Paul moved toward the stairs. He stopped again, phone to his ear as if to come back to her. Was he going to kiss her? In public?

Evidently he thought better of whatever he'd been about to do, pressing the phone more firmly to his ear and raising a hand in a good-bye wave.

She returned the salute as she got in, looking for him in the rearview mirror as she pulled away.

"I'm insane. I slept with Paul Jameson. Holy crap."

She had to call Pam. What was she going to do? Her job . . . Oh, God, her job. They didn't want her.

They'd left her a voice mail. Didn't have the decency to tell her in person.

That put things in perspective on the work front, that was for sure.

On the home front, well, it couldn't be much more of a disaster. Her stomach lurched thinking about the house, the smell of smoke and water, the whole depressing mess. Which reminded her to call Barbara.

"Hi, Barbara, it's Torie Hagen."

"Oh, I'm so glad you called. Listen, I discovered a rider on your policy for jewelry and electronics. Did you remember purchasing that?"

Did she? No, but what did that prove?

"Yes, I think so. Does it cover my new laptop I'm going to have to buy?"

"Oh, yes, and several other things, like printers and the other things, the hickeedoos that hook everything up, the wireless parts."

Hickeedoos. That would be the technical term. Torie was glad to find at least one thing she could smile about in the whole mess of her life.

"And the jewelry? I do remember that." It covered her grandmother's earrings and necklace, several antique pieces. Oh, Lord, she hadn't thought about that. "Oh." She couldn't help the gasp that slipped out.

"Ms. Hagen? Torie?"

"Yes, I'm still here. It's just that, well, there's been so much, I hadn't considered the jewelry. My grandmother's diamonds. They were . . ."

"Special. I know," Barbara said, her sympathy evident. "This is the worst sort of thing. Having to catalog these things, give us lists, keep receipts. All that."

"Oh, the catalog," Torie brightened. "I have that. On disc in my safety deposit box."

"You have an inventory?"

"I do. I made it after an attempted robbery a few years ago," Torie said, then realized she hadn't put that incident on the list she gave Paul. "I put it in the safety deposit box. The key," she began. Well, hell. The key was at her office, locked in her desk. "I'll get the key from my office and get the disc. Should I bring you a copy of the disc or a paper copy?" She would go to the office at the end of the day. She'd call Steve, her boss, and tell him what she needed. He'd understand that much, she hoped.

"Are there pictures?" Barbara said eagerly.

"Yes, and comparable prices for some of the pieces. I'm an engineer, Barbara. We dot the Is and cross the Ts."

"Well, you'll be glad of that in this case, especially with the jewelry. It means a quicker payout for you, too, on getting new furniture and so forth, if you can prove what you had."

"Well, there's one thing that's going right. I have to say, it's about the only thing."

"I know, dear," the other woman commiserated. "I've seen the news. It must be hideous for you." For a moment, Torie wondered if the woman was fishing for gossip, but in the next sentence, she disproved the worry. "All the more reason for us to find you a rental house, get you on the road to recovering from this."

"Thank you. What do I need to do?"

"Contact a real estate agent, someone reputable, and have them set you up with something." She named a price range that insurance would pay, and then said, "And if I could offer one word of advice?"

"Yes?"

"Buy some new clothes, get what you need there. Start car shopping as well so you'll have reliable transportation, but don't overwhelm yourself. Wait to buy furniture. Wait to try and replace the jewelry and dishes and personal items. From everything I've seen over the years, if you just give it a little time, it's a lot better."

Torie sighed. It was good advice. "Thanks, Barbara. I think I needed to hear that."

She'd no sooner disconnected the call than her phone rang again. It was Pam, calling from home. Pam had said she had a client presentation today. Her design business was so popular, so sought after, the days were often so full for Pam that she barely ate lunch, much less had time to talk on the phone.

"Hey, girl," she tried to sound cheerful. "What's up."

Pam's answer was a sob.

"It's Dev."

"What happened?" Paul was in full battle mode by the time he reached his office. "And when?"

"Yesterday sometime, in the evening they think," Martha said as she rose. "Detective Tibbet is here with the cybercrimes officer, a Detective Johnson. They're in the computer center."

"Jameson," Tibbet greeted him as he walked into the center. The other detective was seated at one of the programmer's stations, her hands flying over the keyboard. "Where's Ms. Hagen?"

"Trying to piece her life back together," he said bluntly. "She's being watched over, and the press are off on another trail, so I think she's okay for the moment."

"Yeah." Tibbet grimaced. "The courthouse shootings.

Miracle nobody died. I guess that's more interesting than a car blowing up and some guys getting hurt."

"Lot of crazy people in the world," Paul noted, thinking that whoever was after Torie ranked right up there on the crazy scale.

"God's truth," was Tibbet's pithy rejoinder. "Back to this deal, though," he continued. "Looks like this is going deeper and deeper. You got any more ideas you're willing to share about who might be behind it? Got some skills with a computer, seems like."

"Damn straight," Detective Johnson commented. She glanced up long enough to say, "I'm Johnson, pleased to meet you, and all that." She then went back to hammering at the keyboard.

"I've told you everything I can think of, Detective," Paul said, watching the code fill the oversize screen the programmers used. It was like watching someone knit, each row following closely along to the next.

"No new ideas? No one you know who has outstanding computer skills?"

"I know a lot of people with computer skills. I have good skills, my assistant should have been a hacker, and I have two friends who run software companies. But neither Martha nor my geek pals want to hurt Torie."

"You sure about that?" Tibbet lowered his voice. "Your secretary doesn't like Ms. Hagen. Not one bit."

"Assistant. She's my executive assistant," Paul corrected, thinking furiously. He shook his head. "It doesn't play, Detective. You're right, she doesn't like Torie, but she adored Todd. She really, really thought the world of him."

"Not a far stretch to hate, though."

Paul couldn't fathom how someone lived each day,

worked each day, seeing the worst of society. "I still don't think so."

"Where were you last night?" Tibbet opened his little book. "Just to clear that up, 'cause I'm gonna get asked."

"I was with Torie, helping her get some clothes. We met her friend Pam and her cousin for a—" he stopped, shifting mental gears. "Drink. We stayed at another of their friend's house for a while. Someone she and Pam know. I didn't know him."

Tibbet was looking at him, and had obviously noted the hesitation. Damn.

"Uh huh. So, what time was this, uh, drink, you all had?"

"Around eight-thirty or nine. We'd been out shopping." He rolled his eyes for form. "Then met Pam, Dev, and Carlos. When we finally left there, Torie and I were starving. We picked up burgers and fries from Ted's Burgers over off Maple, on the way to my house. I think I have the receipt somewhere. We were nearly too tired to eat, but we managed it, then went to bed."

"Together?"

Paul's temper flared immediately, but he strapped it down. Tibbet was trying to get a reaction. Paul wasn't going to give him the satisfaction.

"No, Detective. She's my client and she slept in my guest room. She didn't want to endanger her friend Pam, but since it appears that hotel rooms aren't safe or secure, I put her in my guest room." He finished by putting his hands on the table between them and leaning in. "Satisfied?"

Tibbet grinned. "For now." When Johnson made a noise, he whipped around.

"Whatcha got, Johnson?"

"Trace. Not much. Hang on," Johnson muttered.

"What the hell?" A new voice joined the conversation and Paul turned to see the head of the computer department for the firm, Kathryn Tryon, hurrying in. "What's going on? Who authorized this? What are you doing here?" She turned the last question to Paul. She was fired up and mad, mad enough to get up in his face.

"Pratt authorized it," Paul said calmly. "We got hacked. I'm here because it focused on my files from a particular client. Some others were damaged, but Detective Tibbet indicated that Detective Johnson—" he pointed at the madly typing woman—"felt they were decoys. My files were the only ones totally wiped."

"Oh, my God." Her face blanched. "I hope like hell the backups work."

Paul felt his stomach churn. His antacids were in his desk. "What do you mean?"

"We've had trouble with the backups in the last few months. Some disruptions. This is exactly what we were afraid might happen, but the partners . . ." she trailed off, realizing to whom she was speaking. The firm protected its own, especially the partners, and evidently Kathryn realized that she had been about to diss them to a detective.

"Ahem," she said, clearing her throat. "The partners have been reviewing all my requests and fail-safe plans, and were budgeting for the options we would need."

"Does that mean we're shit out of luck in recovering my files?" Paul demanded, not really caring that Tibbet was there.

"No, no. We have backup, it'll work." Kathryn shot a look at Johnson and Tibbet, then faced Paul. "It'll work."

"Don't try and boot it any time soon," Johnson said without turning around. "You got some serious cleaning up to do before you can clear and reboot with the backup." With a last lightning sequence on the keyboard, she turned around and looked at them. "In fact, if your firm can afford it, you may want to start fresh with new drives, load the backup on them. I can't guarantee you'll ever be able to get these clean."

"Really? What kind of virus are we talking about?"

"You've got a three-pronged attack," Johnson began. The two women began speaking what Paul considered to be a deeply foreign language. He could figure out a lot of things, dig down into the code to a limited degree, but it wasn't his first love. The larger databases, like the ones designed especially for the firm, weren't the poison he'd pick.

Wait.

"Kathryn, doesn't this database have markers? Like, uh, special hooks? Don't I remember something about that in one of the presentations early on? You or what's his name—" Paul searched for the former staffer's name—"Caldwell. Didn't you or Caldwell make a big deal about the whatchamacallits that were supposed to protect from hackers?"

"Yes, that was me. Before I took over."

"Where's Caldwell?" Tibbet asked, looking from Paul to Kathryn. "This Caldwell knows the system well enough to do this?"

"Uh, well," Kathryn began, obviously not sure whether to rat out a colleague she hadn't liked to the police, or protect the firm.

"Caldwell left the firm about six months ago."

Tibbet frowned and scribbled. "Full name?"

"Taylor Caldwell."

Tibbet looked up. "Like the author?"

Kathryn grimaced. "Yeah, but it's a guy. He hated that reference. Said his mom just liked the name."

"He got any beef with your client, Jameson?"

"Huh? Caldwell? Not that I know of. Why?"

Tibbet ignored him. "Ms. Anderson, these fail-safe technologies, should they have prevented this kind of intrusion?"

Kathryn looked at Paul. He had no idea what Pratt would have done, but he nodded. Better to tell the truth.

"Yes. They should have."

"I got something," Johnson said. Motioning Anderson over, she detailed how she'd put in a program and how to take it out.

When she was done, she said, "I'm runnin' a search and track program. Like a bloodhound, it's supposed to give me a location for the sender. Like an address in cyberspace. I send the dog out, it comes back with the info." Data stopped flowing off and on to the screen. Four lines of text appeared, but didn't change.

"What's that?"

"The address. Now to backtrack it." She scrambled the keys again and the data disappeared, and was then replaced by a mapping program. The satellite maps that popped up drilled down onto a street in a suburban area of Philadelphia. "Damn."

"What?" Tibbet demanded.

"Cybercafé. Out a ways from town, over the river. Wish it could have been something better. These places are glorified coffee shops. Make more money on food and stuff than on renting the computer time. No cameras, no paying attention to the customers. Kinda like a Starbucks or a McDonald's. Unless we can go in there with a picture and a description, they won't be any help."

Tibbet turned to Paul. "You got a picture of this Caldwell?"

"Kathryn?"

"Uh, Human Resources should have something. There are those ID cards and stuff."

"But they're on the database, right? And it's compromised, isn't it?"

"Uh, no, separate system. HR demanded stand-alones."

"Good damn thing," Tibbet muttered. "C'mon Jameson, let's go to your HR department."

He paced the confines of his office. What had happened? He hadn't been that clumsy. No one should have known the files were gone. Not for months. How could they have figured it out so quickly? He'd seen the police going back in. He'd seen the woman's jacket. It said "Cybercrimes" on the back.

There should have been no way for his subtle tampering to be found in such a short time.

"It's not me," he decided, muttering the words aloud. "Nothing I did should be traceable. It wouldn't crash anything major." He looked out the window, noted the obvious police cars parked across the street. "Don't panic now. This isn't about you. Red herring. Something else," he reassured himself. He needed to find out.

How could he get into the offices? What pretext could he use? It had to be good, normal, natural. It would be too obvious otherwise.

He'd come too far, risked too much to panic now. No one suspected him. No one would ever suspect him.

There had to be something, someone else.

The thought hit him like a bolt of lightning.

What if someone else had hacked into the law firm's computers? None of his tampering should warrant the cybercrimes people. What he'd done was too small, too delicate. Especially at this stage. It should have been months before it was detected.

It should have simply deteriorated the files slowly, oldest documents first, with very little trace. The file names would have remained.

If someone else tampered, would it speed the process up?

"Damn." He whirled away from the window and dropped into his chair, swiveling it to face his monitor.

Chapter Eleven

"Pam, what is it?" Torie demanded. "What is it?"

"He's-he's-he's—" she hiccupped.

"WHAT?"

"Gone," she said on a wail.

"What? Where? Back to New Orleans?"

"I-I-I don't know."

Torie fishtailed around a corner, flooring the Mercedes as she got on the Schuylkill Expressway. She took a moment to appreciate the car Paul had loaned her. Maybe she'd look into a Mercedes for her next car. She hardly felt the excessive speed, and hoped the silver SUV could keep up. She found it in her rearview mirror as she scanned for police cars. She prayed there wouldn't be any cops out looking to make their ticket quota as she sped up three exits to wind through the neighborhoods to Pam's house. All the while trying to get Pam to stop crying, and give her some coherent information.

Pam met her at the door. Her eyes were red and her hands clutched a wad of tissue. Torie had never, ever seen her this distraught.

"Pam, what on earth is going on?"

"I don't know. I mean, I do, but I don't."

"Huh?"

"We had this thing," she sobbed, collapsing on the couch.

"Thing?"

"Yeah, you know." Pam glared at her as she sat down, as if she should be able to know all this already. "A *thing*."

"Do you want some tea or coffee or something?"

"No." Pam's head drooped, any flare of anger quickly extinguished.

That, more than anything, worried Torie. Pam never let anything stop her. Never let anything defeat her sparkling spirit. Certainly not a man.

"You're not . . . you didn't . . ."

"I'm not pregnant."

Torie sighed. "That's not what I was asking." Not that she wasn't relieved to hear it. "You didn't . . . fall in love with him, did you?"

Pam's laugh was harsh. "No, not me. I never do anything like that, do I? Have you ever known me to do that?"

"No, but I've never seen you like this, either." Torie scooted closer, putting her arm around her friend. "Do you know where he went?"

Pam shook her head, then blew her reddened nose with a loud honk. Torie took a moment to look around. It was obvious Pam had been moping for a while. There was an empty tea mug, her drink of choice when depressed. Tissues were scattered around the trash can, which was pulled to the coffee table.

Definitely not Pam's usual MO.

"Did you have a fight?"

"No." Pam's answer was defensive. "I just asked if he would miss me when he went home."

"Had he said he was leaving?"

"No. But he lives in New Orleans, right? So I figured I'd ask."

"Actually, I think he lives in Baton Rouge now, but he's from New Orleans. He keeps a house in both places."

"There, see? I didn't know that. How come you know that? You never slept with him." Irrational questions weren't Pam's usual order of business either, so Torie was beginning to be more and more concerned.

"I'm his cousin, Pam. We share a great-grandmother. He came to my father's funeral. I know a bit about him." She cocked her head. "You never showed any interest in him then."

"I was seeing other people," she said with ill grace. "I noticed him."

"Noticed him."

"Yeah, of course. He's a man. I noticed him, all right? He wasn't interested then. Neither was I, okay?"

Uh oh.

"You talked to him then?"

"Well, of course I did. He's your cousin." She folded her arms over her ample chest and huffed out a breath. "I flirted. He flirted back. But he was lookin' at others, so I backed off."

"Backed off. You?"

Pam rubbed her eyes, letting her head fall back onto the back of the couch. "I have standards, you know." She closed her eyes. "They're more flexible than most people's, but I got 'em." She rolled her head, opened her eyes, and looked at Torie. "I don't hunt."

"Oh, honey, I know. He was so supportive, especially

after the wedding was called off. Really kind. But there wasn't anything between us. You know that, right? Nothing but family."

"Yeah. He said the same thing."

"Jeez, Pam, you asked him?" Torie said, a little stung that Pam thought about her cousin that way.

Not like . . . Torie shied away from the thought. Instead, she focused on her friend.

"So, you fought? You yelled at him, some of your men came by, what?"

"No."

"No, what?"

"Nothing like that. One minute we're rolling around on the floor tearing each other's clothes off . . ." Pam said it with such gusto that Torie blushed. Pam was, after all, talking about doing the horizontal mambo with Dev. Hot as he was, there was a kind of "ewwww factor" in knowing her friend and her cousin had slept together. "Then the next thing I know, he's saying he hit his head, has a headache. I'm getting aspirin, joking about how, well, you know, saying the way I do, that doing the wild thing will cure anything, up to and including hair loss."

"Yeah, as always I agree, but then again," Torie stopped. Her standard answer to Pam's hair-loss quote was that she wouldn't know since she wasn't getting any. She'd gotten plenty just that morning, so she couldn't say that with a straight face.

Fortunately Pam didn't notice the lapse. "Yeah, well. So then his phone rings."

"He answered it?" Torie was shocked that someone could resist Pam in full siren mode, offering aspirin and wild monkey sex on the floor.

"Yeah, that bummed me, too," she said, closing her

eyes again. "He checked the caller ID, then went really funny looking."

"Funny looking?" Dev?

"Yeah. He answered it, really sharp and almost mean sounding. Then he made some bogus excuse, and left."

"Just left?"

"Yeah."

"You're stuck on him, aren't you." Torie didn't ask it as a question. She knew the answer. For the first time since high school, Pam was actually smitten with someone.

Heart touched.

"But why would he just leave? I've tried to call him, he didn't answer."

Torie frowned at that. "How long ago did he leave?"

"Four hours. An eternity."

"Jeez, Pam, snap out of it," Torie said impatiently. "That isn't like Dev. He's too straight-up about things. If he was just here for a fling, he'd have bought you something pretty to remember him by and had you drive him to the airport. That's his style, which is to say, he *has* some style."

"But he just left."

"You're always telling me not to live in the past, Pam. Not to keep living there. You rag on me not to let what happened to me, all the pain of it, rule my life." She drew a shaky breath, realizing this pent-up need to speak was not going to be stalled. "Well, you're right. But don't you sit there and tell me that again, just like you have all these years, and then do it yourself."

"What are you saying?" Pam demanded, her eyes firing with hurt and frustration. "That I ran him off?"

"No!" Torie exclaimed. "Of course not."

"Then what are you saying?"

"I'm telling you that you were right," Torie said, thinking about Paul, about what she'd done to keep him away. Had she been afraid of him all along? Afraid of what they could do to one another? Afraid of the power of their connection?

"About what?" Pam managed around her tissue.

"Not getting over what happened in college. About Todd. Life." Torie got up to pace. "A lot of things."

"Well, halle-fuckin-lujah. This isn't about you," Pam fired back, still angry. "Why are you attacking me, saying I ran him off?" She was on her feet now, the blanket she'd had wrapped around her shoulders dropped to the floor, tissues scattered like mutant snowflakes.

"Whoa. I'm not attacking you." Torie put up her hands in defense. An irrational Pam, wrapped in a blanket, was nothing to fool with. "I'm telling you to take your own advice, and not live in the past. Just because you had some jerk leave you and break your heart doesn't mean every man is going to leave you and break your heart if you get close to him." She was nearly shouting now, standing toe-to-toe with one of her oldest friends in the world. "So just back way the hell down and take a fucking compliment."

There was a heartbeat of silence. Neither she nor Pam blinked. Torie didn't know whether or not to hug her, or duck.

"You said fuck." Pam was wide-eyed now. Amazed.

"So what?" Torie growled. "I think I'm entitled. I have no home, I have no clothes, my laptop's toast, my dog's got a plate and five screws in her leg and is costing a fortune in vet fees, and I slept with Paul." It was Torie's turn to yell.

"You *what?*" Pam screeched.

"I have to go." Torie realized she had just admitted to what Pam might consider the worst sin in the world.

"Oh, no. Uh uh. You opened this bloody can of worms, sister. You're gonna pour 'em in a bowl and eat 'em with me."

"Oh, that's just gross." Torie picked up her purse, and started for the door.

"Bite me," Pam said, grabbing Torie's arm and dragging her back to the sofa. "Spill."

"Dev's missing. I have to let Paul know, tell the cops."

"Yeah, yeah. And I'm miserable because of the bastard. Whatever. We need to find him. Five minutes isn't going to make a difference. What happened with Paul?"

Sorry she'd let it slip, Torie refused to sit. "Five minutes could matter, Pam. If someone were after him, like they've been after me, five minutes could matter a lot."

Pam eyed her suspiciously, which was quite a sight given her reddened eyes, puffy lids, and swollen lips. Now that Torie was taking inventory, she could see that Pam also had a pretty serious case of beard-burn on her neck.

"Is that from Dev's beard?"

Pam slapped a hand to her neck to cover the mark. Torie nearly laughed at the futile gesture.

"What?" Pam protested, the distraction working. "Where?"

"I guess it is. Do you have a rug burn on your ass to match it?"

"Hey," Pam protested, shooting a guilty-looking

glance at the colorful wool carpet. "That's beside the point. We're fighting here. You better sit down and tell me what the hell is going on. How did you sleep with Paul? When? I thought you hated Paul?"

"Cripes, I've never hated Paul. Why does everyone think that?" *Probably because I've said it or shown it in a hundred ways.* Torie answered the question in her own mind.

"Uh, duh." Pam pantomimed slapping her forehead. "You asked your fiancé to ban him from the house. Hello? Pretty strong request for someone you're just ambivalent about." Pam said it, but somehow her mind must have been a step ahead of her mouth. "Hey, is he . . . Oh. My God. You never told me who got you home that night. It was Paul?"

"I'm not doing this now, Pammie. We have to find Dev."

Her phone rang. She'd never been so happy to have it ring, never been so glad of a reprieve. "It's him. It's Paul."

Pam frowned at her as she answered the phone.

"Torie, where are you? Marco said you took off like a bullet, then pulled into some house. Where are you?"

"With Pam. Dev's missing."

"Damn. How long? Since when? Like missing, missing, or he left, like he went home?"

Guys. "If he'd have left, I wouldn't be worried, Paul," she explained, only slightly sarcastically. "He got a call, acted really funny, and left."

"Did he say he was coming back?"

Well, duh. Now Torie wanted to slap her own forehead. "Pam, did he say he was coming back?"

Pam shook her head, hanging on every word of Torie's conversation. "No."

"Well did he say he *wasn't* coming back?" Paul continued to probe.

More *Man Logic*, Torie decided. As if Dev would say one way or the other. "No."

"Christ on a crutch. Just what we need—one more weird thing about this whole deal. I'll call Tibbet. Are you going to come back and pick me up, or should I get a cab?"

"I'll pick you up, I do have your car, after all."

"If you need more time, I can—"

"No, it's okay. I'll pick you up," Torie insisted. It would get her away from Pam's prying. She hadn't meant to blurt out what she'd said about Paul. Hell, she hadn't managed to think about it. About the ramifications. She surely didn't want to discuss what had happened at college, nor what was going to happen next. Especially since she had no idea.

She didn't need anymore insanity, past or present, to add to the mix.

"I have to go. The bodyguard called Paul. Besides, I've got Paul's car. He's going to report Dev missing. I have to call GoodMama," she added, seeing the steel of determination in Pam's eyes. Pam pursued girl chatter like a dog with a bone. The saving grace was GoodMama intimidated Pam, so she backed down. Of course, GoodMama intimidated everyone, including Torie. But it would be far worse to *not* tell her Dev might be in trouble.

Escaping Pam was easier than she'd hoped, given the fierce determination Pam had for getting Torie to deal with her past. Any sign that she'd moved toward that was a bonus for Pam. Dev must have some amazing hold on her to have her give up so easily on hearing all about Paul.

"Don't think I've forgotten what you said." Pam's parting shot made Torie wince. Damn. She wasn't forgiven, or off the hook. "We'll be talking."

"I know. I gotta go."

"Yeah. Call me if you hear anything."

"The very minute."

Torie hurried into the car, whipping out of the driveway with the same speed with which she'd pulled into it. Heaven only knew what was going on with Dev. He was an enigma. On one hand, his specialty was green construction, save-the-planet type stuff. On the other, he had been a bodyguard, and in his wilder days, a mercenary. At least that was her guess. He wouldn't talk about it, and neither would anyone else in the family.

Her phone rang again. Paul.

"Hey, I'm on the way," she told him. "Is everything okay there? What was the emergency?"

"Someone hacked into the company computers. We've lost a huge amount of data. We're trying to re-construct what happened. The partners are meeting about how to respond."

"Aren't you a partner now? Shouldn't you be in the meeting?"

There was a moment of silence, then Paul laughed. "Yeah, I guess I should. I'm not used to that yet."

"It happened quickly, I guess. And with me screwing up your life at the moment, I'm sure it's hard to get excited about it."

"You're not screwing up my life, Torie."

"I'm not sure about that. I seem to screw up everything I touch," she murmured.

"No. Don't take responsibility for something someone else is doing to you. You're not to blame in this, Torie. Anymore than you were to blame in college."

That very phrase had started their knock-down, drag-out fight at the end of their one tempestuous, hot, sexy, and disastrous college date.

"I don't want to talk about that," she interrupted. "It's old news."

"Maybe," Paul said, but let it drop. "Anyway, what's happening now is the work of someone who's really crazy, Torie. Two people are dead, you could have been hurt or killed in the fire. It's a miracle you weren't."

"I know."

His voice dropped into a more intimate range. "I would never have recovered if anything happened to you."

Stunned, Torie missed the turn that would take her to Paul's office. "Uh . . ." She finally got a word out beyond her surprise. "Thank you." Focusing on him, she realized that if she lost him, if something happened to him . . .

"Torie? Are you still there?"

"Yes, yes. Sorry, I missed my turn." What could she say to that? How could she say she felt the same? Did she? What had she done?

"I know we shouldn't get involved, you know that, right?" He didn't sound like that made him happy.

"No, no, we shouldn't."

"You're my client. I'm not supposed to—" Paul started.

"I'm in such trouble, and I don't—" Torie spoke at the same time.

They both laughed. Paul cut off her line of thinking.

"Trouble is what I'm good at, Torie. It's my job. We'll figure this out, get you back on track. I want to help."

"My life just sucks."

Paul laughed, but his voice had turned professional. "Yeah, it does. Oh, excuse me," he spoke to someone in the office. "Okay. Torie? Seems like I am expected to be in that meeting. Just park in the slot, and come on up. Martha's here, and she'll get you situated. You can use my office for whatever you need."

"Okay, thanks."

"And Torie?"

"Yeah?"

"Want to go out to dinner tonight?" Paul said in a rush, his voice muffled, as if he'd cupped his hand over the phone. "To celebrate the partnership?"

"Uh," Torie began.

"Just think about it. Okay?" He quickly said good-bye and hung up.

Torie wasn't sure what had just happened. She circled the two blocks necessary to get her back to the garage entrance, mentally apologizing to Marco, the bodyguard, for making him do the same. She had yet one more civil conversation—almost lover like—with Paul Jameson. Had he just asked her on a, well, a real date?

She was living in his house, but she was a guest. It was temporary. She wasn't . . .

A memory of Paul's amazing hands, the way his body had felt above hers, caressing her, flashed into her mind.

Stress made you do funny things.

She pulled into the garage and parked. Leaning her head onto the headrest, she closed her eyes. What the hell had she done? What had they both done?

They'd unleashed something between them in the early morning. Something that had slumbered for a long, long time.

That something, however, was hemmed in by pain.

Torie felt her body quiver, remembering how deeply she'd felt him, how fully. It had been a mistake. But she'd needed to feel alive, feel like something, anything, was good in the world.

And it had been good. It had been earth-shattering and fabulous. She'd always enjoyed and appreciated sex, but wondered why people would kill for it. Or die for it. Sex with Paul had the kind of dangerous quality that gave her an inkling of why people would have affairs, throw caution to the winds. Do anything to have more.

Had that been why she'd driven him off, accused him of asking her out for all the wrong reasons? He hadn't forced her to have sex. Then, like now, she had started it. Was it her fear keeping them both prisoner?

Maybe.

All she knew was she wanted more.

A knock on the glass jerked her, screaming, from her thoughts.

Her heart pounded furiously as she looked into the eyes of Melvin Pratt Jr. She took a relieved breath, and smiled at him.

"Lord in heaven, Melvin," she said getting out of the car. "You scared a year off my life."

Melvin eyed the car and Torie's face, and smiled. "I'm so sorry, Torie. I was worried about you, just sitting there. I didn't mean to scare you, though."

There was something about the way he said it, the look in his eyes, that made Torie uneasy. Melvin had always been a bit smarmy.

"Thank you. I was just trying to gather my thoughts before I went upstairs. Paul said that your father wanted to meet with me to review everything that's going on." She wasn't sure why she said it, but she wanted to get away from Melvin. He'd always made her feel uncomfortable. He'd asked her out several times after she and Todd had broken up, but she'd always declined. When she'd started dating again, she hadn't wanted to date him.

"Ah, well, I'll walk you up then. I haven't had a chance to thank you for helping dear old Dad the other day when the fire alarm went off."

"You're welcome." Torie didn't know how to keep the conversation going as they rode up the elevator. She always hated the sense of forced proximity of an elevator, and for some reason it was worse with Melvin.

"You seem uncomfortable, Torie."

"Oh, I'm sorry," she apologized, though she wasn't sure why. "I have a lot on my mind." She smiled at him. "There's so much I have to do. You never realize how much you count on the little things you've accumulated until you lose everything."

"Yes, I'm so sorry about the fire. It's horrible to have to replace everything. I know you'll be glad of all the extra money when you get to the point of repairing things."

Torie was puzzled. What money? "Well, the insurance will cover the house. That's the basics, however. I'm afraid I'm going to have to put a lot out and get reimbursed," she said ruefully.

"Oh," Melvin seemed surprised, then wary. "I'm sorry. I thought that you would have . . . the will . . ." He stopped. It was an awkward pause, but the opening doors saved him from having to complete the thought. "Here we are. I'm sure Martha will have whatever you need until Father and the others are done."

He stepped aside, motioning her off. She wanted to ask him what he'd been talking about. What about the will? What extra money?

She vaguely remembered Paul saying something on the beach in North Carolina, something about Todd leaving her something. It made her unbearably sad. Todd had felt so responsible, so determined to make sure that she never felt any repercussions from his decisions. He was just like that. But, as she'd told Paul, Todd had long ago paid any debt he might have owed. She had always felt so strange that he'd paid for everything, given her so much.

The idea that there was more made her heart ache. She'd rather Todd had spent it all, enjoying life in the big way he'd had.

"Good afternoon, Ms. Hagen," Martha greeted her. Still as cool as ever. Torie had no idea what Martha thought of her.

"Good afternoon," Torie began. "Paul had said . . ."

"Yes, he let me know that you were to have the use of his office. Would you like some coffee? Tea? Perhaps a soft drink?"

"I don't want to be any trouble."

"It isn't," she declared with a tight smile. "I would do it for any guest."

Ahh. A guest. Yep. That was the distinction. She was making sure Torie knew she was a guest, not a fixture. Torie almost laughed. Since she felt so little was permanent in her life at the moment, from where she lived to what she wore, what Martha thought hardly phased her.

"Thank you then, a soft drink would be great."

"I'll get that for you. Please go in and have a seat."

Not make yourself at home. Nope. Martha didn't want her making herself comfortable, that was for sure. Torie sank into one of the comfortable leather chairs at the conference table.

Where did she belong?

"Here you are." Martha sat down a coaster and the soft drink can. A glass with ice followed, placed precisely on another coaster. "If you'd like to use the phone, this line at the conference table is available."

"Thank you." Torie mustered a smile.

"You're welcome. Do you need anything else?"

"Might I trouble you for a pad of paper? I need to make some notes."

"Certainly." Martha moved behind Paul's desk, opened a drawer, and produced a leather portfolio and pad. Handing it to Torie along with a pen, she asked briskly, "Anything else?"

"No, thanks."

"Then I'll leave you to your calls. Mister Jameson should be returning within the hour."

Torie waited until Martha left, then stared at the blank page in front of her. She picked up the pen, but couldn't bring herself to write anything.

It all came crashing in on her. The house, the destroyed hotel rooms, her job at TruStructure, Paul.

She put her head down on the table and wept.

Chapter Twelve

"So, we're agreed?" Melvin Pratt Sr. said into the silence following his announcement that their consultants were recommending the same course of action the police technical specialist had mentioned. Full back-up on a new system. "We have the capital budget for a secondary system. In order to protect our files from further encroachment, we'll get it installed immediately. Our technical people and the consulting team will reboot the files from there. In the meantime, utilize the portable hard drives that are being hooked to your computers."

"Sir?" Declan Dowd spoke up. "I take as read we'll be prosecuting these scoundrels to the fullest extent of the law once they are apprehended?"

"Yes. We will. To my significant irritation," Pratt answered in the same pompous tone as his colleague, "the technical specialist employed by the police believes this to have been an inside job."

Paul hadn't heard that news and he sat up, hoping for additional information. There were murmurs of interest and disgust amongst the other partners seated around the long, polished conference table.

"Disgraceful that anyone would have instigated this sort of vandalism to the firm's computers, and that we've paid them to do it," another partner began.

"Indeed," Pratt cut him off as he looked around the table, catching Paul's eye and giving him a wink. The man was a windbag, and might have gone on for an hour without being stopped. "We'll hope that the police gather sufficient evidence, and do it properly, so that they can be prosecuted."

There were more rumbles of assent and several side conversations, which began in the breach of silence.

Melvin Sr. cleared his throat. "One last item of business." The room quieted once more. "Although we have officially welcomed Paul Jameson to our ranks here today, we need to discuss the upcoming celebration event for our newest partner."

People looked his way and smiled, or nodded their approval. He'd been welcomed and congratulated throughout the day, and many of the partners had been amused that he'd been late to the meeting.

"There will be the de rigueur dinner and drinks, with a band at the Bradshaw Mansion in Fairmont Park, since the room we've had in the past at the Ritz was unavailable," Pratt continued. "As usual, any of you who would like to make an evening of it and stay the night are welcome to do so. The adjacent Penn Lodgings hotel has a block of rooms. Just let my assistant know you'll need a spot."

Paul saw several people make notes in their PDAs. There were some sly smiles directed around the group as well. He wasn't privy to their meaning, but having heard the gossip about these dinners, he was sure the stories were fairly infamous.

"Are we finished then?" the senior partner asked, wrapping things up. "Excellent. Thank you for rearranging your schedule to meet on such short notice."

With that dismissal, everyone rose and began leaving the room. Most continued to discuss the possibility of an employee causing the damage. "A moment, Paul?"

"Yes?"

Melvin Sr. was frowning, and he waited until everyone had left the conference room before he spoke again. "Have you seen today's *Inquirer*?"

"No, I've been a bit overwhelmed with client work."

"Your most attractive client's on the front page. Evidently, the press has been digging up more of the former boyfriend's names and injuries, then interviewing the fellows." The older man pushed a copy of the paper across the table. "It's mostly harmless, fortunately. The men sound like whiny Nancy-boys for complaining, and the reporter questions the Philly police and their response to your client's woes. Of course, the piece about the family of the young man who was killed is a bit more damaging."

Paul picked up the paper. The story was below the fold, and small, thankfully. That diminished the impact. Then again, given that she was innocent, Torie really wouldn't be hurt by it. However, in skimming the short section, his anger grew at how her company had attempted to distance itself from her notoriety. The quote they had given deliberately minimized her contribution to the firm, and was an obvious attempt to disassociate themselves from Torie's situation.

"A tasteless bit of face-saving on the part of her

firm." The words were out of his mouth before he could censor them.

"I noticed that," Melvin Sr. concurred. "Don't I remember that your client's been instrumental in Chamber affairs and the United Way campaigns for them?"

"Yes." Paul kept the answer short. It wouldn't do to show just how much her bosses' defection pissed him off.

"Hmmm, shame they don't want to speak up about her good qualities, eh?"

"Exactly." Paul allowed a bit of his ire to creep into his voice.

"Will she be joining you at the partner's dinner?"

Paul hesitated. "I've not asked her yet," he admitted. He couldn't think of anyone else he'd rather have be there. Besides, he had to keep an eye on her. "But with what's going on, if she's willing to go, I'd like her with me."

"I'm sure that's the only reason," the older man said with a laugh and a wink. Then his demeanor turned a bit sour. "If only my son had such good taste."

"I'm—" Paul began, then stopped. He was about to say he was sorry for the old man, but that didn't sound right.

"No, excuse me for mentioning it. Now, do you think this unfortunate development of ours has a bearing on your client's case?"

Paul shook his head. "I don't know, sir. On one hand, since it's mostly my files and some files in human resources on the main server which have been tampered with, it has to be considered." Paul tapped the paper. "All of these incidents however are direct, rather than indirect. As we know, criminals seldom take a two-pronged approach to any kind of harassment."

"So, you think your client's still in danger, eh?"

"I do. Just before the meeting, I was told that her cousin has gone missing, and while that's of concern, it may not be relevant. This computer thing is happening at the same time, but again, that may not be a connection either." Paul appreciated the ability to run his thoughts by the older man. He needed objectivity about the whole mess, and he had already realized he didn't have it. "None of it negates the danger to Ms. Hagen. The police now seem to think her cousin, Mister Chance, may not have been a victim as they originally assumed."

He had to remember to tell Torie that news. Tibbet had let that fall when he called Paul earlier, just before she arrived. "This computer situation may be related, but—"

"But it might not be," Pratt finished. "Awful lot of coincidence, however. Seems as if this harassment of hers has been going on a while." He indicated the article.

"At least five years. Since she and Todd Peterson called off their wedding."

"You mentioned your list of coinciding incidents. May I look at that?"

Paul grimaced. "I have the original notes, but the document I created to match them is one of the ones destroyed by our hackers."

"Interesting. I know we had planned to discuss this today, but with the emergency partner meeting, my time to do so has disappeared. I'd like to reschedule our meeting to tomorrow morning. Let's go over all of these notes together. Perhaps an old set of eyes may see some new connections."

"Some of the connections are fairly obvious, sir," Paul explained as they made their way to the door. "Whenever Todd came home from his travels, both he and Torie experienced some sort of mishap. The dates and times of the occurrences coincide with Todd's visits in the U.S."

"Interesting. Have you shared this with the police?"

"In the main. I'm meeting with Detective Tibbet, the detective in charge of Todd's murder investigation." The very phrase made Paul wince. It still wrenched at his heart to think about his friend.

Pratt Sr. rested a hand on his shoulder, stopping him just in front of the large doors. "Son, it won't be the first friend you lose, but I hope it will be the only one you lose this way. I had a great deal of respect for Todd Peterson. Knowing both of you since before you took the bar through Melvin Jr." Pratt's voice sounded slightly choked. "Well, it's difficult to lose anyone of his age, my son's age. You understand."

Paul could only nod.

"He was a good man. I know I said this to you at the time, but I am sorry for your loss."

Paul ducked his head. He knew the grief would be written plainly on his face. "Yes, sir."

In answer, Pratt simply gripped Paul's shoulder a bit tighter, then let go. "Now, have Martha call my assistant, get us set up for the morning. We'll work something in, even if it's over coffee and breakfast."

"Thank you, sir," Paul managed in a modulated tone, in spite of the memories choking his throat.

* * *

Passing through the halls, Paul acknowledged the hails of his peers and accepted their congratulations. He was thankful for the distraction. With the walk to his office punctuated by such good cheer, as well as some open envy, he was able to recover his equilibrium. Everything was off balance, and it was making him distrust his own judgment.

How could he be objective about anything when he was still grieving the loss of someone he'd known for so long? Then, to have Torie be involved, and to have become involved with Torie . . .

The thought of her hot and passionate beneath him, the image of her, the thought of her delicious moans of completion made him detour to the men's room. It wouldn't do to walk into his office, knowing she waited there, with anything less than a clear mind. Thoughts of her tangled up his senses so badly, he needed a moment to compose himself.

He didn't even turn on the hot water. He splashed straight cold water, nearly glacial, on his face. It helped to clear his mind and divert his thoughts. He pushed the towels into the bin as the door opened.

"Oh, hello, Paul," Melvin said. Irritation was obvious in his demeanor. "Done with the meeting?"

"Yes, thanks." Paul picked up his paperwork, but Melvin blocked his path. "What's up?"

"It's been a long time coming," Melvin said, his eyes hard.

"What?"

"Todd. I'm sorry he's dead, but he lived a crazy life."

Fury clouded Paul's mind to hear his friend dismissed so tersely. For Melvin, whom he and Todd had nicknamed *Weaselboy* when they were pledges together, to say something so carelessly stupid was beyond insulting.

Paul bit back the words that clamored to spew forth. Through his anger, he recognized that Melvin was baiting him, hoping for Paul to say or do something stupid, something rash.

It was a pattern Melvin employed to get people fired. People he disliked. People he wanted out of the way.

Weaselboy. He's such a needy little piss. Paul could almost hear Todd's drawling, insulting voice in his mind. It snapped him out of the fog of reaction.

"He lived a better life than either of us, *Mel-vin.*" Paul managed a calm voice, and he could tell he'd scored a point when he emphasized the other man's name, adding the deliberate twist several of the partners used when speaking of him. "And," he added as he stepped around Melvin to open the door, "he would have beaten both of us to partner if he'd stayed."

The parting shot hit home. Paul nearly grinned to hear the muffled slam of a stall door striking the wall. Todd would have enjoyed that.

Thoughts of Todd and the pain of his loss walked with him the rest of the way to his office. Martha was away from her desk, and he opened the door and walked into his own area, sure he'd find Torie on the phone.

Instead, he stopped dead, shocked to see her sitting at the table her head in her hands, tissue box at her elbow.

"Torie?"

"Oh!" she exclaimed, hastily wiping her eyes. "I was just . . ."

"Crying."

She dropped her gaze. "Yeah. That, too. I guess I got a little overwhelmed."

He closed the door. Locked it.

"Understandable. Here." He pulled out her chair, took her hand, and brought her to her feet. "I think we both need this."

His nerves were sizzling as he eased her into his arms, cradling her head into that perfect spot at his shoulder. As they had that morning, their bodies fit together. He wrapped his arms around her and held on, savoring the sense of her close to his heart.

After a few minutes, he finally asked, "What started all this?"

"I have to go to my office," she said on a hiccupping sigh. Her hands were tucked into his chest, as if she were afraid to hold on, afraid to allow herself to trust. "To get a key. They said, they said . . ." She stopped, drawing a deep breath and burrowing more firmly into his arms. "They said such stupid stuff about me in the paper. How can I go back there?"

"You won't have to. Trust me. Not to work." He eased her away just enough that she looked up at him. All trace of makeup had been washed away by her crying jag. She looked vulnerable and lost. It made him want to fix it. "Do you want me to go with you?"

Hope blossomed in her eyes, quickly followed by confusion. "I . . . I'd love it, but you don't have to do that." She sighed. "It helps just to be able to say how much it sucks."

He laughed. "Yeah, but I'll go with you anyway. Here," he said, getting her to look up again, "this will make you feel better."

Paul kissed her. This time, he skipped gentle and

went straight to desire. He caught her mouth and her quick gasp in a fiery kiss that he hoped left no question about how he felt. Part of his mind was busy planning which stable surface he could lift her onto, and drive them both beyond thinking with fast, hot lovemaking.

"Wow," Torie managed when they paused for breath. He wanted to start again, drive her further, but he knew he had to stop.

"Is that a good wow or a bad wow?" he murmured, resting his cheek on her hair. He could smell the strawberry shampoo his nieces had left in the bathroom the last time they'd visited. It was the first time strawberries had turned him on.

"A good one," she said, her breath coming short as he laughed and kissed her again, briefly this time.

"Take your mind off things?"

"Pretty much," she admitted. "I was supposed to be thinking during that?"

Paul laughed, enjoying the moment. "No, absolutely not. No thinking."

"Okay, warning bells," she said. "I'm thinking now." Torie pushed him away, although she didn't entirely leave the circle of his arms.

"Damn."

It was her turn to laugh. It was still a bit shaky, but it was a laugh.

"I thought we said this was a bad idea. I'm your client, and all that. What about that?"

"It is a bad idea, but pretty much only for that reason."

She smiled but it held a lot of puzzlement. "Not to look a . . . well, let's call it a gift horse, though I could be saucy and call it something else . . . in the mouth, but we don't like each other. Right?"

"Who says?"

Torie laughed, but it was sad again. "Pretty much everyone. Including us."

"Hmmm. Old news. Time to turn over a new leaf, don't you think?"

She smiled, and it was stronger this time. "I didn't get the memo, but hey, I'm willing to get some fresh news."

"Good. So, what do you say to dinner?"

"Dinner?"

"Yeah. As in food. Eating. Together."

"I know what you mean, but—" she began.

"Not burgers. Casual, but nicer than Bob's Grill and Grease."

He wanted to pull her in again, gauge her reactions from the way her body fit. She was recovering from her bout of sorrow though, he could tell. Standing taller, she eased further away. "I'd like that. Thank you. I accept."

"Good." He let her go, knowing she needed to feel stable on her own, but wishing he could shoulder some of the burden for her.

The thought shocked him.

"Is something wrong?"

With a mental shake, he brought himself back to the moment. "No, not at all. I was just thinking that we could kill two birds with one stone. We'll go by your office, pick up that key you need." He stopped. "Is it something you have to get? As your counsel, I have to say that dealing with them right now might not be a good idea. In fact," he said as he sat down at the table, leading her to sit as well, "you might have grounds for a suit, especially if your employers continue to speak to the press."

Torie shook her head. "No. In some ways, it shows their true colors. It's better to know."

"Hmmm, I guess. So, key first. Then we'll run by the house and change. There's a nice family restaurant near the house. We'll go there."

"What kind of food do they serve?"

"What else? Italian."

"Excellent."

"So—" he rose to unlock the door. It wouldn't do for someone to come along and try it, find it locked, and jump to all the right conclusions. "What's on the list?"

He pointed to the pad, covered in neat, precise notations.

"All the miserable details of finding a place to live, and replacing some of my things." She eyed the pad, flipped up several pages to reveal more writing. "You can see why I got a little overwhelmed."

"Yeah, I can. So what's the key?"

"It's to a safety deposit box. I kept it in my desk drawer so I could get it easily if something happened to the house." She looked at him, her eyes dark and sorrowful again. "I never thought I'd really need it."

He pressed his hand over hers. He'd made that gesture a thousand times to clients, to friends who needed reassurance or succor, even to women he was dating, keeping them interested. Never had it felt like it meant anything. Now, it did. He really did want her to feel how much he empathized with her plight. The gesture seemed so very little.

Torie sighed and sandwiched his hand between hers. "Thank you for offering to go. If this is part of the 'Truce with Torie Campaign,' I really appreciate it. I can go by myself," she said, beginning to temporize.

"I know. But won't it be easier if I go with you?" he said quickly, knowing she'd talk herself into facing it alone if he didn't. He didn't want her to go alone. He *wanted* to be there for her.

Another shocker.

She smiled, nodded. "Yeah, it will be easier if I have company when I go. Thanks."

"Oh, so I'm company now," he teased. "Jeez."

"You know what I mean." She pushed at his shoulder and he pretended to be knocked back.

"Wow, you pack a whallop. And yeah," he said and returned to serious mode, "I know. Let me just wrap up a few things here and we'll head out. That way, we get there just before five. You can get the key and get out without a lot of fanfare and gossip."

Torie closed her eyes, winced. "Yeah. Sounds like fun."

"Stick with me, kid. We'll have 'em rollin' in the aisles," he joked, hoping to make her laugh.

Fortunately, she did. He went to his desk and checked the printout Martha had managed to make of his schedule for the next few days. Thankfully, he could indeed leave early.

"Hey," he said, and turned as a thought struck him. "What was up with Pam? Was she any help figuring out where your cousin went?"

"No, not really."

Another thing occurred to him, and he was about to ask when Martha knocked on the door, easing it open.

"Oh, I beg your pardon, I didn't mean to interrupt."

"That's all right, Martha, I was just checking to see what was on the docket for tomorrow."

"You have several clients who are scheduled to come in tomorrow. Did you want me to reschedule those again?"

"Don't reschedule on my account," Torie interjected, hefting the list she'd made as an addendum to her comments. "Obviously, I have a considerable amount to do. And . . ." She forestalled his suggestion that she come with him to the office. "I can do that from—" she stopped her gaze on Martha, then shrugged—"from your house just as easily as I can do it here."

"Very well, then." Martha nodded without waiting for him to reply. "I'll see to it. I have the information on the dinner, as well as several other items. I understand you're having breakfast with Mister Pratt Sr."

"If he says so. His schedule was jammed more tightly than mine."

"His assistant just called to confirm it. His office at seven-thirty."

Paul snagged a pen from the drawer, and wrote the time and particulars on the paper calendar. "Got it."

"Very good, sir. Unless you need me, I would still like to leave early today. Does that suit you?" she added stiffly, not looking at Torie. Paul wondered if she just didn't want the younger woman to know she had a real life, or if she still just didn't like Torie.

"That's fine. I have to assist Torie with a matter about her office, so I'll be leaving shortly as well."

To his surprise, Martha turned to Torie, her lips pursed and disapproval written all over her face. He was about to interrupt, forestall any negative comment, but he needn't have worried.

"Ms. Hagen, I have to say that your firm has not lived up to its obligations to support you. I'm sorry for that."

Torie managed to not look shocked as well. "Thank you."

Martha's nod was sharp and decisive. She was done with that topic. "Will you need me to get your tuxedo sent to the cleaners again?"

Crap. The dinner. He hadn't thought about the tux. When was the last time he'd worn it? Had he sent it to the cleaners? Hell. He had no idea, and said so. "I'll check it." He jotted another note to himself on the paper.

"Very well. Good night, sir. Ms. Hagen."

They replied in unison, and when the door was closed, glanced at one another.

"Did I miss something, or was she just nice to me?" Torie asked.

It was infuriating. That's what it was. Now she was with another man. Again. And who was it? The odious Paul Jameson, whom she professed to despise.

How like a woman to go from one man to the next, turning to the worst possible man if the potential for profit was there. Paul Jameson. The man's very name made his blood boil. He thought he'd gotten rid of the problem, laid out his plans so carefully, and disposed of the bastard who'd caused him so much grief.

He'd been sure, *sure* that he would be able to let it go, with the ever cutesy Torie and Todd out of the way. But she hadn't died. Once again, Paul Jameson had been there to ride to the rescue.

Damn Paul Jameson.

"That's it," he realized, saying the amazing words out loud. "Fuck me, that's it. It was never Todd. It was Paul. Always in the way. Always the one to call the shots."

He leapt from his chair, paced the room, thinking furiously. It had been Paul, then. Damn.

The revelation was startling.

Not that he regretted killing Todd. It had been a rush to kill him, despite having to handle the illegal firearm. He preferred his own sleek weapons, but they were traceable. The twenty-two had been effective, however. He thought of the neat, tidy hole in Todd's forehead. It had been so symmetrical. So clean, in fact, that he'd been surprised. The television sensationalized so much that he shouldn't have believed it about the pools of blood and the spurting spray so often depicted in films and cop shows. It had been remarkably precise, and the blood had been so minimal as to require almost no clean up.

Of course, he'd used a small caliber weapon. He'd done his research on the internet. Off site, of course, never while he was working. Not that it would matter with his safeguards, but everything must be separate.

The twenty-two had been easy to purchase. He hadn't even had to look very far for it. South Philadelphia was so helpful for procuring the things he needed.

That's why he would succeed so brilliantly. He was a master at thinking things through.

"Paul Jameson," he said, returning to his earlier thoughts. He slowed his pacing, glanced at the press release which had come through, featuring a sober looking and entirely too competent Paul. Part of him wanted to shred the noxious document, toss the scraps into the nearest toilet, and flush.

"No. No reaction," he cautioned himself, speaking out loud to help control the impulse to make confetti of the picture. "That's what sets me apart. Cool. Think it through," he soothed.

Sitting back behind the desk, he took up a pen, made a series of notes in his own brand of shorthand. No one could read it. No one but him.

He listed all the points at which Paul had thwarted him. Putting it down on paper, starting with their fraternity, made the pattern clearer. His list had grown so long, he had to use another sheet.

His blood pressure rose as he got closer to the present time. So many incidents.

"It was you, then," he muttered. "Never Todd. Todd was just your puppet, your front man. How did I miss this?"

He had to hand it to Paul. Only now, with Todd out of the way, could he see the pattern.

"Clever, very clever. But as always, I'm a step ahead." He dashed off a few more notes. "I know now, and I'm going to act. This time I'll get you both."

With a giggle, he thought about the Wicked Witch of the West's line from *The Wizard of Oz*. "'And your little dog, too,'" he cackled.

With a last flourishing stroke of the pen, he added his final reason to the list. Right after that, after the sentence about Torie taking up with Paul, he wrote:

"Time to kill Paul Jameson."

Chapter Thirteen

"Martha can be nice," Paul protested, closing and locking his desk. He picked up the paper schedule and several files, and crammed them into his briefcase.

"To you, maybe. She made it quite clear that I was unwelcome," Torie replied, gathering her own things as well. Not that there was much to gather. "Do you mind if I use this portfolio and pad for a few days? I'll get another, and get it back to you."

Paul frowned at it. "Keep it, it's a spare, and I don't think I've ever used it."

"Thanks," Torie said, joining him at the door. Riding down on the elevator with a host of other people, they stayed silent , but once in the car, Torie gave him directions to her office.

"I know where your office is," Paul replied, pulling into traffic. "Did you call ahead?"

"I guess I should." Her stomach coiled into a knot at the thought. "At least alert Tristan that I'm coming by."

"Much as I'd rather surprise him, yeah, you should."

Torie managed the call, even with her hands shaking. She didn't mind conflict, nor did she have a problem with her boss, but this unwarranted distancing of the firm from her personally was new territory. Heck, everything was new territory.

"Tris will be waiting for us," she said, closing her eyes at the thought of being escorted to her desk, watched, stared at.

"Nice of him," Paul said dryly, the sarcasm evident in his tone. "Of course, since it's your desk and they haven't fired you, he really doesn't need to escort you."

"Of course."

The visit was as stilted and painful as Torie imagined. She'd imagined bad. It was worse. Tristan followed them to her office, and anyone still in the building stared at her as she walked in, following her with their eyes. She could feel the speculation building in her wake.

"Torie," Tristan said, his eyes shadowed. "I'm so sorry about this. I really . . ."

"Not sorry enough to vouch for me, stand up for me," Torie said, fighting back tears. She'd never played the weak female card here before, and she wasn't about to now. Nothing would be worse than crying, so she locked it down. "I've worked hard for this firm, helped build its reputation, served on every board or committee you ever asked me to serve on. Given that, I somehow deserve this kind of treatment?" She motioned toward the door, where she could see people peeking over their cubicles to see what was going on.

"No, but—" he began.

"But nothing," she snapped, letting anger take the place of the tears. "This is so wrong."

He glanced at Paul, who up to this point had been

silent. "I know it's tough, but the phone wouldn't stop ringing. We might have lost clients."

"Did you?" Paul spoke for the first time.

"Uh, I don't know," he waffled. "I don't think so, but we were advised to do, um, damage control. Quickly."

"Oh, so putting me on admin leave is damage control? What about saying you believe in me? In my innocence? What about supporting one of your longest-serving, most loyal employees by believing in her?"

"Torie," Tris stuttered. "You've got to see our side."

"No, actually, I don't. You never hesitated to use the fact that I was a woman, and one of the best in my field, to your advantage. From contracts to PR, you made sure everyone knew you had a crack engineer who met the government requirements for gender equality. Nope, never missed an opportunity on that one, did you?"

"But—" Tristan began.

"Yeah. But when it came to trash-talking reporters with no real information sniffing for more, you caved. You *gave* them a story. Don't you realize that? You made this far more of a story than it was originally by doing your little admin leave deal."

"When you come back, we'll do our best to make it up to you."

"Uh huh. That's going to take some doing." Torie unlocked her desk, found the safety deposit box key, took several other items as well, then relocked the desk.

"D'you mind leaving that unlocked? We needed some files earlier today and couldn't find them."

"No. I won't." She turned to Paul. "I don't have to do that, do I?"

"No, and you can press charges if they break the locks."

"It's our desk," Tris protested, shocked.

"Yes, but unless you terminate her employment, in which case she would clean out the desk, the contents can be considered her intellectual property to which you have no right."

Tristan looked at him in horror. "What are you, her lawyer?"

"Yes, actually, I am."

Tris's face went pasty at the rejoinder, and he almost staggered when Paul handed over his card.

"This is Pratt and Legend," Tris said.

"Yes. We're among the best in the city, I believe." Paul smiled.

While the two men were facing off, Torie took a moment to check her files. So far, nothing had been disturbed. Paul's words had reminded her that she had a stake in things. Given that, she selected several items from her file rack on her credenza. The folders contained ideas for breaking into new markets, ideas she was developing to present. They also included her personnel report on all her employees, and the review she'd been preparing on herself.

"Uh, Torie, I don't think . . ."

"These are ideas in development. My ideas. I believe my attorney already indicated I was perfectly within my rights to take them with me."

"Indeed you are, Ms. Hagen," Paul said, nodding with a serious air. He turned a frowning gaze toward Tristan. "So, do you feel you need to be here, supervising what Ms. Hagen is doing? That feels a bit like harassment, don't you think, ma'am?" He turned to her and raised an amused eyebrow when Tristan couldn't see it.

"Uh, no. I guess not. Torie," Tristan said, shrugging helplessly, "I'm really sorry about all this."

She didn't say anything. Part of her wanted to tell him it was okay, that she understood. Since she really didn't understand, she kept silent. Paul's presence helped her keep up the façade.

Tristan backed out of the office, and Paul shut the door behind him.

"Well," he said and grinned. "That was fun."

Torie sagged onto a corner of the desk. "You have an unusual sense of fun."

He came over and put an arm around her shoulders, gave a squeeze. "No, it probably was nerve-wracking for you, but you put on a good show. I would never have known you weren't cool as a cucumber. Except . . ."

"What?" She looked around, looking in vain for something he might be referring to.

"Except for when you nearly cried."

"You're a rat," she said on a weak laugh, punching at his shoulder.

"Hey, don't hit your lawyer. I might sue."

"Yeah, yeah. Sure."

"So, candidly," Paul said, scooting onto the desk next to her, "you should take anything you don't want someone looking at, or pawing through."

"How about everything?"

Paul laughed. "I don't think you have a briefcase big enough." He pointed at the one sitting under the desk. "The nice thing is, you have one here, so you can take whatever files you want to protect."

"Wow, I forgot. I didn't take any work home that night." She sighed. "Lord, it seems like a hundred years ago."

"You usually take work home?"

"Yeah. You?"

"Yeah." They laughed at one another.

"Why didn't you take work home that night?" Paul wondered.

Torie pushed off the desk and began filling her briefcase. Her mother had given it to her when she graduated with her master's degree. "Well you know about the little, uh, escapade with Pam, of course."

"Yeah, I guess that would preclude working."

Torie laughed. "Actually, the snatch and grab didn't take too long. Getting Bear's chain undone from the fence where he'd been tied for the twenty-seventh night in a row took a lot more time." She shoved a file in harder than she'd meant to and gave herself a paper cut. She shook the injured finger, then got back to packing the case. "I was going to call my mom, preempt her usual Thursday night call, and have a nice dinner."

"Your mom calls you every Thursday?"

Torie smiled. "Yeah, since she went into assisted living, they have all this stuff they do. But Thursday nights are always open. She hates bingo. She's lonely," Torie offered, "sometimes she calls three or four times a week. She misses my dad. Still."

Paul nodded. "My folks were close, too. With my mom gone, my dad fills up his time with hobbies." Paul made air quotes around the word hobbies, telling Torie that the hobbies were fairly annoying. "My sister has to deal with it more than me, but motorcycle maintenance?"

"Really?" Torie stopped to stare. "You're kidding, right? He's not—"

"Oh, but he is. Never touched an engine in his life until sixty-seven, but now? Up to his elbows in it."

"Wow. Wish my mom could find some sort of hobby other than calling me. She's been calling every day. She wants Steven to fly back home. I keep telling her—" Torie suddenly realized how it all sounded, and tried to take it back. "I mean, not that I mind her calling, or anything. I'm glad she can, that she does. It's just—" she broke off as Paul laughed.

"Oh, trust me, I know. My dad called virtually every night, right around bedtime, for about a year after my mom died. He was heading to bed, you know? Hated to go to sleep, knowing she wouldn't be there. He'd call and talk for an hour or so, he'd get so sleepy, I'd have to yell at him sometimes."

"Yell?"

"You know, he'd fall asleep talking to me and I'd be calling to him, 'Dad, Dad? Wake up and go to bed.'"

"Well, at least I don't put my mom to sleep."

"Har, har. I'm guessing you said no to Steven and your mom, about coming, right?"

She knew they were both thinking about how easily her frail mother and her brother could be targets. "Absolutely."

"Good. You about done there?" Paul reached for the briefcase handle as she did.

She jerked back. "Sorry. Thanks."

"What is it?"

"I, um . . ." She looked around, anywhere but at him. "It's my office. Seems weird to be in here. With you. Under these circumstances." She hesitated, then continued, "I feel like we're being watched. That's weirder."

Paul nodded. "Weirder. Yeah. Let's go to dinner."

"So what made you choose this place?" Torie asked as they sat, sipping a nice glass of red wine while they waited for their meals.

"For what?"

"To celebrate?"

"I like low-key. Making partner's a big step, you know?" Paul said, buttering his bread, then putting it down to use both hands to gesture. "It's never been my ambition, though. I wanted to build a company, or take over one that's really messed up and make it hum, make it profitable."

"Really? You wanted corporate?"

"Yeah, well more like entrepreneur." Paul shrugged it off, going back to the bread. "Then life intervened. I needed to get into a firm, get some experience. Who knew it would be eight years?"

"Yeah, time flies, and all that. I certainly never expected to work for TruStructure all this time. And now that I have, I guess I'm sorry I didn't branch out more."

"Have you thought about doing your own thing? Everyone knows you. They talk about you a lot at the Chamber, from the board to receptionist. I've heard your name mentioned at the leads group."

"Wow, really? They talk about me?"

Paul smiled at her. "Yeah, they do. I guess you did a talk there about cooperative marketing to build business."

"Oh. That."

"I hear it was impressive. So, you have the contacts and the know-how. I saw for myself that they didn't want you taking potential ideas out of there, especially if they were yours to begin with."

"Yeah. I have to see if I signed a noncompete clause, or something like that. As you say, it's been a while. I started there just before . . . well, you know."

"Yeah."

The waiter arrived with their dinners, for which Torie was relieved. She didn't know how to talk to Paul about Todd. As emotional as they both got over his death, with everything going on between them, how would they?

She wrestled with the thought all through the wonderful dinner. It surprised her that this was his kind of celebrating. They were nearly finished with dinner when she ramped up her nerve to ask about it.

"This has been really nice," she said, looking around the quiet restaurant, admiring the subdued décor. "Nice to go casual, eat good food in good company. Have an interesting conversation."

"But?" Paul questioned. "I hear a big ol' but in there."

She laughed. "Yep. I'm wondering what happened to the party guy. Back in the day, you would have been dancing on the roof of the McClaren building, shooting champagne corks off the roof."

Paul threw back his head and laughed, open and free.

"Yeah, you're right. I would have. Now I wonder who would sue me, and for how much, if I hit them in the head with a cork."

"Oh, come on, you would not."

"No, but you have to admit, making partner is a

bit more of a sober event than passing advanced law practice and principles."

"No." She giggled. "I don't think so. Bigger milestone. I guess that means you should pick a bigger building and something larger than a two-glass split of cheap bubbly."

"Hmmm, let me think. Well what about City Hall? Or the new Liberty Bell museum. That would be fairly high. Not the highest in Philly, mind you," he said, pretending pomposity. "Can't have that. Got to wait for a bigger milestone to do that."

"Absolutely. But the bubbly, that can be the good stuff."

"For the roof? Are you sure?"

They laughed and continued the scenario as they wrapped up the meal with coffee and dessert.

"Lord, this is delicious. Want to try it?" She offered him a spoonful of the tiramisu she was having. It was a date gesture, a comfortable thing to do. When she realized it, she started to pull the spoon back. "I'm sorry, you probably don't like tiramisu."

He took her hand, holding it steady as he leaned in, eyes on hers, to take the spoon into his mouth. "It's nice of you to offer. Thanks. Mmmm," he said, never taking his gaze from hers. "Tastes good."

The teasing was gone. The easy camaraderie faded in the intensity of the thoughts written on his face. She could see desire there. Desire for her, for them together.

And she felt a fire well up within her as she was caught, held in place by the lightest touch of his hand. Every need, every nerve vibrated. The spoon quivered in her hand, and he smiled.

"Shall we?" he said softly. The words were laden with meaning, with passion.

She wanted it. Badly.

"Yes."

He watched them leave her office, followed them to Paul's house. Paul had let the bodyguard go before they went to TruStructure, which was helpful.

It was amusing to think of the time and energy Paul was wasting on watchers. He knew who they were, too. He had his own reasons for hiring them from time to time. It had been child's play to watch Torie leave the building, see what kind of car followed her. Of course, if Torie knew she was safer during the day, it would ruin some of the fun.

He hoped they were coming back out. He didn't want to sit out all night in yet another trashy rental car. They always smelled so *used* somehow.

He saw lights go on in several rooms. It amused him to imagine Torie stripping out of the snug pants she'd had on. He liked thinking of her, standing naked before him. Desperate, helpless. He wanted her that way. Again. And again.

His breathing quickened, and he could feel himself harden under his own seeking hand. It wouldn't do to take care of that now. Not in a car that might be traced to him in some way.

No. Later, he would picture her behind those windows, weeping and helpless, ready for him to come for her.

He would be able to take her as he wanted to. Paul would be dead. Maybe, just maybe he'd keep her alive. See where things went from there. He could always kill her. Later.

The lights changed, with the outside lights coming on. It pulled him from his imaginings, and he eased down in the seat so he wouldn't be seen.

The garage door opened and they pulled out. If Paul were leaving alone, ah, then Torie would be alone. How . . . convenient.

But, no. Irritation washed over him as they passed. He could see that both of them were in the car. He brightened a bit, though, thinking that they'd been in the house such a short time that Paul wouldn't have had time to touch her again. He knew Paul couldn't leave her alone. And Torie was a tease, a woman, after all. He knew Paul would want to have her. Besmirch her.

Unless he had a short fuse. He giggled at the thought of the infamous Paul being an early shooter.

He tamped down the amusing thought as he turned the car on and followed them. Not too close. As interesting as it was to speculate, it didn't help him focus. He had to be cautious, keep his cool. Watch for opportunities.

The restaurant was small. The parking lot was dark, with shadowy corners. Even better, there was a lot above it, rising about six feet to one side. From there he could see the whole building, including Paul's elegant Mercedes.

He curled his lip. As if buying a sleek car made the man better, made him more worthy somehow. Yeah, right.

Pulling the notes from his pocket, he reviewed the distances. If he used the nine millimeter as he had for the hired sedan, he might have enough of a clear shot to hit either Torie or Paul. The twenty-two was too wimpy for this, and it was safely disposed of anyway.

He squinted in the low light, scanning for more details. He wasn't that far away, but he could easily leave the lot and go onto the side street without being seen.

Almost perfect. He would have liked to plan this out more thoroughly. He didn't like chance. It messed things up. Everything that had gone wrong for him had been by chance. More time, and he would have had Torie. More luck, and it would have been him, not Todd, rolling in the millions. If he'd won, if he'd had the money, then all his father's maunderings could have been cast aside like the drivel it was.

Well. Water under the bridge, as his dear old mother would have said. Hmmphf.

She should have known better, too. It had been so easy with her, after all. She couldn't swim.

The doors to the restaurant opened, and a couple came out. He cursed himself for sitting, wallowing in the past. Nothing could be done about it now. Nothing that he wasn't already doing, that is.

He'd never get the shot planned, get the silencer on. His palms began to sweat as he fumbled for the sections of the gun.

"Damn it all."

He froze at the sound of his own voice. Silence was the rule. You couldn't . . .

The couple was getting into another car. Some kind of SUV. It wasn't Torie and Todd . . . Torie and Paul. Todd was dead. Already dead. He'd been to the funeral. Yes.

Now, to get his aim down pat before his real target came out.

Chapter Fourteen

"You're sure?" He slid his hand over the nape of her neck, deliberately repeating the gesture he'd used to bring her closer before, when they'd only kissed the first time.

"I'm not sure of anything right now, Paul. I can't help it, I want this."

"That'll do." Paul pushed the door of the restaurant open, resting a hand on her back to keep her close, feel her. He also registered the cool night air, the feeling that rushed over him as he contemplated taking Torie home, making love to her again.

He helped her into her seat. It was impulse that made him do it, bend to kiss her.

He barely heard the thwick of the bullet whizzing over his back, but the window next to him shattered into a million glittering shards.

"What the—"

"Get *down*," a voice called out of the darkness. Another windshield exploded into fragments, over where the voice had come from.

"Shit!" a different voice yelled.

He heard the sound of an engine, heard the shuffle of moving feet, but all he could see was the glass. It covered his feet, covered Torie's lap. She'd thrown herself sideways, a wise move.

"No." He pushed her back down as she started to shift. "Stay there."

"You okay?" Detective Tibbet appeared seemingly out of nowhere, peering through the blasted window.

"Yeah, I think so."

"You okay, Ms. Hagen?"

Torie turned to look at him. Nodded.

"I heard a car—" Paul began.

"Yeah. I think he beat it. Harry, my partner, radioed for black and whites, but he's probably gone."

"Damn."

"Tell me about it."

Tibbet grilled them about what they had been doing, what they'd heard. He helped Torie out of the car, but asked them not to touch anything else. Within minutes, he had a team out searching for the bullets or any casings.

"What are casings?" Torie asked Paul as they sat together on the tailgate of an ambulance. A crowd had gathered, of course. The owner of the other car, the one hit by the bullet, was protesting the need for his car to be impounded, towed back to the city lot for examination. Torie didn't blame him.

"What do you mean?" Paul asked.

"What are these casings they're talking about?"

"Shell casings," Paul answered the question, but gave her a funny look.

She looked exasperated. "That doesn't mean anything to me."

"Gunshots mean bullets. Bullets mean shell casings. It's what holds the shot while it's in the gun."

"Oh. I didn't know that."

"You don't watch the news? Or TV?"

How irritating. "Of course I do. I simply don't watch a lot of violent TV. I can't sleep when I do."

"Ah." He sounded odd. And a little condescending.

She scooted away from him, just a little. She needed distance. Even that much helped.

How could this still be happening?

"Ms. Hagen. Mister Jameson." Tibbet came over to where they waited, his ubiquitous notebook open and ready for more squiggly notes.

"You were following us," Paul said. She could tell he was a little angry, a little embarrassed.

"Yeah. Obviously someone wants to kill your client. Possibly you, too. You don't torch a house, and shoot a guy, and then stop, ya know?" Tibbet didn't quite roll his eyes, but it looked like he wanted to. "My partner and I had some time, so we've been watching over Ms. Hagen. Saw the bodyguard bug out. Guess we'll have to tag you, too. Now, if you separate . . ." he said to Paul.

"Separate? Tag him, too? What do you mean?" Torie jumped in.

"That shot wasn't meant for you, Ms. Hagen. Whoever this guy is, he had a clean shot at you through the back window. Or while you were walking to the car. Nope." Tibbet looked at Paul, his expression quizzical. "That one was meant for Mister Jameson here."

Torie's heart squeezed in painful understanding.

She had gone to dinner with Paul. That had painted a big fat target on his back.

"Oh, my God," she gasped, horrified at the implications.

"Torie," Paul said sharply. "This could as easily be someone after me for other reasons."

"No, I don't think so, Mister Jameson," Tibbet interjected, cutting off Torie's reply. "We've checked your cases. Pretty much none of your work has been controversial. No divorces, nothing that's big press. Those being the usual causes of a grudge," he explained. "I think your friend, Todd, is the unifying factor, but I can't get a handle on it."

"But why Torie?"

"She dumped him. Or was dumped by him."

"But the accidents . . ." Torie began.

"Were deliberate. Look," Tibbet said, leaning in, foot on the bumper. "I don't pretend to know what this guy's thinkin', okay? But seems to me that the common denominator is your friend Todd Peterson. He wins money, and goes gallivanting off into the wild blue, right? Leaves you behind. If your time line's right, the one you gave me a rundown on?" He directed this toward Paul, who nodded.

Tibbet turned to Torie. "Then the accidents and incidents your friend had began the first time he returned to the U.S. for a visit. You put down on your time line that you were on a date with—" Tibbet references his book—"a guy named Trey Buckner?"

"Jeez, you dated Trey?" Paul shot her an amazed look.

"Yes, I did. He was very nice, but we didn't click," she said defensively, and nearly cursed at how it came out. She'd have preferred to be cool and calm about the whole thing.

"Yeah, that's the guy who had the nuisance complaint, right? Where someone canceled all his stuff."

"Yes. I only found out because he thought I might have done it."

"Why?" Paul asked, turning to look at her. She could see the knowledge in his face. Knowing Trey's reputation, Paul could guess why.

"Because I said no." Torie left it at that.

Tibbet, of course, wouldn't let it rest. "No?"

Torie sighed. "No to his advances, which were fairly aggressive. We got into a shouting match involving a lot of bad language on his part." She felt so prim saying it that way, but she wasn't about to tell them Trey had called her a cocktease, and Todd's throwaway whore of a bride. With the way Paul was already looking, Trey might get a visit, and she didn't want that.

"Bad language, I see," Tibbet scribbled again. "Any pushing or shoving?"

"It's been more than four years, Detective. But none that I remember. Not on my part anyway." She remembered the bruises on her arms where he'd grabbed and shaken her, but mentioning them did no good.

"I've read the notes from the complaint. We weren't very smart about internet stuff or the whole identity thing, even that short time ago." Thankfully Tibbet let it go, but the look he gave her told her he knew more. "And Mister Peterson lost four tires, hubcaps, and a windshield."

"He did?" Torie was aghast. "Wow, he never told me."

"He laughed it off," Paul said, his voice tight. "Said it was probably kids."

"Not in that neighborhood."

"Yeah."

Tibbet nodded, and returned to questioning Torie. "All the other intersecting events took place when Mister Peterson was in the country. I couldn't find anything in our files that you reported or with which you were connected in between those times. Do you remember any?"

Torie thought about it, but was so tired she couldn't dredge up a single thing. "I don't know, Detective. It's not that nothing happened, I just don't know if I can say for sure. Not tonight when all this is going on."

He asked them a few more questions, then told them they were free to go. Paul had already called for a cab, which was waiting.

"Oh, Ms. Hagen?"

"Yes?"

"I can't tell you officially, but you're no longer a suspect."

Paul spoke before she could. "What changed?"

"The time line's too short, and Ms. Hagen gave blood. Even with the gaps in your story, Ms. Hagen." Tibbet's smile was grim. "There's enough weighing on your side to rule you out."

"Why did you need my DNA?" She'd been dying to know ever since they had come to Paul's office and taken the sample.

"Officially, I'm not at liberty to say." Tibbet nodded at Paul.

"It could be," Paul began, watching Tibbet, "that

they found some of your hair at the scene, as I mentioned to you."

Tibbet nodded.

"And possibly your blood? You mentioned the blood just now?" Paul phrased it as a question, and Tibbet answered it with another nod. "Ah. But they've ruled out your actually being there, I guess."

Paul's guesses were confirmed by yet another nod.

"Interesting speculation, Mister Jameson, but you know I can't answer that," Tibbet said as if he hadn't confirmed everything about which Paul had asked. "But the lab will tell us everything in due time. They're especially good with preservatives. Amazing what those crime scene techs can find."

"The shooter would be good."

"Yeah, they would. They haven't gotten anything yet, but today's a new day, ya know?" Tibbet waved toward the two cars, now on tow trucks, headed for the lab. The owner of the other car was still protesting that he couldn't let his car go.

"We'll let you know when you can pick up your car," Tibbet said to Paul.

Paul helped her into the cab, and gave the driver his address.

"Maybe I should go to a hotel again." Torie was beginning to realize how much danger she was bringing to anyone she was with. Paul hadn't been a target before, but he was now. What had she done?

"No. You're safer with me."

But *he* wasn't safer with *her*, was he? What should she do? How could she protect anyone from what she couldn't understand?

It was horrifying to think that someone wanted her dead, or to ruin her life so badly that they would go to these kinds of lengths to destroy her world. It was worse to think about the pain that other people were enduring, the problems and difficulties. All because of her.

Maybe it was all her fault.

But what had she ever done to anyone that was so bad, so terrible, to bring this kind of retribution?

"Tibbet wants to meet with us midmorning to go over some things. Do you have time to do that?"

She nearly sobbed right then and there. As if she had a life, right?

"Nowhere I need to be, unfortunately."

Paul must have heard the despair in her words. "It's going to work out okay, Torie. I promise."

"Sorry, Paul, but that's one more empty promise. You don't know who's doing this. You can't be the white knight this time, and ride to the rescue."

"What do you mean, another empty promise?" Paul demanded as the cab pulled up at his house. He paid the driver and waited until they were in the house to continue. "I've never made you any promises, Torie."

"No, you haven't," she said with weary resignation. "Actually, come to think of it, you haven't promised anyone anything. Ever." She looked at him, thinking about that new insight. She hadn't realized it to be true until she said it. "You stay away from promises and commitments, don't you? Is that why you pushed me away back then? No strings on you, were there, Paul? Nothing to tie you down."

"That's not the point, Torie. Is there something specific you meant about the promises? Did you think that my coming and finding you, getting you out of that room in the fraternity house constituted some kind of promise?"

"No. Never. But you've always treated me like it did. You and Todd both. He took it a different way, after you told him. Yes." She was too tired to glare, but she wanted to smack him. "I know it was you who told him. That's a promise you broke, by the way. I asked you never to talk about it. To not tell anyone."

"I thought he should know—"

"What?" Torie shot back, gaining strength from the old anger which welled up within her. "That his future bride was some slutty girl who was lying around naked in the frat house? That I was too stupid to recognize that I'd been drugged? Just because I didn't get raped, did you make him think I'd gone willingly and got cold feet?"

"No!" Paul protested, tossing his coat onto the couch. "Of course not. I knew the moment I saw you that you were drugged. Jesus, Torie." Paul moved toward her but when she stepped away from him, he halted. "I thought he should know not to leave you alone with any of our brothers. I never did figure out who drugged you. The guy whose room you were in had been out half the semester with mono. It wasn't him. He wasn't there."

"Oh, so you felt you should tell him that, in spite of my asking you not to?"

"Good Lord, Torie, I didn't want anyone to hurt you. Besides," he fired back, "the only one you ever banned from your house was me."

"I didn't ban you, damn it. You keep saying that."

"Well, if you didn't ban me, what the hell did you do? Once you two got engaged, Todd stopped planning to go into business with me. He stopped playing pool with us on Thursdays. I'd hear about parties at your house, parties I got no invite to."

"For crying out loud, Paul, it was six or seven years ago. I never specifically asked Todd to ban you from the house. I just told him I'd be more comfortable if you weren't there."

"Oh, yeah, right." Paul smirked, but there was no humor in it. "Like that isn't a ban. Hell, Torie, if you hadn't said anything, do you think he would just stop, cold, playing pool with us? He was as loyal as could be. If you had a problem with me, why didn't you tell me?"

"You know what? I'm not doing this." Torie was panicking. She didn't want to face this. Didn't want to tell him anything about her feelings, or dredge up the past. She picked up her briefcase and purse. "Thanks for the hospitality. I'll find a hotel in the morning, and we can go back to our unusual truce. Whatever happened, we'll chalk up to stress."

"Stress?" Paul nearly shouted the word. "You call what happened between us this morning a stress reaction? Well, you have a hell of a way of working out your stress, Torie. No wonder guys are dropping like flies around you."

The words cut her to the heart.

The minute he said it, Paul knew he'd not only screwed up, he'd damaged something between them. Maybe destroyed it. The fragile truce, the beginnings of understanding and forgiveness were wiped out in the blink of an eye.

The light of battle went out of her eyes. She looked defeated. Broken.

"Thanks for that reality check." She turned away from him, started down the hall.

"Oh, God, Torie, I didn't mean that."

God, how could he have been so stupid, pushed her away so harshly? "I'm an idiot," he managed. "I didn't mean to say, to imply—"

She froze, and he stuttered to a halt. While she'd stopped in the archway, she never turned around. Didn't look at him.

He felt his own heart crack. Was he having a heart attack? He put a hand to his chest, but felt the steady rhythm. The pain was something else.

"You've never said an unplanned word, Paul. Never," she said softly, but the words carried the power of conviction and he heard them clearly. "You're so . . . careful with your words. It makes you a good lawyer, I guess." There were tears in her voice now, and the pain in his chest and gut burned hotter. How that was possible he wasn't sure, but it did. Her next words arrowed into his mind, burying there to start a second burn. "But it makes you a lousy human being." She paused, gathered herself, shifting the briefcase on her shoulder. "So. You did the right thing in helping me out back then. Good for you. I've paid the price for that help with you. And I never owed Todd, nor he me. So, debt paid. I don't owe you anything anymore." She took several deep breaths before she continued, her voice unsteady. "I wish Todd had finally been able to let it go. I'm going to learn from him, and do it differently. I'm going to let it go." She stopped again, then straightened her shoulders. "I'll be ready to meet with Tibbet in the morning."

He watched her walk away. His chest hurt so bad, his stomach was a tight twist of pain. He couldn't speak. What could he say, after all? She'd been right.

He was careful with what he said, with what he did, what he promised. The idea that he'd somehow broken a promise, done something less than honest in his dealings with her made him cringe. The knowledge that his careless words, born of frustration and fear, had been said to strike at her, bring her down somehow . . .

That was unbearable.

Again.

Once more, he'd found her, had her right there with him, and he'd pushed her away with callous careless words.

What the hell was wrong with him?

On the phone with Pam, Torie sobbed. She had cried more in the last month, in the last few days, than she had in years.

"It was so cruel, Pammie," she whispered, keeping her voice down. As if Paul cared that what he'd said had been so devastating. Didn't he know how responsible she felt? How could he not understand that she felt every bit the Black Widow they dubbed her, and completely accountable for everything that had happened to everyone around her.

"He's afraid," Pam counseled, her voice sounding small and wispy through the cell phone.

"Of what? Don't answer that," Torie said, sighing. "How could he not be afraid? Good Lord, Pam, someone *shot* at him tonight. The detective said it wasn't meant for me this time. That if the guy had wanted me, he could've shot me already. He was aiming for Paul."

"Well that is scary, yeah, but he's afraid of you, as in he's afraid of *you,* the woman. The person."

"Why would he be afraid of me, other than the fact that I'm probably going to get him killed, too?"

"You are not," her friend snapped. "Cut it out. The cops're watching, right? They're on the lookout for Dev, too, though they refuse to consider him a missing person yet. They know something's up, so they are gonna catch this guy."

"You're a heck of an optimist, Pam. They fail more often than they succeed at this kind of thing."

"What, catching bad guys? I think they do okay. Philadelphia's finest, right?"

"I guess."

"Well, better than L.A. or New Orleans, you know?"

"Fine comparison. But yeah, I suppose."

"So, tomorrow I'll take the day off, we'll take care of you. We'll go shopping, we'll find you some property to look at. It'll be great. I called Kuhman, and he's going to meet us at two o'clock to get an idea of what kind of place you want to rent. Then mani, pedi, and dinner."

"Oh, Pam, I'd love to, but I don't want you around me. I don't want anyone else I love getting hurt."

"I won't get hurt. Neither will you. So far, has this guy struck in daylight?"

A startling realization. "No."

"So, we'll go shopping, get our nails done, and voilà, meet with the real estate agent. Got me?"

"Yeah." She lay back on the bed, uncurling from her nearly fetal position. With Pam's help, she could go on. Somehow. "I hear."

"And obey?"

Torie managed to smile. "Yeah. I guess. I have

to ride in with Paul, meet with the cops. Get another rental car." She sat up, wearily jotted notes on the pad she'd taken from Paul's office. "Find a hotel."

"I'll be there with you, honey." Pam said with stalwart firmness. "I think I've kinda let you down over the last few weeks since the fire."

"Never," Torie excused, knowing that Pam had never been hit by feelings for a guy like she had with Dev.

"Nah, don't say that." She heard Pam rustling around, walking through her house. "I haven't done this before. Leaving you high and dry to manage all this."

"No one can manage it for me," Torie said. Perhaps it was all the more painful that she'd begun to feel like Paul was there for her. Standing with her in her hour of need. Again.

She'd mistaken his lawyer duties for caring. She'd reached out in her own need for comfort, and had messed them both up by stepping over the line and making it personal, sexual.

She said as much to Pam who listened to the philosophy and the reasoning and said, simply, "Bullshit."

"What?"

"Look, it takes two to tango. If he felt nothing but a hard-on, as a lawyer, he'd back off. He's too smart to think with his dick. He wanted you as bad as you wanted him, right? No holds barred?"

Thinking of the wild, reckless nature of their lovemaking, Torie agreed. Not that she really wanted to. It was easier to put him back in his old box, the "I dislike Paul" box. If she could pretend he had only been in it for sex, it would be easier to go back to loathing him.

And she desperately needed that distance, that distaste as armor for her heart.

"So, tell me," Pam said. "How long have you had a thing for him?"

"What?" Torie jerked the phone away from her ear, stared at it as if the words were printed on its tiny screen. "Are you kidding?"

Chapter Fifteen

"Credit score, seven-eighty; reason for relocation, fire; size property, two to three bedroom; pet, yes." The realtor talked to himself as he entered all the information into the computer. Pam had picked Torie up in the morning because Tibbet had rescheduled.

The drive into the office with Paul had been tense, loaded with unspoken pain. Paul went to a meeting and Torie immediately called Pam. Within minutes they had been off to meet with Pam's realtor friend.

"So." Kuhman Parshaw swiveled around to smile at them both. "I have many things I can show you. Out toward where you are living now, I have several things. Near your unfortunate current house, I have several things, but they are moving toward the uh, streets that are having more difficulty keeping tenants. Society Hill has many rentals, but something nice in your neighborhood is," he paused, his pleasant, accented voice deepening with regret, "difficult. Most who own in that area sell rather than rent. So the rentals are farther out toward Queen's Village and . . ." Kuhman let his voice trail away.

Torie knew what he meant but couldn't say. Within blocks of her wonderful house, there were some less than desirable neighborhoods.

"However, when we check the areas you mentioned—" he rattled off the more suburban areas— "I came up with six for you to see today. One is even a listing of mine. Friends from my early days in Philadelphia. There will be more as I see what you like and don't like from this list." He stood, taking papers from the printer. "So, we'll go now, yes?"

"That's great." Pam bounced out of her seat and tugged Torie from hers. "Let's go. We need something to keep our minds off our woes," she said.

"Ah, yes. I know of your friend's troubles," he said to Pam, with a nod to Torie. "But you, dear flower, what possible trouble could be darkening your doorway?"

"Oh, it's just that a friend of mine is missing. He's probably fine, but, you know," Pam said, seeming to shrug it off.

"Ah, yes. A friend." He turned to Torie and grinned. "Pam is forever bringing me a friend. I am quite grateful to her, you know. And to you for coming by today. You have brightened a dreary morning."

Torie smiled in return. His boyish humor was infectious, crinkling his merry dark eyes and lined cheeks. Despite the fact that he was nearing sixty, he was handsome, his white hair and eyebrows a contrast to his warm brown skin tone. "I appreciate your willingness to help me," she said.

"We will be sure to get you something nice," Kuhman insisted. "Very cozy, very practical while you wait for your difficulties to mend themselves. We will make sure that even with the dog, you have a good place. Now, do you want to drive with me or follow me?"

"We're going to run errands when we're done, so we'll follow you." They also had to be sure the latest in the series of watchdogs knew which car to follow.

"Very good." He handed Torie a copy of the listing sheets, and they separated to their respective cars.

"This looks nice," Pam said, peering over her shoulder at the first house.

"Big," she commented. She didn't want to look for a place. Not today. Today she wanted to hide her head under the covers and feel sorry for herself.

She knew it was sheer cowardice, but it would have felt good. Even if it wasn't the right thing to do.

"What's up with all that sighing over there?" Pam said. "I'm the one who got tossed aside. You merely got shot at, oh, and had your house burned."

As Pam intended, she laughed. "Yeah, paltry stuff."

"So you gonna kick his ass some more?"

"No, I'm not going to speak to him if I don't have to."

"Mature reasoning," Pam offered, dodging out of the way as Torie punched her arm. "Totally. You can get another lawyer. Hey, do you need an attorney if the coppers say you're off the hook?"

"I don't know. There's still the will and stuff, which he says I have to be present for. And he's working with the police to tie all this together, see if it fits."

"Fits what? The looney profile? I can tell you now that it does."

Trust Pam to wrap it up so neatly. "Yeah. Well, I think we've got no call to throw stones at loonies. We were the ones out stealing a dog. Hell, we're still hiding him."

"About that—" Pam began.

"What? Bear didn't get loose again, did he?" Torie was anxious all over again thinking about it. "Do we need to go over there?"

"No, but Carlos's mama is coming from Chile. For the next few weeks, I'm helping him get his house fixed up so she doesn't catch him in all the lies he's told about what he's done around the place."

She said it so matter-of-factly that Torie sniggered. "And?"

"No dogs allowed. Between the number of workmen I'm gonna have in and out of there, and the noise? Bear will go nuts."

"I'll take him."

"What? Now who's nuts?" Pam pulled to the curb behind Kuhman and turned to face her. "The dog's enormous. He's huge, untrained, and potentially dangerous just because of his sheer mass. Not to mention that he looks incredibly scary with those bicolored eyes. Hell, he's got jaws like a hippo."

"Yeah? And?"

"You're nuts. You don't have a place to—" Pam started. "Sorry, but you don't."

"I have to have a pet-friendly place for Pickle as it is. What does it matter if it's one dog or two? I know what Bear is, and I know he's salvageable."

Pam rolled her eyes. "Please, Torie, be reasonable. Have you seen the size of that dog? Really? In daylight?"

"No, but I know what he is. About a hundred and thirty pounds of misunderstood mutt. He needs a home, I need him. End of story. I'll order a really big crate for him."

To end the discussion, she got out of the car. She

reminded herself not to look for her bodyguard. Focused on that, and on Pam, she hadn't looked at the house on the listing sheet other than to note that it was big.

"Oh," was all she could say. The house was neglected, that was obvious, but it had potential. "It's great."

"The fence is sagging, the gutters are full of crap, the grass is more like hay, and you say oooh?" Pam shook her head. "Maybe we should get your head examined."

"Come on," Torie said, ignoring the jibe. "Let's see inside."

"This is in an estate," Kuhman explained as he removed the key from a heavy lockbox on the front porch rail. "The family cannot decide what they are to do with it."

"It's—" Torie was about to gush and say it was great, but Pam's elbow hit her ribs and Pam gave a warning shake of her head. "In bad shape."

"Yes, yes, but it was a beauty at one point." Kuhman pointed out the details of the wood paneling, the inset brass diamonds in the floor tile.

Pam on the other hand, pointed out the drooping wallpaper, the foyer ceiling that canted slightly to the left, and the multitude of cracked window panes.

Torie let the two of them duke it out, since it was obvious they were enjoying their sparring. She wandered through the dining room, through a butler's pantry, and into a hideously outdated kitchen.

"Oh, Lord, look at this place. No, Torie, you couldn't possibly live here."

She looked at the gleam in Pam's eye and nearly laughed. Keeping to her role, though, she played along. Pam knew her well enough to know that she liked the house.

"It is pretty dilapidated. Especially this kitchen."

"It's right out of the nineteen thirties is what it is."

"No, no, the appliances are new." Kuhman pointed to a stainless steel dishwasher. It was so obviously new and out of place it was like a rocket ship on a sheep farm.

"One appliance," Pam insisted. "Only one. The refrigerator qualifies as an antique. Jeez, Kuhman. Torie's house burned, she's not gonna be bringing appliances with her, you know."

"Yes, yes, well maybe there will be some concessions from the owners. Come and see the rest of the house. They allow pets, you know. The old lady, she was fond of dogs, you see, and had several. They told me . . ." He rattled on about the old lady's chihuahuas as they walked on, but once again Torie lagged behind, checking out the living room with its built-in bookshelves. While Pam and Kuhman argued over the fence and the need for repairs, she mounted the worn and creaking stairs to the second floor.

Light flooded the upper hall, gilding the wooden banister, and highlighting more falling wallpaper. The dust was thick as could be, and the bedroom doors creaked like a movie prop house.

"Wow," Torie exclaimed, pushing open the door to the master bedroom. "Amazing."

The balcony, the light, the huge bathroom, and the massive cedar-lined walk-in closet closed the deal. She could live here.

"Torie?" Pam followed her in. "Oh, check that out." She, too, was captivated by the view of the huge backyard with its oaks and flower beds.

"Look at the closet," she whispered, not sure if Pam was still in her bargaining mode.

"You like it?" Pam whispered back.

"Tons."

"Don't tell him, okay? Let's be dismissive and see some of the others."

"I don't want—"

"I know," Pam said in a louder voice, presumably for Kuhman's hearing. "It's a lot of work, and you already have that to look forward to in your own house. Let's go."

They left Kuhman to lock up, moving on to the see five more of the listings he'd found. By one o'clock they'd exhausted themselves and Kuhman. Several of the houses would be great, but the first was what she wanted, warts and all.

"So, which pleases you? Any of them? Or should we start again?" Kuhman made his pitch.

"I liked the last one, and the first one on Bodia Drive. I like the first one a lot, but they'd have to cut the rent in half for the first six months. With half rent, I could get the place cleaned and painted for them," Torie said, frowning for form's sake.

"You don't want to get into that, do you?" Pam interjected. "I mean, I know I could help you find vendors and all that, painters, someone to do the kitchen, but you've got your own house to worry about."

"If you would consider it," Kuhman broke in, "I could talk to the owners. See if they would trade, ah, work on the house as exchange for rent, or perhaps a small fee to see to bringing it back to its glory, eh? They will sell it eventually." He shrugged, watching both of them for a reaction. "But the way it is?" He made a face. "Difficult in this market."

"Well, maybe if you checked with them?" Torie began, and Kuhman brightened.

"I will, I will. So I can reach you at this number?" He rattled off her cell phone number.

"So, how about lunch?" Pam said as they got back in the car. "We can talk about what you're gonna do with that house, and yours."

"I can't. I need to get back to Pratt and Legend. We're meeting with the detective."

"Oh. Well, dinner maybe?"

"Yeah, that's good. Would you do me a favor?"

"Sure.

"Isn't there a hotel over on Parson? A big one? Like a Marriott or something?"

"Yeah, I think so."

"Go get me a room, bring me the keys. I want to be out of Paul's house tonight."

"You sure?"

"Yeah." Torie had never been more sure. She'd realized sometime in the night that she had always been attracted to Paul, ever since they met under such terrible circumstances at the frat house. She suppressed a shudder. Thinking about that so much lately brought back all the fear, the feeling of being so out of control, without choices. It had been terrible. Every time she thought about it, the "what ifs?" of the whole scenario overwhelmed her with fear.

Fear that she'd transferred to Paul.

"You okay?"

"Yeah, thinking about all I have to do," Torie lied.

"Uh huh."

"Really. It's kinda frightening, you know? I'm crazy, too, to think about a house like that. Have you seen my house?"

Pam gave her a sympathetic look. "Yeah. I drove by right after it happened. It was a huge shock."

"Yeah." She might have said more, but her phone rang. "Excuse me."

"Ms. Hagen?"

"Yes?"

"Barbara at Pawlings Insurance?"

"Yes?"

"We've been notified by the police that your house has been released, and you can start work on it. If you'd like to pick up your preliminary check for expenses, I'll have it ready for you by the end of the day."

"Oh, thank you for letting me know. I'll be by. I'm going to look at a car later today. Has there been any change on that situation?"

"Oh, yes, I'm sorry. I can get a check for you on your car by tomorrow."

The memory of her car, a burned hulk, being towed away, made her shudder.

"Thank you for all your help."

Pam pulled up in front of Pratt and waited as she finished the call. "Insurance?"

"Yeah. Let's skip the rental. How do you feel about car shopping?"

"Love it."

"Good. Then once I'm done at Pratt, let's go visit the dogs, pick up some pizza, and go car shopping."

"Sounds like a plan. We'll talk about the house, too."

Paul and Melvin Pratt Sr. had finished up their morning meeting with more coffee. Paul was wired by the strong brew. Now, back in Pratt's office for the meeting with Torie and the detective, he poured more into his company mug.

"It seems as if the incidents are tied together. The fact that we all knew one another in college and grad school may tie in as well."

"Perhaps we should bring Melvin Jr. in to these discussions. He might be able to add something. He has quite a good memory for those kinds of details."

Paul managed to keep his voice level as he answered. "He might be very helpful. Why don't we meet with the detective and Ms. Hagen, then invite Melvin to join us."

Pratt watched him for an uncomfortable moment, but nodded. "Good. Let's see if either the detective or Ms. Hagen is here."

He buzzed his assistant, and was informed that the detective was waiting and Ms. Hagen was on her way up.

"Send in the detective, won't you?"

Tibbet came in, glancing around at the plush office. His face betrayed nothing of what he thought about all of the awards and photos of Mr. Pratt with various dignitaries.

"Detective, I'm Melvin Pratt Sr. I'm pleased to meet you. Thank you for agreeing to come to our offices rather than meeting at the station."

"Better coffee, sir," the detective quipped. "And better atmosphere."

Pratt laughed. "Indeed. So, please sit. We've been covering the details of the incidents Ms. Hagen wrote down and Mister Jameson remembers, and recorded from their friend, Mister Peterson."

"Your client."

"Yes. I've also discussed bringing my son, Melvin

Jr., into this discussion as well, once we've had a few minutes to reconnoiter."

"Ah, you want him to come in . . ." Tibbet trailed off.

"Mister Pratt Jr. was at college and grad school with all three of us," Paul said. "He was also a fraternity brother to Todd and me. His memory of events might be helpful." Paul was striving for neutrality. Tibbet glanced his way, but it didn't seem as if he'd given anything away.

"Ms. Hagen, sir," Pratt's assistant spoke from the door.

"Come in, please," Pratt said as the three men stood. Pratt directed her to a seat at his right, between himself and the detective.

Paul could see she hadn't slept. The circles under her eyes were carefully concealed, but since she wasn't big on makeup, the fact that she now wore more than usual clued him in. She avoided looking at him as she spoke to the others at the table.

"So, there is some good news," Tibbet began, setting the pace by starting right in. "We have a lead on what might have happened to your computer systems."

"Ah, do tell." Pratt looked satisfied.

"One of your former employees, a Taylor Caldwell, is being questioned in connection with the damage. He may have had an accomplice from the records department. According to your human resources folks, they were both, uh, terminated, on the same day."

"Do you think they're connected to Todd's death?" Torie asked.

"We're investigating both, but they're denying any knowledge of Mister Peterson. Our cybercrimes folks served warrants late this morning."

"I don't know either of them," Paul commented. "I

heard that a couple of people had been terminated in December. I'd never worked with either of them."

"I know. I don't have much call to be in the computer center myself, so I was unaware that these individuals had such animosity toward the firm over their dismissals." Pratt seemed disturbed that he hadn't been aware. "When the firm reached a certain size," he said, "you lose touch."

As he watched, Torie laid a hand on Pratt's arm. "It's difficult."

He smiled at her. "Yes, it is sometimes."

How could she be so empathetic to the old man, care so much for someone she didn't know? How had he managed to screw up so badly?"

"Paul?"

"I'm sorry, sir, I was thinking about the situation. What was your question?"

"I asked Ms. Hagen here if she'd be my date for the partner's dinner. She said you hadn't asked her yet, so I'm preempting you."

"Ah, I see." Paul was flabbergasted. He couldn't believe the old man had slipped that in.

Tibbet was struggling not to laugh. Paul wanted Torie there. Needed her there. He hadn't expected it to be this way.

"She still might dance with you, though," Pratt teased. He and Tibbet, along with Torie, laughed at that.

"Now," Pratt said more soberly, "we should get down to business. Detective, can you give us a written statement saying that Ms. Hagen has been cleared of any charges in connection with Mister Peterson's terrible death?"

"I believe I can do that. Yes."

"Excellent. If you'll get that to Mister Jameson here, it will help us move things along on our end." He motioned toward Paul. "He's got several things to wrap up."

"Detective," Torie broke into the conversation. "They've cleared my house as a crime scene, and I am going to begin work on getting things put back together. I'm hoping that my firm will get past the negative publicity the police caused by leaking the information about the men . . ."

Paul could see she was struggling to figure out how to phrase it that didn't sound terrible.

"Do you have any idea where the leak came from, Detective?" Paul asked. "I'm not saying that I think Ms. Hagen should act on that knowledge, but has the department locked that down?"

"Actually we believe it's connected to the cyber issues. The information wasn't leaked," Tibbet growled. "It was stolen."

"Stolen? How do you steal information from a police department?"

"The same way you do from anyone, Ms. Hagen," Tibbet answered. "You hack into their computers. Public resources don't really extend to hacker-proof software and fancy gadgets, I'm afraid."

"Ah, then our culprits may be guilty of more than destroying data here as well then."

Tibbet nodded. "Could be. We'll see. I wanted to talk with you further about the connections between you and Mister Peterson," he said, indicating Torie and Paul.

"Would you like me to bring my son in on these discussions?"

"Were you close in any way with Mister Pratt's son?" Tibbet asked Paul.

"No. We were in several classes together, pledged the same fraternity, but otherwise we didn't socialize."

"At the time, my son was going through a bit of a rebellious stage," Pratt Sr. broke in. "I believe you got to know one another somewhat in graduate school, didn't you?"

Paul tread very carefully. Technically, they hadn't known Melvin much at all. The invitation to interview with Pratt at Melvin's behest had come as a shock to both he and Todd.

"We did have several more classes together there," he temporized, stretching the truth only slightly.

Pratt took up the story, much to Paul's relief. "When Melvin graduated and passed the bar, he suggested we interview several of his classmates. His judgment there was superb." Pratt smiled at Paul. "The firm hired both Paul here, and Todd Peterson, from the group of six we interviewed."

"Ah, interesting. And did you see any reason to doubt them or their skills, given the rebellious stage you mentioned?"

"No, indeed. Their scores were impressive, their references good. They both worked hard and proved themselves up to the job. Then young Todd made his fortune and left us, of course."

Torie winced, but the old man didn't see it. He was in full storyteller mode. Paul shot her a sympathetic look. She turned away.

Ouch. He'd been given the brush-off a lot, by plenty of women, but it had never hurt more.

"So, that brings us to the present," Pratt wrapped up. Paul was lost in thought again, and had missed most of the speech. Damn.

"Ms. Hagen, from your perspective, how did this play?"

"Pretty much that way. I was more familiar with Todd's friends than anything else," she said. "I believe I met your son at some of the fraternity functions," she said to Pratt. "But he wasn't one to hang out at the fraternity house much at all. Ironically, I might have known him best in those days. He was in at least two of my engineering classes."

"Really? Electrical? Civil?" Tibbet asked.

"Structural and electrical."

"Ah. Interesting. So, Mister Pratt, do you have any reason to believe these two employees that were fired might want to hurt any of these people? So far we've found no connection to Mister Peterson. He was gone before the woman was hired."

"Not that I'm aware, Detective."

"Okay. Well, I don't think I'll need to speak to your son, but if I do, I'll call over, set something up. Ms. Hagen, I think the department will probably send you some kind of official apologies for the lapse in the computers, but I'll say it for them. It was inexcusable and, since it may jeopardize our case, it sucks. So, I'm damn sorry."

"Thanks, Detective. I appreciate it. I hope my bosses will, too."

"Yeah, that's not right. Jameson, you ought to fix that for her, for sure." He prodded the sore spot Paul was feeling. "Harassment and all."

"I'll follow my client's wishes on that one, but yes, she has a case."

"There you go. Haul 'em into court, Ms. Hagen. You're the victim here as far as I can see." He closed his notebook and rose. "Nah, keep your seats. I'll see myself out." He was almost to the door when he paused, looked back. "Ms. Hagen, did Mister Pratt Jr. ever ask you out?"

Everyone froze and looked at Torie. "Yes, he did. I was already dating Todd, so I declined."

"And later?"

Torie hesitated, and for the first time looked to Paul for guidance. Damn. He nodded.

"Yes, after Todd and I broke up, he asked me out several times."

"And?"

"I wasn't ready to date. I declined again."

"Interesting," Tibbet muttered, and walked out the door. A faint, "Thanks for the coffee, Mister Pratt," was his parting shot.

The detective had been to see Torie again. It was insulting. How dare the man get so close? And he'd heard from his little sources that they'd arrested that woman from records, as well as someone from the computer division at Pratt. Wasn't that an ass-kicker? The woman might—no, it wasn't her. She was too malleable, her tits were bigger than her brain. Besides, he knew where she had been.

But the other one. The techie. No wonder the files had dissolved into a puddle of nothingness. Between them, the morons had taken his careful tampering, his brilliant program, and turned it into a visible cancer, a blight.

He snarled. They had to be dealt with. If they told the police they *hadn't* tampered with the files, then his IPO might give him away. Someone might remember him.

Not good.

To add to that insult, Paul Jameson was still walking. His shot had missed, and he'd nearly been caught. His heart still raced at the thought of the shouts, the lights, as the police revealed their presence.

He'd been watching so intently for the departure of the bodyguard, he'd missed the fucking cops.

But Luck had saved him. She was finally on his side.

He swung the gimbaled chair from side to side, listening to the air swish. It mesmerized him for a moment, breaking the spell the anger had built.

He took a deep breath, let it out. He had to plan, shift his priorities. The two idiots who'd damaged the systems at Pratt needed to go.

Then, he'd get back to Paul, and then, to Torie.

Ah, Torie.

Chapter Sixteen

"I'm not going."

"You are if I have to dope you and drop you off," Pam insisted later when Torie told her of the new development.

"I don't think he meant it, Pammie. He's a lonely old man."

"Oh, add influential, rich, and interesting." She paused, fork buried in salad. "Please tell me he's at least interesting."

"Of course, and he's older than my father would have been."

"Not bad, really."

"It's not a date, Pam."

Pam rolled her eyes. "The salad, you goose. It's not bad, as in pretty good, which means you should eat the chicken in it, instead of tossing it around with your fork. Besides, you need the protein—we've got shopping to do."

Torie grinned at her enthusiasm, but resolved not to be steamrollered. She would not be going to the partner's dinner as Mr. Pratt's date.

"Now, it's already settled," Pam continued. "You need to party, girlfriend. You need to get out, forget about all this mayhem stuff, and get drunk. You've got cab fare and a new hotel room, okay? All you need is a dress. That we can fix. Miss Pam, she has her ways." Wiggling her eyebrows, she continued to eat. Before Torie could protest once again, she changed the subject. Typical Pam tactics.

"So, let's talk cars. Big or little?"

"Medium"

"SUV or sedan?"

"SUV, I guess, or something like the small Jeep. What do they call it? The Liberty?"

"Well, we are in the home of liberty, so that fits," Pam joked. "Regular or hybrid?"

"Hybrid, if we can get one that's cool."

"Cool."

"Yeah, and big enough to handle the dogs."

"You *sure* you want to take on that mammoth masquerading as a dog?"

Torie grinned, felt her heart lighten at the thought of Bear. "Yeah. Maybe I'll change his name to Woolly Mammoth, or Woolly for short."

"Ha! That's good. So, we'll hit car shops and talk about the house, okay?"

"About that . . ." Torie pulled out her notebook, flipped pages, and handed it to Pam.

"Damn, girl," was all Pam said as she began reading.

They talked about the house as they finished lunch. Torie had decided it was time for a complete life change. She was going to fix her house, but the more she thought about the rental in Darby, the more she thought she might buy it.

Once she fixed her current house, it would sell

easily. Society Hill was a favorite of young married yuppies and professional singles alike. With two dogs, she needed a yard like the first one on Bodia.

By six, she called a halt to the car shopping. They'd been to five dealerships, in between stopping to see Carlos and making a trip to the vet to visit the fast-recovering Pickle.

"I surrender," she said, pretending to wave a flag. "Pam, I'm dying here. I have to have food."

"Just one more. I wanna drive the Mercedes SUV. The shorter one."

"Who's buying this car, you or me?"

"You, but I'm the one having the fun here, I can tell," Pam teased.

Her phone rang and she jumped, snatching it up to look at the caller ID. Her face betrayed the answer. It wasn't Dev.

"Hey," Pam answered with none of her usual bounce. "Got it, thanks!"

"No word then?"

"None." Pam's bright façade fell and Torie saw the hurt, worried woman underneath. "That was just a vendor."

"Hey," she murmured. "He's smart and strong. He'll be back."

"Did you call his, I mean your, grandmother?"

"Great-grandmother, but yeah. I called."

"And?"

"Nothing. I got the machine."

"Oh."

Into the silence, Torie's phone rang. She, too, looked at the caller ID, but not with Pam's enthusiasm. "Paul."

"I'm right here for you, babe. Go for it."

"Hello, Paul."

She closed her eyes and listened as he asked where she was, when she'd be back, what she was doing. As if he really cared.

"I'll be back to pick up my things. Is eight o'clock convenient?"

Pam snorted a laugh at her formal tone. Torie shushed her, trying to listen.

"Torie, I don't know how I can ever apologize enough. I'd . . . I'd like it if you continued to stay here. I want to know you're safe. I'd be, well, devastated if something happened to you."

"Devastated? That's interesting. Wow." She put a note of derision in her answer. "Somehow I don't feel welcome anymore, Paul. I'll pick up my things. Pam's booked me a room at the Marriott."

"Which one?"

She told him and could hear him fumble for a pencil to jot it down. "I left a pen on the counter by the fridge."

"Thanks."

"No problem."

"Do you know the room number yet?"

"No."

He sighed, and sounded sad, tired. "I'll be here, Torie. Waiting for you. I'll do whatever I can to help."

When she hung up, she didn't know what to say.

"That was long and involved." Pam's neutral comment puzzled her more. After all these years, she was far more used to Pam dishing dirt on Paul, and heaping coals on the fire of Torie's peevishness with him. Instead, she was silent.

"Yeah. He's full of apologies." It puzzled her.

"You gonna forgive him?"

Torie couldn't believe her ears. "What? After what he said? Jeez, Pam, he practically called me a whore."

"But he didn't, did he?"

"No."

"Never mind," Pam said in one of her lightning changes of subject. "Let's go shopping."

"I'm not getting a dress."

"Yes, you are. If nothing else, you'll need it for the Spring Fling for the Chamber, and you literally have nothing you can wear. So shut up and let's shop."

By the time they got to Paul's house, a little after eight, they'd found four dresses. Pam had insisted she buy all four, take them back to the hotel, and think about them.

"All right, all right. I'll do it," she said, finally giving in.

"Good. That black dress will be perfect with the shoes we bought." She grinned at Torie. "I like being your personal shopper."

"Yeah. Well, you gotta help me the way you're helping Carlos. Hopefully, I'll be able to go back to work on Monday, which means I'll have less time to get both houses up and running."

"I should start charging for this," Pam said, joking. "Help people manage all this kind of stuff."

"Yeah, you should," Torie said, totally serious. "You'd be perfect at it."

They rang the bell and Paul answered immediately, hurrying them inside.

"You don't want to be standing out on the porch when someone's trying to shoot you."

"Oh. No. I guess not." Now that she was with him again, in his house, she didn't know what to do with herself. "I'll get my things."

"Let me help you," Paul offered.

"That's okay."

He followed her anyway, after telling Pam to make herself at home.

"I know you need to do this, Torie. I don't blame you."

"Blame me? I should hope not." Torie struggled to find the anger and hurt she'd felt the night before. Instead, she found nothing. She smoothed the covers on the bed, thinking briefly about their incredible lovemaking.

"Torie?"

"I need to get out of here," she mumbled.

"You didn't really get a chance to unpack."

She busied herself tossing the few things she'd set out into the suitcases, stacking the cases together to roll them out.

"Please," he said, blocking her path.

When she looked up at him, his eyes were dark, unfathomable. "Please," he repeated. "Don't do this because I was stupid. I know sorry doesn't cut it, as you said. I blew it. But don't put yourself in the line of fire, Torie. Please."

Damn the man. Why did he have to sound so sincere? So worried about her. Not about his reputation, not about the police, but about her.

If you'd have asked her a month ago who would stand by her, Tristan or Paul, she would have said Tristan. How wrong she'd have been.

"I need to do this, Paul. I've been reeling since Todd was killed. I've let myself be blown from here to there by everything that's happened. I have to find my center, find me again." And why the hell was she explaining it to him?

Because he'd stood by her.

Because he'd apologized.

Because he was so obviously miserable.

She ignored the little voice in her head and put her hand on his outstretched arm, the one blocking the way.

"I need to go."

He moved aside and let her roll the suitcases past.

"Torie?"

"Yes?"

"Will you dance with me?"

"He asked you to dance?"

"Yeah."

"What the hell does that mean?" Pam demanded as they rolled her luggage to the room.

"I guess it means he wants to dance with me at the partner's dinner."

"Duh, yeah. But what else does it mean?"

"For heaven's sake, Pam, I have no idea. I mean, he's all sexy and serious, and he's asking me to save him a dance. How the hell . . ." She caught sight of Pam's face. "What?"

"You said he was sexy," she said, sounding stunned.

"So?" It took Torie three tries to get the door open.

"So," Pam said, shutting the door behind them, going to hang the dresses. "I've never heard you call him sexy before."

"Cripes, Pam, I slept with him."

"I know, but you didn't say it was good. You didn't call him sexy, you didn't say anything about it."

"Well, it's not like I go around detailing my love life."

"Ha!" Pam laughed. "Like you have one. So, I got a question for ya . . ."

"Open those Cokes and pour me one before you start asking your probing questions."

"'kay."

"What's the question?"

"'Do ya love him, Loretta?'"

The movie line, from *Moonstruck*, had never failed to make her laugh. This time, however, it hit Torie like a fist to the solar plexus. She sat down on the coffee table, feeling as if the wind had escaped her and she couldn't draw breath.

"Torie? Torie?" Pam hurried over, crouched down. "What is it?"

"Oh, my God, Pammie," she managed. She felt like she'd been socked in the gut.

When Paul's phone rang, he ignored it the first time. Then thinking it might be Torie, he raced to get it. Sometime in the night, and throughout the day he'd realized the impossible. The improbable.

Not only was he in love with Torie, he had been since his sophomore year in college.

No wonder he had indigestion.

When he checked the caller ID, it was Tibbet.

"Hey, you called?"

"Yeah. We're watching your house. Thought you should know."

"Thanks. Torie's not here."

"What? Where is she?"

Paul hesitated. "If you don't mind, I think I'll text that to you. Try and keep it private. There's someone on watch for her, too."

Tibbet grunted. "Yeah. I get it."

"So, what now?"

"Nothing. Go on to bed, get up, go to work, just like the rest of us slobs," he said, and Paul could hear the ironic twist in his voice. "But if you hear anything, don't be a hero, okay? Call nine-one-one. Call me. You got it?"

"Got it."

"Hey."

"Yeah?"

"What's up with you and Pratt Jr.?"

"We've never liked each other. Even in college. We used to call him Weaselboy because he always acted like one."

"What do you mean?"

"Off the record?"

"Off."

"He was a slinky, sneaky, slimy snitch."

"Tell me how you really feel," Tibbet drawled, making Paul laugh. "He's got Pratt Sr. fooled."

"I don't think so. Senior's not easily fooled, even by his kith and kin. Melvin's not that sly as to fool the old man."

"You'd be surprised how blind a father can be," Tibbet said, adding, "especially when it comes to the eldest son."

"Only son, at that."

"All the more reason."

"So how'd you end up in his good book so much that he pimped you and your buddy to his daddy's firm?"

"No idea, and that still puzzles me. Neither Todd nor I saw that coming, I can tell you. We took Melvin out, thanked him with a nice dinner and all, but it was never comfortable. I think the bottle of Scotch Todd bought him is still sitting in his office on the credenza."

"Really?" He could hear Tibbet scratching notes. "Waste of good Scotch."

"Yeah."

"Okay. I gotta get home. Remember, call. I don't care if you think it's only a mouse farting, if it's out of place, lock the damn bedroom door and call."

"Got it, loud and clear."

He would call because he had something for which to live. He had Torie. He was going to do whatever it took to find her forgiveness.

For the first time, he understood Todd's obsession with making it up to Torie. The difference was, Todd had felt that he'd somehow let a friend down, embarrassed her.

From the vantage point of love—dear God, that was hard to admit, even to himself—he could see that Todd wanted to ease a friend's pain. On the other hand, Paul wanted to win her back, and he didn't give a damn about the short term. He wanted forever. He wanted a chance to be with her, hear her laugh. Have another dinner out. Or in.

It wouldn't matter if it was burgers and fries, or the finest steak and wine. He just wanted it to be with her.

"Christ Almighty, I'm getting sappy talking to myself," he complained aloud.

It was true, though.

Tomorrow he would plan. He would figure out a way.

He'd loved her too long to let her go without a fight.

He turned off the lights in the living room, but sat

down at the kitchen table with his laptop. There was one thing he could do now.

Within minutes, he'd ordered the flowers to be sent. They would be delivered to Torie's room first thing in the morning. The card would have only four words.

"Save me a dance."

That done, he shut down the laptop and turned out the lights. He turned off the porch light, but the other light, the one in his bedroom, he turned on.

That was nearly his death sentence.

He was walking to shut the drapes when he saw a glint of something directly across the street, where the neighborhood kids' playground was located. Someone moving.

Something different, Tibbet said.

As he dove for the phone, the glass shattered.

A whoop of a siren made him wince, and he heard engines revving outside as they tore off toward the park.

He dialed Tibbet.

"What?"

"Your guys hit the sirens." He couldn't help the shake in his voice. "Someone just put a shot through my bedroom window."

"Damn, I was right. Marsden owes me twenty bucks." Paul heard the sound of rustling clothes. "I'll be there in fifteen minutes. Sit tight."

"Okay if I do that on the floor?"

Tibbet laughed and cut off the call. Paul heard the doorbell, and shakily got to his feet to answer it.

By the time Tibbett arrived, the crime scene tech had dug the bullet out of the trim around his closet door and left. Paul was sweeping up the glass, wondering if he had any plastic or a board in his shed to cover the gaping window.

"Hey," Tibbet whistled from the doorway. "Nice room."

"Ha, ha," Paul faked a laugh. "Hand me that garbage can."

Tibbet brought the can and held it as Paul tossed the last load of glass into it.

"So what was the bet?"

"I said the crazy would go for you again. Get you out of the way so your girl was left unprotected."

He let the "your girl" part slide by him. He hoped he could make it true.

"Yeah, so Marsden thought he'd go for Torie again? We both have someone watching her, right?"

"Yep, sitting in the lobby as we speak."

"Great," he said, and meant it. "Mine, too."

Another officer came down the hall and spoke to Tibbet. "No luck, Detective. No casing, no nothing."

"Smart bastard," Tibbet muttered. "Too smart. He's getting predictable. Pushing the time limit. He hardly gave it a day between shooting twice at you. That's what we call an escalating tendency to violence."

"Focused on me."

"Right now."

"Nice. But better me than Torie."

"Yeah, thought you'd see it that way. So," Tibbet paused, eyeing him, "were you schtupping the bride before the wedding? Is that why Peterson called it off?"

Paul stared for a moment. "Hell, no," he protested. "She didn't like me at all."

"I'm not so sure about that. Why was she so hell-bent on keeping you away?"

"Because she didn't like me."

"Didn't. Past tense, right? So, you had this thing for her for a long time? Did your friend know?"

"What? No."

"Look," Tibbet said, putting his notebook away. "Let's talk here, off the record, as you're so fond of sayin'. What's more important, your pride or her safety?"

"Her safety, of course."

"Then spill it."

"Torie and I have a history."

"No shit, Sherlock," Tibbet snorted. "You've known her longer'n most people have known their wives. Just tell me what happened."

"There was a fraternity party . . ." Paul started the story, and found he had to sit down to tell it. His knees were shaking. "We were all drinking, but Torie doesn't drink that much. So suddenly she disappears."

"You two were dating at that point?"

"Huh? Oh, no. I was interested in her, though. One of the senior brothers had invited her to the party, but he was off smoking a—" Paul grinned, realizing he was talking to a cop—"cigarette."

"I'll bet. So?"

"So I was watching to see if I could talk to her. I wanted to ask her out. But she was gone. When she didn't come back in a few minutes, and her date was feeling no pain with a bunch of the guys on the deck, I went looking for her."

"Altruistic of you," Tibbet drawled.

"Not really, though she thinks it's real white knight kind of stuff. I had a vested interest. So, I go upstairs, I ask around. Somebody tells me one of the brothers helped her upstairs, and that she wasn't feeling too well."

"I take it that didn't sit right with you."

"No. The frat was already on probation for violating policies about people sleeping over, and I knew she wasn't with anyone."

"Not a party girl?"

"No. Not that way. She enjoyed a party, but I'd never heard of her going for the wilder stuff. Anyway," Paul said, remembering all too vividly how he'd found her, "I found her in an unused room, tied to the bed, naked and drugged. In the space of fifteen minutes, she'd gone from nursing one beer—to that. Whoever did it worked fast."

"Not Todd then."

"No, not his style. Besides, he was singing karaoke in the dining room with four of the other guys."

"You didn't tell him?"

"No, neither of us were dating her at the time, so it didn't occur to me to tell him. I got her untied and dressed, and took her to my room. Stuck my finger down her throat and got her to throw up whatever shit they gave her." The memory of her quaking body, miserable and shaking, nearly made him sick. "She refused to go to the health center, and I was too dumb and scared to insist. She was sick for an hour. I got her a washcloth, helped her get cleaned up. Later, I sneaked her out of the house and got her back to her dorm. When I checked on her the next day, she said she was okay and only wanted to forget it."

"Did she?"

"Yeah, I think she did, but she never came to another party. I asked her out."

"Did she go?"

"Yeah, we had one date. It got hot and heavy, then I said something stupid, something about the birth-mark she has on her back, and broke the mood. She accused me of only asking her out because I thought she was some kind of kinky tramp. I denied it, and we went at it for a bit at the top of our lungs. We both calmed down and apologized, but it was our only date."

Paul realized now, so late in the game, that he had pushed her away. He'd been so worried about her, but then to have her be so passionate, so sexy, so strong and stable, in spite of the near-rape at the party, had blown his mind. Scared the hell out of him.

"That was a bonehead move, man."

"Tell me," Paul said. "I'm still paying for it eleven years later."

"Real bonehead. So when'd she hook up with Peterson?"

"Couple of months later at a dance. He asked me what I thought of her, and I told him I thought she was great. He beamed and agreed." Paul could still see Todd's happy grin. He had been delighted that elegant Torie Hagen had decided to go out with him. Paul had been stricken. If Todd, with his upper-class ways won Torie, he, Paul would never have a chance.

"You ever tell him you dated her?"

"Yeah, but I told him there wasn't any chemistry."

"So you lied," Tibbet said blandly.

Paul looked him in the eye and with a straight face, answered. "Like a damn dog."

"You have a list of the brothers who were at this party?"

"No. It was eleven years ago."

Tibbet watched him, then cocked his head. "Seems

to me, Mister Off the Record, that you track shit. You watch. Bide your time. Now, if you weren't the one gettin' shot at, I might be looking at you for this. You've got the patience for it." His smile was feral when he turned it Paul's way. When Paul didn't react, he smiled more fully. "Whatever this is, whoever's doing it, it's about real deep anger, backed by a lot of patient planning. This shot tonight was panic. Stupid. He's covered his tracks, but he got rash. He thought we'd follow Torie. Stick only to her."

"Mistake."

"Big one. But back to you. You store information away, keep lists. You kept lists of the incidents that happened to your buddy and client, Peterson, although your buddy blew them off as chance or coincidence."

"Yeah, I did."

"So, this is a woman you have had a thing for. For eleven years. I'm betting you kept a list of all the guys that were there that night. Who it might have been. Who it wasn't. I need that list."

For several minutes, the silence hung between them. They faced off like two stallions, circling one another, deciding whether or not to leap for each other's throats.

Finally Paul dropped his gaze. "I'll dig it out."

Chapter Seventeen

"So, what's on the docket for today?" Pam asked as they drove back toward the dealership.

"Buy the Chrysler, and talk to Kuhman again about the house."

"You want me to come with you?"

Torie looked at her friend. "You'd play hooky again today?"

Pam smiled. "Yeah. I feel like I've neglected you during all this. I got involved with Dev, who turned out to be the great disappearing jerk, and left my best friend in the world to dangle on her own when her house burned down."

Torie scoffed. "You didn't leave me to dangle, Pammie. I was okay until somebody started shooting at me."

"Yeah, so okay that you retreated to North Carolina again?"

"Hey," Torie protested. "I like North Carolina."

"So do I, but you go there to hide. I shouldn't have let you go alone."

"Pam, don't beat yourself up over this. Besides,"

Torie added, "I wouldn't have let you come. I needed the brooding time. I had a lot to think about."

"Seems like you've been doing more thinking lately than you have in a while."

"Since the wedding. You know what?"

"What?"

"I think I've been waiting, all this time, for him to come back."

"What? That's crazy, you have not. He *did* come back, remember, asked you a bunch of times to reconsider, get married."

"I don't mean literally."

"Oh," Pam rolled her eyes. "This is the deep soul-searching stuff."

"Don't knock it. It's the only way I change. You know that."

Pam smiled, despite her grousing. "I know, honey. So what did you learn on the beach?"

"That I was waiting. Waiting to do stuff. Waiting to move, to get out of what had been our house. Waiting to figure out if I still liked working for TruStructure."

"What the hell were you waiting *for?*"

Torie shook her head, mildly disgusted at her realizations. "I don't know. Now that I see that, I feel like I've wasted so much time. I didn't want Todd to come back, but I sure didn't move on with my life, did I?"

"Well, kind of. You dated a lot."

"That turned out so well for everyone involved." Torie shuddered as she said it. "But I wasn't really looking, you know? I wasn't dating people who could have been, well, you know, possible husbands or anything. I dated random people who happened to ask."

"Nothing wrong with that," Pam said, a bit defensively.

"No, there isn't as long as you know it, but I kept telling myself and you, too, that I was looking for Mister Right."

"True. And all of them were Mister Wrong, not to mention Mister Wrong Side of the Tracks."

"Yeah, him, too." Torie laughed, remembering the one date she'd had with a bartender. "You know, I don't think anything ever happened to him. I should tell Tibbet."

"Make a note, but let's do the fun stuff first."

"Sounds like a plan."

For the first time in years, maybe ever, Torie felt free. She was buying a car she liked, to haul around dogs she really wanted. She was going to forget practicality and rent a house that needed massive work while she was simultaneously trying to rebuild her own house. She was, in the deepest darkest places of her mind, considering opening her own business. Given the way TruStructure had treated her when the press was hounding her, she wasn't sure she could go back. If she did, she wasn't sure she wanted to stay.

She hadn't had the courage to tell Pam about the business thing yet. It was too new an idea.

Not to Paul, her subconscious whispered. *He suggested it, supported it. Told you to go for it.*

"Fuck Paul," she muttered.

Unfortunately, Pam heard her.

"What did you say? Did I just hear you use the f-word *again*? What is this, twice in a week? Lord, you've gone years between breaking bad and cussing like that, and now you're driven to fuck twice in one week?"

Torie couldn't help it. The opening for the joke was there, and she took it.

"I only fucked him once, thank you very much."

Pam goggled at her. Then giggled. Then laughed.

Before she knew it, the two of them were laughing hysterically, to the point of tears. Several of the salespeople had looked out of the dealership and seen them, but neither she nor Pam could stop.

"Don't look at me," Pam said, still snickering. She deliberately looked out the driver's side window, up at the sky. "Don't look at me. I'll never stop if you keep looking at me."

"I'm not looking at you," Torie protested, wiping her eyes. She flipped the mirror down from the visor to check her makeup. "Jeez, I haven't laughed like that in—" she stopped to think and couldn't remember a time—"forever."

Pam was taking deep breaths, and Torie started to giggle again. "You look like a dying fish with all that heaving."

"Fish don't have great boobs to heave," Pam said, bursting into laughter again.

They finally got themselves under control. "I needed that," Pam said, checking her own makeup. "Lord knows, you did, too."

"Yeah. So let's go buy a car."

"Wonder if they think we're lesbians?"

The question sent them off into fresh gales of laughter. By the time they finished the paperwork on the car and handed the check over, the salesman was laughing, too. He promised the car would be ready by the weekend.

"Thanks, Pete," Torie said as they shook hands. "I'll look forward to picking it up."

"You're welcome. It was a pleasure." He smiled at her, and held her hand longer than necessary. He also smiled at Pam, telling her he was available whenever she wanted a new car.

"Or anything else," Pam said, still giggling as they got into her car. "Men are so obvious."

"He was, that's for sure."

"They all are, but you're finally noticing it. How do you think I get all that stuff done? I know the signs, and use them to my advantage."

Thinking about all the vibes Pete the car salesman had been sending, Torie nodded. She hadn't paid much attention to it before.

"I guess it's time to start noticing that kind of thing."

"You'll get a lot more done," Pam joked. "And you're gonna need it with all you're taking on. How are you going to do it once you go back to work?"

Torie took a deep breath, and said the words out loud for the first time. "I'm not sure I'm going back."

Horns honked and there was a brief screech of tires as Pam swerved the car, staring at Torie. "What did you say?"

"I have a lot saved, thanks to Todd. I, uh, think maybe I won't go back." It sounded weak, even to her ears, so she tried again. More firmly she said, "They treated me badly, Pammie. I think I might go out on my own."

"You're kidding? Finally?"

Stung, Torie pouted. "What do you mean, finally? TruStructure has been good to me."

"They've sucked off all your ideas, you mean. Any big project has had your stamp on it, whether your name was on it or not. It's about time you hoisted your own flag, and flipped those guys the bird."

Torie laughed at the thought of a flag with a middle

finger raised in salute, flapping over TruStructure's building. That would be fun. She told Pam, which set them laughing again.

"You're killing me here, girl," Pam said, still chuckling. "We're going to have to run by my house, repair makeup."

"Lunch first," Torie said. "I'm starving."

"Okay. We'll call Kuhman while we wait for our food."

The lunch turned into a business meeting. Borrowing paper from the manager, they outlined a business plan for Torie's new venture. Using another four or five pages, they wrote down more ideas they'd had for the houses.

"That upper bedroom, the big one that isn't the master," Pam said, "that would make an awesome office. That balcony would be really cool to enjoy while you're working."

Torie could see it taking shape. All of it, ultimately, due to Todd's generosity.

As if the thought had summoned him, Torie's phone rang. It was Paul.

"Good morning," she greeted him warmly, and Pam's eyebrows rose.

Paul seemed taken by surprise as well. "Uh, it's afternoon, but thanks."

"You're welcome. What's up?"

"Tibbet would like to meet with you. Do you want to go to the station, or meet him here?"

"Your office would be better, if that's okay."

"Does three-thirty work?"

"That's fine."

Paul sounded totally nonplussed as she confirmed

the time, wished him a good afternoon, and told him good-bye.

"Mending fences?"

"Trying it your way."

Pam smiled. "My way's not always so hot. Hasn't been working for me in the last few days."

"Give it time," Torie said, then reached out to press Pam's arm in sympathy. "Still no word?"

"No. I called his office. He called in, asked for vacation they said."

"So he's not missing."

Pam shook her head, visibly fighting tears. "No. Just missing from my life." With a shake of her shoulders, she tossed her hair back and smiled. It was patently fake, but she smiled. "I've gotten the message. It had to happen at some point, I guess."

"What are you talking about?"

"Getting dumped. Now I know what it feels like," she added. "So now I know better. I'll do my own dumping differently."

"Uh huh," Torie said, fairly sure that would never happen. "Either way, I think he'll be back. And he'll have an explanation."

"Yeah, but it didn't matter enough for him to tell me what this was about before he took off. Which means I don't matter, you see?"

"Maybe." It was Torie's turn to waffle on the answer.

Before they could discuss it further, Kuhman joined them at the table.

"Ah, so wonderful to have the company of two such lovely ladies," he said with a slight bow for them both. "I hate to tarnish it with business, but such is life, eh?"

Torie enjoyed the theatrics, and let Pam and Kuhman

battle it out as they haggled over what she could and couldn't do to the house, and what the owners would and wouldn't pay for.

"I want an option to buy at current market price built into the rental agreement," Torie interjected.

Kuhman paused, eyebrows raised, then laughed. "Ah, Pam, my dear, your friend is shrewd. I will include it. I'll put together some current comparables, and we will agree on fair market value, yes?"

Torie winked at him, surprising him. "Taking into account the current state of the property."

"Very good," Kuhman said, smiling. Turning to Pam, he added, "Very, very shrewd, your friend."

Back at the hotel, she surveyed her meager wardrobe. Tomorrow, shopping.

"I guess I should say more shopping," she said, flipping the hangers of the gorgeous dresses she'd been coerced to buy. With them sitting in the closet, she had resigned herself to going to the partner's dinner. "God, I'm tired of shopping."

The lease for the house caught her eye. That was going to be shopping she'd enjoy. Furniture. Wallpaper. It would be a blast to work with Pam to set both houses back to their glory.

Things would change for the better.

It went right along with the other changes she was feeling. It was as if she'd been ill for a long time, and was finally feeling better, returning to health and energy. She felt like she had a new lease on life.

The phone rang before she could think anymore about the dinner.

"Hello?" It was the front desk. They had flowers for her.

"Would you like us to send a bellman up with them?"

"Yes, please." Who would be sending her flowers? Her firm? They'd sent the ones in the hospital, but those had been destroyed at the Extended Suites, after the car fire. She grimaced at the thought. So much had happened in the span of a few short weeks.

"A month now," she counted aloud. "More than a month."

A knock at the door stopped her musings.

The flowers were gorgeous. She tipped the boy, and carried them to the desk. "Wow," she said, burying her face in the roses. They actually had a scent, which was unusual for hot house roses. "Beautiful," she breathed. Taking up the card, she ripped it open.

Save me a dance.

"Paul." She breathed his name. A rush of . . . something, some feeling poured through her. It had been a long time since anyone had sent her flowers, simply because.

She thought of his apology, so heartfelt. Of his concern, his time and energy over the last few weeks. When had they shifted from dislike to . . . something else? Dare she call it love? On her part, anyway.

He felt something, too, though. That she knew.

With a light heart, she dressed and caught a cab to his office for the three-thirty meeting with Tibbet. Once Martha had showed her in, she waited until the door closed before she walked toward the desk.

Paul set the phone down, finishing a call. Without

pausing at the chairs, she walked around the desk. It was a little awkward, but it felt right, so she leaned down to kiss him on the mouth.

She wanted it to be a token of appreciation, a thank you. More intimate, perhaps, than the words, but no more than a happy acknowledgment of his kindness.

Within seconds, it turned into far more.

"Torie," he murmured, sliding his hands into her hair and bringing her close. Without letting go, he stood and took her mouth in a searing kiss that rocked her to her shoes. "I missed you," he said, breaking the kiss long enough to utter the words before diving back in, firing her senses with passionate kisses.

Striving for balance, she gripped his waist, swayed toward him. Just as their bodies met, the phone on the desk buzzed.

They whipped apart as if they'd been shocked.

"Jesus," Paul gasped, nearly falling into his chair. He took a deep breath and pressed the button. "Yes?"

To Torie he sounded breathless, impatient.

"Sorry to disturb you, but Detective Tibbet is on his way up."

"Thank you." Paul was curt, and cut her off. Torie had moved to the other side of the desk, putting distance between them. Paul wasn't interested in distance. He came around to stand in front of her, pull her to her feet.

"What was that?" He didn't wait for her to speak. "Never mind. Come here." He wrapped his arms around her, tucking her under his chin and holding on as if she were a lifeline and he a drowning man.

"Are you okay?" she managed to say, her face muffled into his shirt.

"No," he said, and she could hear the unsteady beat of his heart. "Yes."

"Which is it?" she asked, smiling. It felt good to be in his arms. There were things they had to talk about, but for the moment, it felt exactly right.

"Do you forgive me?"

"I think so. Maybe."

"Then it's both."

"That's a good lawyerlike answer," she said with a lighter heart.

He laughed, and she felt as well as heard the rumble of it.

"Tibbet's probably here." She pulled back, looked at his face. "You have lipstick on your cheek."

"Do I?" he said softly, gazing into her eyes. "I'll have to do something about that." He made no move to let her go.

"Thank you for the flowers."

"Ah, is that what the kiss was for?"

She nodded, adding, "It was supposed to be a friendly gesture."

"Back to the Truce-with-Torie?"

She nodded, unable to read the intense look in his dark eyes.

"Good. We'll talk about that. In the meantime," he said, lowering his head and pressing his lips to hers in a clinging, gentle touch. "We should talk about the past."

Her senses were so fired up, so mixed up, she nearly missed what he'd said.

"What? The past?"

Paul closed his eyes. When he opened them, he looked sober, and Torie could see the traces of a sleepless night in his pallor.

"What is it Paul? What happened?" She put her hands on his face, keeping his gaze on hers, forcing him to face her.

"I had a visitor last night," he said, letting her go when she began to struggle in his grasp.

"What do you mean? What kind of visitor?"

Paul took her hand, led her to where a counter held a coffee area and several bottles of water. Handing her a bottle and several napkins, he said, "You wore the lipstick. Help me get it off, will you?"

He wouldn't say anything until she'd completed the task. It surprised her slightly when he took the damp cloth and dabbed at her cheek. "I transferred some right back to you, it appears," he said, smiling. The smile was warm, open. Different.

The way he was looking at her made her want to shiver. It was as if he were looking through her, seeing something no one else saw. It scared her.

"You said the past. And that you had a visitor. What's going on?"

He led her back to the chairs and they sat down. He continued to hold her hand. "Tibbet decided that perhaps your stalker would come after me. Since the mystery shooter tried for me once, and failed, he decided to stake out my place, lie in wait."

"Tibbet?"

"Not personally, but when shots were fired, he was on scene pretty quick."

"You were shot at?" Torie squeaked. "Again? Last night?" Oh, my God. Would it never end?

"Yeah, but they didn't catch the guy. Problem is, it put our two culprits who messed with the computer systems in the clear as your stalker."

"But Paul, someone *shot* at you. Again. At your

home." She could hardly take it in. The shots at the restaurant were surreal, almost impossible to take in as gunfire. But the fact that someone had deliberately tried to shoot into his home, kill him that way, rocked her.

"Yeah. It scared the crap out of me, I can tell you. One more inch to the right . . ." He stopped short. "Well."

"Oh, my God, Paul." She gripped his hands. He'd nearly been killed. With horrible words between them. "I'm so sorry. So very sorry." He was in trouble, getting shot at because of her.

"I'm okay, Torie."

"No, no. You're not. Nothing's okay about this." She wrenched her hands from his and rushed to her feet, pacing the floor. "I should do what Todd did, go away, get away so no one gets hurt. I don't want to be the reason one more person gets hurt."

"You're not the reason," Paul said, coming up behind her, his hands resting lightly on her shoulders. "This guy's nuts, Torie. Whoever he is, *he's* responsible. Not you. You may be a catalyst, but he's responsible for his actions."

"I need to go. You—I can't have you hurt, not because of me."

He turned her gently, taking her once more into his arms. Wrapped tight, she still resisted. He had to let her go. She had to leave, protect him.

"No," he murmured, kissing her hair. "We started this together, we'll finish it together."

His words took her back. She froze into immobility. Started it?

"What are you talking about?"

"I'm talking about what happened at the party, eleven years ago."

"Nothing happened, Paul," she protested, but her voice was shaking.

"That's not true, Torie, and you know it."

"I'm okay."

"That's not the issue, not right now. I'm not sure it's true, either, but we'll have to get into that later. Right now, it's about who did it."

She wrenched away from him, going to the table, leaning against it, her arms wrapped around her middle. "No one did anything."

Paul closed his eyes, sighed. "Yes, Torie, they did. Someone violated your human rights, your dignity, and your privacy. Someone took your choices away from you, and they nearly did a whole lot more. Why nothing had happened to you when I got there, I don't know, but it's a bloody miracle you weren't raped."

Horror flowed through her. "You told Tibbet."

Paul nodded. "I had to. He thinks this may go all the way back to that incident, the fraternity party. He believes that whoever started that may be the one who is still stalking you. He thinks that inciting incident may have led Todd's killer to murder him, and that this guy is so obsessed with you, he drives off or hurts anyone he thinks is getting too close."

From horror to betrayal, Torie was awash with emotions. She'd come to the office so confident, so full of energy, and it had all disappeared.

Was her life ever going to stop seesawing from one extreme to another? Where would the next blow fall? Her family? Her mother?

"I don't want to talk about it," she finally managed to get out.

"I know," Paul said, starting to move toward her. When she flinched, he stopped. "I didn't want to spring this on you. I didn't want to tell Tibbet, but he knew, Torie. He knew something had happened. Something bad."

"What else did you tell him?"

"I told him everything."

Shame and horror washed over her and she felt faint. From a long way away, she heard Paul calling her name. Sinking into the chair at the conference table, she wanted to vomit.

"Put your head down," Paul ordered. "Breathe, Torie. Breathe."

He'd seen the cop drive into the parking garage when he went out to get coffee. What was the detective going back?

Of course he'd come back, another part of his mind reasoned calmly. There'd been another incident.

Damn it, he'd *missed*. How could he have missed *twice*?

His luck, so phenomenal except for the lottery, hadn't helped him kill Paul Jameson.

The police had nearly caught him. Instead, they'd milled around in the dark, looking for him while he sat in a tree, waiting for them to leave. He hated trees. He was still itching from something which had bitten him, as well as nursing scrapes and bruises from the fall he took getting down.

He had to get to Paul before the police talked to him again. They were digging deeper. Nothing connected him with anything in the past or present. He had no ties to Paul, or Torie.

And yet, they were his main priorities.

Now they both had to die. He'd seen them kiss. He'd seen them together.

She would never turn to him.

Knowing that, he made his plans.

Chapter Eighteen

"I trusted you," Torie whispered, head between her knees.

"I know," Paul murmured, crouching down to face her. "And I betrayed that trust. I didn't mean to, not the first time. I did it deliberately this time, and you can hate me for it, but Tibbet believes that it may be the key to stopping whoever's stalking you, killing people. If that's true, then it might keep you safe, and alive. I can't lose you again, Torie."

"W-wh-what do you mean?"

A knock sounded, and Martha entered at Paul's hail.

"Detective Tibbet is getting impatient, sir," she said. Catching sight of Torie, she shifted from professional to concerned in the blink of an eye. "Good heavens, are you all right, Ms. Hagen?"

"Please," Torie managed weakly. "After all this, please call me Torie. And no, I'm not okay, but I'll get through it."

Martha hurried to the refreshment area to get a bottle of water, pour some in a glass. She glanced at the open bottle, the napkins covered with lipstick, but she didn't say a word. Handing Torie the glass, she went back and tidied up, pulling bottles out of a cabinet to replenish the stock.

"Drink a bit of water, it'll help. Would you like something stronger, Torie? You look like you've had a shock."

"No, the water's fine, thanks," Torie managed, taking a sip.

"Very well. Mister Jameson?"

"Give us a few more minutes, then send Tibbet in, please."

"Yes, sir." She slipped out without looking at Torie again, but Torie felt as if she'd crossed some invisible line with Martha. Finally accepted. How ironic.

"Torie, I'll ask for forgiveness till the end of my days, but if it helps keep you safe, the secrets need to come out. That's what Tibbet used to persuade me. Your safety. I'll do whatever it takes to keep you safe." He said it softly, but defiantly. "The only thing for which I won't apologize is for caring enough about you to want you safe."

Before she could answer that, before it sank in, Tibbet was walking in the door.

"So, you let her know?"

Paul nodded, shaking the other man's hand and motioning him into a chair at the conference table. Since Torie was already there, it was the logical place.

"Did you find your list?"

"I did."

"List?" Torie roused enough to speak. "What list?"

Tibbet stepped into the breach, saving him from having to look even worse in Torie's estimation.

"I figured that being a lawyer type, Paul here would have kept a list of everyone he knew who was at that party where your incident occurred."

"Incident." Her laugh was more of a harsh bark, and it held nothing of mirth. "It sounds so tame."

"It wasn't, I know," Tibbet said in answer. "It was ter-rifying, and you felt shame and guilt. You were afraid everyone would judge you if they knew."

Torie couldn't believe what she was hearing. He was saying exactly what she felt. Exactly what she feared. "H-h-how did you know?"

"Because when something like this happens, it *is* how you feel. And you keep feeling that way until you decide not to, until you decide to put the shame and blame and judgment where it belongs."

"W-where?"

"On the person who was cowardly, nasty, and sick enough to drug a woman, scare her to death, and probably rape her."

"Oh-h-h," Torie managed to say before the tears burst from her. His matter of fact recital of it, his com-plete acceptance, exploded the lock behind which she'd kept her feelings about the attack.

Paul was at her side in an instant, kneeling on the floor, supporting her as she sobbed out all the anger and fear. Both men waited patiently as she re-leased the pent-up pain. Paul offered water and tis-sues, all while continuing to rub her back or hold her hand.

Finally, she began to master the flood, and choke back the tears. "I-I-I'm sorr-r-ry," she said, her breath still catching.

"Take your time," Tibbet said quietly. "You need to

get it out. Lance the wound so it can heal once and for all."

She couldn't answer that, but felt the rightness of it. Wiping her wet cheeks, she nodded. It was long past time she stopped hiding in her fear. Hadn't she already decided that this morning? Hadn't she already decided it was time to stop waiting around for life to come to her?

It was time to blaze a new path without looking over her shoulder in fear, or worrying about who would judge her if they knew.

She already knew who the "judgers" would be. She worked for them. Those who accepted her already knew. And they still accepted her.

Torie managed a watery smile, directed it to Paul, and thought about Pam. They knew. They had known from the beginning. They had never judged.

What she had mistaken for judgment on Paul's part, and for betrayal, had been something else. She shied away from naming it. She had enough to deal with. But it hadn't been disgust, or dislike. Of that, she was now sure.

"If you think you're able, Ms. Hagen, I'd like to go over Paul's list, see if you remember any of the men he's named, if any of them have contacted you over the years, or if any of them ever bothered you on campus."

Torie nodded. She pulled several more tissues, worked to regain her composure. This was important. It might save Paul's life, and that was important.

He was important.

"It's okay," he soothed. "We'll do it together."

He'd said that before. He'd said that a long time ago, too, as he'd sneaked her out of the fraternity house shaking and afraid. "It's okay. I've got you. I'll get you home," he'd said. "We'll do it together."

A sense of peace came over her, a rightness about the time and place of letting this go. Sitting up in the chair, she took several sips of water to clear her throat.

"Let me see the list," she croaked.

Paul rose and went to his desk. Unlocking a drawer, he came back with three copies of the list. His was handwritten, and notes were penned in the margins in several different colors, as if he'd written the notes at disparate times.

The copy he handed to her and to Tibbet was clean, typewritten, and new. "I cleaned it up a bit, took out the people I knew weren't there, or who had been away. I took Todd off the list," he added, for her benefit.

"Thanks," she managed. "It wasn't him. He was singing."

Paul laughed. "We both agree on that. You could hear it all over the house."

"He had a big voice."

"That he did," Paul agreed.

"So, not Peterson," Tibbet agreed, making a note on his own list. "What about the others?"

Torie went down the list.

"I've seen Deke Marshall since college. He came to the wedding, and the funeral. I think I saw him somewhere out, too, maybe when Pam and I went somewhere."

Tibbet made a mark by Deke's name.

"Of course, I see Tru everywhere." She indicated Truman Delacorte's name, a local businessman who was active in every Chamber of Commerce event. He was a pompous ass who seemed to believe he was in every way superior to the general populace. "I think his office is right across the street, isn't it?"

Tibbet marked his name as well.

"Melvin has asked me out, as I told you. I was already dating Todd when he asked, though." She frowned over the list. "He asked me out later, too, after Todd left, but like I said before, I wasn't ready to date. Oh, and Blaine Zamkowski. I saw him at a party two years ago. He and I went to homecoming together freshman year, before either of us pledged anything. I saw him again recently, too, at a building I was working on."

She found five other names of the twenty or so on Paul's list. She didn't feel like any of them were the type to hurt her or to be capable of murdering anyone, much less Todd.

"I just don't see how it could be any of them."

"I know it's hard to fathom, but one of those men was responsible for what happened to you in college, and what's happening now."

"You're sure they're related?"

"I'm getting more sure by the day," Tibbet said with conviction. "It's one of the only things that makes sense." He reviewed the list with her, and asked Paul more questions about his notes and what he remembered about each man.

"I didn't know most of those guys," he said, looking at his notes. "They were upperclassmen. Deke, Melvin, and Blaine were all in my class, but we didn't hang out."

"So you said. You were very careful when you were discussing Melvin with his father, Mister Jameson. You want to elaborate now that we're in private?"

"Not really, no. Melvin's all right. The only thing I

don't know is why he helped me get my job here, or helped Todd. He didn't like us all that much. He said it was payback," Paul remembered.

Tibbet sat up. "What does that mean?"

Paul grinned. "Nothing sinister. The only time we ever got along with Melvin or hung out together was when we were all studying for the bar. He might be a bit of a weasel, but he's smart, damn smart. He's . . ." Paul searched for the right word.

"Weaselboy," Torie interjected, smiling. "Oh, my gosh, Todd used to call him Weaselboy."

"Yeah, he did. We both did. But when it came to studying for that damn test, we were willing to take all the help we could get. Wea—Melvin was willing to take a part of the exam and break it down. We took other parts. Together we figured out the way to study for the damn thing. We probably should have sold the method; we would have made a killing. Instead, we just passed the damn thing."

"All three of you?"

"Yep. Flying colors, for once."

"I remember that," Torie said. "I remember the two of you complaining about him, but saying he was okay."

"Yeah, well, he says we helped him pass, which made him look good to the old man. He says that's why he put us up for consideration. He told us we'd have to get the job on our own, he'd only get us in the door."

"What about this Blaine guy?" Tibbet asked.

"Blaine's a good old boy. He talks a great game, backs it up with hard work, and has a family," Paul said.

"Sorry, that doesn't rule him out these days," Tibbet

said, seeming genuinely disappointed. "It would be easier if it did."

"No, guess not. Now Deke," Paul said, pointing to the last name on the short list. "He's kind of a social misfit, but he's popular anyway. He could say the stupidest things," Paul reminisced.

"Yes, he could," Torie added, but she said, "He also couldn't keep his mouth shut. He was like a bullhorn. If you wanted campus to know it, tell Deke. If not, be sure Deke never found out."

"I know that kind."

"So, that's it. Those are the ones I know or knew, and pretty much what's going on with them now," Paul said as they finished going through the list.

"That gives me a place to start. Thanks." He stood, and Paul did as well. Tibbet ignored him and put a hand out to Torie. "Thank you, Ms. Hagen. I think we've made progress. I hope we can catch this guy soon with the help you've given me today."

"You're welcome," she said. "And no one hopes you catch him more than me."

Tibbet said, "Yeah, I'm sure," then took his leave.

Paul returned to the table and sat next to Torie.

"So, how are you feeling? Do you hate me more than you ever have?"

"I've never hated you, Paul," Torie said for what felt like the millionth time.

"No? That's good to hear."

"I've said it before."

"Maybe I wasn't ready to hear it then."

"What's that supposed to mean?" She looked at him now, instead of the tissue she was folding and refolding in her lap.

"It's a long story. How about I tell you over dinner?"

"I'm not really hungry."

He was instantly concerned. "I know. This was rough. I shouldn't have asked."

She smiled. "It's okay. I did love the flowers, you know. And I'll save you a dance."

"Rain check on dinner?"

"Yeah."

"Okay." He leaned back in the chair. "Why don't I take you back to the hotel and buy you a drink. Just a drink," he teased. "Then you can go on up to the room, order room service, and get some rest."

"If you come over to the hotel and have a drink, do you really think I'll order room service?"

He didn't know if it was an invitation or an honest question, but his libido decided it was an invite. "Oh, better not ask me that one," he growled at her.

To his delight, she laughed. "What I meant was," she corrected, still smiling, "I would feel like I had to go to dinner. I . . . have a lot to do." He didn't think work was what she needed, or was even talking about, but he let it drop.

"Well, why don't I drive you over there and you can tell me about it."

"Thanks, but I don't think that's wise." She stood up, straightening her blouse and picking up her purse.

"Do you really want to be wise?" he said, moving toward her. When she didn't protest, he eased in, slid his arms around her. She felt so good, right there, next to him.

He heard her purse land on the table, and her arms encircled him as well. It was as if they dove into one another, pressing together, letting their bodies speak what they couldn't yet say.

Tongues tangling in heated battle, they kissed and murmured endearments to one another, things that were hardly intelligible, but deeply heard.

"Torie," he groaned, wanting to take her right there on the table. "You have to let me, I need to." He couldn't form the words, could barely form the thoughts behind them.

"Not here," she moaned. "The door . . ."

The thought of someone coming in, finding them wound around each other, clothes askew, was like cold water on a hot day. Paul half-laughed, half-moaned. "You're right. You're right," he mumbled, still kissing her. "We have to stop. Soon."

"Now," she said, breathlessly. "We have to stop now."

He pulled back, the barest fraction. "Lord, woman," he panted, resting his brow on hers. "You wind me up."

"Mutual," she said, taking a deep breath. He was able, from his vantage point looking down, to see the lovely deep V of her breasts as they rose and fell. As if he weren't hard enough, his overworked libido screamed more loudly for release.

"Ahhh, I think I'd better let go," he said ruefully. "Before you take another one of those deep breaths."

"Why?" she asked, puzzlement evident in her voice.

Taking her hand, he slid it down from his waist to the rock hard bulge in his trousers. "That."

"Ohhhhh," she purred, gently squeezing him, her eyes hooded, her lips moist.

"Unless you want to bring me a new pair of pants, you need to stop that," he growled, grabbing her hand and returning it to his waist. Holding it captive there, he closed his eyes. "Not that I really want you to stop, but the circumstances . . ."

"Aren't ideal."

"Hah, no. They're not."

"I really, really want you to come to the hotel, but I think it would be a bad idea." She blurted out the words, as if she were afraid to say them.

He laughed, knowing she was right, wishing it were easy. "We'd never get dinner. Or drinks."

She giggled and it lifted his heart. The wrenching tears had brought him to the brink of breaking down himself. Her horrible shame, so unwarranted, had been brutal to unmask.

Everything within him knew she needed time. But that was intellectual. The part of him that was male, primal, and in need wanted to push the matter, urge her to let him come over, hold her.

The images in his mind were erotic and brought him back to the painful brink.

"I'll have Martha call you a cab."

"Good idea."

They stood together for a few more minutes, breathing hard like marathoners at the end of the race. "Think you're ready?"

"I'd say for what, but that would just start this all over again, right?" He could hear the laughter, so he did the only thing he could. He tickled her.

"Oh, jeez," she nearly shrieked. "Stop that!"

"Shhhh. Martha's going to know exactly what we're doing."

"Don't tickle me then," she admonished, pulling away to put her clothes to rights.

"Not right now, maybe later," he teased, happy to see her smile again.

* * *

Her phone was ringing as she got into the room. She picked it up and the front desk informed her that more flowers had arrived.

This time, they were sunflowers. Fat, gorgeous, and cheerful. The card read:

Save the last dance, too.

Spinning around the room in delight, she clutched the card to her chest. "This is nuts," she exalted. "Crazy. Fabulous."

Flopping down on the bed, she lay back, enjoying the sensation of arousal and delicious sensuality. His reaction to her was instant and amazing. And as always, her reaction to him was heated, wet, powerful. She nearly had an orgasm thinking about how good he'd felt pressed into her body, how marvelous and affirming it had been to hold him, see his muscles quiver as he struggled to hold back his desire for her.

"Ooooh," she drew out the word, savoring the sensations. Tomorrow night, after the partner dinner, she would bring him back here. They would take their time. Enjoy each other, free of the past.

With that thought foremost in her mind, she fell deeply and completely asleep.

In the darkness, he watched. He could see the police cars now, tucked in with the commuters and the travelers. Their Pennsylvania plates and multiple antennas gave them away if you took the time to look. Parked between cars from Ontario and Georgia, the cop cars were conspicuous. So was the latest bodyguard.

The cops would be in the bar and the lobby lounge, watching for trouble. The private hired muscle would be on the floor where Torie was, probably in one of the sitting areas by the elevator.

Excellent.

He smiled. Time for a little fun.

Chapter Nineteen

"Jameson? Jameson? You in there?" Paul heard the pounding on his door, and went from the depth of sleep to instant, hyperaware wakefulness in the space of a heartbeat.

He struggled into jeans as he hurried to the door. "I'm here. That you, Tibbet?"

"Whaddya think, it's a monkey?"

"Hey," Paul complained, pulling open the door. "You're the one who told me to check this shit out before whipping open the door."

"Yeah," Tibbet said, prowling into the house.

"What's up?" He knew it wasn't Torie. Tibbet would have said so immediately.

"Weird shit."

"Huh?"

"Torie's okay, but—"

"What happened?" Paul demanded, grabbing Tibbet's arm to stop him in his tracks.

"You're gonna want to let go," Tibbet said through gritted teeth.

"Not till you tell me what happened."

Tibbet shook him off, but started telling. "I had two watchers on the hotel. One in the parking lot, two in the lobby. I could only keep 'em on for a while. City's busy tonight. We needed 'em, ya know?"

"Budget cuts suck."

"Yeah, you know it." Tibbet seemed relieved that Paul understood. His chief had nearly fried his ass about the cost of manpower.

"So it was time for them to switch around, not be so obvious, and parking lot guy checks in with central. He goes into the bar and next thing I know, I got a nine-one-one to the head over there for the other two to be picked up, intoxicated."

"Drunk? On duty?"

"Somebody wanted it to look that way. Waitress says they were both drinking nothing. One had tonic and lime, the other, an O'Doul's."

"That's the nonalcoholic beer, right?"

"Yeah. So suddenly both of 'em start getting silly. One of 'em's singing with the band, the other guy's picking fights and shit. My third guy walks into the middle of this."

"Hence the nine-one-one."

"Yeah. I roll over there, fast, calling your Torie, but can't get her. She's turned her phone off, by the way, but I didn't know that. Freaked me out."

"You didn't call me?" Paul nearly shouted the words. Now he was upset, and pissed.

"Nothin' to tell till I got there."

"But she's okay?"

"Sound asleep. But I had to call my team in because someone had used our kind of crime scene tape all over the hall, over the doors and exits. I think our boy didn't know which room she was in. She's not registered, so he couldn't get her room number."

Paul frowned. It didn't make sense. "But your guys . . ."

"Were drugged. Someone slipped them something. Both of 'em are at the ER, puking up their guts, getting it out of their systems."

"Oh, that's nasty."

"Yeah, stupid, too. Nothing like an out-of-control cop."

Frightening thought, Paul decided.

"So you were able to call Torie?"

"Once I convinced the front desk clerk that I really was a cop. Seems a slightly built man, blond and brown-eyed, had come in earlier claiming to be a cop and asking for Torie's room. You'd given me her friend Pam's name. I asked for that and the clerk pulled it right up. Perky little twit called her for me."

"You woke her up. What did you tell her?"

"Just that there had been an incident in the lobby, and I didn't want her to worry if she heard about it. I told her to stay in her room, keep the curtains closed. That sort of thing."

Paul let himself sit, let himself relax now that he knew Tibbet had talked to Torie. He looked at the clock. It was nearly three in the morning.

"I'm going off shift. If I don't get some sleep, I won't be fit to catch a one-legged man on a unicycle."

Paul laughed. "Yeah. Thanks for letting me know."

"Welcome. Had to come check on my guys over here, too. Sorry to wake you."

"You'd have been sorrier if you hadn't."

It was Tibbet's turn to laugh. "Figured."

When he was gone, Paul paced the kitchen. He hadn't

turned on any lights in the small room, preferring the dark, preferring not to be a target.

He wanted to call her, reassure himself that she was okay. Hell, who was he kidding? He wanted to go over there.

He had nearly talked himself into going back to bed when he heard his phone trill, signaling an incoming text message.

> "Tibbet said he would tell you,
> but so you know,
> I'm okay."

He read it, glad to see the words, hear them. It was a relief to have Torie confirm Tibbet's assessment. The time stamp was less than a minute ago.

He hit return dial, and waited for her to pick up.

"Hey," she said, her voice husky with sleep.

"Hey, back. You okay?" He slouched into a chair, closing his eyes to see her in his mind.

"Yeah. I guess. I was scared to death when Tibbet called from the front desk. I thought . . . I thought something had happened to you."

Having felt the same, Paul reveled in her concern. "Yeah, I nearly freaked when he pounded on my door."

"Oh, I'm so sorry he woke you," she said.

"If he hadn't, he'd have been hurting in the morning," Paul stated as a blunt fact.

"Paul," she admonished with a gentle laugh, "he's doing his job."

"Yeah. I know." He didn't want to talk about Tibbet, he wanted to talk about her. "You get some sleep?"

"Some. I was asleep when Tibbet called."

"Hmmm. You sleeping now?"

"No." She gave a soft laugh. "I'm talking to you, you goof."

"I wish I was there with you."

"I wish you were, too," she admitted.

"I can be there in fifteen minutes, if you want me to." Please, he thought. Want me. Every part of him wanted to leap up, head for her hotel. The thought that the cops stationed outside his door would know where he was going and what he was doing didn't stop the wanting.

"I wish I could beam you over," she murmured, and he heard the drowsy desire in her voice. "I'd be able to touch you." She yawned and he did, too. The rest of his body was wide awake, however.

"You want to touch me?" he baited her. "Mmmm. That would be good. Then I could touch you, too. Everywhere. Anywhere you wanted me to touch you. Light," he said, waiting so she could picture it. "Or firm, and deep."

"Oh," she whispered. "You're making me crazy."

"Not half as much as you're making me, babe," he said, thinking he was going to need a cold shower before heading back to bed. Either that or he was going to say to hell with all the phone sex, and climb in bed with her for some furious, awesome lovemaking.

"Good," she murmured. "You've been driving me crazy for years. Mmmmm. About time I gave a little of that back."

"Years?"

"Years. I've wanted to touch you like I did in your office today. Hold you in my hands." She lowered her voice to that devastatingly sexy purr. "Feel you touch me. Everywhere."

"I'm going to come over there and let you feel what you're doing to me."

"No, too many police in the lobby," she crooned. "And they'd shoot you if you climbed in the window."

"Yeah, they would."

"So, talk to me."

"I don't want to talk, honey," he murmured. "I want to do."

She laughed. "After the last dance?"

"You got the flowers, I take it."

"They're beautiful, like the roses."

"Like you."

"Sweet-talker," she protested.

"You haven't had enough of that, I think. So I guess it's up to me."

"Hmmm. Impress me."

He did his best. By the time they hung up, it was nearing daybreak. He was so aroused, so ready to explode that only a cold shower would help him. As it was, he climbed back into bed with his hair wet and cold, and his body still on fire.

"Just wait, Torie Hagen," he murmured. "You'll dance with me, and I'll never let you go."

"So somebody drugged the cops? Wow." Pam was shocked by the latest development. "Hard to believe."

"Yeah, scared me," Torie said, then thanked the waiter who served their breakfast plates.

"You should have called me. I would have come over."

"I know." Torie ducked her head so Pam wouldn't see the blush that stole over her cheeks.

"What? What is it?" Pam eyed her with suspicion. "You're blushing. Who did you call, Paul?"

When Torie didn't answer, Pam laughed. "Can't fool me, girl. I can see right through you. How long did you talk?"

"An hour," Torie admitted. "Maybe more."

"At three in the morning, eh? Well, well, well."

"Stop that."

"What?"

"Being so smug and I-told-you-so."

Pam attempted to look serious, sliding her sunglasses off her head to perch them on her nose in professorial fashion. "Now reaaaaallly, darling," she drawled with dramatic skill. "You muuuuust tell me everything. All the delectable details."

"No," Torie protested. "That's personal."

"Uh huh. Personal. So you're going tonight, right?" In one of her lightning changes of subject, Pam shifted to the party. "The partner dinner," she said, snapping her fingers under Torie's nose. "C'mon, keep up here. You're going, right?"

"Yes, I'm going. I wish you could be there, too. I could probably get you a date," she said, trying for a sly look.

"God, don't do that, your face might freeze that way. Who, some hunky, rich partner drooling to get his hands on little ol' me, or merely another skanky lawyer?"

"You have dated a few."

"You have no idea. So?"

"How about Melvin? He's single."

"Weaselboy? Uh, no way."

"Did everyone call him that? I thought it was just Paul and Todd."

"It was. Todd told me to stay away from him one time, at a party for a bunch of the frat brothers. Said he was trouble."

"I guess he was for a while. Seems like he's straightened out now."

"Don't get me wrong, I like a reformed bad boy as much as the next red-blooded American woman, but that one? I don't think so."

Torie paused, her breakfast forgotten for a moment. "Yeah, what is it about him?" Another thought distracted her. "Hey, do you remember Blaine and Deke?"

"The Big Blue Ox and Mister Muscles?" Pam asked, using the nicknames she had for them. "Yeah, I remember them. I ran into Deke at that Chamber thing you dragged me to. He hit on me, hard, but I didn't have the time. And Blaine, seems to me I've seen him around, but I don't know either one of them that well."

"We looked at a list yesterday." Torie explained about the list and the questions the men had asked of her.

"Oh, baby." Pam's eyes were wide with shock and glistened with tears. "Why didn't you call me? You shouldn't have had to go through that, relive that alone."

Torie closed her eyes on tears of her own. How like Pam to think that way. "Thank you," she said, her voice catching on the tears. "I wasn't alone, though. Paul was there."

"I see."

Torie laughed at the dry rejoinder. "Pretty much, yeah."

"So, I repeat my earlier questions, which you *so* did not answer."

"Which is?"

"Game plan, girl. Game plan."

"Okay, okay. Game plan. I'm calling the bank today about a business loan. I've already signed the lease with Kuhman on the house in Upper Darby, and I've got a builder/remodeler guy coming to the house on Sunday."

"Darby house or Society Hill house?"

"Both. Society Hill first. The sooner I get started there, the better." The keys to the padlocks were a weight in her pocket. Sorrels had dropped them off to her, asking her to replace the locks with some she'd bought, and return the existing ones to him.

She hadn't been back home again, sure that her stalker would follow her there and finish the job he'd started with the fire.

"So, you've made a list, right?"

"Yeah." It was in her purse, five neatly folded pages of stuff to do.

"Good. Then we can get you ready for tonight."

"What does that mean?"

"It means we go get a massage. We have lunch, we get our nails and toes done. Yours are a mess, by the way. And then we get you back to your room in time to pamper yourself and get ready."

"Thanks for the compliment," Torie retorted. "Pam, I've got a ton of stuff to do. I don't think I can spend the whole day goofing off getting ready for this dinner."

"Since when is spending the day with me goofing off?" Pam pretended to be insulted. "Besides. You have waited for eleven long years to get your hands on Paul Jameson."

"But—"

"Don't 'but' me, girlfriend. I was there. I know how

excited you were and what you said when he asked you out. I know how horrible you were to live with after the two of you fought over nothing. Pushed each other away."

"All these years," Torie exclaimed, blindsided by the information. "All these years, and you didn't see fit to tell me you thought I should go for him? What, all that Paul-Jameson-is an-ass talk was for show?"

"He's a *man*." Pam stressed the final word. "Of course he's an ass. They all are. Some are bigger than others. And honey, he did make some stupid moves back in the day. And said some stupid shit. He's making up for it. I'm simply saying that you care about him. If you do this, you'll either know he's the one for you, or you'll wash him out of your system. You know?"

"I guess." The steamroller was moving, and Pam was in the driver's seat. Torie decided it was time to get a bit of spine. "How about a compromise. I'll spend the morning getting some things done. You get us salon appointments for one o'clock over at L'Artiste on Chancellor. We'll do girl stuff and have fun. That'll get me done by four and back to my room to dress. My date," she said, and grinned at Pam, "is sending a limo, I'm told. Mister Pratt's assistant left a message this morning."

"That's a kick. I'm glad you're going with the old man. He sounds nice."

"He is, and I like him. I kind of feel sorry for him, too. He's lonely since his wife died."

"Sucks, doesn't it? Falling for someone, then losing them?"

Knowing that Pam wasn't speaking entirely about Pratt, she answered, "Yeah, but he had a long time with her. Some people get that blessing before the loss."

"So," Pam began as she took a deep breath and straightened her shoulders, "one o'clock it is. Need me to take you over to the dealership?"

"Thanks, that would be great. I've got a check for you, too, for the room."

"Cool. You can pick me up in the new ride, chickiepoo."

"Sounds like a plan."

It wasn't until Torie was pulling back into the garage at the hotel in her new car that she called Paul. She'd wanted to call him first thing, but didn't know if he'd been able to sleep in or not. She worried that . . .

"Nothing. You're worried over nothing," she told herself.

"Mister Jameson's office." Martha answered the phone with professional precision.

"Hello, Missus Prinz. Is Mister Jameson in? It's Torie Hagen."

"Hello, Torie. I'll see if Mister Jameson is available."

"Thank you, Martha." Evidently the casual address had survived the night and Martha's ideas of propriety.

"Torie." Paul's voice was warm, welcoming, a sensory treat. "Where are you? Are you coming over to the office?"

"No, I'm back at the room. I thought I'd work in their business center and in my room. I replaced my car, and I found a place to rent. It's an incredible house. Since they released my place, I need to start getting estimates on that, too, so I wanted to get started."

"Sounds productive. How are you feeling about TruStructure?"

"Uh, I'd love to talk to you about that also. You had said something to me, something that got me thinking."

"Ummmm, I love to get you thinking," he teased.

"Stop," she said, though she loved hearing it. "I'm trying to be serious."

"Serious. Okay. Hit me with it."

"You said I should go out on my own. Not go back."

"Have you decided to do that?"

"I don't know. I'm going to sit down with the new laptop and work on the pros and cons, make a list of all the potential customers, and all that."

"What about all the projects you took with you? Are all those your original ideas? Are they viable for production?"

He'd switched gears to lawyer now. It was nearly as exciting as his teasing. He believed in her.

"I've made an appointment to talk to a small business banker the first of next week. I have a lot saved, but I want to keep the business separate."

"That's wise," he said, but she heard a laugh in his voice. "I don't think you'll have a problem. You should keep Monday open, if possible. I think we've finally gotten everything we need to read Todd's will, and get all that straightened out."

"Oh, I'll call back, change the appointment until Tuesday."

"Sound's good. Now about the house you're renting—where is it?"

"Not too far from your house, actually. It's in a good neighborhood. It's got room for the dogs—a big fenced yard, and all that."

"Wait, dogs? Plural?"

She paused for a second, wondering how he'd react. "I, uh, I'm taking Bear."

"Holy shit. He's a moose. How do you think your pup's going to react to him?"

Her heart melted. He hadn't told her she was nuts,

he hadn't asked if she had thought it through. He asked about Pickle. "Uh, she loves company, so I think they'll get along okay. He's really a big teddy bear."

"More like a grizzly bear."

"Pam called him a woolly mammoth."

Paul laughed, a booming delightful sound. "That's perfect. So what are you going to do first at your house?"

"I don't know, I'm kind of . . ." She hated to admit it, but he'd been so understanding so far. "I'm a little afraid to go over there until there's been some kind of resolution."

"On your stalker? Yeah. I don't have any say in the matter, but I hate to think of you over there by yourself. If, uh, you'd like me to, I'll go with you tomorrow. We can see if there's anything else you can salvage. Get it out, and start getting workmen in."

"That would be great." Relief lightened her heart. Going over there was imperative, but it would be so much easier to have him with her. "Oh, but we shouldn't, right? We have to be careful. I don't want anyone taking a shot at you again. No, I'll go alone."

"We'll go together," he said, firmly. "We're not going to live in fear, Torie. Marco's still watching you, and he can watch us both. So what else?"

Torie let that sink in for a moment, but decided protesting would get her nowhere. "I'm having lunch with Pam, getting my nails done. Getting ready for my date with Mister Pratt."

"Should be some night. Old Pratt's a wild man. The rest of the crew are pretty crazy, too. The fraternity parties have nothing on Pratt and Legend."

"I'll bet. So, how much dancing is there?"

"Enough. I'll be claiming that dance, Torie." He

let his voice drop. "And a few other things, if you'll let me."

"I think something can be arranged."

"Excellent." He returned to his professional tone. "I'm so happy to hear about your plans. If you'd keep me abreast of your progress, I'll see what I can do."

"Someone came into your office, didn't they?"

"Indeed."

"So should I talk dirty to you so you get really embarrassed while Martha's standing there?"

"Uh, no. I'm fine, thanks." She could hear the amusement in his voice.

"I'll talk to you later. Call me on my cell if you need me."

"Will do."

Still smiling, Torie parked and enjoyed the fun of beeping the locks on the car. Briefcase in hand, she headed to the business center.

She'd been working for several hours when the door opened yet again. The place was busy, with a conference in the ballroom and the usual general weekday traveler business.

"Is this seat taken?"

Torie swiveled around, looked at Paul. He stood there, big as life. In his hands he carried yet another vase of flowers. These were weeping over in a fabulous riot of color and form.

"Oh, those are beautiful."

"I'd like to say something clichéd like, 'They're not as beautiful as you,' but that would sound sappy."

"Go ahead, be sappy."

"No," he said, setting the flowers on the table and leaning down to kiss her. "I'll be as sappy as you want. Later."

"Okay."

He sat down in the other chair, looking over the notes she had spread all over the table. "You've been busy."

"It's been fun," she said, surprised to find she meant it. "Here, let me show you." She turned the pad around and showed him the outline of the plan for her business. "If I were to capitalize enough, I could get office space pretty quickly."

"I don't think it'll be a problem. What are you going to do about TruStructure?"

She copied his posture, leaning back in the chair. "I don't know. Part of me wants to call them and say screw you. Another part of me is scared to death to start this whole thing, and I want to call them and say, 'Hey, I'm exonerated, when can I come back?'"

"You really do have grounds for a lawsuit, you know, especially since you have been cleared of all charges. We got the letter this morning, by the way."

"Oh, good. But do I want to do that? Open that can of worms?"

They discussed it for a while, and his insights were right on target. She showed him the listing sheet for the house, too, and told him about Kuhman and the walk-through. He didn't seem surprised that the house was near his place in Lansdowne.

"That's a lot of work to take on, especially if you're starting a new business as well." He leaned forward, elbows on the table. "With both houses, the dogs, everything changes."

"I know." She hesitated, not sure how to tell him what she was feeling.

"But?"

"It feels right."

Paul leaned back again. "Then it's the right thing to do."

"Wow. Really?"

Her expression must have been shocked because a grinning Paul shifted forward to tap her lower jaw, pat it back up into place. "Really. C'mon."

"Where?"

"Pack up, I'm taking you to lunch. We'll start our celebrating early."

Chapter Twenty

"Good evening, my dear." Mr. Pratt greeted her in the lobby later that night with a satisfied smile and a single rose. "Beauty needs no adornment, but I thought you might enjoy this."

"You are delightful, Mister Pratt."

"Call me Pratt, my dear. My late wife was fond of that, and I find I like it."

"Well, then, Pratt, shall we?"

"With pleasure." He offered his arm, and they strolled out to the limousine parked under the portico of the hotel. Torie tensed slightly, scanning the parking area and the street. "Something wrong, my dear?"

"A little nervous, I guess, about the bodyguards."

He patted her hand where it lay on his arm. "Not to worry, they're there. No worries, either, about the group. They don't bite. Quite the contrary, in fact. They're a remarkably friendly crew for lawyers."

"For lawyers, yes. I guess I don't want anyone to feel that there's an outsider in their midst."

"Nonsense. Here we are," he said, holding the door.

She slid into the limo to find a small table holding hors d'oeuvres and champagne. She also found a smiling Paul Jameson.

"Hello, Torie."

She couldn't help it. Her heart began to race.

"There now, my dear," Pratt said as he settled into the seat. "Have a canapé. We'll ask Paul to pop that cork so we can have a little private celebration. I quite surprised our Paul by inviting you to be my guest, you know."

"I'm sure you did."

"He's a stubborn lad, our Paul," Pratt said, smiling fondly at Paul. "I've told him that life is short. He listens politely, then does what he wants, much like any young man."

There was a muffled pop and Paul directed the frothing bubbly into flutes clipped into the small table.

They each took a glass and raised them.

"To friendships long and dear. To life, and new beginnings." Pratt raised his glass and drank, and she and Paul did the same.

"So, Torie dear, are you going to let us represent you and harass your employers?"

He said it with such jovial good humor that she almost agreed before she realized what he was saying. "I'm not sure, Pratt. I'm considering . . ." she hesitated, but Paul gave a subtle nod. "I'm considering going out on my own. I've built a reputation and have been asked several times if I would consider jobs outside the office." Once she got started, it all came out in a rush.

"Well, not to push our business on you, but we're here to help with that as well. Still," he mused, "you ought to at least let us get you emotional damages from the bastards."

Paul laughed. "Sounds good. Don't worry, Torie. I won't let them get too mean with it, but you deserve something for all they've put you through. They haven't called you to come back yet, have they?"

"No."

"There we go," Pratt said. "That's settled then. Paul tells me you'll be in on Monday. We'll talk about it then. For now, it's an evening to put work aside and have a little fun. Will you let me steal her for one waltz, Paul?" The older man was enjoying himself playing the matchmaker, Torie could tell.

"Of course, sir."

"No *sirring* tonight, Paul. I'm just Pratt. So, have some more champagne. Now Torie, tell me about your plans."

Their enthusiastic interest buoyed Torie's ideas for her business so much that she was nearly giddy by the time they arrived at the exclusive mansion near Fairmont Park. The limo let them out at the door, and Torie entered on Pratt's arm with Paul coming in behind them. Most of the invited staff were already there, sipping cocktails and holding full plates of hors d'oeuvres. When Pratt and Torie rounded the corner, the volume of conversation dropped, but picked back up again.

"Paul!" Several people hailed him, one dubbing him the man of the hour.

"Thanks for the excuse to have a party on the old man," another partner said as he slapped him on the back and shook hands with Torie. She never got his name. She, Pratt, and Paul made the rounds, and when the chimes sounded for dinner, the two men escorted her to her seat, flanking her at the table.

"This is lovely, Pratt. I feel like a princess."

"You look like one, too, dear."

Melvin Jr. and his date, an attractive dark-haired woman, sat down. "Hello, Father. I believe you remember Sylvia."

"Yes, good evening." Pratt's welcome was less than warm, but he was courteous. Introductions around the table got to Torie, and Sylvia's eyebrows arched nearly to her hairline.

"Ah, you have been in the papers of late."

Before Torie could speak, Pratt rose to her defense. "We won't be discussing that tonight. We're here to celebrate."

"Of course."

The meal progressed, and Torie found it hard to keep her mind on the conversation. Underneath the table, Paul had found the slit in her dress. He wasn't doing anything that could be seen, merely running the tip of one finger up and down her leg as far as the fabric would allow.

She was about to die from wanting him.

When she thought she couldn't take it anymore, Pratt stood up. At that signal, the soft music the band was playing died away, and a microphone was brought to their table.

"We're here tonight to celebrate another fine partner at our firm," Pratt began. He outlined some of Paul's achievements, introduced him, and joked with him a bit. "Thank you for coming out to celebrate with us, everyone. Let's clear that dance floor and enjoy, shall we?"

As if conjured by magic, staff appeared to clear

several tables and reveal a wooden dance floor in the heart of the room, near the band. The band struck up a waltz and Pratt held out a hand to Torie.

"If I might have this dance?"

"Of course."

Paul cut in as the music finished, and Pratt selected another partner as well. The music ramped up to a faster pace, but Paul kept their dance slow and sensual.

"Paul," she whispered in his ear. "People are staring."

"So?"

She laughed. "So, you have to work with these people."

"Uh huh," he said, but didn't change the tempo one bit.

When the song ended and the band started on rock, he relented and led her back to the table.

Martha stopped them on the way there. As a long-standing employee, she had been invited as well.

"Hello, Martha," Paul greeted her warmly.

"Good evening, Paul. Torie."

So, it was still friendly, Torie decided with an inner smile. "Hello, Martha, you look lovely tonight."

"Thank you. I wanted to tell you that I admire you."

The words came as a total shock to Torie. "I beg your pardon."

Martha's smile was prim. "You've been dealt some difficult blows. I was not, I confess, a fan of yours. I cared very deeply for young Mister Todd, and I wasn't as fair as I should have been about the situation between you."

"Oh," Torie squeaked out. What the hell was she supposed to say to that amazing statement?

"However, I believe you to be a woman of considerable courage. I want you to know I wish you the best." With that grand pronouncement, Martha bid them a good night and moved off through the maze of tables.

"Did she just apologize?" Torie asked.

"Sounded like it to me," Paul said with a smile, guiding her to the table.

"Your phone rang," Melvin spoke up as they approached. "I had to catch your purse to keep it from falling off the chair. You must have it on vibrate."

"Oh, I do," Torie admitted, thinking it was weird that Melvin had noticed.

"He almost spilled my drink when it fell on his foot," Sylvia complained, coming up beside them. The ill-disguised whine in her voice grated on Torie's nerves. "You haven't asked me to dance, Melvin." She now turned her attention to Melvin. Torie could see that he was irked, but he set down the glasses and led her away.

Torie yanked the phone from her purse. The caller ID said Pam. The last three digits were nine-one-one. It was urgent.

"I'll be right back," she nearly shouted to Paul. The music was reaching the higher levels, and she could feel the thump of the bass in her bones. "Pam called. Something urgent."

"I'll come with you," he began, only to be distracted by a man patting his back, bringing his wife over to meet Paul.

"No worries, I'll be back."

Weaving her way through the tables, she readied the call. As soon as she slipped through the ballroom doors, she hit send.

"Pam?"

"Torie! You'll never belie—"

Noise from the opening doors blocked out all the sound.

"Hang on, Pammie, I'm walking outside so I can hear."

She managed to find a side door leading to the pool, and opened it with her elbow as she continued to try to hear what Pam was saying. "Pam, honey, slow down."

"He's okay!"

"What?"

"He's okay, Dev's okay. He's on his way over. He texted me, then called. He's okay."

"What? That's great news. Oh, thank God." Relief made her knees weak, and she managed to get to one of the benches and lean on its back. She didn't want to mess up the dress by sitting down, but it felt good to have something solid under her hands. "Is he okay, physically? I mean he didn't hurt anything again, did he?"

"I don't think so," Pam yelled, as the signal suddenly became clear. Torie jerked the phone away from her ear. A noise behind her startled her nearly as much as Pam's continued shouts about what Dev had said.

A hand covered her mouth, a cloth pressed over her nose as well, and she sucked in a deep breath to scream. The drug-laden fabric was wet on her cheek, and she felt a firm arm grip her under the bust as she sagged forward.

"Not bad for an old man, eh?"

She heard the words, but her eyes had begun to blur. A dark shape in a tuxedo loomed over her, draping her arm over his shoulder. He dragged her away from the mansion, aiming for the darkest area of the parking lot.

"You are such a pain in the ass, you know?" he mocked, unlocking the door to a plain, older SUV with a push of a button. He managed to open the door and shove her in without ever releasing the cloth from her mouth.

She knew his voice. She *knew* him. Tibbet had been right. It was someone she knew. Her thoughts circled like bats, flitting from theme to theme. Where were the bodyguards? Where was Paul?

The voice kept droning on about the frat party and Todd. He put two hands on the wheel when they got to the main road. He waited for the light, and whipped the car into the darkness, away from the city and its lights.

"You never could let well enough alone, could you? Getting involved with Todd, moving in with him. Nobody else was good enough for you, Miss Hoity-Toity. And now Paul. He's trash. Raised in a trailer, he comes from nothing. *Nothing*, do you hear me?"

He slapped at her face, but the awkward angle and the fact that he had to keep one hand on the wheel made it difficult for him to actually hurt her.

That won't last, a clear corner of her mind reasoned. *He's got you now. You're dead.*

". . . kill you," he ranted. "But, no. I thought, hey, she turned me down before, but I'm successful now. And Todd's off doing his thing with all that *money*." He spat the word. "It should have been mine, do you hear? *Mine*."

It made no sense. The money was Todd's. He'd won it. Hadn't he?

"I bought the tickets that day. I bought all the

lottery tickets for the whole office that day. I handed them out. They were all mine. Every one of them. But did he thank me? No. Did he offer to share the money with me? No. He gave me my five dollars, and he *walked*."

The car was weaving now, turning this way and that. She felt it bump, bump, bump along the road. The only light was from the dashboard.

Wasn't there a song about that? Torie's mind wandered with the drug. Every few minutes she'd feel more connected to her body, get snatches of what he was saying.

"And then Todd came back. Again. Why couldn't he just leave? Huh? Well, it was the last time he was going to rub all that money he *stole* from me in my face. You get it? Huh?"

The car lurched to a stop. "He stole it from *me*," the man said, slamming his way out of the car. He jerked her door open, took her arm, and yanked her up. With a quick twist, he swung her legs out, and pulled her up to stand woozily at his side.

"I took the cloth away, so you should be coming around. Nice thing about that drug, it's effective but fast acting. You'll know me before I kill you. Just like Todd."

The voice rang in her head. The voice . . .

He finished chatting up the Martins, and looked around the ballroom for Torie. He was ready to dance. With her. Then, he decided, as soon as he could, he was going to steal her away, up to the room he'd reserved. There was already champagne chilling, and more flowers. Maybe somehow, between her change of heart and his abject groveling, she would forgive him.

It might take a few more months of courting to heal the wounds he'd caused, but if he did it right, cared enough, loved enough, then perhaps she'd agree to marry him.

He thought of the ring he'd looked at earlier in the day. It would suit her.

He pressed open the door to the hallway, felt the rush of cooler air. It felt heavenly on his heated skin. Tuxedos were dashing, for sure, and fairly comfortable, but with all the dancing and alcohol, he was well warmed up.

Thinking of Torie again, he decided he was way past warmed up, and moving well toward open flame.

He saw Martha leaving the alcove marked for Ladies, and waylaid her. "Hey, Martha, you look lovely. Did you see Torie in there?"

"Thank you, Paul. No, no one else was in there."

"Okay. If you see Torie, would you tell her—"

He didn't get to finish. A shout went up from a nearby seating area. He turned in time to see Pratt toppling over, off the sofa, and onto the floor.

"Good Lord," Martha exclaimed, and ran to help.

Suddenly, Paul had a terrible feeling in his gut. Torie was missing. Pratt was in trouble. He remembered the cops in the hotel lobby.

He had to find Torie. Now.

Rushing toward the reception area, he looked in every nook, every seating area, near all the phones.

A mansion employee came up, asking if he needed help.

"Have you seen a woman from the party? She's wearing a dark blue short dress. Long blond hair. She was taking a phone call," he said, putting his hand to his ear as if answering the phone.

"Ah, yes. She went out the door, there."

The young man pointed to an exit which led into the gardens, and Paul wasted no time. Whipping out his own cell phone, he rolled through calls till he found Tibbet's, then redialed.

"Tibbet, it's Jameson. Torie's missing. Old man Pratt collapsed, and I can't find Torie." Damn, he was repeating himself. Where was she? Why couldn't he find her?

"You're sure? She's not just—" He cut himself off. "You're sure. Never mind."

Paul rattled off the address. He heard Tibbet start his car.

"Hang tight," Tibbet said. "I'm sending black and whites. I'll be there as fast as I can."

His dress shoes rang on the concrete walkway as he searched for Torie. A bench loomed out of the semi-darkness, and he heard the faintest sound of voices.

On the ground, half-buried in a flower bed, was Torie's phone.

"Hello? Who is this?" Paul demanded.

"Paul, is that you?"

"Pam? What's going on? Where's Torie?"

"I don't know. She was there one minute, talking to us, then she was gone."

"Us?"

"Dev's back."

"That's good," Paul acknowledged briefly, then hurried on. "How long ago?"

"A couple of minutes."

Paul ran into the parking lot, spun in place checking the exits. Searching for any sign of Torie. Where the hell was Mike? He'd hired Mike to watch the exits, keep Torie in his sights.

As he worried, he searched. The driveways were long and twisting. Way off in the distance, he saw a car turn on its headlamps as it sat at the traffic light. When the light shifted to green, it turned left.

"I have to take the chance."

"What? What are you talking about?"

"Somebody's taken Torie. Kidnapped her. I think I saw him leaving. I gotta hang up, call Tibbet, and tell him where I'm going."

"Call us," Pam shouted as he turned that phone off and opened his own again.

"Jameson? That you?" A man hurried over, his tuxedo rumpled.

"Mike, where the hell were you? You were supposed to be watching the lots, making sure she didn't get snatched."

"I have been. I've been out front. One of the staff came out, said you were looking for me. I went inside and saw the commotion. No one knew where you were, so I figured there was trouble. I'm sorry I let you down."

"Never mind that now. Where's your car?"

"Right here," Mike said, and pointed to a silvery gray Oldsmobile. "I was going to—"

Paul cut him off. "You drive. Go out that way," he instructed, pointing to the exit. "We're following a car that I think took Torie."

He redialed Tibbet as he flung himself into the passenger seat, and they peeled out after the phantom car.

"He's got her, I'm following."

"Who? Who is it?" Tibbet demanded.

"I don't know," Paul snarled. "Turn, turn," Paul

ordered Mike as they got to the light. They squealed through on red.

"Where are you?"

Heading north on Kelly Drive along the river. We just left the Bradshaw Mansion. I'm with the guy I hired for tonight," he said.

"Shitty hire if he let somebody get Torie."

"Agreed. The tags are—" he began, then turned to Mike.

"R-S-A-three-two-five," the bodyguard snapped, taking the turns on the winding road with competent speed.

Paul relayed to Tibbet.

"Okay, keep me posted. There's a black and white on the way to intercept. I've notified the park rangers as well, but their patrol's in another area. I'm en route. I'll be there as soon as I can."

"Hurry."

Paul dropped the phone into his lap and searched the night.

"There!" he shouted to Mike. Faint taillights off a side road betrayed the other car's direction. They'd been pretty close; it must be him.

He prayed it wasn't kids out for a little nookie in the backseat. They searched for a way to follow, and passed the overgrown entrance to a rutted road.

"Stop," Paul insisted, pointing to the road. "There."

"Got it," Mike grunted as he cranked the wheel to turn the car onto the overgrown drive.

A faint dust cloud was the only other clue that anyone had gone that way.

It was enough. It had to be enough.

"Tibbet, you still there?" Paul picked up the phone.

"Yeah. Black and white's closing in on your location."

"We're turning off onto a dirt road. There's nothing marking it, but I saw taillights. I'm pretty sure it's him."

"Wait for the black and white."

"No. He's got Torie. I can't. I just can't." He let Tibbet's protests fade into the background as he focused on the bumpy, pockmarked, and narrow way. Mike doused the lights as he rounded a bend.

It was his worst nightmare.

Torie in her glorious dress, with her blond hair cascading over her shoulders, was silhouetted in the glare of the other car's headlamps. The shadows concealed her kidnapper, but it was obvious that she was afraid. She wobbled where she stood, and he heard an indistinct shout of anger.

"Go back to the road, flag down the cops," Paul ordered.

"I'm trained—" Mike began.

"Shut up. I think I know this guy, and I have a chance to talk him out of this. I hope. You don't. Go back, make sure the cops find the damn road."

Reluctantly, Mike agreed, and like a ghost, he disappeared into the darkness. When Paul tried to slip out of the car the same way, the sound of the door opening gave him away.

"I'll kill her, Paul. I know it's you. Only you would have come looking. You're such an idiot. Get over here, and let me do it properly and kill you both."

He sprinted to her side, as well as he could in the patchy light, turning his ankle as he did. He stood in front of her, blocking the gun he could see. It was steady, held firmly in the gloved hand of Melvin Pratt Jr.

"Are you okay?" he asked her, reaching back to grip her hand.

"Woozy," she slurred. "He drugged me. Horrible taste. I think I'm going to be sick."

"Quit bitching," Melvin ordered. "Now kneel. I want to get a clean shot."

"No."

"Paul, you've gotta run." Torie was still slurring but her voice was stronger. "It's me he wants."

"Oh, no, that's where you're wrong, beautiful Victoria. I want you both dead. I originally thought I could kill Todd and marry you, which would let me finally claim the money Todd stole from me. But noooooooooo," he mocked like a teenager would. "You weren't ready to date, you said. But you were," he accused. "You dated that nasty Trey Buckner. It's no wonder you got labeled a slut and a black widow. He's trash, and you lowered yourself to his level.

"So I planned something else. I knew I wouldn't get the money, but it didn't matter. I'd get my revenge."

"Revenge?" Paul baited him, hoping he'd get a chance to overwhelm the angry man, get the gun. "For what? Todd won that money fairly. He lived fairly and gave back. That's more than anyone can say about you."

"Shut the fuck up," Melvin shouted. "You don't know. You never saw what he was. What he did."

"He never did anything but help you."

"He hated me, despised me. Called me Weaselboy." Paul betrayed himself with a glance at Torie.

"You *knew*, you bastard. I should have killed you first. You knew it was me, didn't you, back then, in college? I could have had her then, if it hadn't been for you."

"At the fraternity house? You drugged her? It was you all those years ago?" Rage nearly overwhelmed Paul as he realized that he'd never seriously considered Melvin. All those years . . .

"Nothing too strong," Melvin chuckled, and a shudder ran up Paul's spine. With all of this, he knew Melvin was crazy. Now he knew Melvin was capable of worse things than killing. His next words drove the point home. "She was so easy to drug, so willing. She has a beautiful body. I've never forgotten it."

"How could you? How could you pretend all these years?"

Keep him talking; Paul's thought was scattered, nearly panicked as he felt Torie sag onto his back. "Hang in there, honey," he muttered, trying to get her to respond.

"Pretend? I'm not the pretender, Paul. *You are.* I found out where you came from. You're the son of a trailer trash whore and a deadbeat father. You're nothing next to me, do you hear me? Nothing."

"I never made any secret of that, Melvin. I never lied. You lied. You're still lying."

"I am not," Melvin nearly screeched. He hated to be called a liar.

Behind Melvin, Paul saw the barest movement. If it was help, he needed to be sure Melvin didn't know it was there.

"Shut the fuck up, Weaselboy," he taunted, keeping Melvin's attention directed his way. "You were never up to the standard. How you ever pledged Delta Phi, I'll never know."

"You shut up," Melvin screamed, and the gun wavered, then steadied. "Stop it, Paul. You think you're so clever, baiting me, trying to get me to lose my temper. Uh uh uh." He waggled the gun like a scolding finger. "I'm not falling for it.

"You need to die quickly, and so does she," he said, pushing back the top of one of the gloves to check the time. "My father should be loading into the ambulance about now. I'll get back to the mansion in time to speed off to the hospital. Oh, gosh——" he pretended to be shocked and appalled—"whatever happened to dear old Dad? Heart attack?" he roared with laughter, but the gun never wavered.

"Now, do as I say. Move aside so I can kill her first. A nice little murder-suicide, I think."

"Drop the gun," a voice called out of the darkness.

How the cops had crept up so quietly, Paul had no idea. He didn't care. All he knew was that the cavalry had arrived, and he could tend to Torie.

"Don't move," Melvin ordered. "You come any closer and I put a bullet through both of them. Come out into the light where I can see you."

"I said, drop the gun." The disembodied voice was insistent.

"I'm never going to jail," Melvin said, as if they were having a conversation over lunch. "I'd rather die. Hell, my father would rather I die before I disgraced his name." He laughed. "Oh, if he only knew."

"Drop it, Pratt," a new voice called. Tibbet was over to Paul's left, beyond the circle of light made by the headlights. How he'd gotten through the city and out to them that fast, Paul didn't even want to know.

"I'm taking both of you with me," Melvin said, calmly. "These bullets are a little special. They're Sampson bullets. They're loaded hot. They have enough extra oomph to penetrate your body and kill her, too. You made a mistake, Paul. You should never have put her behind you."

"Drop. The. Gun," Tibbet ordered again.

Everything happened in slow motion. Paul saw Melvin smile, and knew the shot would kill him.

But it didn't have to kill Torie. With a wrench, he tossed her down, throwing himself over her body just as Melvin fired.

Shots rang out and he heard a scream, but he didn't look up.

"Paul? Jameson? You okay?"

He felt Tibbet's hand on his shoulder.

"Oh, God, Torie? Torie?" He rolled off her as Tibbet turned on a high-beam flashlight. "Torie?"

"Paul?" She put her hand up to shield her eyes from the glare. "Are you okay?"

She struggled to sit up, far more quickly than he could have guessed, and launched herself into his arms.

"Torie," he breathed, holding her tight, stroking her hair over and over. "Oh, I thought I'd lost you."

"No, Paul, no. You've found me."

Epilogue

"We've got to stop hanging around in ambulances and hospitals," Paul quipped, sitting on the seat in the back of the emergency vehicle, wrapped in a blanket. He had no idea why they'd given him the blanket, since he wasn't cold. He was glad, though, because it gave him something to hold onto as they loaded Torie onto a stretcher, and readied her for transport to the hospital.

"You're right," she managed around the muffling oxygen mask. "This sucks. And I didn't get my dance."

He laughed, but felt tears rise up as well. The emotion was so new, so raw, it choked him as he looked at her. Her sexy dress was dirty now, and her hose torn.

Her shoes sat in a bag at the side of the stretcher. It seemed so odd.

"He was so angry," he heard her whisper. Tearing his gaze away from the strappy dancing shoes, he nodded.

"Yeah. How could he have gotten that twisted up?"

"Don't know," she whispered.

* * *

In the hospital room, Dev, Pam, and Paul perched like birds around the small space. Pam had the lone chair, but Dev, still looking battered, sat on the arm. Paul was as near to Torie as he could get, one hip on the bed itself.

"You," Torie said as she pointed at her cousin, "have some 'splainin' to do, Lucy." She put on a Ricky Ricardo accent.

"To a lot of people," he drawled. "We'll get to that, you know?"

"Yeah." She focused on Paul. "When are you getting me out of here, hmmmm?"

"Doctor has to clear you. Besides, Tibbet wants to talk to you."

"I'll bet."

"He should be here any minute."

"That's what they all say," she joked, then sobered. "How's Mister Pratt?"

Paul's face fell, and his eyes were sad. "Whatever Melvin gave him kicked off a massive heart attack. He's still unconscious. They won't tell me anything else, because I'm not kin."

"Oh, that's terrible." She reached for his hand, both giving comfort and seeking it.

"Did you get any sleep, Torie?" Pam finally spoke. She looked happy, in spite of the circumstances. Torie had to smile at the possessive hand Dev was keeping on her shoulder.

"Some, once I stopped, well, you know." She didn't really want to talk about how much she'd thrown up. The drug Melvin had used made her sick. Between her first bout with it after the fire and now, she'd thrown up more in the last six weeks than she had in the past eleven years.

"Yeah. What—" her question was aborted as Tibbet knocked and came in.

"Good morning. Looks like you've drawn a crowd again," he said with a smile.

"Yeah, but it's my crowd, so I'm okay with it."

"I can see that. I'll make this brief and get out of your way. The warrant on Melvin Pratt Jr.'s home was served, and we were able to find enough evidence to link him not only to Todd Peterson's death, but to the fire at your house, Ms. Hagen. He kept journals in a funky shorthand, but it only took our guy a few minutes to figure it out. Had 'em in a safe, too, but that was easy. Evidently, he's also partially responsible for the computer crash at your office." He directed the last bit to Paul.

"He was," Torie said. "I was in and out in the car, but he planned the thing at the frat house. The one we discussed? He wanted to marry me."

"Ah." Tibbet flicked a glance at Pam and Dev. "You said something last night about the lottery as well?" The ubiquitous notebook was out, and Tibbet was jotting things down.

"Yes, he had been the one to buy all the tickets that day for everyone in the office. He said that Todd stole the money from him, since he had been the one to actually purchase the winning ticket. He believed Todd got me to marry him as a slap, in addition to the money."

"Ah, okay. That makes more sense when you put it that way."

"I guess I wasn't all that coherent last night."

"You did fine," Tibbet praised. "I've just got a couple of other questions. Do you have any idea what he might have given his father?"

"No." She paused, trying to remember exactly what Melvin had said. "But I'm sure it was him. Melvin said that he'd kill me and get back to the hotel in time to ride with the old man to the hospital."

"Hmmm. Very good." He closed his book, looked over at Dev. "What about you, Mister Chance?"

"Me? I'm living life, Detective."

"Uh huh." Tibbet didn't look convinced. "You now think the attack on you was unrelated, you said."

"Oh, yes," he drawled. "Totally unrelated. Nasty coincidence you might say. Worried my poor cher cousine half to death, though. I scolded the people responsible quite harshly."

"You did, eh? You know you shouldn't tell me that."

"No, I reckon not. But you're okay, for a damn Yankee Philly boy," he fired back. "You come down south to the Big Easy, I fix you up with the best meal and the best time you ever had. Payback for taking care of my girl, here."

"I may take you up on that." Tibbet grinned. "I had family down there, once upon a time."

"You ever had roots there, they still there, you know?"

"Detective?" Torie asked. "Do you think you could find out about Mister Pratt for us? They won't tell us anything."

"I think I can make that happen," Tibbet said. "Why don't you two walk over to the nurse's station with me," he said, pointing to Dev and Pam. "We'll find out and you can relay. Ms. Hagen, I can't say it's been a pleasure, but I appreciate all the help you've given me. I'm sorry for all the trouble you've had."

"Thank you, Detective. I appreciate you as well."

"A regular lovefest," Dev drawled, getting to his feet. Torie could tell he was sore; he was moving more slowly than usual. Pam rose as well, and shot her a smile.

"We'll be back."

They trooped out en masse, and Paul rolled his eyes in mock relief. "I thought they'd never leave."

"Oh, stop."

"Never." He bent down and kissed her. "I need to tell you something. I don't want it to change anything between us, but we've had too many unspoken issues, over so many years, that I can't not say it."

"What?" Torie frowned, worried now that things would turn upside down yet again.

"With Pratt in the hospital, the meeting on Monday may be postponed."

She rolled her eyes. "I thought it was something serious."

"It is. You're Todd's sole heir."

The words registered, and Torie's mouth dropped open. "I'm what?"

"Other than a few charitable gifts, you inherit everything," Paul said.

"Ah."

"I don't want it to make a difference between us. And I don't want you to think that, like Melvin, I want you for—"

"Shhh." She rested a finger on his lips, stopping the flow of words. "You're nothing like him and never have been. In fact, you're the opposite in so many ways. If it will make you feel better, I'll give it all away."

"I could help you start a foundation."

"How about we do it together?" She waited, hoping to see the truth in his eyes. He gave it to her in the gleam in his eye and the smile that blossomed on his face.

He bent to capture her mouth in a searing kiss. "How 'bout we do that? How about we do a few other things together, too."

"Like what?" she asked, not really caring what he said, as long as he kept looking at her that way—and kept kissing her. It made her feel so alive.

"Like buy a house, get married, play with the dogs, go on vacation. Stuff like that."

"Wait." She tuned in to his words between kisses. "What did you say?"

"I said—" he began.

"The middle part."

"Ah, I, uh, well. What would you say to getting married?"

"I'd say yes."

Thrilling Suspense from
Beverly Barton

Available Wherever Books Are Sold!

Visit our website at **www.kensingtonbooks.com**

Romantic Suspense from
Lisa Jackson

See How She Dies	0-8217-7605-3	$6.99US/$9.99CAN
Final Scream	0-8217-7712-2	$7.99US/$10.99CAN
Wishes	0-8217-6309-1	$5.99US/$7.99CAN
Whispers	0-8217-7603-7	$6.99US/$9.99CAN
Twice Kissed	0-8217-6038-6	$5.99US/$7.99CAN
Unspoken	0-8217-6402-0	$6.50US/$8.50CAN
If She Only Knew	0-8217-6708-9	$6.50US/$8.50CAN
Hot Blooded	0-8217-6841-7	$6.99US/$9.99CAN
Cold Blooded	0-8217-6934-0	$6.99US/$9.99CAN
The Night Before	0-8217-6936-7	$6.99US/$9.99CAN
The Morning After	0-8217-7295-3	$6.99US/$9.99CAN
Deep Freeze	0-8217-7296-1	$7.99US/$10.99CAN
Fatal Burn	0-8217-7577-4	$7.99US/$10.99CAN
Shiver	0-8217-7578-2	$7.99US/$10.99CAN
Most Likely to Die	0-8217-7576-6	$7.99US/$10.99CAN
Absolute Fear	0-8217-7936-2	$7.99US/$9.49CAN
Almost Dead	0-8217-7579-0	$7.99US/$10.99CAN
Lost Souls	0-8217-7938-9	$7.99US/$10.99CAN
Left to Die	1-4201-0276-1	$7.99US/$10.99CAN
Wicked Game	1-4201-0338-5	$7.99US/$9.99CAN
Malice	0-8217-7940-0	$7.99US/$9.49CAN

Available Wherever Books Are Sold!
Visit our website at www.kensingtonbooks.com

Thrilling Suspense From
Wendy Corsi Staub

__All the Way Home	0-7860-1092-4	$6.99US/$8.99CAN
__The Last to Know	0-7860-1196-3	$6.99US/$8.99CAN
__Fade to Black	0-7860-1488-1	$6.99US/$9.99CAN
__In the Blink of an Eye	0-7860-1423-7	$6.99US/$9.99CAN
__She Loves Me Not	0-7860-1768-6	$4.99US/$6.99CAN
__Dearly Beloved	0-7860-1489-X	$6.99US/$9.99CAN
__Kiss Her Goodbye	0-7860-1641-8	$6.99US/$9.99CAN
__Lullaby and Goodnight	0-7860-1642-6	$6.99US/$9.99CAN
__The Final Victim	0-8217-7971-0	$6.99US/$9.99CAN

Available Wherever Books Are Sold!

Visit our website at **www.kensingtonbooks.com**